PRAISE FOR

THE MAN WHO HEARD TOO MUCH

"The action is swift and brutal . . . his sense of characters is powerful. As ever with Granger, the prose is the opposite of the bloodless stuff of techno-thrillers."
—*Chicago Tribune*

"Granger's plots can be as intricate as the best le Carré. . . . Granger is a master of fooling the unwary reader."
—*St. Louis Post-Dispatch*

"Bill Granger is a rarity among writers of serious novels. Each of his books seems better than before. That is particulary true of his latest, *The Man Who Heard Too Much*."
—*Minneapolis Star-Tribune*

"Lovers of espionage novels will applaud the latest case of Granger's agent Devereaux . . . moves at breakneck speed."
—*Marlboro Enterprise/Hudson Daily Sun*

more . . .

AND PRAISE FOR
BILL

"The November Man yarns just get better and better."
—*People*

"A novelist of superb talent who has mastered the genre. . . . I hope the shining promise of the November Man will be kept forever and forever."
—*Chicago Sun-Times*

"Since his debut, Devereaux has reappeared annually in a new thriller, each better than the one before."
—*Buffalo News*

"America's best spy novelist."
—*Ed McBain*

THE MAN WHO HEARD TOO MUCH

BILL GRANGER

WARNER BOOKS

A Time Warner Company

WARNER BOOKS EDITION

Cover design by Jackie Merri Meyer
Cover illustration by Joe & Kathy Heiner

Warner Books, Inc.
666 Fifth Avenue
New York, N.Y. 10103

 A Time Warner Company

Printed in the United States of America

This book was orginally published in hardcover by Warner Books.
First Printed in Paperback: November, 1990

10 9 8 7 6 5 4 3 2 1

For Lori,
who was the woman of all these places

Little Lamb, who made thee?
Dost thou know, who made thee?

—William Blake

I'm very, very good
And be it understood—
I command a right good crew.

—W. S. Gilbert

AUTHOR'S NOTE

This book is concerned with the questions of Soviet Jewish emigration and the political fate of Lithuania. The book is set in the period before the open Lithuanian Republic push for total independence but after the first glimmers of what is called "glasnost." It reflects both political and religious entanglements true at the time. This book like others in the November chronicles, also brings up the continuing and real problem of computer security versus computer virus programs.

The first book in this series, which is a sort of history of cold war politics and the bureaucracies that direct them, was *The November Man* and concerned a plot by IRA terrorists to assassinate a cousin of the British Queen while on his boat off the Irish coast. The book appeared a few weeks before Lord Mountbatten was assassinated by terrorists off the Irish coast. The prescience was unintended; it was my attempt to turn reporting observation into a study of future logic. It appears this book, written in 1988, also focused on aspects of an international story before the story actually began to unfold.

THE MAN WHO HEARD TOO MUCH

ONE

Stockholm

The fog from the Baltic Sea came in waves across the city of islands. The spires of the palace and the national cathedral and all the other churches and temples of man and God were detached from the earth and held in the clouds, where they disappeared. Silence came down on the narrow, crooked streets of the Old Town section and extended into the harbor. It was October, and the air was damp with expectation of winter. The sun had not set, but the fog made everything beneath the city spires full of gloom and foreboding.

Viktor Rusinov, twenty-four, seaman aboard the Soviet cargo ship *Leo Tolstoy*, slipped along the outside passage on two deck toward the radio room. The cargo—Swedish machine parts from the factory at Göteborg—had been loaded, and the *Leo Tolstoy* would sail in the morning for Gdansk, on the Polish north coast.

Viktor Rusinov paused on the passageway and sensed his fear. He stood very still to make his fear subside. He smelled the sea and the city beyond. He heard a church bell toll. He blessed himself with the Orthodox sign of the cross because he was a religious man. The fear was suppressed in that ritual.

There were two political officers assigned to the *Leo Tolstoy*. They were both ashore now, probably gorging themselves at the smorgasbord served at the Opera. The political officers—who were, in fact, members of the Committee for State Security, the KGB—were totally privileged men.

Viktor Rusinov had nourished his rudimentary communist hatred for the upper classes during five years at sea. He hated the KGB men and he hated the captain. He hated every superior officer. He hated people with money, and those who could buy goods in the special stores set aside for foreigners. He hated with the fine, certain passion of the committed Christian. He knew God would destroy his superiors in time (and in a particularly cruel way). He was certain hell awaited them for their sins of having more than Viktor Rusinov. Development of this hatred had not been enough for Viktor; he had decided, in the end, to enjoy the benefits of his superiors in the only way left open to him. But there was risk to it, and that made him afraid.

Viktor came from a small village a hundred miles south of Moscow. He had dreamed always of the sea. He loved the life of it. He loved the company of his fellow seamen. He loved to drink and to fornicate, and he saw nothing in those activities that compromised his religious beliefs. The women he had were not important and did not figure in his complex scheme of good and evil and envy and retribution. He was strong and tall and his eyes were blue. He could have been Swedish or Polish because of his fair complexion.

He was going to slip over the side in a few minutes and disappear into the fog of neutral Stockholm. He had had only waited for his father to die, and his father had obliged him two months earlier in a cancer ward. He had no one left and no obligation to return. He saw it that way, in those correct, legal terms.

He would have preferred to defect in New York, but Stockholm was here and now. He had been in New York harbor once but had not been allowed to leave the freighter. The immensity of that city thrilled him as well as the constant rumble—the city noises conspired to create a constant sound like that of a train passing in the distance—and he knew it was his destiny to return there sometime. Stockholm was the first step. Besides, in the last few days the KGB men had spent a lot of time watching him. Now was the time. He knew the location of the American embassy—101 Strandvägen, which was the broad street on the harbor in Norrmalm, the northern sector of the city.

The red flag was limp on the standard at the stern of the ship. The ship was silent, full of a thousand tiny noises that were as comforting as lullabies. The ship rode the slight swell of the harbor, the bulkheads rubbing against the pilings, making soft, purring sounds against the ropes.

He opened the door of the radio room.

Yazimoff was there as he should have been. Yazimoff looked up at Viktor.

"So, it's now?" But not really a question. Yazimoff almost smirked. It was very annoying, and it made the tense knot in Viktor's stomach that much more painful.

Viktor inclined his head without a word. He reached into the pocket of his coat and extracted the wad of rubles, deutsche marks, francs, dollars, and pounds. A lot of money, some of it quite valuable. All he had saved from the liquor trade. Viktor Rusinov, when not counting his resentments and nursing his jealousies, was both a maker and seller of illegal vodka. Nothing had helped his business more than the crackdown on vodka by the Gorbachev government.

Yazimoff stared at the money with reverence. It was quite a lot, more than he had ever seen in his life.

"This," Yazimoff said.

Viktor stared at the handwriting on the paper. It was Yazimoff's. He did not understand the message, but he understood clearly it was in code.

"What is this?"

"Oleg? You know, the fat one? He took the message and he decoded it right away. And he used this."

Viktor took the second sheet of paper. The key. It was covered with numbers arranged in sets of four. Viktor didn't really understand how it worked—but so what? That was someone else's problem. Viktor wanted to defect to the Americans. The coded message and its key would be a gift, to show his good intentions and to make certain the Americans would not send him back.

"Is it worth this?" Viktor asked, holding up the bills.

Yazimoff made a little shrug but held out his hand. He took the roll of bills and put it in his pocket without counting.

Viktor folded the two sheets of paper carefully into a waterproof envelope attached to a chain around his neck. He rebuttoned his shirt.

"The water is cold," Yazimoff said.

"I've swum in colder water," Viktor Rusinov said. He had a tendency to brag about his abilities, including his prowess with women and his gargantuan need for drink. No one on the *Leo Tolstoy* much liked him, but as a bootlegger, he was tolerated.

Viktor closed the hatch to the radio room. It was 1600 hours, and the ship was caught in that curious, sleepy time between the workday and the evening mess. No one was on deck. He went carefully and quietly down the ladders.

When he reached the main deck, he looked over the side. The *Tolstoy* rode low in the oily, dark water. The fog made his skin wet. He wiped at his lips. He would drop off on the seaside and swim around to the end of the pier, where it would be safe to climb up the old ladder to land.

"What are you staring at, Seaman?"

Viktor turned.

The first mate of the watch was on the deck, scarcely six

feet from him. It was Doesniov, a particularly loathsome specimen in Viktor's pantheon of hated superior officers. Doesniov was a big, boastful man with a bullying manner. He strutted down the deck to where Viktor stood at the rail.

"Well? What are you staring at? Do you see something in the water, in all this damned fog?"

Viktor felt intimidated, not by Doesniov's size but by his rank. Viktor's intense hatred for those in superior positions did not alter his almost religious respect for rank.

"I thought I heard something—"

"What? Heard a mermaid?"

"Something in the water." He was not a very good liar. But Doesniov looked over the rail. There. He was looking over the rail.

Viktor couldn't move.

Doesniov turned to look at him. "You've been drinking your own stuff, Viktor Ilyich."

"I don't . . ." So Doesniov knew about the illegal liquor trade. Why not? Everyone knew everything. "Look—"

"Are you ill? You look ill."

Viktor felt the color drain from his face. He felt fear and cold. He felt the weight of the documents in the waterproof envelope on the chain around his neck. He could give them back, say it was a mistake—

That was stupid! Yazimoff wouldn't give back his money. What would the two pigs from KGB do? They already suspected him, he was sure of it.

"Look!" Victor pointed down at the water, as though something had caught his eye.

Doesniov turned. Again, he looked over the rail, his head lower than his shoulders.

Viktor had to do it. God offered him no choice.

Both hands locked into a hammer of flesh. The hammer came down hard on the base of the skull. Doesniov grunted, his chin broke on the rail, and he slid to the wet deck.

God offered no choice. There was only this one way and no other.

Viktor slipped out of his wool coat and dropped it over the side.

Not a moment to spare.

He scarcely made a splash when he hit the water.

TWO

New York City

Sixteen days later, Devereaux climbed out of the yellow cab in a pouring rain in front of the old Algonquin Hotel on Forty-fourth Street in Manhattan. He pushed two twenties through the open window on the passenger side and turned to face the entrance. He carried one small brown canvas bag, which contained all his travel equipment—the clean clothes, the spare sweater, the pharmacopoeia, including uppers and downers and penicillin and cyanide capsules. He had also packed a 9mm Beretta automatic of the design now issued to the U.S. military as well as to "authorized agents of the intelligence services."

He crossed the sidewalk and paused at the entrance. The rain was sheer gloom; the chaos of traffic and noise, an audition for hell. Brutal sirens, horns, the screams of ambulances, the belches of buses—it rolled over him in hopeless waves. The sidewalks were temporarily empty because of the rain and because it was the middle of the afternoon. But the fullness of the city noises suffocated him.

He thought for a moment of refusing to enter the hotel and meet the man who controlled him. He would just turn and run until he could not run anymore, and if they found him, he would kill them.

The doorman decided for him by opening the door. He went inside the old lobby full of overstuffed chairs and old ladies. He walked to the Blue Bar to the right of the entrance. The barman was wiping a glass, and the waiter was reading the *New York Post*. Devereaux stood, dripping raindrops on the carpet, staring at the bar. And then he saw Hanley at the little table in the corner.

It was just after 3:00 P.M.

He crossed the room to Hanley's corner. Hanley looked up from the folded front page of the *Times*. Devereaux stood a moment and then shrugged out of his wet raincoat, folded it on a chair, and sat down. A thick carpet covered the floor, and rows of glittering bottles rested on the shelf behind the bar. The barman was Chinese, and he looked as sour as the waiter who approached the table.

Devereaux ordered a vodka. Hanley, clearing his throat, asked for another bowl of nuts. The waiter made it understood with a pull to his mouth that he was extending himself. He nodded without a word and went back to the service bar.

"Tell me," Hanley said.

But it had been a long flight and the days of interrogation had worn Devereaux out as certainly as if he had been the one being questioned. He didn't feel in the mood to respond, and something about Hanley's tone irritated him. Devereaux knew he was a mere cog in the great intelligence machine, but he suddenly wanted to insist he was human, that he was tired, that even a cog can break down. Instead, he looked at Hanley and smiled. "You arrange these meetings in places like this."

"What's wrong with places like this?"

"Old New York. Club 21 or the bar at the Algonquin or the lobby of the Plaza. Doesn't it ever occur to you that you're living in an old movie?"

Devereaux's sarcasm made him feel better. Hanley was struggling to understand. It would come to him in a moment, and then he would blink like a startled rabbit, and Devereaux knew that would please him too.

Hanley blinked.

He was small, bald, and he was very rigid after a lifetime in the service. He believed in R Section, which made it that much worse. He had fixed his beliefs and ideas when he was a boy in Nebraska, dreaming through storybooks or at the weekly picture show. New York was such and such; here was China, and here was the way of Chinamen; here was London, full of knights and kings; and here was Washington, seat of power in the world and true to Manifest Destiny, full of dedicated men given to ferocious patriotism. That his view did not reflect reality then or now was the spark that drove the engine.

"I like this old hotel and this old bar," he explained. "I like old things. I am conservative, and it seems that the old things were better."

"Silk stockings and segregation," Devereaux said. His voice was weary, but Hanley always revived a sleeping sarcasm in him. "The best of times."

"We make the best of times," Hanley said.

The waiter brought two drinks and a metal bowl full of nuts. He put them down on the little table along with an absurd bill and went out of the room.

"Viktor is a genuine," Devereaux said after sipping his vodka. Vodka numbed him all the more now because he had refused to drink on the long flight back from Stockholm. He had taken a pill and slept most of the way across the Atlantic, even through a patch of bad headwinds. It did no good. When the stewardess awakened him thirty minutes before the plane touched down at Kennedy, he felt as though he had never slept in his life.

He had kept at Viktor Rusinov for eight days. The CIA station chief had his turn as well, and R Section had been called in to "share" with great reluctance. But part of Viktor's coded documents demanded R Section involvement. And the participation of Devereaux.

"Are you sure? That Viktor is who he says he is?"

"Nothing is sure." Devereaux put down his drink and leaned forward. "He's a hateful man, really. He explained to me his envy as a theory of unfairness directed at him. He has justified everything in his life, every act, every petty revenge. His hatreds are rooted in a ferocious kind of religiosity. In His heart, God knows Viktor is right."

"He sounds deranged," Hanley said.

"Perhaps he is. Perhaps he's only being normal by Soviet standards. He said the KGB men on the ship suspected him of wanting to defect. He thought he'd killed the first mate when he hit him. He's a big boy, Viktor. I told him the Soviets insisted he stand trial for mutiny and murder. It scared him, but it also made him angry, and he went on about how unjust the world was to deny Viktor Rusinov his due. Maybe he's that simple, just crazy." Devereaux's voice softened. "He can come to America and join his fellow lunatics living out of their shopping carts on the streets."

Hanley lowered his eyes and sipped gin. "Which are not made of gold."

"Viktor's message had two names. 'Skarda.' 'Henry McGee.' Viktor simply does not know either name or how they connect. He's the messenger," Devereaux said.

Henry McGee. Nothing else in the defection incident had interested R Section as much as the name of Henry McGee.

Henry McGee was now in federal prison, thanks to Devereaux. McGee had penetrated R Section for years as a mole from Moscow—which also made him an American traitor because he was born in Alaska. McGee had been set the task of destroying the credibility of R Section and had nearly succeeded.

When Viktor defected to the American embassy at 101 Strandvägen in Stockholm, the message had been turned over to CIA, which had bucked it to the code breakers at National Security Agency. Very routine. All the intelligence services were alerted to the results: a message fragment in which only the names "Henry McGee" and "Skarda" and the routine wording "no operational difficulty in any connection for penetration of Eagle" stood out. "Eagle" was the current Soviet euphemism for American intelligence. What did the American services make of this message? Was it genuine? Was Viktor genuine?

So Devereaux, because he had broken the penetration of Henry McGee, was the logical man to send to Stockholm to question Viktor, to see if he was genuine, to see if he understood more than the coded message fragment. Henry McGee frightened the brass at R Section, even now when he was buried in a fifty-year sentence in a maximum federal prison.

"Skarda," Devereaux said, breaking a moment of silence. "Person or operation or both. Unresolved. But Viktor doesn't know."

"That is your assessment."

Devereaux said nothing.

"So," Hanley said, shifting in his chair.

Silence ticked into the room. The Thurber drawings on the wall next to the bar portrayed the Algonquin lobby with old ladies shaped like overstuffed chairs, wearing lamps for hats. The roar of the street did not penetrate this silence.

Vodka filled Devereaux with false warmth. Autumn was bleak now that he did not live in Washington, where the colors were languid and sullen and suffused with sexual stimulation. It was not the colors, he realized. It was the warm, languid, sullen, sexual remembrance of when he lived with Rita Macklin there. He was certain this final separation was inevitable, which made the separation so much more bleak. Rita Macklin was a journalist, and her name in a magazine or in an op-ed piece in the *Times* was a constant reminder to him. She never tried to reach him, though it would have been simple. She could call the Section number, and they would patch her through to the safe house in Manhattan. . . . House, safe house—three rooms in a West Side neighborhood full of shabby, rent-controlled apartments. Orange-lit Manhattan enclosed him, but he had to be here, waiting for the next assignment and the next, away from the color and comfort of the only woman he had ever loved, who could have been his if only he could renounce this bleak shadow life. He could not. He could explain it, the life, but he could not renounce the life.

Hatred was so strange in all its forms. Devereaux had marveled at Viktor Rusinov's hatred, which spewed out from time to time in words as foul as sewage, blaming this or that circumstance or member of the bureaucracy for his lack of advancement, blaming the American agents for keeping him locked in the velvet prison of the Stockholm embassy. He wanted to go to New York.

Devereaux had no such hatred. Not for Section, not for Hanley. Not for Rita Macklin. Hatred was scorched out of him, twisted as a burned forest, blackened to charcoal into fossil remains of what he had been. The only thing that remained was the pain of separation from Rita Macklin because she could not live anymore with a man of secrets.

He had to stop thinking of her. He turned back to Hanley. "Skarda as a man, not an operation. Think of it."

"I've thought of it," said Hanley. "We run through files and find one thousand six hundred thirty-four Skardas. Primarily a Czech name. There was a Skarda who was running agents from Berlin in the sixties, during the Dubczeck regime. But nothing in computer links Henry McGee to any Skarda."

"Then consider it as an operation," Devereaux said.

"We have no reason to do so," Hanley said.

"No reason not to. When we put Henry McGee away two years ago, we didn't get a flutter from the Russians. Not even an informal contact. He was their agent, a ranked agent inside KGB. It's not like them to not recover their lost lambs."

"Even Henry expected more," Hanley said.

"Perhaps they plan to spring Henry," Devereaux said. He did not look at Hanley but at the room, at the soft light, tried to feel the warmth of the place. "Skarda is some future thing that needs the presence of Henry McGee. Or his cooperation.

Or Skarda is some ongoing operation that Henry knows about and they are worried he told us.''

''Why send such a message to the *Leo Tolstoy*?'' Hanley countered. ''It's not a spy ship, just a dirty freighter with no secrets.''

The *Tolstoy* had ''political officers,'' of course, as all Soviet ships did, ostensibly to answer questions and provide instructions on matters of faith and morals in the communist religion. They were the KGB men who had spooked Viktor into defecting in Stockholm.

But *why* this defection by this Soviet sailor? Why in Stockholm? Why was he bringing the gift of a coded message fragment hinting at a link between Henry McGee, a jailed spy, and something or someone called Skarda, and a penetration of Eagle?

''We don't understand this message—'' Hanley began again, signaling for his third drink of the afternoon.

''Therefore, it must contain the germ of truth,'' Devereaux finished for him.

Hanley nodded. ''Is it disinformation? That seems unlikely, since disinformation must be understood to disinform. We don't understand. Unless you missed something, Devereaux, and Viktor is a spy and you believed him to be genuine.''

Devereaux took his second vodka. The vodka burned the back of his throat.

''Could you have made a mistake?''

Could he? He made mistakes all the time. He let her go. Now Rita Macklin haunted him in the Manhattan streets in this bleak, treeless autumn. He was certain he saw her on Broadway, hailing a cab in the rain . . . in the doorway of Lutèce . . . saw her at a sidewalk table in the St. Moritz, talking to a man. . . . He knew they were just ghosts, but they were genuine anyway. Yes. He made mistakes all the time, about important things.

''No,'' Devereaux replied. ''I didn't mistake Viktor. Just

as I didn't mistake Henry McGee when Section believed him and let itself be penetrated.''

That was meant to sting, and Hanley squinted in pain.

"Then perhaps it is a matter of place,'' Hanley recovered. "Viktor defected in Stockholm. Scandinavia. Soviet submarines are probing at the Swedish coast again, violating the waters.''

"But the Swedes never find them.''

"They want to turn the Baltic into a Soviet pond. That was clear in the last Soviet naval secret directive. They don't have to own the shoreline of every country, just make their presence felt long enough and often enough.''

Devereaux considered it. "So Skarda might be a plan directed at Scandinavia. Some bait to make us react foolishly.''

"What about the political officers on the *Leo Tolstoy*?''

"They were followed while the ship was in Stockholm harbor. That's not easy to arrange on short notice. The report said they split up several times and were lost more than once.''

Hanley said, "Two weeks, the secretary of state meets with his Soviet counterpart, the foreign secretary, in Malmö, Sweden. The talks are . . . about freedom of the seas in the Baltic. But there is a secret agenda.''

"What?''

"We don't know. Either the secretary isn't telling the intelligence services, or he doesn't know, either. The initiative came from Moscow.''

They all did nowadays, Devereaux thought.

The administration was fumbling in a dozen places in the world, grasping at every Soviet straw proffered. The intelligence services had advised against meetings with "secret'' agendas, but the administration was not listening to them right now; it was listening to the popularity polls published at intervals in the newspapers. If the Soviets wanted to throw Washington a bone, it might have meat on it.

"You'll have to go to Malmö for the conference. To observe.''

"For whom?'' Devereaux said.

"Section. Maybe this Skarda thing involves the conference. Maybe it will come up."

"I was going to take furlough," Devereaux began. He had not thought of such a thing until now. He was very tired, and he did not want to go to Malmö, and he did not want to think of Henry McGee or try to unravel another riddle. . . . He wanted to sit in the shabby three rooms in New York and wait for a telephone call to be patched through from Washington. What would he say to her? What had he ever been able to say to her?

"You can have furlough when you come back. It's not such a difficult matter—"

"None of them ever are, Hanley," Devereaux said.

"Is that sarcasm?"

Silence again except for the rain against the windows.

Hanley said, "There's an opening. In Bangkok."

Devereaux's eyes became heavy. He had been recruited for Asia during the Vietnam War. He had loved Asia. He had been locked out of Asia for twenty years. What new irony did Hanley intend?

"You've been cooled off," Hanley said. Why was he offering this? "No one objects to your going back to Asia. We need a man there."

"You don't need a man. Everything is Sigint now. Spy satellites, transmitter interceptors. It's Fort Meade's show now." Fort Meade was home of the gadget-laden National Security Agency. "I don't need Asia, Hanley. Not anymore. No promises because I've been a good boy."

At the beginning of the world, Devereaux had been professor of Asian studies at Columbia University. Until a man in bow tie had met him on the steps of the library one sunny afternoon and explained that he could give him all of Asia in exchange for his soul. That's how simply his recruitment into R Section had been handled.

"We have to talk to Henry McGee," Devereaux said. He put down his glass. "Before Malmö."

"Henry won't talk to us," Hanley said.

"He's a federal prisoner. He'll talk to anyone we tell him to," Devereaux said.

"I don't want to hear his lies again."

"We never asked him about Skarda. Maybe that will jar him."

"How will you know if he tells you the truth?"

But Devereaux did not speak. He could not. Henry was just the next step leading to Malmö, leading to Skarda, leading to the next step and the next, that much farther away from Rita Macklin and the ghosts of New York City.

THREE

Lewistown, PA

The first six weeks inside prison, Henry McGee did not think he would survive. His faculties were intact, though the shock of the sentence—twenty-five to fifty years in federal penitentiary for treason—had not sunk in. But prison was a very different place from all the places he had been in the world.

When he had first defected to the Soviet Union seventeen years before, they had put him in detention, but he had understood that world and his role in it. He had been a defector in a party of Eskimos lost on the straits between Alaska and Siberia. So it seemed. He had known exactly what he was doing then, always had known what he was doing.

They had questioned him, over and over, to see if he was a plant from the American intelligence services. They became convinced he was what he seemed—a traitor to the Americans and a convert to the Soviet side. He gave them good information. He knew the location of radar installations and the secret Alaskan naval and air bases that were not listed on any map but are all over Alaska. He knew them as a native knows the secret places. After he told them many stories that they believed, the detention was lifted and he was merely observed closely at all times. They stripped him of all knowledge, and later they built him back up again, this time with the tools of a counterspy. He became the mole who nearly tore apart R Section.

But this place, set in the gentle hills of Pennsylvania, this was prison as punishment—that was the difference. A cold, dehumanizing mechanism ran life inside the walls. The new prisoners were not even people, not even animals. They were called fish. They were chum for the sharks who had survived their own infancy as fish and now cruised the blocks and tiers for victims.

Henry McGee, fifty-one, had the body of a thirty-year-old. He was thin and dark and very mean. The mean aspect showed clearly in his coal black eyes. A coldness in his manner set him apart from the others. In the evenings, in his cell after supper, he did exercises—one hundred situps and one hundred pushups. The evening hour of his exercises was his surrender to age: it was easier to move his body in the evening as opposed to the morning, when it was stiff. His body had scars and his hands spoke of strength. He thought he would be left alone. Anyone could see how mean he was if anyone had looked hard at him. Still, in the first week, a large black prisoner attempted to make him perform fellatio in the dark of his cell.

Henry had already fashioned a cutting weapon from a spoon. Nearly everyone had such a weapon. They were routinely confiscated in sweeping searches several times a year. The weapon was sharp, but the cutting edge was still jagged. When Henry fell to his knees before the black man as he had been told to do, he took two passes to cut off the right testicle. The black man staggered to the common tier. He was screaming so loudly that the rest of the prisoners turned down their radios and fell into an uncommon nighttime silence. He ran along the metal tier, pursued by guards with rifles and clubs. They clubbed him to unconsciousness to stop the screams. His body fell at the far end of the block, and the guards saw the blood on his legs, on his trousers, on his lower belly. One of the guards was sick at the sight of the blood.

There was both an official and an unofficial inquiry. No weapon was found. The code of the prisoners was silence. Henry McGee was left alone after that.

This prison, like all others in the country, was segregated by its inmates. Blacks and whites formed their own societies, and bloody encounters between the societies were not unusual. Hispanic prisoners, when present in numbers, formed a third society. Societies of Nazism and black supremacy and Islam formed spiderwebs of structure inside the larger divisions of racial segregation. Complicating the sociology was the strong homosexual community—willing and unwilling, resigned in any case—that was both black and white. In many cases, the younger, smaller males—usually white or Hispanic—were attached as "women" to the black society.

Henry McGee tried to understand the sociology of the place, and it buried him in despair. As he saw the hopelessness of prison life, the weight of his sentence began to drown him. His mean, black eyes lost luster, and for a time he could not eat. He sat in the darkness and stared, listening to the animal noises of the prison at night. He was certain he would not go mad; he just might not survive. He thought he was less afraid of death and the endless oblivion beyond than survival for months and years in this stupid, self-limiting place.

He tried to be patient about the Soviets and to have understanding of the real politics. The Soviets always took care of their own. It was the great unspoken tenet of Soviet espionage, the ultimate reward for the secret soldier. He had been a colonel inside KGB; he had status as a mole in R Section for nearly ten years. He had been a faithful servant to their cause, and his reward must be his freedom. Even a freedom in retirement in Moscow, with its intricately layered society of privilege.

He had been certain he would be traded in time. He had boasted about it to Devereaux of R Section, his antagonist and interrogator. Just before he'd been transferred to this prison, Devereaux had arranged to interview him one last time in a small room in the federal courthouse in Washington.

"You'll do the time," Devereaux said. He had said it without a note of vengeance. There had been curiosity in the gray eyes, a catlike quality that wonders what pain is like to the bird in his paws.

Henry McGee had smiled and said nothing.

"They don't want you very badly," Devereaux said. "We marked your trail. You gave us too much information about too many things. That's what they think. They think you betrayed everything, and they don't want you back."

"You know I didn't."

"You confessed," Devereaux had said. "We made a nice package and spread it around. The embassy here thinks you're the reason we sent home seventy-four KGB-GRU 'clerk-typists' from the embassy and the United Nations. We gave you full credit. They're discussing you tonight in Moscow Center."

Henry McGee had let the smile fade exactly as Devereaux wished. It was personal with Devereaux, and Henry McGee knew the disinformation could be carried out. There was no reason to "frame" Henry McGee as a willing betrayer of the Soviet operation inside the U.S. It was too petty, too personal, too vindictive. But he had seen something in Devereaux's eyes that chilled him. Perhaps the man was capable of coming down to that.

"They'll still want to trade for me."

"They have nothing to offer us, Henry. You're used up. Empty." The words tolled. Devereaux's face held only contempt, without pity.

Henry was as tough as Devereaux, was the toughest man alive. He let the meanness in him sustain him for a moment.

"You'll do all fifty, Henry. You'll be a hundred and one when you come out. It'll be a different world."

"You get your kicks out of this, don't you? Something I said? Or you just a generally sadistic son of a bitch? You want to scare someone, start practicing on little girls. I don't scare, not from men or bears or anything.''

Devereaux had smiled. The bastard had smiled, and it unglued Henry. ''I just wanted you to know, Henry. It was me. I wanted you to know that so that it could comfort you all those days you got ahead of you.''

He became a prisoner in late winter of one year. The winter-brown fields in narrow valleys, sullen with ice and streaks of dirty snow, melted at last to spring. And spring turned to the sticky, hot Pennsylvania summer. The trees bloomed, the fields were full of corn. The corn tassled, and pollen filled the air. Fall broke the stalks in the field. The cold days came and the prisoners wore naval pea coats in the yard. Their breath came in clouds. Henry McGee went to movies and watched television. He read a book every day. He went to the dentist. He worked in the laundry first and then transferred to the library when one of the librarians was paroled. At Christmas, there was a show and some of the he-shes wore their best clothes and sang and danced and shook their fannies on the stage. Everyone loved it, even the straight cons. There was a knife fight in the laundry and two prisoners were killed. A prisoner died of AIDS in the hospital. It snowed Christmas day. Winter howled until March, and then it was spring again. Twelve months. Twelve months turned into thirteen.

Henry figured that twenty-five years had three hundred months.

He wrote to the Soviet embassy in Washington six times. He wrote twice in code. He wrote four times in clearspeak. There must have been some misunderstanding because, after four months, he began to receive the picture monthly called *Soviet Life*. It enraged him.

The words. It came down to Devereaux, sitting quietly in that small room, explaining how he had smeared Henry's name with the Soviets and they would never want him back. . . . Henry could not stop the dreams, and Devereaux's words came back in dreams. Everything else was an act of will, but he could not stop the dreams. He awoke some nights with sweat covering his body in a fine sheen, so that he had to towel himself off.

There were communists in the prison, but they were mostly black. Henry tried to engage them in political discussion, but their perspectives and his were very different. They talked the politics of liberation and fulfillment of a race. Henry was beyond all that. Politics was a real thing, not a wish list. It was money and power. Power turned into money, and money was power from the beginning. You just needed a certain number of chumps behind you, and you could buy the world. He couldn't get these black guys to understand it because they came from a real world, knew too much about how real things were, and turned to Communism as Christians turn to God.

He finally discovered the mob on the sixteenth month in prison.

He had been aware of them. Everyone was aware of the members of the Mafia and respected them, even the guards who provided them with weekend passes to nearby motels for visits with women, and large, pasta-filled dinners.

Very cold for May. The clouds scudded on a wild blue sky. The wind shivered down the valleys. Exercise time and the blacks were playing their endless game of basketball, their shoulders shining with sweat, their swift and elegant dances done back and forth, up and down the court, the round ball arcing in triumph to the basket, the bodies crushed beneath the net. Shouts and shoves, grown men laughing like children in a prison yard. It was full of beauty and melancholy and life.

"Don Anthony," Henry McGee said. "I want you to know me so that you can trust me and so that you can help me."

The olive eyes seemed amused, but nothing else in that large, stolid face gave any indication of the mood of the man.

They were watching the basketball game in the sports yard. Don Anthony did not stand alone, but when Henry approached, they stood aside, as though what they had to say to each other was in confidence.

"Maybe I know you, you ever think of that?" Don Anthony said. Softly. The New Jersey accent was there, but so was the whispery shadow in the voice. Everything was softened in the presence of Don Anthony. He walked in his own time, in his own music, and everyone respected it because of the alternative. Henry McGee guessed that his music was *Il Trovatore*.

"I know you know everything. But stories got stories sometimes. I tell good stories."

"A man of stories," Don Anthony said. He paused. He had tried to make it sound profound, but it had just seemed stupid. Henry McGee caught that.

"The *melanzane*, they play basketball. I swear the fucking game was invented in Africa—they brought it on the boat with them," Don Anthony said. For a moment, Henry was puzzled by the common Italian slur for blacks—he had never heard it—but figured it out.

Henry said nothing. His hands were bunched inside his pea coat. He stared at the game. He hated games. He had noticed that morning this was his sixteenth month in prison. Two hundred eighty-five more just like this one and maybe they would parole him. He would be seventy-six years old. The thoughts of time pressed him too hard, and he had to say something to Don Anthony.

"I got five hundred thousand," Henry said.

The olive eyes went very wide and loving. Without looking at Henry, Don Anthony put a little burr of interest in his soft Jersey City voice: "That's more money than God. How come you didn't get a better lawyer? There ain't no way anyone has to do time with money like that."

"It wasn't a question of the lawyer," Henry McGee said. "Sometimes when the government goes after you, there's not a damned thing you can do about it."

"When they wantcha, they gotcha," Don Anthony agreed. He was a realist. He shrugged. "Yeah. Well. You could make it more comfortable with money. Spread it around. These guards are only human, they got families to support. You want a little something nice, they can make it nice. You can buy anything in this joint, you know that.''

''If the government finds out about the money, they take it.''

''Ain't that just like them? They don't play fair.''

Henry stopped. Was Don Anthony making fun of him? He waited for a moment to let the silence talk. They heard the shouts from the basketball courts. Black kids played the game in the ghetto, now they did it in prison; life was all the same.

''Well, you made it tough on yourself, Henry McGee, playing the spy. You're a spy, I hear.''

''I was a spy,'' Henry said.

''Yeah. You ain't a spy now,'' Don Anthony said.

''No.''

'' 'Cause you're inside and there ain't nothin' to spy on.'' He turned to Henry McGee. The face was cold, not amused. His skin was like gray pebbles. '' 'Cept me. You spy on me, huh?''

''Jesus,'' Henry said. Jesus. It was the last thing he had expected. ''I want to get out of here.''

''Apply for a parole.''

''I want to get out of here. I got five hundred thousand.''

''Is that right?''

''I give you a number and you check it out. Bank of Hong Kong, it's my account. I'll need fifty thousand to set up when I get out. You get four hundred fifty thousand.''

Olive eyes made the face a shade warmer. Money was definitely a woman taking her clothes off. He couldn't help it. Sometimes it gave him an erection, thinking about money. ''Why you figure I can get you out when I got my own ass in here for nearly two years?''

''Don Anthony. You're one of the guys. You run your business affairs from here easy as from there. You got home here. You got your boys with you, you guys play cards, eat pizza, have parties with the broads. It's better than being home in some ways, at least your wives aren't around.''

Don Anthony tried a precise smile. Unfortunately, his lips were thick and his large head with the olive eyes and the gray pebble skin made the gesture grotesque. "You do your homework about us. What is it? You working for the G? You working for yourself, maybe see if you get something? You cut that *tutsone*'s nut off, but we ain't niggers and we don't mess with you. Don't mess with us. Beat it, McGee. I got nothing to say to you." And he turned then, and Henry felt the stone in his belly again because the interview was ended.

The black faces shining with sweat moved up and down the court. The black legs churned. The round brown ball arced again and swished through the basket.

Luis Miranda became Henry McGee's mark.

Luis was doing bad time. He had gotten into three fights that involved staving off homosexual advances. The last fight had earned him a very bad scar on his left cheek, which, unfortunately for him, did not mar his beauty enough. He was a painting by Raphael and should be hung on a wall in the Vatican and not wear prison clothes and get those looks from large men.

Luis was a hard-luck kid all the way. His parents were migrant workers, and he had grown up in a lot of places between the apple orchards of Michigan and the berry groves of upstate New York. His hands were hard from all the work he had done in his first twenty-two years.

His twenty-third year started out with a bank robbery.

The bank was in Hagerstown, Maryland, a branch of a larger bank out of Baltimore. Luis decided that year he would not get old and stooped like his father and have nothing to show for it. His father had said he should go into the army, but he flunked the test. Even the fucking army didn't want him.

He acquired a Spanish-made .22 automatic knockoff of a

more reliable gun by Smith and Wesson. He went into the bank at 11:12 A.M. Monday and terrified the young teller, who gave him all her money. She put it in a McDonald's paper bag he had carried into the bank with him.

Luis Miranda raced out of Hagerstown down old U.S. 40 without a problem. The robbery had so upset the young teller that it was nearly six minutes before she came out of a terrified trance and informed Mr. Drexler, the vice president, she had been robbed.

Sixteen minutes later, Luis pulled into the same McDonald's where he had breakfasted before the robbery on milk and sausage biscuits. He had to use the lavatory. It was typical of him, his father might say, to go in and rob a bank without first going to the bathroom. He left the engine running and went inside.

A moment later, two teens emerged from the restaurant and went to his car. They looked inside. They opened the doors.

All this was laconically observed by two Maryland state policemen eating their lunch in an unmarked highway patrol car at the south end of the McDonald's lot.

"What the hell those kids doing?" one asked the other. The other, Wilbur Dasher, said, "Fuck you think they're doing?"

Both cops got out of their car as the kids pulled something off the front seat of Luis's car. It was a McDonald's paper bag. The first kid saw the cops approach and said something to the other. They turned and the first kid dropped the sack, tearing it. The money was caught in a light breeze and floated up before the surprised eyes of all four of them.

"Jesus," said both cops simultaneously.

The kids turned and ran and the cops stood motionless. Money in the wind.

And then Luis Miranda pushed open the door while buttoning his jeans. He saw the cops and the money and he thought about it and then put up his hands.

The cops began to draw their pistols at that point. Later on, the cops made a point of telling Luis they had no intention of arresting him for anything until he put up his hands. The cops thought it was comical that Luis was dumb enough to surrender even before he was asked to.

Every time Luis told the story to Henry, Henry tried to sympathize. It seemed as downright funny to him as it was to the cops, typical of all the fuckups of the world. Henry had a use for fuckups, though, and Luis would work out just fine.

It took a few weeks to get around Luis, but Henry had patience when he saw a plan forming. It was just another story to him then, and Luis was a character in it, without flesh or blood. He was just someone to be used.

Luis liked the nose candy, and Henry could get that. Anybody could get that if he had the price. There were a couple of dealers, but Henry used Amos Amad, a large, strapping black man from Chicago who was doing five to ten for importing narcotics. Amos had the best stuff.

Luis got very heavily into it. Luis was grateful to Henry, not just for the nose candy, but for protecting him. Nobody put the hit on him anymore because there was Henry and nobody wanted to fuck with Henry McGee. Some of them figured Henry had turned Luis into his woman, but it wasn't like that. It was just friendship, and Henry got good, really good, absolutely fine shit that put you on the moon or something.

Henry would watch him get his turns at night, taking the stuff up his nose. Luis liked it that way, not freebasing, not doing some of the other silly things you could do with it. Shit, it was like smoking unfiltered cigarettes—just do it. And Henry would see Luis get weaker and weaker.

Henry wanted him to kill someone, and Luis had to be weak enough to do it and strong enough to follow through on it.

Luis had a homemade knife and it was good enough.

Two days before the hit, Henry told him what he wanted him to do and told him he couldn't have any more shit until he did it.

Luis practically pleaded. Henry gave him one little line the first day, but that was that, just out of the goodness of Henry's heart.

The hit was a small man, smaller than Luis, named Giorgio Fontanelli. Fontanelli was the clown of the outfit guys, the runner and the gofer—and the pimp when it came down to it. He got the girls, got the coffee, went out for pizza. Once, in a comic weekend at a nearby motel on one of their frequent weekend furloughs, the guys mated Fontanelli with a 250-pound hooker named Sweet Sue. It would have made you die laughing. The woman practically smothered Fontanelli.

Fontanelli worked on the garden. It was a good job if you had a feel for the soil and growing things, because you could grow just about anything in this part of Pennsylvania. Fontanelli grew tomatoes as big as this. He would like to have been a truck farmer in New Jersey, but his uncle and his brother and everyone else were employed by a different firm in a different line of work, and so he had gone into the mob the way some Irish kids become cops, because there's an inevitability to it you don't fight.

Luis worked on the garden project as well. It was noted in his file he had been a migrant laborer, and the guidance counselor at the prison thought it would be good for Luis's self-esteem to do work he was good at. It was not noted in his file that he hated it, even if he did it well. He felt the first pains in his limbs now from all the stooping; he would end up like his father. But in the joint.

"I don't understand, Henry, why I got to kill him?"

"It's kill or be killed in this life, Luis," Henry McGee said. He spoke as calmly as a teacher. "But, actually, you just got to pretend to kill him."

Henry said it that way, just slow and simple.

Luis shook his head. He wanted a rush right now real bad. It was the empty time of evening when they were all watching

"Leave It to Beaver" reruns, and the tiers were full of noises made by caged men.

"What I gotta do it for? I don't get it, Henry."

"Bless you, Luis, you don't have to get it." Henry spoke in a country voice with a wide smile. It was his way. "I got a favor asked me and I said I'd do it. It's a fucking joke, Luis, don't you get it? Like the time they put Giorgio on that fat whore out at the motel. A fucking joke, but he won't know it till I step in and end it."

"I don't like to mess with dose guys. Dose guys is by themselves, they don't let no one fuck with them."

"Ain't no one fuckin' with them, Luis. Don't I tell you straight? I been taking care of you, boy. Don't you feel a lot better about everything?"

"I feel better with some of that," Luis said, not pointing.

Henry nodded. "So you want to do me this favor, Looey?"

"What you want me to do?"

"In the garden. You just pretend to go off your nut out there, and you swing your hoe at Giorgio."

"Shit, I could get shot doing that."

"I'm gonna be right there. Don't you worry. I'll grab your hoe and wrestle you down, and we'll watch the little guinea shit in his pants. Mr. Anthony is gonna be out there, all the guys. It's a joke."

Luis had two more lines and felt better about it. Henry was his friend. Henry was a tough dude, and he wasn't no fag, so he never asked Luis for anything. Henry was the kind of guy Luis wanted to meet on the outside, someone who had it together, someone who could show Luis how to do the thing right. Like a father.

Luis reasoned it through that night.

It went just right.

Giorgio very nearly got clocked by the sharp edge of the hoe, because Luis was higher than the Empire State Building when he took his swing.

Henry saw to that. Not the white lady this time but the

standard tees and blues, and it just about put Luis over the moon.

When Henry knocked him down, it was just the way he planned it.

Don Anthony wasn't there. He heard about it later. It was no joke to him.

He called Henry to conference that night and explained that the world was a matter of favors. Luis was sleeping soundly in his own cell, dreaming his cocaine dreams. Luis was a friend of Henry's. Henry should ice him. That was a favor, Don Anthony explained.

Henry very nearly could not keep the excitement out of his eyes.

FOUR

Chicago

The plan was to get Henry McGee out of Lewistown prison, which would not have been very difficult. Don Anthony lived in the federal prison as though it was his summer home. He had his friends around him; he had women when he wanted them; always there were pasta, cards, and telephone calls to the sports betting people in Las Vegas. As Henry had observed, why would Don Anthony want to escape from that?

The escape was planned for October 19. It was a variation on the hidden-in-a-laundry-basket theme. The simple plans always worked best. The escape was planned for Sunday, so that it would take the authorities nearly a full day to realize Henry McGee was gone.

Henry earned his escape by dint of $450,000 and by killing Luis Miranda. Luis's death saddened him for at least thirty seconds because he and Luis had been close. He killed Luis in his sleep as a favor to Luis. He pushed a pillow over Luis's face and pushed down until there was no breath in the thin body. Someone found him in the morning before breakfast, and his death was attributed to substance abuse because an autopsy revealed the presence of great amounts of cocaine in his system.

The neatness of the murder—as well as the quickness of it—pleased Don Anthony nearly as much as the thought of $450,000. Don Anthony, who specialized in interstate theft, particularly theft from airports, was probably worth $10 million. But money was more than a way of life, it was a way of counting. If Henry McGee had been a *paesan*, Don Anthony would have made him pay anyway.

The trouble with the escape plan was that it came too late.

On October 14, federal marshals came for Henry McGee. They prepared him for travel. They put leg irons on him, so that he could only walk with small, waddling steps. They handcuffed him with heavy metal. And then they took him out of Lewistown prison.

All his belongings were sent with him. They found the homemade knife and confiscated it. They did not find the cocaine. At least, none of the search party acknowledged finding cocaine, and Henry thought they had just confiscated it for their own use.

Henry McGee was taken by car to Philadelphia International. The plane to Chicago departed at 7:00 P.M. He asked one of the marshals why he was being taken to Chicago, a place he knew nothing about. The marshal suggested he shut the fuck up. The flight took ninety-four minutes, and the plane descended through bumpy clouds to land. It was raining in Chicago. The marshals walked Henry through the long, glittering corridors of O'Hare Airport to a gray government car parked in a no-parking zone at the lower level. The marshal opened the back door and guided Henry in, putting his hand on Henry's head so that he would not bump it on the door frame. The gesture was humane, but there was something very threatening about it as well, because it made the prisoner feel the hand of the guard, which reminded him of his manacles and his utter helplessness.

Henry stared at the rain out the side window of the gray government car all the way into the city.

They told him nothing. They barely tolerated his existence. When he had had to use the toilet facility on the airplane, he thought one of the marshals would hit him for the crime of having a bladder.

Henry McGee wore a prisoner's look. His black eyes seemed to focus on some middle distance. He stared into tomorrow, which was fifty yards away. Five days before his sure-thing escape, and they were moving him. He wondered if it was Don Anthony's doing.

The car delivered him to a high-rise triangular building on Van Buren Street. The building had narrow slits of windows and resembled three old-fashioned computer cards leaning against each other. The Loop elevated tracks permanently shaded the entrance of the building. Henry was disoriented by the noise of the El train passing overhead and by the silence of the federal marshals.

They passed him through security and turned his papers over to a man behind a gun-metal gray desk.

Henry didn't ask any questions. They weren't going to tell him.

They put him in a single room on the ninth floor of the high-rise prison called the Metropolitan Correctional Center. It was very collegelike, much softer than Lewistown. Henry looked around the room. The guard said that since he had eaten on the airplane, there would be no further food until breakfast.

He looked out the window. It was a window, and the glass, while thick, was merely glass. He looked down at the glittering city. The Loop shone with light in the soft rain. The streets were full of cars. He could see trains. He saw the lights stretching out to the horizon, grids of light on lights. It saddened him inexplicably to be imprisoned so close to so many people.

"Hello, Henry."

The interview room had no windows. It was in the federal court building one block north of the prison. Henry McGee had been escorted to the building by two somber federal marshals who handcuffed him, pushed him into another gray government car, and drove him one block.

"I coulda walked," Henry said.

"Streets are for free people," one of the marshals had said.

Henry McGee wore handcuffs and stared at Devereaux. The Devereaux of his dreams faded into the real dimensions of this man. God, Henry hated him.

Henry rested his manacled hands on the table.

"Can you take these off?" he said.

Devereaux got up, went to the door, and summoned the marshal. The marshal removed the handcuffs and looked hard at Henry, as though he regretted doing this. He closed the door on the two of them.

Henry tried to keep down his excitement. Devereaux. There was going to be a trade after all. The Soviets had come through. The Soviets kept their promise, and Devereaux was going to have to eat crow about it. That's the only thing this could mean. And to think he paid Don Anthony all that money to escape from Lewistown. Now he would go back to Moscow. He would still have fifty grand left. In Moscow, money could buy anything, the same as it could anywhere else in the world.

Henry McGee's eyes were shining again, and he felt good for the first time since they took him out of Lewistown.

"The trade," Henry McGee said.

"There's no trade."

"You're shitting me. What am I doing here?"

"How's life inside?"

"You couldn't hack it."

"Penitentiary."

"What?"

"They call them penitentiaries. It's a place for penitents. For bad people to regret their bad deeds. Do you regret yet sufficiently, Henry?"

"Come off this shit."

Devereaux said, "We want to know something."

He dealt the words like cards.

Henry stared.

"Skarda," Devereaux said.

The name lay between them. Henry picked it up and examined it. "Skarda," he repeated. It burned right back into the darkest part of his memory.

Devereaux waited.

Henry put the name back on the table. He stared at the man across from him. The walls were white, the room was a perfect box. If other humans existed, they were not aware of it. The room was the world and nothing was beyond.

"What's in it for me?"

"Your cooperation is appreciated," Devereaux said. "It shows a degree of penitence. The Lord loves a sinner who repents his sin."

Henry waited.

"On March twelfth last year, you attacked and mutilated a prisoner. Henry Lewis Jackson. You cut off one of his balls."

Henry McGee didn't blink.

"We suspect you murdered Luis María Miranda. He was your buddy in Lewistown, Henry. A hit was put on him, and it was probably you. You were his pal, Henry, how could you kill a pal? But then you stuffed that Eskimo girl in the trunk of a car in Anchorage—"

"Shit, Devereaux, I was probably the lead pilot in the attack on Pearl Harbor, too," Henry McGee said. "Let's clean up the blotter."

Devereaux went on as though Henry had not spoken. "We're afraid we might lose you, Henry. We're considering sending you to a maximum-security institution." The words were flat cards again, laid out like solitaire, all the words strung out across the table with no kings or aces showing. Henry stared at them and he didn't have a play. Time to shuffle the deck.

"Marion. It's our maximum prison. It's in southern Illinois, Henry. You've heard of it."

Everyone had. Everyone knew about the bad places. Marion was the worst. They had the kid spy—the one called Falcon—locked up down there, and it made him so crazy he was fighting in the courts to get out. The other spy, the guy who gave the secrets to the Israelis, he was there, too. The only way you got out of Marion was to die. Everyone was hard-core, everyone was doing maximum time. Marion was the waiting room of hell.

Henry McGee had seen the inside of Lubyanka once. He had gone into the basement rooms where the Cheka had beaten Reilley, the British spy, to death. He had smelled the hopelessness of the basement rooms, the smell of blood spilled and death torn out of living bodies. Marion would be like that, only he would not be tortured in a brutal manner. The torture would consist of days dropping, one by one, drops of rain on rock, wearing it down through the endless days of the endless millennium. Christ! Henry thought. He was scaring himself. He had to get control, grab the cards.

"What do you want?"

"Skarda. Tell us about Skarda."

"Honestly don't know what the hell you're talking about." Skarda. What if he played Skarda now, just a card in a friendly game, and it turned out once they got Skarda, they screwed old Henry? Play a cool hand and don't give nothing away. "Honestly don't know." Just to show he was lying.

"Honest Injun?" Devereaux said.

"Skarda. You want me to make something up?"

"Go ahead."

"Skarda. Skarda was this old fella in Alaska, used to trap on the slope, was part Inipu'it. Ran into him in Fairbanks one winter—"

"That's not good enough," Devereaux said.

Henry blinked. "Skarda is a plan. Skarda is an operation to populate the north coast of Siberia with—"

"Henry, stop fucking around with me."

"I ain't fucking around. You wanna know something. I'm trying to tell you—"

"You're hopeless. You couldn't tell the truth if your life depended on it. It does, Henry, by the way. Depend on it. Marion is not a threat. It's the reality of things. You think about it, Henry, and you get in touch with me when you've got something to say."

"Shit. You want something from me, but you don't want to give me anything. That ain't fair, Devereaux."

"Fair is for games," Devereaux said. "Fair is what we are not about. You want to work with us, we can make life tolerable. You want to fuck with us, we can make you wake up screaming every morning. We make the nightmares, Henry."

"You gonna scare me or just talk me to death?"

Devereaux smiled. "Skarda, Henry. Think about him." He got up, went to the door, called the marshal. Henry sat still at the bare table and thought about Devereaux. His back was turned. Henry could get up and hit him real sharp on the neck below the skull. Practically guarantee that he'd kill him. Then what? Then Marion for sure and leg chains and all the rest of the shit. Henry tried to keep down the violent hatred. He tried to keep Skarda clearly in mind.

The marshal put the large, heavy handcuffs back on his wrists and led him out of the room. He went down in the prisoner's elevator, back into the gray car, back to prison. The Loop was around him. Girls in bright dresses, men in suits, children, cops, taxicabs . . .

He blinked at the self-pity welling in him. He pushed it down.

Skarda.

He sat in the common room on the ninth floor and stared at the television set. The dumber the program, the more they liked it. They were like children, really, and Henry had to hold back this edge of contempt for his fellow inmates. They lined up and they marched when told to march, and they schemed in the most childish ways, schemed for little favors or treats. They pretended to be men and women, and the endless perverse cruelty and kindness of that fantasy infected so many lives that reality was blocked out.

Skarda. If he had to play Skarda, how could he make it work for him? He had thought Skarda was dead in the water when he was picked up after the first part of the plan failed, the Alaska part.

"Sam Ricca," the man said.

McGee turned. His gaze was level, waiting for a challenge or an invitation.

Sam Ricca was short and wide. He had big hands that had once hung a man on a basement meat hook. He had been a butcher once, working in a West Side abattoir, cutting steers into steaks. Then he was a butcher in a different trade. He did a greedy thing and stole more from an interstate shipment of television sets than he could get rid of. The G found the sets and nailed Ricca for them. Racketeering. It was laughable to Sam Ricca, but the seven to ten were not. He was fifty-five years old, and you started figuring out how many years you have left when you get that old.

"You're Henry McGee," Sam Ricca said.

Henry wasn't making it easy. Maybe this fat greaseball was a fag.

"I got the word from a mutual friend."

"Is that right?"

"Da fuck," Sam Ricca said. Who was this jagoff? Little guy like him make about a half-dozen steaks and a few chops. He could cut this guy with the side of his hand, didn't need a saw or knife.

Henry waited, seeing the hostility. He wasn't afraid.

"Don Anthony told me to help you," said Sam Ricca.

It was amazing. He had been in Chicago for only two days.

"He said you were trusted and that you and him had a deal. He said he didn't do nothing to queer your arrangement, it was one of those things. He said it was easier in a way for you to get out of here."

Henry didn't want the hope rising in him any more than

he wanted self-pity. You had to stay rational inside or you'd start believing any kind of fantasy.

"Tell me," Henry said.

"Don Anthony said you were to get out. I get you out. That's what it's about."

"What's in it for you?"

"A debt I owe Don Anthony. It's nothing to talk about."

"What if I thought Don Anthony set me up?" He thought about Devereaux and thought about Marion maximum-security prison in southern Illinois.

"Then my debt is relieved, you piece of shit. So is my obligation to you. If that's the way it is with you, then fuck it, I gave it a shot. I only had to give it a shot." Sam Ricca got up from the folding chair.

"Sit down," Henry said.

Sam Ricca sat down.

"How do you get out of here?"

"You afraid of heights?"

Henry blinked and shook his head.

"You strong? You look weak."

"I'm strong."

"What d'you press?"

"My shirt," Henry said. "Don't worry about it."

"I don't worry about nothing. You get outta here tomorrow night. I'm supposed to give you money, five dimes, help you on the road till you get to your bank." Sam Ricca smirked, as if he had said something funny.

"If it's so easy to get out of here, how come you're here?"

"I'm a local celebrity," Sam Ricca said. "The newspapers call me Sam 'The Butcher' Ricca. Newspapers. Well, I was a butcher in the trade. So I'm sitting a little time out till I get paroled, and I play cards, enjoy myself. I can do time. You got twenty-five to fifty hard, I hear. Don Anthony said you and him got an arrangement. Good. Anything I can do for Don Anthony is done."

Henry waited for the commercial to end.

"All right. Here's the easy part for me. I got a hundred feet of electrical cable. Black. I got a glazier's knife. You get them both tomorrow night and you do it."

"Do what?"

"Cut the fucking window and throw down the cable and shimmy down the side of the building, just like Batman and Robin."

"You're crazy."

Sam Ricca let that go with a shrug.

"Ten years ago this fall, exact same thing happened. Two guys got out. They were out for a year before they fucked up, got caught in Kentucky or something. Same way. They put TV cameras on the roof now so that it won't happen again. Except it don't work that good when it's dark. You just shimmy down the cable and you catch an El out of here."

Henry thought about it. It was as crazy as the laundry basket idea at Lewistown and just as simple. He knew he would go along with it.

He cut the window. It took a half hour. Sweat formed on his face and forearms as he cut at the thick glass.

It was one in the morning and it was raining. The rain was perfect, Sam Ricca said, it made it hard for the TV cameras on the roof. Sam Ricca was fucking cheerful because he didn't have to slide his 275 pounds down a skinny piece of electrical cable.

And where do you get a hundred feet of electrical cable inside a federal prison? Sam Ricca said the hardest part was getting broads in, that electrical cable was easy.

He pulled the glass inside. It came inside without a sound, stuck to the suction cups. He put the glass on the bed and covered it.

He wore his pea jacket and watch cap. He wore tennis shoes. He went out the window. One end of the cord was tied to the door of the cell.

He skipped down the side of the building, rappeling quickly, his feet against the wall here and here and here. He felt no fear. The concrete floor of the city yawned up at him, and the buildings were all around like narrow mountains that formed narrow, crowded valleys.

Ten feet short.

Henry dropped to the sidewalk, cushioning his fall with bent knees and then letting his body roll onto the sidewalk, taking the shock of the fall on his buttocks, shoulders, hands.

He stood up and felt a sharp pain at the back of his left ankle. He took a step, and the pain was not as bad. He could handle it.

He looked around. A bum slept in the doorway of a transient hotel. The bum smiled in sleep. Rain fell from the glowing red sky. An elevated rumbled overhead, lights winking.

He took another step. The pain was there but it was muted. The hell with it. He was free, and it scared him and pumped him up at the same time. He hurried across the street. He was free, by God! The dull months of prison fell away. He felt alive for the first time in nearly two years, alive in a way you can't be inside. It was dangerous to be free, to have this feeling of power.

He saw the blue and white police car turn into the street ahead of him. He ducked into a dark doorway and waited for the car to pass. He had civilian clothes on and had left the jumpsuit in his cell, but a prisoner gets the feeling that anyone with a badge and gun can see right through the civvies and see the soul of the con.

The rain matted his black hair and streamed down the angles of his face. He raised his arm and hailed a cab.

He climbed inside. "Airport," he said.

"O'Hare?"

"That one," he said. He wanted to settle back but he couldn't. He sat on the edge of the rear seat, and the cabbie looked back at him once or twice.

"You got a plane to catch?"

"Yeah," Henry said.

"What time's your plane?"

"Three."

"Shit, you got two hours. Don't get anxious."

The cabbie looked at Henry in the rearview mirror. The man hadn't moved. He seemed really nervous, and that made the cabbie nervous. John Mozart regretted picking up his fare. You never knew. Someone on the street when the bars were closed and you never knew. The guy was a white man, but even a white man could be dangerous.

The cabbie took the Eisenhower Expressway west under the post office to Spaghetti Junction, where the strands of three expressways connected in a bowl of ramps and cross-overs. The cab climbed and then dropped and shot onto the Kennedy Expressway and headed northwest. The roadway was nearly deserted. The city was slick and empty beneath the orange lights of the side streets and the gloom of the rain. The skyline from Sears Tower north two miles to the Hancock Building tilted up and away, winking in the eternal nondarkness.

Shit, John Mozart thought, just give him the money. He played it out in his mind, because the guy didn't say anything and sat hard on the rear seat and was staring straight ahead. Give him the money. Only don't get hurt.

Henry was still on the edge of his seat, thinking about it. Two hours, would probably be that long before the first morning flights went out. Nobody caught a plane at three A.M. And where the hell was he going anyway?

He thought about a flight back to Alaska. He knew Alaska. He could use Alaska to get back into the Soviet Union, it wasn't that hard.

But they knew that, too, didn't they? They knew about Henry McGee right down to the nth degree. Bastard like Devereaux would have that covered. They'd sew up Alaska from Anchorage to Barrow, close it down at the airports because all the harbors were frozen now.

Henry stared at the back of John Mozart's neck while he figured it out. Skarda. Where the hell had Devereaux come up with Skarda? Someone had put Skarda on Henry McGee's back, and Devereaux wanted to pound it out of him. Skarda was buried sixty feet down an abandoned mineshaft of memory, and now they were digging for it again.

The thought crossed his mind almost casually. He looked at the face on the hack license attached to the dashboard. John Mozart. Should ask him if he played the piano, Henry thought.

He knew what he had to do a moment before John Mozart knew it.

"Is this a stickup?" Mozart said, his eyes on the rearview mirror.

"Yep," Henry said. His hands were below the back of the front seat.

"Jesus. I thought it was."

"You guessed right, son."

"What do you want me to do?"

"Pull off this road and find a quiet street and pull over. Then give me your money and I go away."

"I swear to God I will, but don't hurt me. I got a wife and two kids."

"I won't hurt you," Henry said.

John Mozart believed that almost to his last moment.

FIVE

Malmö

It began with a series of mistakes on the day after the officials ended their conference.

The conference had taken an unusual turn on the second day, and the public agenda was replaced by a secret agenda.

The public believed the U.S. secretary of state and the Soviet foreign secretary were discussing freedom of the seas as it related to the shallow, frigid waters of the Baltic Sea.

Sweden had alleged abuse of that freedom by the Soviet Union when a T-class Soviet submarine grounded itself on a rocky shoal six hundred meters off the city of Stockholm. It had taken two Soviet trawlers three days to pull it off while the Swedish navy watched from Stockholm harbor.

The incident had led to an American show of strength on the eastern Baltic, off the Latvian coast, that consisted of two older frigates and a destroyer. The gray ships had sailed up and down for four days in the gray sea, shadowed all the time by Soviet submarines. The dangerous game had been called off when the conference on the Baltic was agreed to by the American president and the Soviet president.

That is what the demonstrators who gathered in Malmö on

the Swedish southern coast believed. There were no more than sixty demonstrators, but they were very colorful and the city tolerated them.

They urged the Soviets to free Lithuania.

They urged the Americans to sever relations with South Africa. They sang folk songs, and their eyes were sad.

The negotiators ignored them. Nearly everyone ignored them. They were mostly Swedes and still wore long hair and jeans. They were very sincere and passed out buttons and petitions, even in the rain.

It rained all that Saturday morning after the conference ended and the principals had gone home. The rain came straight down for a time, and the demonstrators gathered in the pedestrian street behind the Savoy Hotel and tried to attract the Saturday shoppers. But the rain was very cold, and the tolerance of the Malmö residents did not extend to catching cold. The shoppers hurried on.

It was just after eleven in the morning. At noon, Michael Hampton would collect his things—his tapes, his equipment, his translation books, which helped him look up the precise word in a precise context—and carry them down to the train station. The train for Stockholm left Malmö's old red station on the waterfront at 1340 hours. There was plenty of time.

Because of the rain, the immense room in the rear of the Savoy Hotel was colored in gray light. The room made them feel sleepy. They lounged on the wide, soft bed and held each other. They were naked. The rain made them feel dreamy and romantic and very tired of the rest of the world.

Outside the hotel, the demonstrators chanted for Lithuanian freedom and South African censure.

Rena Taurus, whose parents had fled Lithuania after the war and after the Soviet Union had swallowed up that Baltic country, pushed her hands above her head so that he might better see her nakedness. Her hair was so intensely black that it was almost blue. Her body was pale, and her eyes were deep, blue ponds. Her mouth was formed by generous, pouting lips. Sometimes, in a moment of pleasure, her lips formed a circle that made her look vulnerable, and yet the vulnerability was belied by the voluptuous touch of those glistening lips.

She drove him crazy at times, those times when she stretched her arms above her head, times when she looked at him in a certain way when they were both in a crowded room and could do nothing about her look. It pleased her to excite him, and it pleased Michael Hampton. He was blond and large and, she thought, clumsy. He spoke in a soft voice, even when they drank too much together in one of the noisy bars and it would have been better to shout.

Now her lips, wetted by her tongue, pouted to be kissed. He bent and kissed her, lost his lips in the hunger of hers. Her lips sucked his lips as her body relaxed to yield to him, to draw him on her lap.

There was a knock at their door.

He waited, poised above her, holding his breath.

"Oh, answer it," Rena said. She smiled. The moment did not pass, it was merely suspended. "I'll wait here for you."

He grinned. "I'll have to put my clothes on."

"Not too many," she said.

He pulled on his robe and went to the door. It was Rolf Gustafson, the equipment man from the temporary news bureau that had been set up in the Malmö city hall. He was some sort of employee of the town. He pretended to know all the secrets of Malmö and where the women could be found and what the price of dinner was in a particular place. He was annoying, but he was useful to the journalists who had attended the conference, as well as useful to people like Michael and Rena, who were translators and interpreters. Rolf stood in the doorway. He had two small equipment cases that belonged to Michael Hampton.

"I didn't expect this," Michael said in fluent, if not unaccented, Swedish. "I was going to pack up myself."

"It was my pleasure, Mr. Hampton," Rolf said. He had packed up everything for everyone from the journalist's lockers—he had the master key. He had earned himself several tips as a result.

Michael fumbled for a tip and held out a twenty-kronor note. The equipment man said thank you and tried to look around Michael at whoever was in his bed. Michael said thank you again and closed the door.

"That saves you time," Rena said from the bed. "We have more time." Her eyes looked curiously at his bag.

"I wish you could come to Stockholm," he began, untying his gray robe. He let it fall to the floor. Rena pulled her eyes from the bag and looked at Michael. The room was decorated in the permanent, old-fashioned style of so many provincial hotels. The Savoy was somber, gray, formal. From the front windows, you could see the blustery waves of the Kattegat that extended across to glittering Copenhagen on the other shore. "I wish you didn't have to go back."

"It's only six weeks until the winter break," she said. She was thinking of Brussels and the European Community, where she worked as a translator. Like all legislative bodies, the European parliament had frequent holidays. The EC was slowly accumulating a bureaucracy with real economic and political power, and she was an *apparatchnik* there, translating the Dutch demand for free trade into French, and the French demand for wine controls into English, and the English demand for open butter markets into German. She spoke every language well and was paid a good salary for her talents. Michael did not make as much.

After they made love again, they slept a while.

Then Michael awoke through instinct. He never set an alarm but he was never late. It was nearly one. He went into the bathroom, which was as large as some modern hotel rooms. He took a quick bath in the large tub and washed himself, remembering her scents. He was so in love with Rena that it made him helpless to think of her. If he thought of her eyes—azure and deep, innocent with all the world's secrets behind them—it broke his heart because she was not there to be touched in that moment.

He dressed, and she still slept.

He opened the two equipment bags, just to make sure everything was in order.

He discovered the mistake almost at once.

He had five tapes from the official summaries and the official "final statements" of the conference. The tapes were routine, because it was a way to double-check the accuracy of his typed translations for the various press associations he worked for. Everything was routine. His principal client had wanted him to attend this conference; his principal client had paid for information that was so inconsequential that Michael could not believe it. His principal client was a cardinal of the Vatican who demanded information on many things from time to time. Money was money, and his principal client was generous and always paid promptly. His language skills were not as rich as Rena's, but he had more range in some of the lesser languages used around the Mediterranean rim.

His hand trembled.

He picked up the sixth tape.

He knew he had had five tapes, but now there were six.

"The damned fool," he said aloud.

"What is it?" Her voice was low, full of shadows. She was on her naked belly on the bed, and she raised her shoulders slightly, and those cloudless eyes held him in a sleepy embrace. Her lips pouted the question to him, and he saw her lips were wet again. He desired her again in that moment, desired to feel her breasts beneath his fingers. . . . He looked at her and said nothing.

The rain was beating against the tall windows now. There was some anger to the sound of wind and rain. The demonstrators in the malled streets had gone away, and Lithuania was not free and South Africa was not censured.

"Six tapes," he explained.

She propped herself on one elbow in the bed and stared at him with those incredible eyes. Even if she were not attractive in face or body, her eyes would have made many men fall in love with her.

"Now I have to find out where it goes," he said, not looking at her but looking at the tape.

"What are you talking about?"

"Should I miss the train?"

"What are you talking about?" Rena seemed anxious. "You can't miss your train."

"I'll take it with me," he said, still talking to himself. He dropped the tape into the case and closed it. "Busybody Rolf packing up everyone and getting it screwed up. What if I can't return the tape?"

"It's only a tape, Michael. Don't worry about it." She sighed. "Give me a kiss good-bye, OK?"

He kissed her a long time and smelled her passion and felt her moist mouth open on him. He wanted to lie down with her again, just to hold her against him and to feel her lips on his flesh. It was ten minutes after one. The train station was just across the street.

He said, "I miss you more every time we have to split up."

"I miss you more, Michael," she said in that wonderful low voice. But her gaze was focused over his shoulder on the equipment case.

The countryside was flat and thick with pine trees. The train rocked along through the narrow valley formed by the right-of-way. Raindrops drizzled on the windows, forming patterns before they blew away. The cars were brightly lit and the warmth of the train made everyone feel a little sleepy. Michael closed his eyes and slept a while, leaning his head against the window frame. The conductor awoke him to take his ticket. They gossiped a while about the various soccer teams. When the conductor went on, Michael rose and stretched and went to the next car ahead to get a sandwich and a beer. He took them back to his compartment. He ate the sandwich slowly, staring out the window at the bleak,

chill countryside. Winter was so long in Sweden. It began
with the last breath of summer—even while the children were
still at the beach—coming one morning and blowing on the
leaves of the trees to begin their brief time of blushing and
dying. It made the summers so much more precious to know
how brief they were.

Michael fell asleep again, lulled by the warmth of the car.

He dreamed of Rena. He always dreamed of her when he
left her. He knew she treated him at times like a pet, but it
didn't bother him. She was the reward. She had come to the
Malmö conference from Brussels, for certain unnamed
clients, funded by this or that European Commission payroll.
She was so vague that Michael dropped it. He wasn't interested anyway. Rena was always mysterious, perhaps delib-
erately. She would speak of Lithuania—a place she only
knew through the experience of her father and mother—and
she would be annoyed if Michael did not understand her deep
patriotism.

Lithuania . . .

Michael woke with a start. He shook his head slowly. He
felt bad and did not know why. He had been dreaming of
Rena of the black hair and skin like alabaster.

Michael opened the paper and saw the photograph in which
the American secretary and the Soviet foreign minister shook
hands and smiled for the cameras of the world. Michael made
a face. Frauds. They were all frauds. What had his principal
client in Rome warned him?

Cardinal Ludovico had been a father to him these past few
years. They had sat in the great brocaded room in the tomb
of a building on Borgo Santo Spirito and ordered cappuccino
and ate the little, dry cookie-breads and talked of Malmö. Of
the conference. Of being aware of secret agendas by great
powers. "You are God's spy." The cardinal had smiled at
him, and it embarrassed Michael because his Catholicism,
which lingered in guilt, had long ago fallen away from the
skin of his soul.

"Watch, Michael," the cardinal had said, resting a bony

finger on his wrist. "Try to see those things at the conference that are left unsaid. Hear their silences, Michael, and judge them for me."

He was not a spy, but he would not protest to the old man. The old man was kind, not like the fools who had tried to run him into the CIA from Army Intelligence.

Michael stared at the photographs. Secret agendas.

Yes. Rena had said that night in bed, after love, after the city was asleep and they were awake . . . something. . . .

"Michael, would you love me if I had secrets?"

"Do you have secrets?"

"Would you love me if I must keep secrets from you?"

"Do you, Rena?"

"But answer."

"I love you. . . ."

Secrets. He hated the thought of them.

Michael closed the paper in disgust. He stared out the window at the dusk. There was nothing to do and ninety minutes to Stockholm Central. And then he thought of it.

He took out the sixth tape.

Stupid thing. One tape too many. But perhaps it was merely a copy of the other tapes.

He put the cassette in the black Sony machine and closed the opening.

He connected the earphones and slipped them in place. He pressed Play.

For a moment, there was nothing but silence, and then he heard the clear and careful voices.

The train rushed through a dark forest as Michael listened.

SIX

Brussels

By the time Rena Taurus left Malmö, it was nearly six in the evening. She took the hovercraft ferry across the gray, choppy Kattegat to Copenhagen and then transferred to a cab for the ride to the airport. She need not have hurried. Kastrup International, outside Copenhagen, was filled with travelers delayed by the bad weather that had blown across the North Sea from Scotland. It was a terrible time of day, and Rena felt miserable. She thought of Michael and felt a pang of guilt. She should have clung to him, given him another day together; she should be with him now beneath the sheets. . . . It was his fault as much as hers. She did what she had to do, just as Michael served his principal client, and Michael's client knew very well what this was all about, didn't he?

She smoked two cigarettes and drank a very spicy Bloody Mary while she waited in the lounge.

Sabena Air's flight back to Brussels finally took off an hour late. The 727 bucked in the headwinds on takeoff and then gyrated dangerously side to side as it struggled above the clouds. The pilot spoke in French, Dutch, and English and tried not to sound frustrated. They all wanted to go home and be safe on earth again.

The plane was full of the clammy humidity of tired people jammed together in plastic and vinyl seats. Every seat was taken. The flight attendants seemed cross as they dished out food and drink. Rena Taurus had the ability in such situations to withdraw from her surroundings and wrap her thoughts in a tight, dark cocoon that would not let mere discomfort interfere.

She did this now. The blue eyes closed for a moment and then focused inward so that she really did not see the interior of the cabin around her. She thought of a song she had sung when she was young, a song of infinite sadnesses that always moved her to tears. Her mother had taught her the song one afternoon. It was from the old country and her mother had learned it as a girl living in one of the flats in the old part of Vilnius. The song linked her to her dead mother, to the dead country she knew so little about, to the idea that her blood was Lithuanian and that the beauty of her skin, her eyes, the perfection of her mouth were all due to the beauty passed through her mother and her mother's mother and so on, back through ages when Lithuania had kings and warriors. . . . She smiled, eyes closed, seeing the connection that pleased her almost sensually. It comforted her. Had she used Michael? Yes. But she had not harmed him. She could never harm him. She was smiling but didn't realize it.

The man across the aisle was watching her, and she didn't realize that either.

A woman sat next to the man across the aisle, annoyed with him for watching Rena.

The authorities had discovered the mistake in Malmö at four in the afternoon. There had been a security alert, and the Russians and the Americans blamed each other for the missing tape. Both sides had rushed to put their agents in place. Everyone was suspect, and the interrogations had begun in the Malmö city hall. The great honor given Malmö to host the meeting of the superpowers had turned into an annoying fiasco. What was on the one tape that was so important anyway? Ah, at that question, neither side answered the confused Swedes. It was just important to put an agent on anyone who might have it, for KGB and R Section to work to solve this mystery. The man across the aisle from Rena Taurus was such an agent.

The possibilities were narrow. The mistake involved either theft or carelessness. The results were the same. There had been ten secret tapes of the secret meetings, five for each side. Each tape consisted of the actual words of the participants, as well as the simultaneous translations of the interpreters for each side.

Now there were nine tapes. The missing tape was one of two that contained the secret agreement. It was typical of the Americans and Russians to distrust each other so much that even their secret accords had to have a trail of evidence.

By design—or again, by carelessness, it didn't matter which—one of the Russians' tapes had "disappeared" from the safe room and "floated" (in the agency slang) into the possession of an unauthorized person.

The "floater" was identified as Rolf Gustafson. That was at 4:31 P.M. He seemed to want to cooperate freely with the security forces. He explained how he had made a little extra money packing all the equipment of the translators at the conference, as well as the state television's technical crew.

Were there tape recordings?

Of course.

Who got tape recordings?

The list was short. One of the names was Rena Taurus. Another name was Michael Hampton. There were no more than six other names.

The man across the aisle in the crowded jet had gray eyes framed by a pale face. There was a touch of winter in his look.

Rena opened her eyes and saw him looking at her. It wasn't so unusual. Men looked at her all the time; let them look. She gazed at him openly, as though he were naked and she wore too many clothes, too much silk, as though pleasure were stretched like satin across her belly. Everything in the universe of her gaze was created for her pleasure. Naked man, said the azure eyes. A smile of pleasure formed on her lips. It was the pleasure derived from seeing interesting or beautiful things, especially when least expected. Men interested her. She studied them the way some men study women. She was fascinated by his look and glanced at him again. He was nothing like Michael, who was generous and young and very, touchingly innocent. He was not those things. There were secrets in his eyes. Her smile faded; she was puzzled by those November eyes.

He stared at her when she glanced at him, but did not speak.

The plane broke free of the clouds only in time to begin a long descent to Brussels. The North Sea, always gray and angry, chopped in vicious waves below the wings.

She thought of going home alone to the place where she lived near the park. The apartment was small and precise. Her father, who was still alive, had visited her there once and exclaimed that whole families in Lithuania did not have so much room to live in. She knew his stories were true. She once had gone to Lithuania to find the broken thread of family memories. She had searched for names her father gave her. She found some, and was sorry she had gone back to that place her parents fled. The conditions in Vilnius had made her angry, and she had not expected anger.

The jet bumped again through the lower elevations of clouds. The attendants had picked up the empty miniature bottles and plastic glasses and paper cups and plates and were bracing themselves at the front of the plane. The No Smoking light was on.

Rena glanced again at the pale man.

In such moments of rough landings, everyone on a plane deals with fear of death. Rena believed this, but she had long since resolved that particular fear. This is what she told herself. The plane shuddered at some invisible restraint. Landing gear whirred down and locked with loud bumps. The plane tipped, rolled to the right. The farmlands of Belgium were divided below, and there were streams of traffic on the roads.

The man across the aisle only stared at her.

She thought she would take a warm shower when she was safe at home on the rue du Lavois, on the hill above the center of the town. After the shower, she might drink some of the Stolychnaya vodka she kept in her refrigerator, in the freezer section. Bread and brie and an evening to listen to music, perhaps Grieg in honor of the week she had spent in Scandinavia. She smiled at that, a dazzling smile and very out of place on a plane careening down through the clouds with 121 passengers strapped to fragile plastic chairs. But Rena was in her cocoon again: she would fall asleep and dream of Michael or the tape, and not think of Vilnius or anger or the wolf in winter. She would dream only of her pleasure.

The tires bumped and the brakes shuddered. Flaps went up, biting at the wind to slow the hurtling steel. The air slammed against the wings, and the engines whined in their familiar complaining voices. In that violent moment, they were down. Relief shrugged out of the crowd on the plane. Even as it taxied to the terminal, the plane was filled with sounds of voices again, the clicking off of seat belts, the slam of overhead baggage doors. Everything routine; piece of cake; we weren't really afraid.

The gray man did not move.

The aisles clogged before the plane made contact with the terminal. The jetway snaked out from the terminal and clamped to the bulkhead.

People pushed against each other in the narrow aisle to be first out of the plane. Rena thought it was like the ungentle queues in the fruit markets or in lines at the cinemas. She had spent four years in England once, where people waited in patient lines. She could never again become used to the aggressiveness in lines on the Continent.

Rena waited, and so did the man across the aisle.

The plane was nearly empty when she got up. She stretched and took down her weekend bag from the overhead compartment. Was he watching her? Of course, he had waited to watch her stretch and take down this bag. She was totally honest about her appearance and the effect it created. She made her way up the aisle. Near the front of the plane, she turned back.

The man across the aisle was still in his seat. He was still watching. His look was curious, even familiar. How could he presume that intimacy? But it wasn't that, Rena saw. It was a familiar look but a sad one as well, as though he was staring at a sick child or a grieving mother. And there was something else in him. Yes, she thought, exactly like the wolf. But where had she ever seen a wolf in winter? In that moment, she felt the satin stirrings inside her belly, felt a warmth that was not intended. She pouted at him in that moment, and her wet lips opened, and she looked tentative and uncertain and confused. And then she looked away.

"Sorry for the delay. Fly Sabena next time," the attendant was saying. Rena turned, nodded, stepped onto the jetway and followed the windowless corridor to the terminal. Was it raining in Brussels? She would have to get a taxi all the way to her apartment below the Palace of Justice. Brussels would be full of Saturday-night revelers.

It never occurred to her the man was following her.

She climbed the carpeted stairs to her apartment on the third floor. The stairs were narrow and the banister was elegant, sculpted in the French style of the last century. She had tall French doors for windows in her flat, and there was a small gas fireplace in the main room which bore a ridiculously ornate marble mantel. She stepped into her rooms and turned on the light in the small kitchen. The telephone was on the kitchen counter as well as the recording machine. No one had called her in a week away. It disappointed her for a moment; maybe the tape machine was broken. She would have to ask M. Claude on the fifth floor, who was a genius at that sort of thing.

A moment after she closed the door of her apartment, the doorbell rang.

She had just taken off her coat and hung it in the armoire in her bedroom. She made a face. The doorbell rang again. Claude on the fifth floor probably had seen her come in and he wanted to . . . well, he wanted to see if she needed anything. Claude was sweet, a gentle, divorced man who was a bureaucrat in EC in charge of counting such things as wheat crops in France and pea crops in Britain—but she really wasn't ready to go to bed with him.

She opened the door to the hall, and he pushed her inside. Her breath caught. It was him, the man on the plane. The wolf was very near, there was blood on his teeth.

"*Qui êtes-vous?*" she demanded.

"Sit down," he said. His voice was low and flat but without any softness. No blood, but the savage feeling was in the room now. Whatever was her in the room was beaten back to shadows in that moment. "I want to see if you took something by mistake."

"Who are you?"

He stared at her a moment. "Don't be afraid." He tried to make the words gentle, and they sounded grotesque. "There's been a problem, in Malmö. From the conference. Something is missing and it's a mistake, but we still need to have it back. I'm from the conference, and it's a little matter of security. I want to see if you have it."

"How did you follow me?"

"That was difficult, even with a police driver. Brussels taxi drivers have their own rules." Devereaux smiled again, but it did not assure her. It is one thing to have a man stare at you, to admire you, even to follow you for a while down a sidewalk because you are what you are. It is another thing for a man to be on this side of the door. . . .

"I want to see identification—"

He showed her a card. It might be identification. She would remember the U.S. Great Seal on the plastic card. He seemed slow and intent on not threatening her. She was not assured. She thought of Michael suddenly and the sixth tape.

Her bags were in the middle of the living room. He picked up the weekend case and opened it.

"This is monstrous, I'll call the police—"

He glanced at her then. The glance was almost an afterthought, as though he had decided something she would not understand.

He took out her blouses and put them gently on the couch. He took her nightgown and put it on the blouses. She had worn the nightgown when she slept with Michael in the big room at the Savoy. Her perfume was on the gown. He really was looking for something, she thought. He moved his fingers like chess pieces. They probed her case and clothing. Whatever it was, it was small, the thing he was looking for.

She saw Michael in her mind's eye. He was checking his luggage in the room at the Savoy, and he held a tape in his hand.

She saw Michael and felt chilled. Would he be in danger? But there was to be no danger, least of all to Michael.

What did he say? It was the wrong tape? He would have to return it? But she had reminded him he had to catch his train.

This could be handled with civility, then. She could tell this man about Michael and they would get their tape back and the matter would be over. She had no intention of letting Michael be in harm's way, none at all.

Rena said nothing. She folded her arms across her chest in a defensive way. She took a step back. She was very alert to the stranger filling the middle of her room. If he didn't find what he wanted, what would come next?

He was going through her equipment bag now. He opened her translation books. He looked at the tapes as though looking for a marking on them. Each cassette was turned over twice. He put them down on the couch.

She stood near the door with her arms folded, waiting. Her intense blue eyes, full of fury a moment before, were calm now. She willed the calm center that filled her, stilled every thought but this single feeling of immense calm.

He looked up at last.

"You slept with Michael Hampton. Did he mention a piece of equipment? A tape cassette that didn't belong to him? The equipment manager, Rolf Gustafson. He packed Michael's bag. Did he check it before he left you? You slept together. He must have packed his bags to leave you."

The words were careless, brutal, as though a man has the right to accuse her of making love to someone and then demand that she tell any secrets exchanged with her lover. He didn't care now if he frightened her.

"I don't know what you mean. You insinuate—"

"You shared room 343 in the Savoy Hotel in Malmö, but he was registered in a room at the Medallion Hotel. He left the hotel to catch the 1340 train for Stockholm. Did he mention anything when the equipment manager brought his bags?"

She stared. The lazy American voice was less soft now because he spoke like a policeman. All policemen speak the same, no matter what their language. It is the dialect of power.

"I don't know what you mean."

Devereaux sighed. He was on one knee on the floor in the living room, holding the equipment bag. She pressed her arms across her chest very tight to hold in her fear of him. She would not be afraid. He got up and crossed the room toward her.

He was very close and stared into her face as though studying it. She felt like a child in school again, confronted by a particularly vile teacher who wished her nothing good.

"Why do you want to lie to me?"

"What? Are you accusing me of being a liar? You are an insulting bastard. But you must be used to that. Being an American, you don't know how crude your manners are or your questions."

Devereaux reached into his pocket and took out a card. On the blank card was written a telephone number in ink. "You can call—night or day, it doesn't matter. Someone will be there."

"Why would I call?"

"You might have a reason. Sometime. We want our property back."

"I'm not a thief."

"Is Michael?"

"You are insulting."

The gray eyes let the pity seep out. "That's the least of it," Devereaux said.

SEVEN

Copenhagen

Coffee. Drank more damned coffee in the last week than in the last two years. Or at least what passed for coffee on the inside and which was nothing but bat piss anyway.

Coffee warmed him. Coffee kept him alert. Had to stay awake and stay one step ahead. Sitting in the open window of this café on the Stroget, watching faces pass, watching rain. Rain was careless, almost soft. The sheen on the pavement of the pedestrian street off Radhus Pladsen was like the sheen of makeup on a pretty face. No traffic here, just footsteps, voices, laughter.

First thing Henry McGee did after Chicago was get $50,000 out of the Bank of Hong Kong. Don Anthony had kept his word, had taken the $450,000 and left the rest. Seed money. Henry McGee thought he had to seed very, very carefully in the next few days to see where Skarda stood and where Henry stood. There had been no reason for Devereaux to suddenly bring up Skarda in that interrogation room in Chicago, no reason at all. The bastard was connecting Henry to something that nobody in the world was supposed to know about. Except him and Skarda and a dozen people on the committee inside KGB.

He had gone to the Honest Broker in Frankfurt after stealing all the necessary documentation to get an international flight. Frankfurt via New York, London, and Edinburgh, necessary detours. He felt he didn't have time to go through the riga-marole of checking out cemeteries for likely birthdates and then applying for birth certificates that could be turned into social security cards and driver's licenses and, finally, pass-ports. That was the classic way to get good paper. The other way was fairly classic too. You waited out at Kennedy for a nice planeload of tourists to come in from London or there-abouts, and you got one of the right age and size and all that, and you became his friend. Like the English director who hung out in the Algonquin Hotel bar, where all the stage people hang out. Son of a bitch hadn't heard about the AIDS crisis. Was still looking for young pretty boys.

Henry McGee had learned all that fag talk inside. Knew just enough of it anyway and said he knew where there were young and beautiful men who would do things for you. Up-shot was they got drunk together and told stories and went down to SoHo and Henry put six inches of West German steel between those thin, elegant shoulder blades, staining a Savile Row gray pearl sports coat on the way and utterly ruining a handmade Maida Vale button-down mauve shirt. This happened in the entry of a townhouse. Eric Harp. Well, play on Eric Harp and John Mozart.

He was on the morning British Airways flight out of JFK. He traveled first class and even enjoyed the service, especially Brenda the blond stewardess, who was very attentive. He liked the way her legs joined up to her body beneath the skirt. She had a nice accent to go with the legs and a bright smile that was as open as a door. He would know just what to do with a girl like Brenda over three or four days, maybe more. He was an old friend by the time they landed in London, and he almost decided to spend the night with Brenda and see how the door opened and see how her legs exactly did join her body—but that could wait. It was raining at Heathrow. He took a British Caledonian flight north to Edinburgh. It was time for the first message.

There was no point in evasion or even politeness. The Soviet consulate in Edinburgh wouldn't be able to make heads or tails out of the message, but he knew there were people there who would know the people to contact. He made the message plain to let them know he was out and running and that this was about Skarda.

He dialed a number from the telephone box at the central station off Princes Street in the heart of the old Scottish city. The spires of Edinburgh castle loomed on the hill above the railway culvert. Henry let the phone ring three times and then hung up. He dialed again. This time, they picked it up on first ring.

"Coordinate 31 Moonwalker," Henry McGee said in perfect Russian. "Skarda plus six. Henry McGee flies."

He replaced the receiver. They got the message all right. Everything was taped. He went back to his room at the Station Hotel and took a long shower. In the morning, he went out in search of a likely-looking American. Eric Harp was getting old, and he shouldn't overstay his welcome.

He found the American at noon coming out of the tour of Holyrood Palace. They became old friends within minutes and drank at one of the pubs off Princes Street. Great friends, in fact. Henry regretted another murder, especially of such a jovial companion, but Americans were always checking their fucking wallets to make sure they hadn't lost their passports, and there was an American consulate just up the street. If the missing passport number got passed on too quickly to the computers, then Henry would be up a creek again. He needed a place to hide for a while, to await contact from KGB. Did they want him home? They damned well better want him home.

Copenhagen. It was the perfect place for spies. KGB ran so many watchers and agents out of the Russian embassy there that their presence on the trams and buses was almost ubiquitous. Sweden disapproved strongly of the strong Soviet staff presence, but that delighted Denmark, as did the constant American protests about the overpresence of Soviet "diplomats." Denmark frequently conceived of its international role as class clown or social irritant.

It wasn't a matter of just running. You kept running and someone noticed it after a while and started chasing after you. The point was to stop running at the right time and start chasing someone else.

Skarda.

When Devereaux had said the word, Henry McGee felt deeply shocked, as if he had no secrets left at all. Skarda was buried so deep in Henry's consciousness that it was like a second skin.

He went to the Honest Broker in Frankfurt, the sort of man who arranges everything. He paid a handsome price, and the Honest Broker came up with three different sets of identification. The broker also took the second and third parts of the message to the Soviet stationmasters in Bonn. Let them gnaw on that.

The message came back to Henry in Frankfurt, and it was very specific about time and place. Copenhagen. On the Stroget. In the café. By the window. Rain or shine. Five P.M.

He was there a few minutes before five. Another cup of strong coffee. The Danish waitress with the flat, blond hair and tight sweater reminded Henry McGee how horny he was. The whole deal inside—the rampant homosexuality—turned Henry off, and he had pushed his erotic mind down into a hole. He didn't even want to touch himself inside. When it raged up in him, when he knew he couldn't stand it and even one of the pretty boys turning tricks inside could look good to him, he took to the yard and ran and ran until his legs cramped and his breath came in painful gasps. God. Now he was a free man, and this Danish blonde with flat hair hanging to her shoulders like the beatniks used to do was practically swinging her tits in his face. He'd like to lick those tits until she screamed.

"You are American?"

"And you're Danish, like a Danish and coffee?" Henry McGee said. He smiled. He had a nice face, and the mean in his eyes just made him more intriguing. His smile was crooked enough to make girls smile back. The blonde smiled.

And sat down.

She wore jeans that might have been as tight as the sweater. Pale skin, pale eyes, not over thirty yet.

"My shift is over, huh? You come with me and we can talk someplace. I don't like to sit in here where I work." The voice lilted, the blonde smiled at him, practically told him what was going to happen. Henry felt very tempted and then thought about being careful. There were plenty of blondes later on.

"Can't, honey. Waiting for someone."

"Your wife? Your girl?"

"See a man on business."

She smiled at that. "Not a man."

Henry paused.

"Maybe me," she said.

"Maybe you?"

"My name is Christina."

"That's nice."

"Come with me, Henry. It's all arranged. Even me. I'm part of the arrangement."

"Is that right?" He was still smiling, but the blade was out already, beneath the table, six inches from her crotch, pointed right at the seam that joined the legs of her trousers. "Is that right?"

She had about five seconds to finish it.

"The message is: *Solidarnocz* is not a union but an idea."

Just in time.

He put the knife back into the little holster inside his trousers. She was young and probably thought she was supposed to fuck him around a little, hold him on a string, before she put out the message. Dumb. But Henry thought he might like to crawl between her legs anyway and start doing business.

"Just fine, honey," he said. "Next time, put the message out up front, don't fuck around. I'm a careful man."

"So am I careful," she said, hurt.

"Where do we go?"

"I show you."

Just a girl picking up a guy in a coffee shop, taking him for a little Danish sex up the street in her rooms. Maybe she'll charge him and earn a little unreportable money to spend on beer. The lights were on; the sun was down; the rain was very gentle on a pretty, brittle city of canals and towers.

Henry wrapped his left arm around her waist. It was small, and he could feel her bones. She didn't mind. It made it look right, just the two lovers going off to do it.

They veered off left to the Skindergade, which led into Köbmagergade. Up the broad street to the canal and across into a tangle of streets. The houses were narrow and ornate and gloomy in the faded light.

"Here," she said.

They went through a gate into a garden and up wooden steps to a paneled door decorated with painted flowers. Christina looked at him and wanted to smile again. "Just like lovers," she said.

All right. "Part of the arrangement?"

"If I like you. If you treat me well."

"I like you, Tina, I do."

"Are you young or old? I can't tell."

"I'm seven inches and that's about all there is to it," he said. He said it to be as crude as possible, to make the statement in front the way you had to do inside to keep your space.

She licked her lips in a gesture learned from movies but long since part of the bag of tricks she carried around. She was committed to the cause, had been committed since she was in school. She had this stupid job, but sometimes she was given certain little assignments and it thrilled her to think she might be a spy.

The door opened and a grandmotherly type in a print dress

and short, gray hair stood in the light of the entry. She frowned first at Henry and then, in a more disapproving way, at the braless girl with long, flat hair.

"*Solidarnocz*," said the woman.

Christina started to enter.

"Not you," said grandmother. "Him."

Christina pouted on the step.

Henry stepped inside and looked back. "You working tomorrow, Tina?"

She nodded.

"I'll stop by," Henry said.

She nodded, and the door closed in her face. Grandmother held an Uzi pistol in her right hand. It wasn't pointed at anything.

"Upstairs."

The house creaked with age. A grandfather clock drummed below, the banisters squeaked when you leaned on them, the narrow stairs led up to narrow rooms. He opened the door, and there was light from a small coal fire, and a table and a chair and a man with a wide bald head dressed in black leather. Exactly like a spy, down to the leather epaulets. Henry was amused. He kept a sense of the grandmother just to his right and the leather spy at the little table just in front of him. Grandmother had the automatic weapon, probably set on single shot so that it didn't get out of hand in such a narrow room, and the fat leather spy wasn't showing a piece. Henry made these calculations as naturally as he thought about breathing or screwing Tina. After all, despite the messages and the threat implied, there was always the possibility that Mother Russia would not welcome him home with open arms. He had bent a few rules and regs in the business in Alaska, but that's what you had to do in the field.

"We are very pleased that you made your escape, Henry," said the fat leather spy. "Directorate is delighted, I might say." He spoke Moscow English, which is learned in schools where people try to talk like Peter Jennings.

"You want to know about how they know about Skarda,"

Henry McGee began. He wasn't much for booga-booga with leather raincoats and little coal fires and shadows on the wall and a middle-aged lady in a print dress carrying an Uzi. Cut the crap. "I don't know. I don't know a thing. I know they walk in one day and ask me, and it hits me as big a surprise as if they told me I was being traded out." The last sarcasm went unnoticed; Henry saw that.

"They never got it out of you in all your interrogations?"

"You know they didn't, or Skarda would be dead meat now instead of whatever it is," Henry said. "I kept the faith, even when the church wasn't lighting a candle for me. How long was Moscow Center going to let me sit in that goddamn place?"

"Henry, you caused the problem of your incarceration. You were too clever. You set out to wreck R Section and ended up dangling in it. Then you tried that escape from the Section debriefing camp in Maryland—"

"That was a setup. I didn't escape. I was set up that time in Maryland after they had arrested me."

The fat spy waved his hand to dismiss the protest. "It didn't matter, Henry. Prior to that, we could have worked a deal. After that, it became more difficult." He said "deal" with the precise reverence for slang common in all who speak English as a foreign language. "We had our eye on you. Which brings us to this point: how did you manage to escape? I mean, really escape this time?"

"Do I get to sit down?"

"Grandmother has an Uzi."

"I noticed something out of place about the way she looked. Goes nice with your dress, honey."

Grandmother spoke in Danish to the fat leather spy, and Henry didn't follow it.

"Sit down," said the fat spy.

Henry sat hard on a straight chair. This was what you called examination time. All the cards on the table, everything above board. Students will sit five feet apart. You will have forty-five minutes. Go.

Henry told the fat leather spy everything from the Lewistown penitentiary to Chicago to rappeling down a building in the middle of the night to a flight to New York to one fag Englishman and then on to an American in Edinburgh and a flight to Frankfurt and the Honest Broker. He didn't leave a thing out and didn't add a thing.

"This Devereaux brought up Skarda out of the blue?" More colloquialism, more reverence. But the words were skeptical, and Henry felt sweat bead on his upper lip.

See, even when you put down the right answer, it may not be their right answer. Like a fourteen-letter word for a man in charge of a plant. They want *superintendent*, and you put down *horticulturist*.

"I thought about that. You got to have some other kind of leak."

"Activity in the United States is normal."

The Soviet Union had several thousand agents, subagents, watchers, couriers, and paid doubles in the ranks of the combined KGB and GRU (the military espionage agency) in the United States. Key espionage centers were in New Jersey; New York City; Washington, D.C.; Miami; San Francisco; and in Los Angeles. The whole machinery of intelligence against the common enemy was itself monitored twice—at the station level and at Moscow Center level by specialists who did nothing but study the theory of espionage and intelligence gathering by Soviets against America in America. The fat spy meant that there was no reason Skarda would have been leaked to anyone in American intelligence in the United States.

Henry McGee felt naked. The knife was in his belt, but grandmother could put twenty-five rounds into his body cavity before he cleared his blade.

"All right. Here's the other scenario. Everything I told you, or the important stuff, is a lie. I gave them my piece of Skarda, and they waltzed me out of prison. They told me to go home to Russia and say hello to Ivan for them and settle into my retirement. If, along the way, I happen to kill a few citizens, well, no matter, it just makes my story look more plausible.''

"That is what some people think." Words like letters dropped in a postal box on the street.

Henry waited.

"It is not logical," said the fat leather spy. He barely seemed to move his lips when he talked.

Henry let himself breathe.

"Skarda is in motion. Skarda has been in motion for two months.''

"Well, then," Henry said.

"How convenient for you to escape from prison during the show. Now you can play your part in it. Is it not convenient?''

"Skarda was summertime.''

"Winter must serve," said the fat leather spy. "You will stay in this house until 0900 tomorrow, and then you will be moved to the operations center. Events are taking place, and you will be put in the picture at operations. You will also be reexamined," the spy said.

"All right." Very cool, let it relax. Grandmother made a face at him. He looked at her and smiled a crooked smile, the one that had charmed the blond girl.

"Grandmother will be downstairs. You will find a cot in the next room. Do you need anything?''

The fat spy rose. He was just a lackey, Henry decided. That's why he wears that Herman Goering outfit and why he shaved his head. "A bottle of whiskey would be nice. I know you can't get bourbon, but a little Johnnie Walker Red would be fine. And one other thing.''

Eric von Stroheim nodded.

"Tina. Get me Christina, the blond girl. I ain't had a piece of ass in two years.''

"What am I? A procurer?''

"The word is pimp. I get the feeling I just been put through the booga-booga by a couple of third-class couriers who have as much to say about things as Brezhnev. Just get me Tina or a reasonable facsimile and tell her she has to fuck for the cause. And a bottle of whiskey. And some of that *smørrebrod* that passes for food.'' He stretched and felt pleased with himself. He had worked it this far, and he could let his guard down for a moment. ''When we go traveling in the morning, I want to feel relaxed and nothing relaxes me like a night with a girl.''

''This is immoral,'' said the fat leather spy.

Grandmother said, ''Do as you're told.''

EIGHT

Stockholm

The report filed by the Soviet agent Krykin was precise but no less damning to himself:

At 2014 hours, the passenger express from Malmö arrived in Stockholm central station.

Your agent Krykin waited on the platform on the level below the waiting room for Michael Hampton. Hampton was observed almost immediately. He carried two small bags in one hand and a large suitcase in the other.

He appeared agitated and looked around himself several times as he headed toward the waiting room stairs. The agent would characterize him as seeming to be nervous or afraid.

Because of the crowds, your agent decided not to apprehend the obviously distraught translator in the train station.

The translator exited the station, and because it was raining, there were no cabs in line. The translator walked in the rain to the subway sta-

tion on Vasagatan and descended to the train.
Your agent also followed. The southbound subway train carried both men to the subway station
at Centralbron in the Old Town. The translator
emerged from the subway station and crossed to
Lilla Nygatan, where he picked up a taxicab. The
taxicab was number 2134, and your agent was
unable to follow it directly. Instead, your agent
signaled by pocket transmitter to the backup ve-
hicle, which arrived nine minutes later. The ve-
hicle then proceeded to the residence of the
translator at 26 Bastugatan on the south side of
the city. Your agents waited fifteen minutes in
the event the taxicab had been delayed, and then
it was decided to enter the premises.

The translator was not at home, but his bags
were in the foyer. The bags and rooms were thoroughly searched. It was then decided to locate the
driver of taxicab 2134, who, after some difficulty,
was found at home. The driver told your agent
that he had driven the translator back to central
station and that, for a tip of thirty-five kronor, he
had taken the translator's bags back to his home.
Your agent questioned the driver closely, and he
admitted that the translator had removed some
small object from one of the bags and placed it in
his pocket. He could not describe the object because
the light was bad and because it was raining.

It is always raining, the control said to himself. It is always
done in bad light. It is always someone else's fault.

There is now an ongoing attempt to locate Michael Hampton in Stockholm, although it should
be considered probable or even likely that Michael Hampton has left the country.
Krykin; Sunday, 0330 hours.

NINE

London

The message bringing Devereaux to London did not explain and did not allow for an explanation in return. What could Devereaux explain?

He had spent a long time in Rena Taurus's apartment. He had gone through her armoire, opened drawers, strewn out her secret places. She trembled with rage, she broke long silences with curses, she followed him around from place to place. She picked up the phone once to call the police, and he took it from her hand with such brutal directness that she was even more terrified. Her childlike eyes widened and her lips pouted then, not with sexual desire but with horrified fascination. He was the beast, and her rooms, her secrets had been torn from her.

He did the dirty things he had to do, and when he was finished, he sat her down and talked to her. He probed at the edges of her answers. She told him about Rolf Gustafson over and over again.

"But why would he come to your room with Michael's bag?"

She turned her eyes away. She was silent for a moment.

She looked up at him. "They knew. In the news pool. About us. It was not a secret. There was a journalist named Evelyn Jaynes there. He was a fat Englishman and always drunk. He made a pass at me. . . . I told him to leave me alone. He knew. . . ."

"Rolf would know where to find Michael."

She stared at him. "Are you a moralist? We are nearly in the twenty-first century—people sleep together, they make love without benefit of marriage. . . . Or are you a priest? Even a priest knows these things." And she thought, suddenly and unwillingly, of Michael.

Devereaux had asked her the questions over and over again until her exhaustion overcame her and she could barely speak above her yawns. Finally, in a last moment of anger, she had said, "What do you want from me?"

"The truth of things."

"I tell you the truth. What do you want? I'm exhausted, I need to sleep, I'm going to bed. I'm not even afraid of you now, not the way I would be afraid if I were awake. You can do anything you like. I have to sleep."

And he had left her at the moment before dawn. She collapsed on the couch, and he had covered her with a blanket from the bedroom. He had stared down at her beautiful face. Her lips were wide and open, and her teeth were bright in the moonlight. Her black hair lay in tresses about her on the pillow. She began to haunt him in that moment, and the obsession had continued along with his insomnia.

He would see Rena in unlikely places—on the flight from Brussels to London, sitting in Heathrow, on the underground to Victoria Station—but she did not haunt him like the illusions of Rita Macklin he saw in the streets of New York. Rita Macklin had been part of him. He understood that psychic urge to fill in the empty space. But these hallucinations of Rena Taurus were symptoms of mere exhaustion. He had been awake, day and night, Friday and then again Saturday, and now it was Sunday morning and he was taking pills to prop himself up. But the message which ordered him to London did not permit explanation that Devereaux's body was failing the mission.

The elderly black Austin cab chugged up the empty Sunday-morning length of Victoria Street. At Trafalgar Square, the cab made the wide circle left and then picked its way through the pigeons into the Strand. Ben Jonson and Lyndon Johnson and Dr. Johnson . . . tired of life, tired of London, tired beyond belief or ability to sustain life. . . . He closed his eyes a moment and pinched the bridge of his nose.

He realized he was permitting the confusion to overcome him. The pills could not stave it off. He had to collapse, to sleep, to fall through a nightmare and emerge back into consciousness with a sense of being whole.

Rena. She had reached for her case in the overhead compartment, and her breasts strained a moment against the sheen of her white blouse. Well, what was she supposed to do? Devereaux stared at her, and she was beautiful in all her parts so that the whole of her was hard to consider. What color were her blue eyes? Blue, of course, but something like the color of the sea on a bright day beyond the beach at Nice.

Christ, he thought. He rubbed his eyes, and when he removed his hand, there was a reddish glow about the world, which previously had been gray.

The Strand led into Fleet Street, and Devereaux reached into his pocket for the fare. Below Fleet Street, at the viaduct that runs down to Blackfriars Bridge on the Thames, he could see the dome of St. Paul's. Shabby old Fleet Street was no longer the same; perhaps his memory of it had been an illusion as well. Fleet Street's press had fled to break the union grip on printing papers. The life had gone out of the street, and Sunday morning seemed like a wake.

"Here y'are, surr," said the cabbie.

He leaned forward, saw the meter, looked dumbly at the notes in hand. He had lost the ability to count. Five-pound notes, this must be Britain. There were Belgian francs as well in his hand and Swedish kronor. What could he make of it? One plus one is . . .

He handed over two ten-pound notes.

"I don't have change—"

But Devereaux lurched out of the cab like a drunk. He carried the single overnight bag to satisfy customs. If he had arrived without a bag, they would have detained him. The bag contained nothing of value, certainly not the pills he left behind in Brussels. Nor the 9mm Beretta automatic. The English were peculiar. They required a six-month quarantine of animals in case the dog or cat was rabid. . . .

They should have quarantined me, Devereaux said. He thought he said it aloud.

The safe house was not a house at all but rooms let on the third level of the grimy black building a hundred yards west of the old Daily Telegraph Building. Sunday morning dozed in London, dozed in England; it was church bells and nothing on the telly and a thirst building up to pub opening time and sleep across the land. The sky moved clouds to sea slowly, like a church procession.

Devereaux climbed the stairs because the lift was locked. The stairs were marble, the banister black wrought iron. A single fifteen-watt bulb lit the entry of each floor. His feet were stone and the stones clanked on the stairs.

At the end of the hall, he saw the light under the closed door. He knocked and waited for the inevitable television camera inspection. He saw the camera stare at his haggard face, and he suppressed an urge to smash it. Just to smash something, to see it crack.- . . .

The buzzer clicked.

He turned the brass knob and opened the door. It was the last person he expected to see.

Hanley sat behind the desk. Director of Operations for Section come all the way from Washington to the edge of field operations. What the hell was going on?

Devereaux stared at the pale-eyed rabbit for a moment and then sat down heavily on a straight chair. He dropped the bag of props on the floor beside him.

"You look awful."

"Thank you."

"You took pills—"

"They run out on you, Hanley. You reach a point of hallucination."

"There's a cot in the other room. How much do you need?"

"A week at least," Devereaux said. He lurched again, sitting in the chair. Damn. He felt almost drunk. He looked out the window and saw Rena Taurus in the doorway across the street, stretching to reach her bag in the overhead compartment.

"We had a tap on her phone. We made this four hours ago—"

"I talked to her all night. She wasn't clever and things didn't fit right. I believe she's become convinced something bad is going to happen to Michael Hampton. I'm convinced she knows he has the tape. But she's stubborn."

"We don't have time for stubborn girls," Hanley said.

"She was too pretty to break."

Hanley pursed his lips. "That's crude."

"What you suggest is crude."

"I suggested nothing."

"No. You never do."

Silence. Wind. Panes rattled. Silence and silence. Devereaux yawned.

"She had a telephone call four hours ago. We recorded it," Hanley began again.

"Why did I have to come back here? To hear a tape? Why are you here?"

"I flew in twelve hours ago. I haven't slept much myself." Hanley looked for sympathy and found none. Their faces were both composed of gray ash. "There were developments. On this matter and on the other matter as well."

"Henry McGee."

Hanley nodded. "All the points began to converge."

"Lines converge, not points."

Hanley did not bother to frown. He put the cassette in the small Sony tape recorder and pressed the play button.

Devereaux stared out the window. Suddenly, at the sound of her voice, he was alert. All the tiredness seeped out of him. Rena's voice cut through him, and he could see her, standing at the phone on the counter in the small kitchen in that Brussels apartment, talking in her clear, assured way. He saw her lips, saw the curl of her tongue, saw the teeth flash as she spoke into the mouthpiece, saw every part of her. She touched him and he felt desire like a spark alive in the black hollowness.

RENA: Who is it?

MICHAEL: Rena.

RENA: Oh, Michael. I called and called, and there was no answer.

MICHAEL: I couldn't go home. I was followed at the train station. [Muffled.] I knew I was followed. Oh, Rena. This is the most terrible thing in the world.

RENA: A man came here when I got home. He pushed his way in. He had been on the airplane, he stared at me. It was a terrible flight. Late. We had storms. I took the hovercraft to Copenhagen. . . . Raining. . . . He followed me—he might have been on the hovercraft. He went through my bags, and he said he was from security, and they—he meant the security people—were missing something. He opened the armoire, all my drawers, and then he questioned me. Over and over. All night he questioned me, he wanted to know about you and me, about the tape.

MICHAEL: Christ. They know it already, they know I have it. This is the worst thing. It's what I was afraid of in Stockholm, and later I thought I was paranoid, but it was real, wasn't it?

RENA: What is it? What is the tape?

MICHAEL: I can't tell you. I hoped you weren't in it. They went after you, too. [Mumbled; unclear.]

RENA: I thought about that cassette. In the room at the Savoy. You said it didn't belong to you.

Devereaux hit the stop button. He looked at Hanley. "He has it. I was sure Rena knew."

"It seems so."

"Where is he?"

"We don't know. A Soviet—we presume a Soviet—team trailed him to Stockholm. He gave them the slip. He could be anywhere in the world."

"He listened to the tape."

Hanley spread his hands to show his sincerity. "It seems the only thing to believe."

Devereaux shook his head. "Then Rena is in the clear?" He would not go back; he would not see her again.

"No," Hanley said in a very quiet voice. "That's why you have to hear the whole tape. Why we have to devise a strategy." He backed up the tape and then pushed Play again.

RENA: I thought about that cassette. In the room at the Savoy. You said it didn't belong to you.

MICHAEL: I was going to return it—

RENA: Why can't you?

MICHAEL: I can't.

RENA: He asked me, the man, he asked me if you had a tape that didn't belong to you—

MICHAEL: Christ, what did you tell him, Rena?

RENA: I didn't tell him. I didn't, Michael, believe me. I was going to tell him, but I didn't for some reason. . . . Michael, what's so terrible? What could have happened? I saw you less than twenty-four hours ago. . . . [Pause of five seconds.] Michael?

MICHAEL: I have to get out of here, out of Stockholm, I don't know where. This is a terrible thing, I see it now, I listened to the tape. What can they do? Their hands are tied. If I hadn't listened to the tape . . . Sometimes you're better off not knowing. I was sitting on the train, I was bored, I thought I'd listen to it. My God, I could never convince them, could I? Do you think I could? What am

I talking about? They're professionals, and I don't mean a damned thing to them.

RENA: Michael! Michael, get hold of yourself.

MICHAEL: I'm terribly scared, Rena.

RENA: What can it be that's so terrible? You're just upset.

MICHAEL: This isn't going to be all right tomorrow or the next day. The clouds don't have silver linings, Rena —listen to me, for God's sake. I've got to get leverage. There has to be a way to deal with them so they'll have to back off. Who can I get leverage with? I'm crazy with being scared, Rena. I can't think—

RENA: It was an American. He showed me some sort of identification. I remember the eagle, the American symbol—I'm sure of that. He pushed me into the room first, but he didn't touch me after that. You know what I thought. I knew he was the man on the plane. I thought he was going to do something . . . sexual. He went through all my bags—it was humiliating.

MICHAEL: I know what was on the tape.

RENA: Give it back to them.

MICHAEL: It's not a question of that. My client . . . that old man suspected all along something was going to happen. . . . It's not just on the tape, Rena, it's not a matter of giving it back. They could have it today, this minute. It's in my head. I know what was on the tape, Rena. I can't give them my memory.

RENA: What could be so important? It was a conference about naval security, about freedom of the seas in the Baltic, what could be so important? I don't like to hear you talk like this, Michael. You're making yourself sick.

MICHAEL: It makes me sick to my stomach. I want to give it back, I don't want to know their dirty secrets. Why'd that fool Gustafson pack the tape in my bag? It's terrible, Rena, a terrible and cynical thing. It has nothing to do with what we reported, nothing about the Baltic or freedom of the seas. . . . Those were just lies. I thought they were frauds, I've always thought that, all the goddamn politicians. Everything you told me about Lithuania— Goddamn the bastards, the lying political bastards.

RENA: What was on the tape? About Lithuania? Start with that. You must tell me, let me help you.

MICHAEL: I can't tell you, or then you'll be in trouble too.

RENA: Michael, what are you going to do?

MICHAEL: I don't know. I have to get out of Stockholm first. I'm still in Stockholm. I have some money, traveler's checks, my American Express card. Rena?

RENA: I'm here, Michael.

MICHAEL: Do you remember the weekend on the canal?

RENA: Of course I do.

MICHAEL: I need money, Rena. I need some time to think about what to do. Could you meet me there on Monday? At the old hotel? It'll take me that long to get out of here. Could you bring me some money?

RENA: I love you, Michael. The man gave me a telephone number to call if I needed help. Should I call it? You can't be alone in this—

MICHAEL: Rena! This isn't a game, and they're not the good guys, even the ones with American accents and white hats. They've made a devil's deal, and they had it on the tapes so that neither side could ever back out of it. That's the point of the tapes. Except . . . except I have one. I didn't want to know this, I really didn't want to know this.

RENA: Tell me, Michael.

MICHAEL: Then you'll know. Then they'll have to come after you. Don't you see that?

RENA: I'm not a child.

MICHAEL: Monday. In the afternoon, it'll take me that long. If I can come straight to Brussels—well, there's no point in figuring it out ahead of time. Be careful no one follows you.

RENA: Michael?

MICHAEL: I have to go. I love you, honey, I love you more than myself.

RENA: I love you.

Hanley turned off the machine.

The office was consumed with the sudden silence. The place was shabby, temporary looking, as though someone were running a mail-order boiler room out of the place for a few months and expected to move on.

Hanley let the tips of his fingers form a tent.

He studied the tent by turning his little gray head to the side. His eyes were so intent on the fingers that he might have been dreaming of something else. He let the silence go on until the bells of Westminster began their song.

"Rena Taurus. Is she likely to help Mr. Hampton?"

Devereaux said, "I don't know."

"What's she like?"

"A woman. Intelligent." He thought of her lips, the innocent look in her eyes and the blue blackness of her hair, white marble skin, perfect in every part. . . . He was this close to her, smelled her tiredness and fear and, yes, the odor of sexuality. "I can't say."

Devereaux stared at Hanley, not the triangle of fingers. His own hands rested flat on the arms of the wooden chair. There was no tension in his body, no sense of incipient movement to upset the shabby balance of the rooms.

"Michael is in grave difficulty," Hanley said.

"So you know what was on the tape?"

"No. I don't know."

"Then why is he in trouble?"

"Because the tape is missing. Because all hell is loose in Washington. Because the secretary of state is furious with the lack of security at the conference, security performed by R Section agents."

"I was not involved."

"That's true," Hanley said. He was talking like a lawyer now. "You were an observer in black, a secret watcher. But the security was provided out of Eurodesk by R Section. Section is to blame for this breach. In the eyes of the secretary of state, who is beyond being furious. I thought he would physically attack Mrs. Neumann.'' He referred to R Section's chief.

"A gentleman does not strike a lady,'' Devereaux said.

"As you demonstrated in your frustrating interrogation of Rena Taurus. Did you suspect she would not respond to pain?''

Devereaux knew he could not speak for a moment. When he found his voice again, he said: "What's the agreement on the tape? Hampton said they made a 'devil's agreement.' ''

"I don't know,'' Hanley said again.

"But you came all the way to London just to ride the ponies.''

"I was instructed.''

"By Mrs. Neumann.''

"Yes.''

"And does she know?''

Hanley spread his hands again.

Devereaux said, "This is crazy. There are nine tapes instead of ten. We have five, they have four. It's their responsibility to get the last tape back.''

"No. It's a mutual responsibility,'' Hanley said.

"Why?''

"To show our good faith.''

"Fuck good faith,'' Devereaux said.

"Yes. You put it so well. But in this case, we cannot.''

"Who is Michael Hampton?''

Hanley smiled. It was as thin as the sunlight breaking through the pearl clouds.

"That is the nub, Devereaux. You hit upon it. If it had been Rena Taurus, it would not have mattered. She is a technocrat, an EC bureaucrat, and nothing on earth is as controllable and predictable as the destiny of a technocrat. But Michael Hampton is a wild card. Or a loose cannon.''

"In what way?''

"He has no clearance, none at all, except to represent the press at such conferences. I know for a fact that he could not have any higher clearance. Couldn't get clearance. He is accredited with three small, obscure agencies, news organs of the Third World, two of them in the Middle East."

"Not in Israel."

"Decidedly not in Israel. Doubtless the Third World has every right to access to news—"

"Come on."

Hanley frowned. "You're right. There is no urgency to a conference in faraway Sweden held on Baltic security and 'freedom of the seas.' Unless something else was under discussion at the Malmö conference. Alas."

Devereaux said nothing. Tiredness was in his bones, but in the past ten minutes, something was struggling to replace it below the patient, sealike exterior. Perhaps it was the sound of Rena's voice. Just her voice and not the frightened drama of the words caught on the wiretap tape.

"And they won't tell you."

"No. State is very close on this."

"What is it we want?"

"The tape. Before it falls into the hands of two Middle Eastern news agencies which are not Israeli."

"And the third?"

"I beg your pardon?"

"Who was the third agency Michael Hampton was accredited with?"

"The Congregation for the Protection of the Faith," Hanley said.

Devereaux stared at him.

"The eyes and ears of the pope. The semiofficial, totally secret, and utterly deniable Vatican agency in charge of what the more mundane world calls counterintelligence. The Vatican's intelligence agency."

Devereaux shook his head. "This is absurd. I'll take a nap, and you can wake me up later and share the joke."

"Michael Hampton is a free-lance translator and part-time 'journalist' for relatively unsavory organizations, including the Congregation for the Protection of the Faith. I trust my Methodist upbringing has not led me to a perverse form of anti-Catholicism, but we have dealt with the good people of the Congregation before. When Cardinal Ludovico dies, they will have to screw him into the ground."

"Who financed his trip to Malmö?"

"We don't know."

"Is anyone trying to find out?"

"The assumption is that it came from the Middle East agencies. Perhaps not."

Devereaux shook his head again. "You take too much on faith, Hanley. Why are we working with KGB to track down Michael? Why believe there even is a missing tape? Why aren't you on the loop?" The loop was the current bureaucratic slang for the small number of people who would be permitted to sign off on any particular secret project or read a secret document.

Hanley made a sound and his head resumed an upright position. The tent folded. He stared across at Devereaux. "Is this an exercise? I don't know. CIA is digging our grave again, whispering in State's ear about our security incompetence. The conference in Malmö was Section's game. Maybe this is all a phony war, and we are chasing the red flag of the other side. But I don't think so." He stopped, wanting to say something more profound, could not find words.

Devereaux did not speak.

Gloom settled on their shoulders. "Security becomes a monster when it's left untended," Hanley said. "The matter of Henry McGee, the escape from prison in Chicago . . . You see, I can't believe in too many coincidences. First the tape is reported missing. Then we find the wide and open trail of Henry McGee. Which leads him here."

"Where is he?"

"He landed in Copenhagen forty-eight hours ago. Exactly

forty-five minutes by hovercraft from Malmö, Sweden. Isn't that a jolly coincidence?''

Devereaux stirred. Henry McGee always interested him.

Hanley continued, ''He was lost in the U.S. for thirty-six hours, and then we found his trail again, going out of New York with an English passport. We kept just far enough back to watch him. He entered Copenhagen, Denmark, a day ago using a phony American passport under the name of Henry Miller. Occupation: writer.''

''Where is he now?''

''We don't know.''

Devereaux sighed. It was as though he suddenly collapsed. ''Did he use the Honest Broker in Frankfurt?''

''Yes. That's one of the ways we followed him.'' There were a dozen men in the world like the Honest Broker in Frankfurt. If you had the money, they could arrange ''matters.'' They were go-betweens uniting arms dealers and revolutionaries, traitors on the run and the passports they needed to keep running. They were men like Felix Krueger in Zurich and the Honest Broker, men trusted by every side in the way every side trusts the American dollar or a bar of gold in a Liechtenstein bank. Hanley went on: ''Three sets of ID. The point is, why Copenhagen?''

''It's a good place to make Soviet contact. The Soviet embassy is Spy Central there.''

''Copenhagen is just west of Malmö, Sweden.'' There. He did not believe in coincidence. ''Henry McGee's name surfaces on a code sheet. A sheet delivered to us by a Russian sailor who defects in Stockholm more than four weeks ago. The name McGee is linked to something called Skarda. Now McGee escapes our prisons and is next seen in Europe in a city thirty-one klicks west of Malmö. Where a tape recording of a secret conference has disappeared. These things don't just happen this way.''

''Is there a connection between Skarda and this conference? Maybe with this tape?''

Hanley shrugged.

Devereaux started to speak but said nothing. He stood up and went to the window. Fleet Street held no answers. He did not see the illusion of Rena Taurus. Or Rita Macklin. Ghosts had fled his thoughts, and his tiredness was nothing more now than an irritation with his body. He saw Michael Hampton and a cassette tape and Henry McGee and whatever Skarda was.

"So what's the key?" Devereaux said.

Hanley stared at the slate-gray wall opposite him. There was a calendar on the wall put up in 1979. It was turned to August.

"Rena. If Michael eludes the KGB, the key is Rena. We don't know where Michael is—"

"I was assigned to Rena Taurus," Devereaux said.

"Yes. And they were assigned to Michael Hampton. Do you suppose that was coincidence as well?"

"I don't know what to suppose."

"I don't trust the bastards," Hanley said.

The unusual epithet—Hanley never swore—made Devereaux smile. He turned from the window and felt much better.

"Which ones?" Devereaux said. "Who put the clamp on our need to know?"

"It came from the highest levels."

"The president."

"The president wants something and it is apparently involved with whatever secret agenda was agreed upon at Malmö. We shall know at the pleasure of the president. In the meantime, Section is in deep doo-doo. Is that clear enough?"

"No. Not yet. What about the two Middle East news agencies? Where are they?"

"Tripoli. Our friend the colonel. The other is in Riyadh. Our friend the king. Michael Hampton is quite the Arabic scholar. Why would they send him to Malmö for a tedious conference on the right of American ships to intimidate the Lithuanian coastline?"

"You asked me that before," Devereaux said.

"In time we discover all the secrets," Hanley said.

Devereaux said, "I'm going to lie down now."

"You have to get back to Rena today—"

"The banks are closed on Sunday. If she has to get money for Michael, she'll have to wait until morning. The point is, anyone sharing this tap?"

Hanley said, "My orders are to cooperate fully with the security forces of the Soviet Union in recovering what is, essentially, Soviet property."

Devereaux stared down at him.

Hanley opened his hands to see if they were empty. "The answer is no. They have their games and we have ours." He looked at Devereaux's haggard face and tried a small, tight smile.

TEN

Berlin

The Air France jet from Hamburg had only been aloft thirty-five minutes when it began its steep dive through East German airspace for the tiny dot that was Tegel Airport, the link between West Berlin and the West.

Michael Hampton felt the plane strain downward through the surging nighttime clouds, and he closed his eyes. He hated landings; he was still as terrified as he had been on his first flight twenty years ago. He had flown hundreds, perhaps thousands of times, but the landings always induced this suffocating panic.

He thought of God. He thought of Rena. He thought of the moment of impact when the billions of molecules that made plane and passengers and crew and baggage exploded into eternity.

The jet bumped down, and the plane raced across the smooth tarmac to the terminal building. This is Sunday night, this must be Berlin. He opened his eyes and smiled. It wasn't really funny, any of it, but the strain of running was beginning to make many things seem funny to him.

He took the small bag from under his tourist-class seat and

joined the crowd now in the aisles, waiting to get out. He wore a plain blue parka—he had bought it in Göteborg at a ship's chandlers—and a dark sweater. The bag had underwear and socks and a bottle of aspirin and a cassette.

He pushed toward the jetway and then into the customs area.

There were six policemen and two policewomen in the wide entry between the baggage claim room and the rest of the terminal. They were large and German, with flat foreheads and marble blue eyes. They were body searching the departing passengers in little curtained cubicles set up as part of the exit way.

Michael felt a wave of panic. What could he do, run back to the plane? He gripped the handle of the little bag tighter.

He had his own passport and his own identification, and they were looking for him here, in Berlin. It was—

"*Bitte*, Herr . . . Hampton." The policeman read the passport for a moment, stared at the picture, stared at Michael Hampton. He held the passport open with his thumb. The cold eyes of the big German policeman stared right through Michael. The policeman looked like a statue or a recruiting poster. "Are you here for business or pleasure?"

"Pleasure."

The clipped German accent made the English words fall like hanging bodies. "Are you here long?"

"Two days."

The policeman looked at the bag. He put the bag on the table and opened it. He searched the bag with careful fingers and went through everything. He fanned the pages of a paperback thriller in the bag. He opened the plastic bottle of Bayer aspirin.

"Aspirin," said the policeman.

"Aspirin."

Michael started to make a joke about drugs and paused. It was exactly what you never did. Especially in an airport. Especially to a policeman.

"And a tape cassette?"

The policeman held up the cassette and looked at it and then at Michael. Very cold eyes now, very curious and cold eyes. "You have a cassette?"

"Yes."

"And where is the player?"

"I beg your pardon?"

"Your cassette player?"

Jesus Christ, Michael thought. What a stupid thing to do, carry a tape without a player. "I broke it. In Hamburg. I came in from Hamburg."

"What is on this tape, then?"

"Songs. I tape songs I like from the radio—" He felt miserable, he thought his voice was pathetic.

"So," said the German policeman.

He stepped forward into a booth where he would be searched. The policeman had barely glanced at his passport. What the hell were they looking for? He felt the metal detector as it glided over his clothes. He took change out of his pocket and held out his wrist so that the technician could see his Seiko watch was the cause of the detector's alarm.

And then he was free, on the other side of the barrier. He felt lightheaded suddenly because he had been running for more than twenty-four hours and he wanted to sleep. They had let him go, they weren't looking for him. He crossed to the entrance way and found the taxi ranks.

Berlin seemed sinister as the Mercedes pulled away from the glitter of the airport and plunged onto the autobahn. The wide parks were dark; the silence of the immense woods reached to the edges of lighted roads. Why Berlin? But it was the next plane out. Hopscotch. Göteborg. Then Kastrup. Then Hamburg. Now Berlin. He'd wanted to go direct to Brussels, but the flight had been canceled and he had this . . . feeling. They must be right behind him; they would sweep down on him a moment before he stepped on the plane. . . . Berlin was easy to get away from. He had to sleep and to kill time until he could meet Rena. Money, time, had to get the tape south. He thought again about the plan he had in his mind, and he thought it was good. It was going to be all right if it all worked out.

Down into the glitz of the Kurfürstendammstrasse, the Ku'damm Sunday night, and the crowds surged beneath the glittering rows of electric signs promising food and drink and dancing and love and all the goods of the world. The taxi slowed, the driver humming a song to himself. The girls wore bright raincoats and showed their legs as they strolled on the broad sidewalks. Punks with bizarre haircuts and haunted eyes darted in and out of the lines of slow-moving traffic. Everyone on the Ku'damm was on parade, everything was made up and a trick. Girls watched for boys and boys watched for boys and middle-aged men strolled with the young. Michael watched the homeless and supperless line up at the charity soup truck near the Kaiser-Wilhelm Chapel ruins, and he realized he hadn't eaten all day. Hunger was greater than tiredness—he would have to eat.

The little hotel on the side street had no dining room, and they would not accept the American Express card. He paid out in deutsche marks and looked at what he had left. He asked directions for a place where he could get a wurst and a beer, and his German was good enough to please the woman behind the front desk. She relented her Teutonic armed stance and gave him a very good corner room and told him about Otto's *bierkneipe* up the street. It was a good enough place, and they still served food, even on Sunday night.

He thanked her absently, and she took a good look at him at the door of his room, looked at him and at the bed in the good corner room. She said her name was Ernestine. She had a wide, generous mouth, and he realized what it was Ernestine was really saying, and he almost started laughing again.

"There were policemen at the airport . . ." he said.

"It's on the radio. Terrorist sweep." She shrugged. "It is supposed to be over tonight. They found arms and explosives yesterday on an Air France flight."

So.

All routine, nothing to worry about, piece of cake.

He closed the door on Ernestine and went into the room and put his bag on the bed. He took off his clothes and went into the bathroom and tried the old-fashioned shower in the claw-footed tub. Water under pressure wailed up through the pipes, and it was hot and soothing. God, it felt good on him, massaging him. His skin tingled and he closed his eyes and held his head up to the water pouring down.

Ten o'clock. The withered autumn linden trees were stark against the glowing sky. The clouds reflected all the thousands of lights on the Ku'damm and the streets that led to it.

Michael hunched his shoulders against the damp and shoved his hands deep into the pockets of the parka. He was bareheaded. He had thought about nothing but the secret of the tape since that moment in the compartment on the Stockholm train. Why had the accident happened to him? Some stupid clerical mistake, probably by that fool, Gustafson, and it was coming down to finding a way to survive. Not that anything had happened yet. Maybe he was just paranoid, thinking he had been followed on the subway in Stockholm. No. He had seen the man twice, he was sure of it. They were following him.

The little tavern was warmly lit, and they did have wursts served on paper plates with bits of mustard and a hard roll. He sat at the table and gratefully ate the small repast and listened to the roil of voices around him. He held the hard roll in his left hand and the wurst in his right and dipped at the mustard in the approved German way. The action of eating, filling his body, slaking his thirst with beer settled him. He fell almost into a trance, thinking randomly of things beyond this room.

In such moments—it could happen anywhere—he would suddenly see the link between himself and the little boy he had been who had grown up in Cody, Wyoming, a thousand miles from anywhere.

The reverie happened now, precisely as it had happened a hundred times before. The same reverie presented in his mind in the same way, the collection of his past laid out as orderly as pages in a scrapbook. He turned the pages while he ate and drank.

He had not been a good student in the cheerful, go-along sense of the word. Not a good student, but he had this astounding facility for language. It was so easy that he could not comprehend how others could not fall into the habit of working and even thinking in other tongues, so easy that he was declared a prodigy. His brother, Will . . .

Michael closed his eyes tight. No matter where he was, the time of day or night, the presence of friends or strangers, when he thought of Will he first had to cry. It only lasted a moment, this first painful memory of Will, but then it was all right. He opened his eyes and they were wet, but he was not going to cry now. It was part of the reverie; it came at precisely the same time each time he remembered.

Will was big and easygoing and handsome. Will wanted to be a cowboy and nothing more. Will rode well but Michael never did. Will was two classes ahead in school and protected Michael when his *peculiarities* came to the attention of bullies or teachers. Will was his big brother, and he'd do anything for Will. Except he couldn't stop Will from hurting himself. Will signed up for a three-year hitch in the last part of the war. Will loved country and flag and being a cowboy and being a soldier.

"Will," Michael said aloud. He toasted his brother with the beer.

He put the stein down and stared at it and saw Will. Will in the army. Will home on leave, showing his uniform to the girls. Michael said nothing to Will, whom he loved, but he wasn't going to join any goddamn army.

Army. The stupidity of it. One of the last to be drafted, Michael had tried to volunteer for a National Guard company, and he thought it had been fixed, the deal was set. . . .

Army Intelligence. Oxymoron. Top-secret clearance. He didn't want to know any secrets. Then Captain Guthrie had let Sergeant Peterson explain it to him: "You don't want intelligence duties and we don't want reluctant troopers, so we come to an impasse. But right now you got a big brother sitting over there in Da Nang who gets to fly in helicopters to these here fire zones and gets to shoot gooks. 'Course, it's only fair they get to shoot back, and he's got another nine months out there, and there is every chance that some dirty little fucker in black pajamas might just get lucky and nick a big fella like your bro'. Am I going too fast for you, Mike? Intelligence has got its clout and little privileges, and it just might be that your bro' could actually be assigned to heavy duty in Bangkok, which is called Bangkok because that's all cocks do there all day long, bang bang bang. You like my joke? So if you want to think about your bro' slogging his sorry ass through the jungle of 'Nam or getting laid on a nightly basis in the rottenest lovely city in this whole world, you think on it, because that's what your intelligence is for."

Jesus, he loved Will. Pa didn't understand him, but Will did. Ma was dead, and he never thought about her. Wyoming was as big as the universe, and there was no point to touch in it except for Will.

Shit, yes, he'd shovel shit for Will.

They cut him a thousand times with razor cuts that year, the spooks in Army Intelligence. He heard too much, he knew too much, and he tried to keep it out of his mind. He tried to be secret, he tried to hold back his contempt for them. For Guthrie and Peterson and the men who came down from DA in trench coats and cheap suits and made him earn his mess . . . all the spooks. Do you know what they did? But no . . . you don't tell anyone those things. Because he was so skilled at languages, he became the man who heard too much, and it was pain, after a time, a continuing pain in the gut that never went away.

And thirteen months into service—he was stationed in D.C. at the time—he got a call from Pa in Cody. Pa was sober like always and said Will was dead. Said it flat, the way Pa said the yearling died or Ma died or the wind smelled of snow or there was fire in the mountains from the lightning storms. What? Will was dead. How could he die?

Got run over by a deuce-and-a-half in Bangkok in broad daylight. Dead as in dead.

Sergeant Peterson said he was sorry, but DA had lived up to its end. People did get run over sometimes in city traffic.

"But, Sergeant Peterson, sir, you don't seem to understand a fucking thing. I sent Will to Bangkok and I fucking well killed him. And I don't have to do shit for you no more, Sergeant Peterson, sir."

Peterson started about how he, Sergeant Peterson, worked for a living and you didn't "sir" a sergeant. But he saw tears in Michael's eyes and stopped.

"I understand, son."

"You don't understand a fucking thing."

"You're crazy, boy," Sergeant Peterson said a moment before Michael Hampton decked him, sent him tumbling ass over backward out of that goddamn swivel chair, sliding across that lovely government-issue tile floor into the green (army green) filing cabinet, which took a nasty gash out of Sergeant Peterson's head.

Goddamn right. Court-martial—no goddamn Article 15 for your sorry pink ass, soldier—and a disfuckinghonorable discharge from disfucking army. Now, you go out there with a DD and try to get a job, you candy ass.

Which he did. He could speak in tongues and not many men can do that. He went to New York, where the towers of babble needed his services in a variety of low-paying jobs. The Voice of America came to him one day and said there was a way to make up the DD, that nothing was forever, that his facility with Arabic tongues was—

"Get the fuck out of my life, you bastards."

They watched him in New York. He knew they watched him. He developed the instinct of knowing when he was watched. They cut the claws off the cat and then put it outside. What are you going to do now, without your claws?

He was very stubborn those two years in New York, living in Brooklyn near the Williamsburg Bridge, hustling all the time, living in a special crowd that drank its way through First Avenue bars after the UN shut down for the day. . . .

His father fell off a horse and died.

Michael blinked when he got the telegram. He did feel something but could not explain it to himself or anyone, not even now after all these healing reveries that came to him in strange places and helped him find his point in the universe. Saw the vast empty Wyoming world without any fixed point. No universe. Ma dead. Will dead. Now Pa. No one to smell the coming of snow on the wind, no one to hunt deer in the hills, no one to count days forward and back. All time was lost time now.

Then the man from Washington came to him. From a bureau of a bureau. He had to talk to Michael Hampton.

Michael was working in a subsection of the UN Agency for International Relief part-time. He was doing some radio work for ethnic stations. He was translating reports for some oil-wealthy sheiks. What are you doing, Michael? his friends asked. Everything. He worked in a daze because all time was lost.

The man from Washington said he would make a good spy. He didn't say "spy" but that's what it came down to. He said the matter of the DD could be resolved. He said many things.

When it was over, Michael told him to take the government of the United States and stick it up his ass. Or something like that.

He lost the UN job the next day. He lost a lot of jobs. They were making it plain to him.

The man from Washington came to him again and said he could have those things back, those jobs and perks, and all he had to do was work a little for Uncle. On the side. For real money. Serve his country and serve himself—that's what America was all about. Hell, wasn't he patriotic?

Michael told him to go to hell again.

"You won't hold out," the Washington man said. "When we wantcha, we gotcha."

But his friend, the sheik who lived on Park Avenue, said there were other places to live. He could live in Sweden. He could live in Saudi Arabia. He could live in a country that does not do the bidding of—

Sweden by way of New York and the UN and then London. He became a journalist. A little money here and a little there. It was oil time in London, and he got caught up in it because that's where the money was. Arabia was money and sheiks in white gowns and black Rolls-Royces and Western girls without any clothes on who did all the things you could not demand of your wife. It was the way to make some money. The Arabs liked him; they were his friends; they told him jokes they told each other about the Saudi royal family and which members were complete idiots and which thought only with their pricks. He could read the London papers and trans-late them into Arabic. He was the London correspondent for Radio Amman for a while. He was apolitical. It wasn't a bad life, and he had rooms near Paddington Station.

He wished everyone well; he wished to be left alone. He hated that dirty thing, the thing called espionage, the thing they wanted him to do in the army and after, the thing they hounded him about, the dirty and filthy thing that was all lies and deceits and mockery of decency. He would not be a spy, not for any side, not for any price. He would not know secrets. Espionage was the fatal virus that infected the world until there was no life in anything. No decency, no God, no truth or justice or freedom, just lies and lies and lies, until the world was buried to the depth of a thousand feet in the ashes of lies. Rena had said she'd love to visit America. Michael said nothing. The country was a cold place in his heart. He did not hate the country, he did not feel anything for it.

"Do you want another beer?"

His scrapbook closed. He said something and took change

out of his pocket. The barman poured the draft slowly, and it took some minutes to fill the stein. The beer was warm and full. Michael yawned suddenly, and the black thoughts passed. It was no good to think about things you couldn't do anything about.

"American?"

He looked up, startled. The man was at the next table with a Berlin paper spread out before him.

Michael nodded.

"You speak good German. You must be military," he said in German.

"No. Not at all. Not that."

"Ah. Then you are a spy?" Very sly, meant as a joke. The man cocked his ear in a pantomime of secrecy, then smiled and chuckled.

The black thoughts came back. It was ludicrous. "The last thing I would ever be. I'm a journalist."

The old man shrugged. He lost interest. Michael really thought he was a journalist most of the time. Then he would get a call from one of his other clients, and they would pay him good money to translate accurately this report or that. Perhaps reports that had fallen into the wrong hands. Reports full of numbers and estimates, reports of things he wished to know nothing about. It was a precarious living, but he liked it because it kept him apart. And the cardinal was a good man, a friend. Only with Rena had he even thought about living with another person and sharing his bleak life.

Rena. He saw her as she was in bed, her eyes wide open with a cat's curiosity, her lips open in a perfect oval of desire, her arms open, her belly straining with desire. . . .

He didn't want to drink anymore. He got up. He put down a small tip and turned. He went to the door of the tavern and looked out at the dark street that led down to the Ku'damm near the Ka-De-We department store. It was time to go to his room and sleep all night. Perhaps it would look different in the morning.

* * *

Berlin side streets seem darker than in any other city. The night was full of noises, and the trains shuttled back and forth from East to West across elevated viaducts that festooned the city like black ornaments. Michael pulled up his collar and jammed his hands back in the pockets of the parka. He was tired now, tired enough to sleep. The bleak remembrance of Will had steeled him to what he would have to do. With himself and with the tape. They were after him again, and it was going to be the last time. They would stay away after this, no more visits from Washington men, no more threats.

The two men began to converge from opposite sides of the street.

At that same moment, four customers of the *bierkneipe* emerged on the corner, gathering before going home. One was the old man with the newspaper. "A good cool night, what do you expect for this time of year?" he said to no one.

Michael turned. "What is the weather supposed to be tomorrow?"

The old man blinked at him. He had offered the remark on the weather for his own amusement, not for the comment of others. "I don't know," he said.

Michael pressed him. He saw the two men out of the corner of his eye. As long as he engaged these four strangers from the tavern, nothing could happen to him.

It was impossible, they couldn't have followed him so easily.

The thought that they were here—already just behind him despite his run across northern Europe—gave him a moment of despair. He should surrender. He should just give up and try to explain. The world couldn't be that unreasonable. When he was a child, he had learned to surrender, to give up when a game was too hard for him to master.

"Herr Hampton?"

He turned to the first one as he passed under a street lamp.

Michael saw the glint of steel in the hand of the first man.

Impossible. They couldn't do this, not on a street in the middle of a civilized city, in view of these witnesses.

"Herr Hampton—"

The voice purred.

Michael turned to the customers from the tavern. He looked at their faces. A couple of the men were drunk. What could any of them do?

What would they be willing to do?

He suddenly pushed into the group, and the sly old man went down with an angry shout.

The first agent revealed the pistol. The second agent fired from across the street.

The shock of sound stunned the tavern crowd.

Michael heard the shot, felt pain, and then realized he had not been hit. The pain had come because he had expected the shot and expected to be hit.

His footsteps echoed down the empty street. The tavern customers were shouting. Window lights winked on.

A second shot broke. The brickwork ahead of him splintered, and a piece of brick shrapnel cut his right cheek. He did not feel the pain this time, only the wetness.

He turned into an alley and knocked over a garbage can. It signaled with a clatter on the bricks.

He staggered, nearly fell, ran to the back of the alley.

Surrounded by brick walls from three buildings.

Dead end. He leaned a moment against the wall and pushed and sobbed, as though he could push the wall away.

The breath burned his lungs.

He turned to face them. His breath sobbed out of his body.

They were a hundred feet away, at the mouth of the alley.

He ran to the shadows under a ledge and cowered.

In that moment, he felt the grasp on his ankle. He nearly jumped away, but the grasp was too firm. It was a rat. He wanted to scream, but the sound was strangled in him.

He shouted.

He turned to see the creature that was fastened on his leg.

He couldn't see in the darkness. The creature had no teeth, only this devastating grip. The creature pulled, and Michael nearly tripped and fell.

The creature spoke in German: "Are they after you? The police?"

"Yes," he said, horrified by the touch of the creature. There was no face, no body, only voice and darkness coming from an opening in the bricks. He tried to pull his leg away and the creature held him. He could not escape, and the killers were coming down the alley in the darkness.

The thing around his leg tugged again, and this time he fell.

Michael fell to one knee and then felt himself sliding back. His knees were dragged across the bricks.

He bruised his face on the rough bricks, and the metal opening struck his head. He thought he wanted to scream while the creature devoured him. He had no words left to scream. He was passing out in a slow, dreamy way, and he was sliding down and down into real darkness. He heard metal bang above him, and then he surrendered. He surrendered in his mind. He explained to them that it was all a mistake and that he could be trusted not to reveal the contents of the tape. They agreed. They were so reasonable. They smiled at him and told him to go home. They told him to see Rena and have a good time. But it was a lie, a deceit, because there was Will. Will was crossing the street, and the big truck was rumbling down on him, crushing him beneath the immense wheels, cracking his bones and his big handsome face, taking his life when they had promised him, promised him, promised him. . . .

ELEVEN

Helsinki

The portholes were dirty, dirtier than the weather that hustled flat rainclouds over the water of South Harbor. The *Leo Tolstoy* was lifted by the tide against the wharf, and the ropes squealed and groaned. For the last twenty minutes, he had been watching the modest spires of Uspenski Cathedral rise and fall, according to the movement of the freighter. It was something to do.

The other thing to do was to listen to the fat leather spy ask his dull, probing questions. It was like being operated on by a surgeon using a spoon.

They were in a cabin without amenities. The table was steel, and so was the bench Henry McGee sat on. There was no coffee, no whiskey, no warmth from the bulkhead walls. Bursts of rain splattered the portholes and then were beaded up and blown away by a drier wind. He had been on the ship for twenty-four hours from Copenhagen, across the shallow Baltic almost to the doorstep of the Soviet Union. But they had anchored in Helsinki instead, and Henry McGee couldn't figure out why. Or why the fat leather spy was still trying to see if Henry McGee was the real thing.

"Shit," Henry McGee finally said.

The leather spy stopped. He bowed his massive, bald head and stared at him.

"Did you speak?"

"I said 'shit,' " Henry McGee said in plain English.

"What do you mean?"

"I mean I'm being pecked to death by a duck," Henry McGee said. "I picked you for a nobody the day before yesterday in Cope, and I was right then and I'm still right. I ain't gonna answer any of your questions, and I'm not gonna sit here on this goddamn baby-ass bench giving me a blister on my balls."

It was too fast for the fat spy. He blinked, translating the English words slowly. He got to balls just as Henry got to the hatchway.

"You cannot—"

But Henry stepped on deck and felt the wet wind on his cheek. It felt good. He looked down at the water and then out to the islands in the harbor. The islands were wearing winter brown on grass and trees, and they seemed fragile things in the surging cold water. The spires of Helsinki crowded around the harbor. It was a small city of simple charms and electric trollies and brick roadways. There was a spartan elegance to it as well, as though each piece were made to exactly fit the next piece—in the way the brick walks were mended each spring, brick by brick laid in sand until a perfect path was made.

Uspenski Cathedral, up on the hill, had stopped going up and down in the porthole window. Henry smiled while the leather spy stood next to him. He felt the hand on his arm.

He turned, and his mean eyes were the color of prison.

"Keep your fucking hands to yourself."

The spy said, "Please."

Henry let the mean look wash down the leather spy.

"I am to detain you only a little while." The bald man was pleading. "At 1300 hours, the other comes. Please. I was doing what I was supposed to do, to question you, to see if you had told the truth."

"Just so I have to do it again for the next guy," Henry said.

"Please. It is my responsibility."

"Go fuck yourself."

"I did bring you whiskey. And that woman, it was no small thing—"

Henry lightened up. Actually, Fatso was right. Tina was no small thing. First time out of the box in two years—or in the box—and it must have taken Henry five or six seconds to do it. But then it got interesting, and Tina was a regular encyclopedia. There was that, then: Fatso had brought the girl like he was told.

"I need air, Fatso. Had to come on deck. Why we in Helsinki anyway?"

"Because it is ordered so—"

"Look, Fatso, you wanna get along with me, don't use that Moscow Center jargon. You don't want to answer or you can't, just say so, but don't give me the dumb German."

Fatso couldn't follow that for the life of him.

Henry smiled. He thought about Tina in parts. Tits were great, but he had known that from the moment she had swung them in his face in the café on the Stroget. She could do things with them. And when she put her mouth on him . . . well, it was good to think about just now, standing on two deck of this bucket of rust. He looked down at the figures moving along the wharf and the street beyond. The rain wasn't so bad, but the wind was having its effect and they bent to the wind. The cold didn't bother Henry; it wasn't like the deep-down, bone-cracking cold you got in Alaska, where your fingers could fall off like dry-rotted wood and you wouldn't even know they were gone. He smiled.

Fatso said, "I will tell you: I have made my report on you. Based on your answers."

McGee turned.

"Is that right?"

"It is so."

"Who you report to?"

"It is forbidden—"

Henry turned away. Boring. He'd rather watch the pedestrians. When you were on a working ship, standing on a deck in idleness, and you were in port, you watched the landlubbers the way a child will watch an ant hill. They seem insignificant because they are limited by the edge of land that clings to the sea, whereas you are from the sea, which stretches across the world.

The black Volvo pulled up opposite the ship on the wharf.

Three men got out, front and back. Doors slammed, and the Volvo started away.

Three men in black overcoats and black hats. McGee saw Fatso stiffen in his leather spy coat, and he made a guess. Not that it was so hard to guess.

Henry leaned on the railing and looked down at the three men passing through the Helsinki port guard and then the guard at the hatchway.

"Them," Fatso said.

"About time," Henry said. He stretched, scratched at the hairs on his stubble and turned back to the cabin.

They came in minutes later. The cabin was suddenly filled with bodies, and the air turned warm and moist.

The men removed their overcoats, which shone with raindrops. They were sweating.

Henry recognized the middle one immediately. He had hoped for it. It was Skarda come all the way from Moscow to do a deep inspection on him. Or maybe something else. He didn't say a word, and the three men did not look at him until they had removed their outerwear.

Skarda, the middle man, was gaunt, as though he had been sick for a long time. His face was pale, and his eyes were framed by wide, owlish glasses. He looked at Henry McGee and sat down in the chair previously occupied by the fat leather spy.

The other two were big men. Maybe just beef, maybe not. Henry wasn't sure.

"Colonel McGee," said Skarda.

The greeting said a lot. His KGB rank. Said without irony. Henry McGee nodded.

"I did not expect to see you so soon."

"Or ever," Henry McGee said.

The gaunt man did not respond. He opened a briefcase and took out a file. He was the only one in the room with paper on the table, and this made him superior.

"The problem is in the order of things," the gaunt man said. "You plan your escape from this Lewistown place. You are taken to Chicago. The Section agent in Chicago brings up the name of Skarda. You make your escape."

"It would sound less pat if it was you climbing down nine floors on the side of a goddamn skyscraper like one of those clowns in an old movie."

English again. The gaunt man looked up and then turned to his colleagues and the fat spy. "Leave us," Skarda said.

The three men obediently left the cabin and closed the hatch.

"What went wrong the first time?"

"I got snookered. The same man. Agent named Devereaux in R Section. The son of a bitch just didn't ever believe me. I never counted on him to pull an illegal. He arranged to kidnap me more than two years ago out of that interrogation camp in Maryland and damn near killed me. He got it on tape, and there I was, trussed like a Christmas turkey. Got fifty years in prison. But you know that."

"Yes," said the gaunt man. He had dark hair and a mole on his cheek and looked a little like later portraits of Lincoln, except he was beardless. "We made our inquiries about all you said. The problem is in what to believe; there is always too much information."

He looked at his file folder and placed a delicate hand on the paper.

"Devereaux," he said.

McGee stared right through him.

"In a matter you do not know about, Devereaux plays his assigned part. He is in Brussels—he was in Brussels at last report—to guard the life of this woman, Rena Taurus."

"I don't know a thing about her."

"The choice is to bring you back to Moscow. Quickly. Or, perhaps, more slowly, in stages."

Henry McGee said nothing. He waited with a cool expression on his face.

"It is my decision," the other said. "We had to meet you again to be certain you did not compromise the plan when you were . . . an American prisoner."

"And quickly means I get squished like a bug in Moscow. And slowly means I get to work on the plan," Henry said. "Why not just say it plain like that?"

"Some in Moscow Center feel you have compromised it."

"And you?"

"I reserve judgment." He tented his fingers. "They asked you about Plan Skarda, didn't they?"

"They transferred me out of a sardine tin I was gonna escape from."

"I'm sorry we spoiled your plans."

"You did? You spoiled them?"

"We planted . . . a message. If the Americans knew of Skarda, the plan named for me, they would not react. They reacted, Henry. It saves your life."

"I sure am glad, Skarda."

"Yes," said the thin man.

"Skarda was supposed to be the Czech computer genius of Moscow Center. You, in other words."

"And the name of the plan. Plan Skarda. To once and for all compromise American intelligence to the point where it would take a decade to put it back together again."

"I was supposed to work on R Section," Henry said. He

relaxed now. He was beginning to understand. "I laid down a trail for Section, and they got jittery looking for me because I had moled them once and they were afraid it'd get out. Sent that asshole Devereaux after me, but Devereaux wouldn't play my game, wouldn't let me kidnap him in Alaska and float him to the Soviet side of the Bering Straits."

"So we assumed. Of course, at that point you could have betrayed Moscow," Skarda said.

"Yeah. Made such a good deal with Section they got me twenty-five to fifty in federal prison. I'm a lot smarter than that, Skarda."

It had almost worked two years before, the plan to compromise R Section, make Washington believe the bureaucracy was riddled with moles and traitors from Hanley on down. All by "defecting" Devereaux to the Soviet Union against his will while he was on the trail of the mole, Henry McGee, whom everyone had thought dead and buried.

"You failed once, Henry," Skarda said. "But you did not betray Plan Skarda."

"I didn't know the whole thing—"

"But you could have guessed, given them a trail to follow. To save your life and keep you from prison—"

"But I didn't, did I?"

"Do you want to know what the second part of the plan is?" The smug Czech leaned back in his chair as though entertaining a class full of awed undergraduates. Henry kept the half-smile of friendliness on his face and just waited.

"A recent 'superpowers' conference in Sweden. There was a secret agenda."

"There always is," Henry McGee said. He knew enough about how these things worked.

Skarda frowned him to silence. "The Americans have been made aware of our advances in securing our computer files. They cannot raid us as thoroughly anymore from their equipment in the American embassy. They do not understand the software technology that I have perfected. What if, in the spirit of *glasnost*, we were to offer them the technology in exchange for lesser funding for SDI program?"

"For Star Wars," Henry said. He thought about it. "They wouldn't trust you."

"Oh. I assure you. This is above the board. They can examine the program. They can test it in their computer systems. I assure you of this."

"I'm assured," Henry said. What was this leading to?

"The files of the Central Intelligence Agency are completely computerized now and interconnected with the files of the great Western intelligence agencies. Let us presume that in their testing, all went well. They would keep testing and begin to share their results with their allied agencies. And then, one fine day in spring, the virus in the program, hidden in the sequential configurations of the program, would destroy most of their system, their records, their abilities to recall their records from ghost files, the memory of CIA. Do you understand what memory is to intelligence?"

"Like Alzheimer's disease. Lack of memory makes intelligence helpless," Henry McGee said.

Skarda smiled. "Exactly. An apt simile. By which time, of course, the second part of the secret agenda would have been completed. An ancillary project to give the administration a bright eye to its public."

"A bright face," Henry corrected.

"So," said Skarda, annoyed, "we will announce this shortly."

"What will you announce?"

"To release the Jews. More than ever before. More than the forty-nine thousand of last year—many, many more in the name of *glasnost* and democratic freedom."

"In exchange for what?"

Skarda smiled then. "That is the secret of the second part. The human part. The interference with our Baltic states by certain parties would have to be ended. . . . Well, it is not of as great importance as the first part."

"People never are," Henry said, but he was smiling. His even white teeth sparkled in the dim light.

Skarda suddenly ended his lecture. The class sat in rapt attention. Skarda said, "You have to find a man, Henry, and there is no time, no time at all. His name is Michael Hampton, and someone tried to sabotage the secret agenda. It is contained on a tape which this man has. A little tape recording, and somehow he got it. He is running to somewhere and we wish to stop him. And, I might add, so do the Americans, because if the details of the tape are made public, the administration will fall."

"It don't work that way, that's in England, but never mind. Where is he?"

"He escaped us in Berlin last night—"

"Berlin? What's Berlin got to do with this?"

"Berlin? We don't know. We know he has little money and his run is expensive. He has made contact with his friend in Brussels, a woman named Rena Taurus. He seems to know what he will do with the tape, and we suspect he will sell it to someone. Perhaps the press."

"You could get someone more familiar with Europe—"

"But the man who guards Rena Taurus. Is it not fitting?"

"How?"

"It is your November man."

Silence. The ship groaned against its restraints. Ropes slid up and down against the wharf, and the hull echoed with the slaps of waves against the rusted metal.

"To kill him?" Henry said.

"Let us say you could disappear him. Back to the original first part of Plan Skarda. Disappear him to Moscow. It would assure you of your welcome back to the center."

Gorki was his code name, always the code name of the current chief of the KGB Committee for External Observation and Resolution. He was small, a Eurasian with wizened features and a broad forehead. His skin was the color of parchment and as dry; his eyes glittered with the intensity of fires lit on the steppes.

Gorki glared at Skarda, but there was a coolness between them that did not admit to hot emotion.

"How is Henry McGee?" Gorki said at last.

"Useful. I am convinced of it."

"What did you tell him?"

Skarda said, "About the computer virus that we will use to destroy the records of the CIA." He smiled.

Gorki did not return the smile. It was his plan, and he had no doubts that Skarda could technically carry out the computer trickery necessary. But Skarda was not in counterespionage, not trained for it. Gorki felt nervous using the dark, arrogant computer genius in a role not suited to him. Besides, Skarda was a vain man, and the world of spies had no use for vanity or arrogance.

"Did he believe you?"

"Of course," Skarda replied.

"Henry McGee is not a fool," Gorki said.

"It will work as you planned it," Skarda said. There was an impatient tone in his voice. "The Americans—or your agents—have only to recover the tape, and the secret agenda will be in place."

"Do you wonder why it was missing in the first place?" Gorki said. It was the question he had asked himself over and over.

"An accident by that clumsy janitor—"

"So it would appear. So we might think. Do you believe in such accidents?"

"That is a question for you to answer, isn't it?"

Gorki permitted himself a small sigh. He glanced at a paper on his desk just to look away. He spoke while he stared at the sheet of paper. "National Security Agency will test your program. They will examine it for viruses that might harm the computer systems of the Central Intelligence Agency. They will run it through many tests to discover the sabotage in the program."

Skarda smiled. "And they will not find it."

"Because they will look for the wrong thing."

"There is no virus in the tape to destroy the record-keeping capacity of CIA. There is only a virus to destroy—"

"Not destroy. To misdirect the test launching of the sophisticated SDI antimissile missile," Gorki said. He still did not look at Skarda. "If your program works."

"The Americans have committed six billion dollars to the test of this 'Star Wars' missile. The missile launch is under control of the National Security Agency. But my program in NSA test computers will make that money worthless because they are connected to CIA."

"So," Gorki said.

Skarda waxed. He could feel his strength now, in explaining again to one who had heard it before how brilliant he was. "The whole program is a virus designed for one thing. To give the wrong sequence of orders to the NSA computer controlling the test missile. So that when it is fired, the missile will not only fail but will direct a rain of death—"

"Very dramatic, Skarda."

Skarda flushed. After a moment, he said, "In any case, the SDI will be a failure, and the administration will save its face by agreeing to scrap the program in exchange for more refugees from 'Soviet tyranny.' "

"A good bargain," Gorki said.

Skarda said, "Yes. Because we will control the terms of it."

TWELVE

Brussels

Rena awoke suddenly, as though someone had flung the lights on. But there was only darkness. She blinked in the darkness but couldn't see. What had wakened her so violently? It had been raining all night, and the bedroom window was open a crack. She could smell rain on the wind, and the sill was damp.

She lay on the flat, soft mattress, her pillows bunched under her head and neck. Her raven hair was splayed out on the pillows, her soft breath was scarcely a sound in the silence. Her fingers touched the rough-edged pages of a paperback novel that lay open, spine up, on the coverlet beside her. The page was opened to a passage describing a ship entering the pestilential harbor in Calcutta. . . . She had fallen asleep dreaming of a black freighter in the tropical heat, wallowing in deep, malevolent waters to the city of death—

She was wide awake in the darkness.

The combined stillnesses of the apartment were so intense that it made a whispering sound in her ears. The rain fell against the window glass. She held her breath and she didn't know why.

Then a sound.

Someone else shared the darkness.

She reached out her hand to the lamp in panic. She fumbled for the switch on the cord and suddenly pulled the lamp over with a crash.

She sat upright.

"Who is it?"

He moved into the small bedroom. His figure was large and his presence suffocated her. She had to get out of this bed. She decided it was a dream, one of those very realistic dreams that strays back and forth between reality and absurdity. There was no one in the room.

He sat on the edge of the bed.

His hand was wet. His coat was damp. She heard him breathe in the darkness. The breath of the beast.

He put a finger to his lips.

She thought of Michael, thought of the danger.

"You—" she began because it was him again.

She had to scream. Even in the darkness, in the sleeping district nestled below the Palace of Justice, someone would hear a poor woman screaming in the night and—

He put his large hand on her mouth.

She bit him and tasted his blood, but he held his hand as tight as a gag on her mouth. Her scream was strangled. She had heard that sound before, and then she remembered another time, in the darkness, in the countryside, when the bluebird had been pounced upon by the night-roaming cat. The bluebird made a pitiful, sobbing scream—once, twice, a third time—and then, finally, a small peep of death and acceptance. The cat dragged the broken body to the doorstep, where they found it in the morning.

He still held his hand over her mouth. "Two men in the street below," Devereaux said. "You're in danger from them."

She was so close to him. The male smell enveloped her. She was afraid and fascinated. She knew she had bit him hard enough to draw blood, but the large, suffocating hand was still against her lips. She would not struggle, not for the moment.

"KGB, do you understand? We just learned they tapped your telephone in time for your conversation with Michael."

She trembled.

Slowly, he took his hand away. She was sitting upright in bed, her shoulders covered by the shiny white gown. It was the darkness that made their intimacy more terrifying. They did not see each other as much as felt and smelled the presence of the other. Like beasts of the night.

"How do you know—?"

"Two hours ago, we caught their transmitter signal. We know what they know." He paused. She held her breath in the brief silence. "The agents in the street. Someone is bringing a team to back them up. They're going to follow you in the morning, follow you to Michael."

"Why—?"

Her voice was loud. She saw he held his finger to his lips.

The whisper was harsh. "Why do I believe you? You break into my rooms twice. You're here like a thief now. Worse. I don't believe a word you say!"

"Where is the canal where you meet Michael?" Devereaux's voice was gentle. "Where is the old hotel?"

She said nothing. She felt a strange, warm sense of embarrassment, the kind she had not experienced since she was a little girl. A child has no privacy, no rights—a creature of mistakes and reprimands, encaged in a world of rules she does not understand. How many times had she been wrong and the same creeping flush of embarrassment overcome her, starting at her cheeks and burning down her body until she wanted to hide?

"I'm not going to harm Michael. I told you that."

Devereaux stared at her. They both became accustomed to the darkness. They were shadows now, but recognizable shadows. His voice was flat, he was not pleading his sincerity. "There is grave danger."

Grave danger. In all her languages, the words that most

conveyed a sense of casual terror were the warnings the French posted on electrical junction boxes: *Danger de mort*. A simple warning rendered with a shrug of Gallic shoulders. *Danger de mort*.

"I believe you?"

"You have no choice. I know you're going to meet him; they know. If they mean to follow you, they'll follow you. You don't have the skill to elude them. And if they're bringing another team, then it's more than to recover the tape."

"Michael said—"

"Michael said he couldn't give them his memory. He listened to the tape. It's original sin," Devereaux said.

Danger de mort. A standard warning; ignore it at your peril, but don't say we didn't post a notice. People die in stupid ways—lighting a gas stove, touching a wire, leaning out the train window to be decapitated by the express train running in the opposite direction. . . .

Very soft, very full of pity. He was so close to her that the room was filled with the smell of him, his voice was a thick whisper, and yet she could see him as he had been on the airplane, staring at her, the hard eyes growing soft the more he stared at her.

She thought the thing that was too terrible. "They will kill him."

"Yes." No pity now; no absolution. A simple explanation and warning.

"And why must I trust you?"

"Because I won't kill him."

"And I believe you?" Again, the question was only half asked.

For a moment, he sat in the darkness and did not speak. She felt his weight at the edge of the soft mattress. Her body fell toward him, and she was next to him, not by choice but by his weight at the edge of the bed. Close to him, feeling his hesitation at the words he wanted to speak. The blind experience through smell, sound, touch; only those who can see blind themselves to the other senses. She sensed his hesitation, though she could not see through the darkness. She felt the struggle in the silence.

Devereaux had awakened in the safe rooms in London. Hanley sat in a straight chair and watched him as he sat up and yawned and looked at his watch. He had slept long enough to feel the hangover of the pills. He yawned again, and his mouth was a dry hole of foul smells.

"Michael Hampton was given a dishonorable discharge from the army. He had a top-secret clearance. He ran with a radical-left crowd in New York. He worked for the United Nations." *Hanley had gone on in the same dull monotone.* "He has associates in too many places where we have too few friends. He has been approached to enter into service, but he refuses. He lives in Stockholm and has friends in the down-with-America community. This comes from Comp An, and I knew these things this morning, but it didn't matter then."

"It matters now."

"Erase him."

"Get a hitter."

"Erase him. They want to erase the girl as well."

"I won't be a hitter."

"The word comes from State. Cooperate with KGB. We've done it before."

"Fuck you, Hanley."

"Erase them and recover the tape."

"Fuck you, Hanley."

Hanley said: "We do not kill. We erase. We suspend a case. We deal in wet objects. We will not compromise ourselves or our principles."

"Fuck you, Hanley."

"The Soviets want bodies."

"How about their heads in brown boxes? How about their tongues?"

"We can erase them humanely. It will be different if the other side gets there first."

Devereaux had dressed. He had taken a little of the stale tea in a paper cup. When he rinsed his mouth with cold water, his teeth hurt. When he had stared at Hanley in the ghastly light, he had seen how defeated Hanley had become.

"Do you understand the mission?"

"Do you understand me?" Devereaux had said.

And curiously, Hanley had then said, "Yes. I understand perfectly."

The silence held for half a minute, and when Devereaux spoke again, his voice was neutral. He did not want to sell anything; he wanted to explain. He sounded like the history teacher he had once been, long before he became mired in history.

"Michael was right. He heard too much, and it's in his head. The Soviet team means to brainwash him in a permanent way." There was no humor intended in the words, and Rena felt sick to her stomach.

Had she betrayed Michael in Malmö? For the first time, she felt the consequences of everything she had done. But she had no wish to hurt him. It was such a simple matter; no one should have known. . . . He was her pet, her lover, he was her pleasure in company and in sex. Now he was running. He was running away from her as surely as if he intended to.

"What time is it?" she said.

"Six. If you get dressed, I'll get you out of here. Past them. We can get—"

"The bank. I have to wait for the banks to open—"

"The money's taken care of."

She stared at the form in the darkness. She could just see him. Already, very pale light was inflating the clouds over the city and the black reaches of the narrow streets were turning to a dingy ash color. Soot was rising again from the old fireplaces and drab, somehow very human Brussels would stir itself to make another day.

"Can I turn on the bathroom light?"

"There's a window?"

"A little one."

"Don't risk it. There's one of them in a car down the street. The other's in back. If there's only two—I don't know. I don't know what time the backup team comes. I don't know how many watchers there are."

"How did you get in?"

No answer.

"You must have come in the back."

He did not speak.

She felt this silence as well. She was becoming as sensitive to silence as a blind person.

She went into the bathroom, fumbled for underclothes on the retractable line above the tub. How strange the darkness makes familiar things. She brushed her hair. She wore a sweater and jeans and tall black boots. Her purse and passport in hand, she looked at her bedroom.

He was the ghost by the window, barely outlined by the pale light beginning to fill the room. It was not raining. The room was cool and damp. She felt sleepy, the way she did on rainy mornings. The ghost by the window was looking down at the court behind the building. His remembered words calmed her now. She would be able to do it.

"I'm ready" came in a whisper. She shrugged into her raincoat and tied the belt.

"Do you have a scarf? Wear it on your head. In case they see you."

There was a rear entrance, but it was always kept locked, and there was a small gate beyond, which was also locked. Both locks were open.

"You had a key—"

"Of sorts."

Down the old stone back stairs. The stairwell was painted a bluish gray. Back doors of sleeping neighbors watched them.

In the little court, she saw the shapeless bulk of the man lying on the stones. He was a pile of clothes hidden under a porch.

A pile of flesh and clothes. There was a little blood on the stones. She must have made a sound, because he put his hand across her mouth again and pressed her against the building. This time, she saw the cold thing in Devereaux's eyes and saw his lips drawn to bare his teeth.

"No sound, Rena. I told you there were two. Maybe more of them. I don't know, I have no way of knowing."

He pulled his hand away.

She shivered and he held her.

She felt cold, lost, alone in a storm without beginning or end. Her momentary bravery in the apartment dissolved. Michael was not in danger, not running. She was not going to rendezvous with him. He would not die. The world would be made fresh tomorrow. . . .

Frantically she struggled to escape the death in the pile of clothes and flesh under the porch. And yet the killer—she clung to him.

"You. Killed him."

"Maybe he isn't dead," Devereaux said. It was so terrible that she felt angry. She would kill him or hurt him and just tear the flesh of his face. He was hateful.

Death felt so close.

Michael. She saw Michael dead. Hands out, like this one. Blood on the stones and his pretty mouth broken. Michael's eyes wide from looking at eternity. What had she done?

At the end of the court was the street. She saw the car at the end and the man behind the wheel, but why should she believe anything?

"This is your fault," she said.

Devereaux looked at her. They were as close as lovers, pressed against the bricks of the next building. He was watching the driver and deciding something.

"Your fault. Security. You said you were security at the conference in Malmö. Where was security? How could the wrong tape get into the wrong hands?"

He did not speak.

"What was the point of your security? You lost the tape.

The tape went to Michael because of that odious little man. He worked for you.''

"What man?"

"What was he? A Swede. Gustafson. He worked for you—"

"And brought Michael the tape," Devereaux finished. "We questioned him, you can believe me. He didn't know what was on the tape."

"But he brought it to Michael."

Devereaux stared at her, at the deep pool of her Lithuanian eyes. She was as delicate as porcelain and the blue in her black hair framed her oval face as perfectly as if she were a statue and had always stood on this spot in the little courtyard.

Something jarred him. He closed his eyes and let memory go back a few moments. There, it was there. He heard her voice and played it back.

"*He brought it to Michael,*" Devereaux repeated. He had only slept once in nearly three days, but it had refreshed him, and he could think now as he could not have yesterday. *He brought it to Michael of all people.*

The car pulled out of the last space at the foot of the street.

She made a sound.

He turned and saw the car.

"What are we going to do?"

"I don't know."

Dawn filled every shadow. Streets glistened in sullen, damp light. The city was empty, sleeping through the rainy hour of morning, dreaming. Rena looked at the sleeping apartment buildings and wondered about life behind the gauze curtains, about the disheveled beds, men and women caught in sleep and dreams, about lovers turning over to their women, touching them, caressing them with their tongues and little kisses until desire overcame sleep and dreams and they were unguilty children indulging in pleasure. . . .

"I love him," Rena said. It was meant to explain everything.

Devereaux stared at the face of the beautiful girl and saw the car and saw Rita Macklin saying the same thing. She had come to him a long time ago and said things about love, even knowing that he believed words were for lies. But that was far away. This was death on a gray Belgium morning, a dead man stuffed under a porch until only his hands protruded. . . .

Devereaux gently held her and then slipped his hands through the opening of her raincoat and held her thin waist. He cupped his hands behind her back to pull her close to him. The gesture was intimate, arrogant. The movement startled Rena; she started to pull away.

"No," he said, watching the car over her shoulder. "Let's see if he passes."

She understood. It was morning and time for lovers to part—reluctantly. A common sight in this French-speaking city. She buried her face on his shoulder. She closed her eyes. She smelled his clothing, his male smell. All men carried different smells, but she delighted in their differences, especially men who wore no perfume or cologne, who let their scents mingle with their clothes, with the weather, with the time of day. . . .

The car was a washed-blue Peugeot and its headlights were off. It moved almost without sound; the immense low pressure of the night muted the faint *putt-putt* of the engine crawling in first gear.

"Hold me," he said, softly as a lover.

She put her hands and arms around him. She was so close to him, as close as she had been to Michael, but all she felt was her knotted fear. They were pretending to hide by holding each other. Would it fool anyone?

He took his right hand from her back. His hand was still hidden by her coat.

He wore a worn, blue corduroy jacket that was damp with rain. He reached under his jacket.

His hand reached again through the opening in the front of her raincoat. His hand returned to her waist but not to embrace her. She clung to him almost with desperation. He held something very hard in his right hand. The metal chilled her and she knew it was a weapon.

The blue car slowed as it approached the entry of the courtyard. The driver rolled down his side window. He stared at the two lovers.

The driver was Russian with a grizzled growth on his fat cheeks. His eyes were bloodshot. He was damned tired. He had taken a little vodka to keep him company, and maybe he had dozed off. Maybe he felt guilty about it. Maybe he wanted to make sure everything was all right.

Arkady was supposed to be in the courtyard at the back of the building, but he was probably asleep; it hadn't been easy the last two days with only two men on the job. Control didn't understand that, none of those fucking bureaucrats ever understood the field.

Look at him. His hands under her coat. Getting a good feel for himself, rubbing her all over. It made you crazy to watch another guy having his way. It reminded you of the times when you had girls. It reminded you that you were sitting in a goddamn car all night in the rain, and here he was, probably was screwing her all night, sleeping with her, putting his hands and tongue all over her, nice and warm in the morning—

Where the hell was Arkady? Didn't answer the radio, sleeping in the courtyard. Missing the action with these lovers.

Lovers.

The agent in the car pushed the brake pedal. He had sat at the end of the street, and they had not come from the opposite direction—he was sure of that. So where had they come from?

Standing in the entry of that particular courtyard. He couldn't see the girl, she wore a scarf over her hair. Dark hair. So what, that doesn't mean anything, ninety percent of the girls have dark hair—

He slipped the pistol out of his coat pocket and unsnapped the safety. He put the car into park.

On the other hand—

He brought up the pistol almost to the level of the side window.

Devereaux felt her form beneath his hand. Felt her breath on his neck. Felt her breasts molded against his body. Felt the loveliness of this woman in her fear and in the smell of her freshness, and he brought the pistol up. Under her coat. Until the last moment.

He saw the pistol at the level of the side window. The driver was opening the door.

He had not told Rena the truth. The agent crumpled inside the courtyard was completely dead, without any doubt.

He fired once from the Beretta pressed against Rena's waist. The round bulged the back of her coat and tore a small, dirty hole in the fabric. She started, even screamed like the bluebird. It was as though the shot had gone through her. The recoil bruised her lowest rib. Her eyes were wide, and she held him very tight in that moment.

The second agent—the driver—fell forward. Black scorched his cheek. There was almost no blood. He fell forward, and his left arm pushed the automatic transmission lever. The car slipped into slow reverse, describing a small semicircle across the narrow street until it crashed quietly into a parked Mercedes. The driver's door was half-open, and he slumped out of the car.

It began to rain hard and morning became darker.

He looked down at her, and there were raindrops or tears on her pale, delicate face.

THIRTEEN

Malmö

Jaynes lay in bed. He was fully clothed and quite sweaty under the covers. He was past the point of absolutely raucous snoring, which came early in the pass-out; his snoring was routine now, droning like a chain saw.

It was two hours into Monday. They had sent him payment via American Express on Saturday morning, and there had been no stopping him since.

The conference was successful from the standpoint of supplying the large London Sunday newspaper with enough drivel to fill six columns and enough lies to appear plausible. Jaynes still had the old touch, still had the old connections. At least, at times.

Jaynes had celebrated Sunday in the way he celebrated every day in his life. He began with no good intentions and proceeded to follow them. He ate the barbaric Scandinavian breakfast, or at least as much as he could stomach: soft-boiled egg, hard rolls, dark crackers, tasteless pale cheese (what he wouldn't have given for a good cheddar!), and some sort of salami. He would have preferred bangers and toast and a

Bloody Mary, but the restorative juices did not start flowing early in the Swedish countryside.

The hotel was cheap and not very close to the city center. He decided to stay over the weekend and go up to Stockholm and dredge some new Sunday newspaper sensations out of the Olof Palme murder of three years ago. Palme was the leftist Swedish prime minister who was gunned down as he walked home with his wife from a movie. The ineptness of the Swedish National Police had just about obliterated any chance of satisfactorily solving the case until international intelligence connected the killers to Iranian extremists. The Swedes had arrested someone else. Couldn't a journalist as talented as Evelyn Jaynes shake the Palme tree for a few more coconuts of scandal? The Palme tree. He had offered the pun twice during drunken Sunday, and both times had managed to offend a table full of Swedes. Bloody people had absolutely no sense of humor.

These thoughts blurred, mixed, filtered, passed back and forth through his brain as he numbed mind and soul with stunning amounts of vodka and aquavit. No one said he had too much. He knew how to handle his liquor. He might occasionally fall down in the bar or fall asleep sitting on the crapper, but those were occupational hazards. The journalist, by definition, was a drunk if he was any good at it at all.

Bloody clerks taken over the business. Bloody fact checkers. Bloody fucking—what'd the Americans call them?—bloody bean counters.

Resentment entered his dreams, and he groaned through the snores. His nose played the snores like a cathedral organ. His nose amplified and extended his snores.

The knocks insisted their way into his sleep and he finally connected the knocks of the dream world with knocks at the door.

"Go away," he said. He groaned and rolled over. The covers were bunched under his belly. He groaned because the damned knocking went on and on.

He would throw something at the door, but there was nothing at hand. More horribly, he was waking up. He knew the signs. Enough of the alcohol is passed out, and there is this musty, fuzzy feeling that descends in the middle of the bloody night. Three o'clock in the morning and the naked soul is shivering under the interrogation lamp.

Knocking, knocking.

He opened both eyes and saw perfectly, not the double image of the world in his previous incarnation. He stared at the bottle of vodka on the nightstand and measured it with his eye. Enough, possibly, to get him through to the next moment of unconsciousness.

He got to his feet and the pain in his head began. Or perhaps it had been there all along. He steadied himself on the table that contained the vodka bottle and went around the bed. He had an inside room and the window overlooked a courtyard full of steam pipes and other gadgetry. Lovely, lovely, he had told the clerk.

He opened the door without any fear, even if it was three in the morning. This was Sweden, and only the prime minister was not safe.

He blinked at the apparition. The hall was lit by a twenty-five-watt bulb, and the apparition dissolved into a very thin, very short Swede with damp brown hair and large, worried eyes.

"Mr. Jaynes?"

Jaynes blinked to better his vision, but it refused to get better.

"I know the night clerk, he told me your room," the little man said.

"Then goddamn him and goddamn you," Jaynes said.

"Do you know me?"

"Is this a commercial or a bloody American quiz program?"

"My name is Rolf Gustafson." He let the name lie between them as though it meant something.

Jaynes shook his head.

"At the conference. I was the man in charge of equipment. In the press area?"

"Were you? Then I didn't notice."

"The security people . . . they questioned me over and over. You are the last reporter left in the city, the last who covered the conference. I thought I should talk to you."

The non sequiturs caught Jaynes's attention. His head throbbed, and he thought he could feel the membranes that held his brain in place stretch and snap. But something in Rolf Gustafson's presentation intrigued the reporter buried inside Jaynes's habitual sloth.

He stepped back, and the little man scurried into the shabby room.

The little man stared at the place. The bed was rumpled, the half-empty bottle of vodka seemed sad. The room was cold. The window was nearly wide open to the chill Malmö night.

"It's very cold," Rolf said.

"Close the window and the stink of the place will drive you out," Jaynes said. "I've seen it before." He made a theatrical gesture. "Same in Zagreb, same in Mexico City . . . bad drains."

Rolf blinked.

"Civilizations rise or fall not upon the actions of men but by the way men get rid of the actions of their bowels."

"Something happened," Rolf said, holding a cap in his hand.

"Go on," Jaynes said. He stood near the table that held the vodka bottle. He was tempted to take a drink, but then politeness or convention would require that he offer Rolf a tot as well. And what if the bloody Swede accepted? What then would sustain him through the wee small until the morning light?

"On Saturday afternoon when the conference was ended, the police questioned me. Not Malmö police but the national police. And then they gave me to the Russians."

"And the Russians ate you up?"

Rolf had no time for humor. "The Russians and the Americans, they questioned me. I didn't know who they were, to tell you the truth. I didn't know what they wanted until they said I had taken a tape—a tape recording from the minutes of the conference—and that the tape was secret and that whoever had the tape had access to the gravest secrets. I understood then, and I told them whose equipment I packed. There were four reporters, sir. And two translators and interpreters."

"A tape is missing."

Rolf nodded.

"The crux is, they want their tape back. Did they get it?"

"I don't think so, sir. They questioned me again this afternoon. Russians this time. They asked a lot of questions about the two of them."

"Two of whom?"

"The translators, I call them. I suppose they are also interpreters, but I don't understand the difference. The translators who were packed. I packed them. I must have packed the wrong tape. It was an honest mistake."

"You know what's on the tape?"

"No, sir."

Jaynes sighed. What was the point?

"Well, I'm sure they'll get it back."

"They didn't seem certain. They showed me a map. They showed me the places he had gone in the last twenty-four hours—"

"A map? Who had gone?"

Rolf made a face. "The translator. The one they think got the tape recording by mistake. He went back to Stockholm where he lives."

"Swedish."

"No, sir. An American."

Jaynes let the glimmer shine ever so slightly. He moved into the room to crowd Rolf into the single armchair by the window. The cool night air flowed into the room, and the tattered chinz curtains floated like faded white flags of surrender.

"An American?"

"Michael Hampton."

Jaynes tried to think. Memory created forms, voices, faces in the hall. The fat-faced Russian and the long-faced American secretary. Men and women around, the little people of all great conferences. The Americans wore blue suits invariably. The Russians wore brown or olive or, more formally, black. There was a very attractive dish, black black hair and blue blue eyes. Retina or something, lovely Swede.

Yes. Michael Hampton. Next booth but one. Jaynes had sized up the competish, and he wasn't in the running. Worked for some Middle Eastern organizations and even the bloody pope. Very earnest young man, and blessings on him, he wasn't a problem to Jaynes.

Michael Hampton.

The missing tape.

Headlines began to form in Jaynes's thoughts. He saw stories as layouts, pages, bonuses, back into the big house from the dog house, no more chasing his tale in dreary resorts like Manchester and Malmö. Mr. Jaynes, if you please, and a suite at Connaught's for the duration of the international conference. . . .

Visions of sugar plums.

He stared at the little man. "Well, I scarcely know what to say, Mr. Gustoff."

"Gustafson, sir. This map they showed me, I have a good memory, I can tell you where Mr. Hampton has been the last thirty-six hours. The Russians told me, and they wanted me to guess where he would go next. They asked me about her, as well. Miss Taurus, the other translator. She was there when I brought his bags. It was her room."

"Her room."

"Sir, they were lovers."

"I see." That explained why she stared right through him

during the conference. Uppity bitch, would serve her right to
have her tits plastered on page three. Mystery woman of secret
naval conference! Mistress of the man who stole the tapes!
Tits and sunglasses and whispers in the corridors of power!

"You seem to know an awfully lot about so many things,"
Jaynes suddenly soothed. The change in manner from vodka-
wreck contempt to solicitous geniality seemed to frighten Rolf
Gustafson. He shrank back in the armchair as far as he could
go. The surrender of the curtains fluffed at his face.

"I know what I know. I know that the Russians and Americans are very worried about this matter, and this is why, I
think, it is worth money to you to let me tell you what I
know."

That had been bothering Jaynes the last few minutes. Mo-
tive. Like most journalists of any experience, Jaynes had an
inherent mistrust of altruism. Money was perfectly under-
standable.

"What sort of money, Mr. Gustafson? For your
exclusive—and I mean *exclusive*—cooperation?"

Rolf cleared his throat, ducked his head like an estate
gardener, and mumbled something.

Jaynes said, "What did you say?"

"A thousand kronor, sir."

"You're crazy," Jaynes said, figuring it into pounds. Not
a completely ridiculous figure, but that would come off the
top of whatever he would be able to flog the story for.

"Sir—"

"Five hundred. Not a farthing more."

"All right, sir."

The surrender surprised Jaynes. He was annoyed. He
should have suggested less. No matter. It was agreed, and
so Gustafson was now a paid servant, not a guest, and one
did not have to offer the claret bottle round to the staff. Jaynes
poured himself a drink and took it down with a fierce face
and burning gut. But ah, it gives a lovely light in the belly
of the beast.

"Well, where should we begin then, Rolf?"

"With the five hundred kronor, sir," Rolf said.

"That is a technicality. In the morning—proper morning, when the offices are open—I'll make a telephone call to one of my . . . clients . . . and you shall have your money by afternoon."

"Are you certain? And this cannot be traced to me, sir. I don't want to go round with those Russians again."

"Protected by the sanctity of my word, Rolf," said Jaynes, who meant it at the moment. At least, the part about sanctity of words, if not the five hundred kronor.

"Where has Michael gone, Rolf? Why do you suppose he's running away? Perhaps he's had assignments—"

"The Russians. You should have seen them. They are very serious men."

"Yes, they tend to be, don't they? Unless they're drunk and become playful in the manner of bears. But what about Michael?"

"Michael Hampton is in Göteborg, then Copenhagen, then Hamburg, then Berlin, where they cannot find him. All in twenty-four hours. They ask me many things. About the canal, a thing I don't understand, where Michael would meet Miss Taurus. Where is the canal? they ask me."

"Bloody canals everywhere," Jaynes said. "Are you sure you don't have a clue to what is on the missing tape?"

"After they talk to me again, I return to the press room and I look over the log, sir. Perhaps this has a clue, because I do not wish to be pressed again by the Russians."

"Unpressed in the press room?"

"I beg your pardon—"

"Nothing," Jaynes said. One tot of vodka demanded another. He poured the clear liquid in the water tumbler, and Rolf watched him in the faintly disgusted manner of a tee-totaler.

"The telephone lines are for the convenience of the press, sir, and there is a log kept of the telephone calls."

"So you know who Michael called?" Just the edge of excitement.

"The calls are merely logged, sir. The telephones, you must remember, were part of the common pool. There were no exclusive telephones except for the gentleman from that New York newspaper."

"The *Times*, the bloody *New York Times*," Jaynes said. The *Times* man had studied at Cambridge, wore Savile Row clothes, and affected the sort of accent Jaynes should have been born to. There was no worse snob than an American snob, not even in Scotland, Jaynes thought. On the other hand, at least in most of Scotland.

"That's right, sir," he said. "I went through the lists. Many telephone calls for only four days."

"Never offer a journalist a freebie," Jaynes said.

"I don't understand."

"Pray continue."

"For his credentials, Mr. Jaynes, Mr. Hampton showed letters of identity from his regular clients. Two are Arabic news agencies, one in Tripoli, Libya. The other in Saudi Arabia."

"Libya. I like this better and better. The American connection to Colonel Qaddafi." Headlines formed again in mind. He wanted to write them himself, position the byline just so, lay out the page, and dictate the play.

"The third client was the only one he called. The Congregation for the Protection of the Faith."

Jaynes gaped.

"Mr. Hampton called this number seven times. It is at an address in Roma. In Italy."

"I know where Rome is," Jaynes said.

"The phone number is listed there. I . . . I checked it. I was curious. Number sixteen, Borgo Santo Spirito," Rolf said. "I have a good memory."

"Except when you're packing tapes, eh, Rolf?"

Rolf looked blank.

Jaynes saw the headlines vanish from screen. Qaddafi bashing was one thing, bashing the RCs was a bit trickier. Not that a touch of antipopery was all bad, but in this day of ecumenicism and the other nonsense of the churches, it wasn't well to put all your eggs in the same Easter basket. And what on earth did something called the Congregation for the Protection of the Faith care about a naval conference in the bloody Baltic?

"Who knows this? About the list?"

"I know this."

"But who else?"

"I put in the press area. I kept the list to submit for the expenses, since the national telephone exchange will receive the international charges in time. I'm careful, Mr. Jaynes. I am curious. I try to make certain all charges are honest."

Like bloody hell you do, you conniving thief, Jaynes thought. You keep the list to see how much you can inflate the final bill to the Swedish government for the privilege of hosting a meeting of the superpowers. What had Jaynes written? "Fiercely neutral Sweden wishes to assume a greater, more serious role in world affairs by presenting a sober alternative to pro-Western and pro-Eastern factions." In fact, Jaynes thought Sweden was terrified of the coming merger of the Common Market into an integrated economy and didn't want to close any doors to a future alliance of convenience. Perhaps Rolf worked for Swedish security. Perhaps they had wanted to know whom the journalists called.

"So perhaps Mr. Hampton is going to Rome, is that what you imply?"

"I imply nothing. You cannot say that, not now. You must have the proof—"

"I have your list, your telephone list—"

"There is no list."

"You just said—"

"I said nothing." Rolf let it fall flat.

"Oh, bloody hell, Rolf. What was that address in Rome again?"

"This afternoon, Mr. Jaynes. When you meet me again in

Skane Park at four. And you give me the five hundred kronor that you promised—"

"My word, dear fellow."

"I have worked with journalists before," Rolf Gustafson said, and this time there was no question that he would have his way, even if Jaynes had to scramble all morning to tap a friendly editor back home.

Which is precisely what Jaynes had to do.

FOURTEEN

Berlin

Michael Hampton opened his eyes and saw the knife. He felt the tip of it against his left cheek. It was on the side of his nose, just below his left eye. He could just see it. He stared at it cross-eyed for a long moment without making a move or a sound. The strain of staring at it gave him a nauseous feeling, to go with his raging headache.

The knife was very long and sharp.

The handle was gripped by a bony, pale hand that extended back into a thin arm, into a thin shoulder.

The creature, Michael thought. The creature disappeared at the point where arm met shoulder; he could barely discern a form, but it might be large or small, hideous or not. He remembered the grip on his ankle, he remembered the two men at the mouth of the alley with their pistols drawn. He remembered falling and something striking his head. His head was ringing. He blinked and tried not to think of the sharp point of the knife on his face. Wherever they were, the place had no windows. There was a candle somewhere in the room, but the thin, wavering light only accentuated the darkness. The place smelled damp and old. He was in a tomb, he thought, and he wanted to shiver, but the prick of the knife on his flesh made him sit very still.

The creature spoke German. The voice was high and mocking.

"What are you? A thief or a murderer?"

"I'm not."

"The police don't shoot at people if they aren't thieves or murderers."

The voice smiled in the darkness. He could make out the shape of a head now as he blinked in the light, but no features. The light was behind the figure holding the knife.

"You must be a murderer. Or a very poor thief. You have only sixty marks in your wallet."

"I'm not a thief. Those men wanted to kill me—"

"Of course they did. That's why they shot at you."

"Where am I?"

The creature laughed a screeching little laugh. It wasn't very pleasant. "You are at the point of death, Herr Hampton. That is your name?"

"My name," he said. He wanted to retch.

"Don't you have any more money?"

"I was—I was going to get more."

"Where?"

"I—I'm meeting someone. Someone with money."

"In Berlin."

"In Belgium."

The small, ugly laugh again.

"Believe me," Michael began.

"I believe you, Herr Hampton, you are much too simple not to be believed." And the hideous laugh came out of the darkness again.

"They were going to kill me. How did I get away?"

"I saved your life, Michael. Is that worth anything to you?"

"How did you?"

"Do you know this place?"

"No—"

"It is one of my places, you might say. One of the places where the rats are at home."

There. He had not noticed it before until the other spoke the word. He could hear the rats scurrying in the darkness, crooning to each other. The darkness was alive with rats. The rats ran along, stopped, sniffed, stared at him. The rats watched him.

For no reason, the creature laughed again. The laugh shattered the darkness and remade it into a more sinister form. There were rats, and there was this maniac with the high-pitched voice who laughed at nothing.

"I am the Rat. Do you know me?"

"I don't know you. Please take the knife away. You might slip—"

"I might slip on purpose, Michael, and cut your eye out. I might do it anyway because you have a credit card in your wallet. If I killed you now and left you here for a week, I could use that card for many things. Many, many things." The creature paused. "So stop games, Michael, and tell me the truth about the money—"

"I have to go to Belgium, I—"

"You said that before, and I didn't believe you." And the knife slipped a little, cutting the flesh below his eye.

The sudden pain made him want to vomit.

The creature pulled the knife away.

It was just enough, and Michael was just desperate enough. He lunged forward in that moment, upsetting the candle, plunging the windowless tomb into darkness.

He grasped the creature's hand.

The knife plunged into his arm.

Pain like heat. Blood in warm waves from the wound. He held on and the creature hissed. The rats in the blinding darkness scuttled away, making angry sounds.

The hand. He had to turn the hand. He wanted to break the wrist.

The hand opened, finger by finger, and the knife clattered to the damp concrete floor.

But the Rat bit down in that moment, and Michael cried out. The bite was deeper and it hurt more than the two knife wounds. The Rat had torn his flesh again.

Anger filled him. A day of running—of real, shaking fear—had transformed him. He was a mild man, a lover and listener. He never thought of himself as a creature who could howl with rage or pain, who could fight to the death, who would intend to kill another man. . . . The Rat fastened to him, and he felt a thin throat beneath his hand and squeezed. Kill the Rat and kill the life and the screeching laughter in the darkness. . . .

The Rat squeezed his testicles with a bony hand. White pain. The Rat squeezed again, and Michael let go of the throat and then hit out, striking something, making the white pain from the center of his body turn into mere red rage.

The Rat was thrown off and came back to the attack. The Rat was sinewy, all hands and teeth and feet, twisting and pulling and biting.

Michael grasped hair and pulled.

The Rat howled and kicked out. Pain boiled in Michael's bowels. He pulled the hair back and down and felt the creature's body falling.

He pounced then, the cat upon the bird in darkness.

He squeezed at the creature and produced another scream.

Michael grinned in the darkness.

He wanted to cause pain. It was pleasant to cause this pain, to strike and kill and hear the howl in the darkness, the rage and pain mingled until the last sound became a death gurgle, a mere whisper before eternity.

He hit the creature again. And then again. He held the creature's hair and struck at what must have been the creature's face.

Unexpectedly, the Rat bit again, despite the pain.

The teeth cut into the fleshy palm of the striking hand, and Michael cried out now.

"Goddamn you!"

And he slammed the thin body down on the concrete floor and fell on it, sought to smother it with his weight and size.

His bleeding hand found the other's neck.

He could still the head and the slashing teeth. He had the neck and controlled the creature now.

The creature writhed beneath his grip a moment.

Then, curiously, it was still. Death, coming as the last whisper in all the sounds of the world.

Michael stopped squeezing.

Had he killed?

Without meaning to, he let out a great sob.

His hand pulled away from the still form of the creature. He scrambled in the darkness and found the candle on the floor. He found a wooden match in a dish and lit the candle.

Darkness retreated before the pale light and went to the corners of the immense room where the rats roosted, waited, watched.

The creature did not move.

Terror filled Michael's heart for what he had done.

All his life was filled with gentleness. He had become tender from the earliest age, he could not harm a creature. His father had found this disgusting. Will was a hunter who killed for food and without philosophy. They needed the food; they never killed more than they ate. In the autumn, they hunted deer on the ranges, in the snow, killing in the vast loneliness of those pastures and open lands. But not Michael. He went with them; he could gut the deer and did so. He would be as bloody as a butcher at the end of the hunt, and it did not bother him, nor the glassy eye of the dead deer, nor the skinned meat hung in the meathouse. But the moment of the killing—from the point of life to the point of death, a bridge of just an inch of time—could not be crossed. His father mocked him, but Will understood his tender heart all his life. Was it that easy to be transformed into a killer? Turn a man loose and then hunt him over two days, through three countries, make it absolutely sure he understands that the object of the game is to kill him and the only way the prey can escape death is to kill in turn—and then what will happen to his gentle nature and quiet voice and placid manner?

And now he had stilled that creature, squeezed the life out of it with his large hands.

He brought the candle across the floor to the place where the creature lay.

He gasped.

The face was dirty and perhaps, in life, it was hardened. But now it was so young, so soft, the eyes shut against the darkness. Death softened, he thought.

He held his hand to the creature's face.

He put his hand against its neck. Beneath the skin, he felt the slow, steady beat of the heart.

Not dead. For a moment, he wanted to cry because of the release he felt.

He tore open the creature's shirt to better listen to its heart.

He felt so glad in that moment that his eyes teared. The creature, whoever he was, had saved his life.

And then he stopped.

He looked down at the pale, dirty skin.

He felt dizzy again.

The bleeding hand and arm and cheek ceased to pain him in that moment by the shock of it.

Breasts.

Young, budding breasts, with dark nipples.

With horror, he saw the eyes slowly open. They blinked in the darkness. The eyes were tan, almost without color. They stared at him for a moment as he knelt in open-mouthed shock.

And the creature smiled without any humor at all.

It was a woman.

FIFTEEN

London

The Americans stood before the palace and watched the bright British troops perform the changing of the guard. The old, cheerless Buckingham Palace was not occupied by any of the royals this grim November Monday. One was in Ulster, continuing the tradition that held that the six counties of northern Ireland were part of the heart and soul of Britain. One was in the West Indies, beneath the Caribbean sun, showing the flag to the natives, who had been bloodlessly freed of British rule less than forty years earlier. One was in Scotland, living the life of a hermit on a sun-dappled crag called Ben y Vrakie above the valley that contained Pitlochry. He was studying the works of Thoreau and longed to be freed of his aimless, stupid, and extremely wealthy life. In another age, he would have scourged himself in a cell. Throughout Britain and the empire and the commonwealth, the royals embodied flag and history and displayed themselves as museum pieces or caged creatures in a sort of royal zoo. The Americans who watched the British troops in blood-red uniforms shout and march and wheel so smartly did not know any of these things; nor that, less than a mile to the east, across Hyde Park and Park Lane, in the very formal building at the corner of Grosvenor Square, the director of operations for an intelligence agency was being told stories of murder.

"There's no question—"

"No, Mr. Hanley, no question."

The second man was Vaughn Reuben, director for special projects in the Central Intelligence Agency. Vaughn Reuben—in that Langley bureaucracy of intelligence gatherers, disinformation dispensers, go-alongers, dirty tricksters, political policy planners, and all the rest—was simply a spy, the master of spies for the Langley Firm.

They were in the glass room inside the U.S. embassy. The glass room was also called the clear room. The Central Intelligence Agency had offices and staff in the embassy, and it was to the CIA that the director of R Section had been called. That was a humiliation in itself. And the humiliation was intended. Langley was putting the bad-mouth on R Section for fumbling security at the Malmö conference, for jeopardizing a new and secret relationship with the Soviets, for dragging its collective feet.

The master of spies for Langley wore a tweedy jacket, brown-striped shirt, plain blue bow tie, and smoked a pipe. He was a Yale-professor-type out of central casting. His image was as carefully calculated as a presidential candidate's. He was in the bureaucracy, but he had been moved up rapidly because of his friendship with the ambitious man who was chafing as vice president of the United States. Whenever they could, they played golf together. The vice president confided in the Yale professor and spoke of his frustrations—principally his frustration with the secretary of state. The secretary of state had the president's ear, his heart, his balls, and his trust, while the vice president had none of these things. In six years, it would be the vice president's turn, but the secretary of state seemed determined to make sure that eventuality would not happen. The vice president, in his weak frustration, was very useful to Vaughn Reuben.

Hanley's eyes were rimmed with red. Everything in his

manner seemed pale and subdued. His suit was extremely ordinary, a serviceable government gray. It might have been a uniform. His fringe of hair was white and his rabbity appearance was aided by the inevitable cold that visitors to Britain in November manage to acquire in the first few days. His nose was red and sore. His cheeks were flushed. He felt like a man in front of a furnace one moment and in a rainstorm the next.

"I know what's going on in Washington," Hanley said. "The matter of this missing tape. . . . Langley is utilizing our embarrassment to further . . . to further what, Mr. Reuben?"

"We have no secret agenda," Reuben said. He sucked dryly at the stem of his pipe but produced no smoke. His eyes gazed on Hanley as he might have gazed on a prized student in the first row of Philosophy 210.

"Every agenda is secret in the trade," Hanley said.

Vaughn Reuben pulled at his pipe again. To Hanley's relief, he did not draw smoke. The glass room permitted no sound to intrude or to leave. The problem was, it was damned stuffy as well.

"Two Soviet agents, Arkady and Viktorinov, were murdered about 0700 in Brussels, in the area of Rena Taurus's apartment. What was your man's mission exactly?"

"To observe—" lied Hanley. What was it exactly? He was getting whipsawed—first by Mrs. Neumann, who had express orders from the NSC, which got them, in turn, from the secretary of state with the blessing of the president; then by the well-known buddy of the vice president. This was a setup, but Hanley could not see the dimensions of it.

"Observation is not resolution, is it?" A little joke. Vaughn smiled. Hanley didn't bother. The Soviet directorate for "direct action" abroad was called the Committee for External Observation and Resolution. It was in charge of wet contracts.

"You forget the Russians are involved in this circus as well. R Section had joint security at the conference in Malmö with KGB. So R Section pursues its mission, which you know very well—to get back that damned tape. We are cooperating at every level with KGB.'' The lies came easily. "I have no idea what transpired in Brussels.''

"Yes. That's the problem, isn't it?'' Vaughn stared through the glass walls at the opaque walls. "CIA was frozen out of Malmö. I can't understand why. R Section had a chance there, a real chance to shine, and you muffed it.''

"And you were sent here to harass me.'' It was not a question.

"Yes. That's what I was sent for. The heat is terrible, isn't it?''

"Stifling.''

"What was your man's mission? In Brussels.''

"That's no business of yours.''

Reuben smiled. It was the pleasurable, chilling smile of the cat. "A man named Henry McGee was linked in a message delivered to our Stockholm station by a Soviet defector. He escaped from prison a few weeks later. A very suspicious escape. Henry McGee was a mole inside R Section for a very long time, the most traitorous double agent in your history. . . . Quite a long time . . .''

Hanley stared and said nothing.

"Quite a long time . . . And now this business in Malmö, a missing tape recording of minutes of a secret agenda and delivered to a man who is clearly a security risk. Michael Hampton, dishonorably discharged, former top-secret clearance in Army Intelligence, worked with unsavory people at the UN in New York, skipped to London, questioned by the Brits—''

"At whose behest, Reuben?''

"I don't know.''

"Little Langley pressure? You were after his body once, weren't you?''

"That's gossip, isn't it?''

"Perhaps.''

"Oh, come off it, Hanley.''

They were just crossing swords now, circling, touching metal to metal to probe for reaction and weakness.

"The point is, there's supposed to be cooperation between Section and KGB."

Hanley looked at him. "It doesn't sit well on your tongue, either, does it?"

No reaction. Pipe stem prop, bow tie prop, tweed jacket prop, and no reaction except for a blink. Vaughn Reuben said, "We are intelligence agencies. We don't set policy and we don't have secret agendas."

"Vaughn, your section ran the war in Nicaragua for nearly nine years."

"Is that true?"

"You supplied the arms to the Afghanis."

Blink. Blink, blink. Silence.

"The point is, Hanley, the Russians will take it all terribly badly that one of yours wetted two of theirs on the streets of Brussels this morning. Instead of going after the girl, the way he was told to."

"He works in mysterious ways."

"November," Reuben said.

"I don't know what you're talking about."

"Devereaux," Reuben said. "A dangerous man. Some might judge him a psychopath. Certainly a sociopath."

"November," Hanley repeated, hearing the word for the first time.

"Damnit, Hanley—"

"Civility, Reuben. The 'damnit' doesn't go with the professorial clichés you affect, unless you're turning into a John Houseman portraiture," Hanley said.

"I'm doing as I'm told. Told to put the screws to you to get the tape back."

"And ice two probable innocents," Hanley said.

"I don't know about that." Blink. "We don't sanction people."

"No. We never kill."

"Except there are two dead in Brussels."

"Hardly innocents. Russian agents in a hostile environment. Maybe the Belgians did it."

"Your man killed them. And he snatched the girl."

"Did he?"

The question was never answered.

"The point," said Reuben. "The point is that we have to get the tape." He lit the pipe up.

SIXTEEN

Berlin

Michael understood some of it. There had been an opening in the side of a building for a disused coal chute. The metal door was hinged at the top. The creature—the girl, the woman, Rat, whatever she was—had opened the chute as he stood by the building waiting for the gunmen. She had grasped his ankle and jerked him to his knees, and then he had slid down the chute, banging his head on the closing door. The girl had pulled him from a shelf alongside the chute. She must have been very strong.

But then, she was strong. She had nearly killed him. And he, in desperate rage, had nearly killed her.

He touched the bite wound on his hand. His hand was swelling. She was probably infected. She was dirty, thin, and her eyes were wild.

He had been sitting on a box for thirty minutes, watching her. He had his wallet and passport back, along with the sixty marks and a small quantity of leftover Swedish kronor.

He had the knife.

He held it in his left hand because of the swelling of his right.

"What are you thinking about?" she asked. She had scarcely moved, not even rebuttoned her dirty shirt. Her hair was short, not so much cut as hacked to that length. It framed her face and made her look androgynous. Perhaps she intended that. She had an air of severity and contempt, even sitting half-naked in this coal cellar.

He spoke. "You saved my life when you pulled me in. Then you could have killed me later. Why did you trouble yourself?"

The same harsh laugh. "It was no trouble, Michael."

He stared at her.

She stirred and sat up. "Cops. Pigs. Fascists. I wouldn't raise my hand to help one. They were chasing you, and it pleased me to frustrate them." She glared at him in the candlelight. "I didn't give a damn about you. Another innocent lamb born to be fleeced. I should have just cut you when I saw the credit card. I'd be living high now, instead of sitting here listening to your voice."

"How do you live?"

"How do you think I live? By wits and cunning, that's how a girl lives. Even a streetwalker knows that. You give until you can take."

"Don't you have anyone?"

"What? Should every woman be some man's pet? Keep me and I'll obey you, kneel before you, kiss your filthy feet. The hell with it. Men are pigs who think with their pricks, that's all. Use them for pleasure when you have to. No, I don't have anyone, little lamb. I have me. I'm sufficient for myself."

"I can't call you Rat."

"You don't have to call me anything. Get out of here. It must be morning, and those morons called cops won't be waiting around. You can go up the stairs this time if the chute doesn't suit you." And the little laugh again, just as horrible as it ever was. He knew why. There was no amusement in the laugh, no humor, even no satisfaction. It was just punctuation used by an illiterate.

He took thirty marks off his roll of bills and held them out.

The girl crouched now, staring at him with the wild look of a bewildered animal.

"Take half. I need some cash. I can use the credit card to get out of Berlin, go to Frankfurt, get a flight to Brussels."

"What do you want me to do, lamb? Suck your prick for you? That's all right. There's girls on the Ku'damm do it for you cheaper. Or boys if you'd prefer them."

"Are you crazy? Are you from some insane asylum?" He made a face. "You talk crazy."

"I talk sense, lamb. I talk to you the way you need to be talked to. A couple of pigs want to off you up there and you talk like a lamb going to the slaughter."

"I'm not dead yet."

Sober silence for a moment.

The girl rocked on her heels and examined him with those tan, glittering eyes. A little smile curved on her thin face. "Little lamb. Who made thee?"

Michael blinked.

"You really are in trouble, aren't you?"

"Trouble enough," Michael said. He watched her carefully.

"You're really going to Brussels," she said. "I should have known you were Johnny Square. Too square to lie even." She laughed again. "I'm getting too clever for myself."

"Take half," he said. She had saved his life. For a moment, he had understood her in her bleak universe of deprivation, pain, fear of authorities. What was he now but another creature like her?

"I will," she said and snatched at the paper money and crumpled it in her thin hand.

"I'll leave you the knife. I can't take it with me."

"Why, Michael? Why are they chasing you?"

He began to tell her. He had to tell someone. He had to enlist sympathy. From somebody. Rena seemed a million miles away and the idyll of that gray bedroom in the old Savoy Hotel was a century ago.

The words tumbled out in the same soft, low voice that Rena loved. His moment of rage and his scream of anger had passed so completely, it was as though the moment had never happened.

"So what was on the tape?"

"If I tell you, they hunt you as well."

She smiled. The sharp teeth glinted in candlelight. "They hunt me down every day. It is part of life, like eating or drinking or taking a shit. What do you think I do?"

"You live by your wits, like all women," Michael said.

She nearly snarled and then stopped. "You mock me, but it's true. One day the old father beat me up, and he shouldn't have done it—but that's the way he saw you treated women and children. So I cut his heart out." She made a face. "I should have cut off his balls."

"Your father."

"That's what he said he was. I don't remember."

"I don't understand."

"When I was twelve, they said I had an accident. Fell down the stairs. Coma. For two months. Then I didn't die." She laughed. "There was this man who said he was my father, but I couldn't remember a damned thing. I just lived with him, cooked for him, cleaned after him, never went to school. . . . Can you imagine such a thing in such a modern, progressive society? He wanted to touch me all the time. Well, I let him. Why not? I didn't care. But I thought I would just have to take it. *Kinder, kirsch, kitsch*; a woman's lot. My lot. He got crazier, though, and that's when he started beating me, and I hurt very much. I had the headaches back. I wondered if I really had fallen down the stairs. I got the idea he pushed me down the stairs. I told him that once, and he beat me. So I killed him. Cut his heart out, and it was still warm. When you do that, you have done everything."

Silence. Tomb. Damp. Even the rats made no sound.

"I believe you. You must be the strongest woman who

ever lived. I thought you were going to kill me. It was like fighting with a cat, a leopard or something.''

"You surprised me, that's all. I didn't mean to cut your cheek, and when you cried out, I pulled the knife back. I shouldn't have.''

"I have to get out of here. My friend will meet me. Get me some money.''

"And then what? Just keep running? If you're going to just keep running, you might as well stay in Berlin. I can show you how to live here. There are many places, and you can always find shelter and a little food. And if you need some money, wait until the taverns close and find some amiable drunk who wants to give you his marks as long as you put it to him nicely, and that means putting the knife to his throat.'' She smiled at him.

Michael shook his head. "I was a translator and interpreter. Two days ago. A million years ago. I shouldn't have gotten involved in anything, but it was my curiosity. And it was their carelessness, I see that now. It was their fault. They want me to run because I'm the scapegoat. I won't. I've thought about it and thought about it. There's one chance. A place of sanctuary, you might say.''

"Sanctuary," she repeated. Her eyes glowed in the candlelight, and her whole being seemed to soften.

He lowered the knife he had held at the ready.

"Can you make it safe? Should I really believe that, that there is such a thing? I don't believe in anything, little lamb,'' she said.

He felt strange. He felt detached from himself and his words. He reached across to her. He touched her hand. She pulled it away. He reached to her, and she let him touch her hand. He looked into the tan, violent eyes. "I can't run forever. I don't have the wit. I can see one way out of this, just one. If I can get out—"

"Sanctuary," she said.

"Yes. There's a chance. I think I can.''

"How?"

"Use what I know. What I learned on the tape."

"How can you use it?"

"There's one way."

"Sanctuary," she repeated. It seemed to warm her in the damp of this coal cellar.

"If I can get there," he added.

"Is it far?"

"Far."

"Take me," she said.

He was startled.

"Take me," she repeated.

He shook his head. "It's dangerous."

"You're an innocent," she said. She smiled at him and took her hand away to button her shirt. "What would you have done if there had been no coal cellar? *Bang bang*, lamb, and you are slaughtered. These agents after you. Already in Berlin. Do you think you walk out of Berlin like a stroll in the country? They are already looking for you, Michael. You won't survive getting to the airport. I'll get you to Belgium, and you'll get your money and you'll take me to sanctuary."

"But they aren't after you." And he paused because it was so egotistical.

"They are after me every day, Michael. I told you that. Six years running, Michael. Do you think you could do it for six years? I have. I know everything, Michael. I know how to cut a throat so that they can't make a peep, and I can walk out of the delicatessen with sausages under my dress and have the grocer open the door for me. I steal and I survive, little lamb." She smiled at him in a dreamy way, as though considering something faintly regrettable. "Six years. You have only been on this side of things for two days."

The desperation in her words cut him.

He stared at her. For the first time he saw the vulnerable creature behind the tough facade. Her eyes were wide still, but they had lost the wildness. Her small mouth was not so grim.

"You don't have a passport—"

"I have everything I need. Passports are the least of my worries," she said. "What do you say, little lamb?"

"Then why didn't you leave before?"

She let the smile happen again, almost against her will. Her eyes glowed. "I know this Berlin. This old city is my mother and it hides me. Berlin is the world, lamb. Maybe I'm such an old case the cops don't look for me too hard anymore. Maybe I didn't cut his heart out of his body. Maybe nothing I just told you ever happened."

He stared at the crazy creature who rocked on her heels just at the edge of the darkness.

He shook his head. The girl touched him. In her rage, he could see his own. "What can I offer you?"

"Sanctuary. You know sanctuary, and because I have survived six years running does not mean that I want to survive another day in this filth and degradation. I told you I'm not crazy. I had a man once for almost six months. Very gentle to me. He took me in and bought me things. I wore dresses. I put on such lingerie. . . ." She was dreamy again. "I was sixteen, not so long ago, and he took me to the best restaurants on the Ku'damm. I was going to love him all his life, so gentle to me, so kind. He didn't know I would have done anything for him. He woke one morning and gave me a kiss. We had a wide bed and always slept close to each other. I would have done anything for him." Soft, softer than the crooning of the rats. "Emil went to his shower. He came out wearing a dressing gown, all glowing and pink. He looked like a baby. I heard him fall in the foyer and I went to him. 'Emil, Emil.' " Softer still. Her eyes were wet, tears on her cheeks. "He was dead. Only forty-seven years old and he was dead. . . . I had to get out of there, I saw it. I stayed with him all morning. I turned him over and put a pillow under his head. I closed his eyes for him. I told him I loved him and I would do anything for him. He never answered me."

"I'm sorry," Michael said.

The girl looked up at him through the tears. The eyes

glittered again. "You don't believe that, do you? How wonderful you are, Johnny Square. I come to your store and put sausages under my skirt, and you beg me to take more. I think you are a lamb after all." And she laughed without any mirth, rocking on her heels.

"My sanctuary is not certain. Not certain at all. It's just a hope."

"You need me, Michael. I need hope. You need experience. I'm surprised you've survived at all."

"I can take you to Belgium. If you have a passport. That's as far as I can take you. I'll give you money there—"

She scuttled away into the darkness. The rats crooned at her. She came back into the light with a West German passport. She handed it to him as though he might have been a control officer.

He opened it and stared at the gamine's face.

Marie Dreiser.

"Is this you?"

"It looks like me, doesn't it?"

"As much as passport pictures look like anyone."

"But it looks like me, doesn't it?"

He stared at her.

"Is it you?"

"For now. It's me for now."

SEVENTEEN

Bruges

*R*ita Macklin had red hair and green eyes, and she had loved him for a long time. Perhaps she still loved him, but he wouldn't think about that. She had decided something the last time, the time they had almost come back together. They had made love, and when it was over, it was over. She didn't even try to explain that to him. Dead. If not dead, then it would be killed. Put in a box and buried under the dirt of everyday life. Life goes on, life is compromise. . . . To save your life, leave your love and find another. They had parted one day and they never expected to see each other again.

The train rocketed along the track across the broad, rolling face of Belgium, where a thousand armies had marched in all the years of history, back and forth from France to Germany or France to the Netherlands, back and forth in ceaseless battle from the beginning of man in Europe. Not an acre of ground was without remembrance of bloodshed. Devereaux sat across from Rena Taurus and did not see her but saw his memory of another woman.

The train lurched from side to side. Kilometer posts flashed by, the ground near the train seemed to stream away from it like the wake of a ship. The train was grubby, close, damp. The heaters worked too well. Dirty windows were streaked with beads of rain.

Rena's coat was open, her arms were folded beneath her breasts, she stared out the window as though she found the bleak, brown countryside utterly fascinating.

Rita Macklin had said to him the last time: "Run away tomorrow and I'll run with you. If we have to run for the rest of our lives to get away from them. I don't need my career. We can live on a beach in Tahiti. We can live outback down under. We can live in the Alaskan bush, I don't care. Pioneer wife. I'll make you children. I'll wash your clothes and clean your house. I'll make love to you all day and all night. I'll bury myself in living with you. Just you and me. Just us in the world. Maybe we'll have ten years or thirty, I can't tell. Then we die. I hope we die together, but even with the sadness at the end, it would be worth it. Ten years, fifteen, twenty years. We'll quarrel and get into long, stupid arguments, that's all part of it. But we'll sleep together every night in the same bed for however long it lasts, until we are dead."

That was the choice. She stared at him with her brave green eyes and waited.

Of course he would do it.

Except it was a fantasy.

The train swayed back and forth through the drizzle that streamed across the windows. The conductor would come into the car from time to time and tramp up and down the aisles, checking tickets, examining each one as if he were a border guard. The forests along the way bent to the wind. The ground was flat and stretched to the unseen sea. Bare branches were raised like arms from the tree trunks; the trees shivered in the wind; the deluge had come again to the world.

Rena stared at him as he stared out the window, and saw the bleakness in him. She shivered at it and spoke to warm herself. "Michael and I went to Bruges. It was the first time we were . . . together."

He said nothing, made no sign that he had heard her.

The shot in the courtyard had deafened her, and the deafness was louder now in the silence between them. She remembered the morning past in vignettes that were not connected. He had bought tickets at the train station. He had taken her arm on the platform. The train was moving. She must have told him about Bruges, about how she and Michael had first gone there as lovers, but she could not remember it. It was the place where she was supposed to meet Michael with money and comfort. Had she betrayed him again to this American agent? But then, she had betrayed him in Malmö, and now he was in danger because of her.

In that moment, her heart was as bleak as Devereaux's face. What had the nuns taught her when she was young? It was evil to do the wrong thing, even for the right reason. The ends did not justify the means. She had agreed to all that when it had not meant anything. And now what had she done to Michael, even for the purest of reasons?

"We stayed at the Hotel Adornes on the canal. It was so beautiful, even in the rain. We walked all over the city," Rena said. "I was in love."

I was in love, Devereaux repeated to himself. Am in love. Was it past for Rena now? Had something happened in Malmö between her and Michael? He turned from the window and searched her face.

"We went to the museum on the Dyver Canal because Michael wanted to see the Bosch there. He loved the chaos of Bosch—it freed something in him, a part I never saw. . . ."

Now it was fantasy, Devereaux decided. She was rattling on to run away from the deaths of two agents in the courtyard of her building in Brussels. She would talk and talk until those two men were not really dead. Like Rita Macklin's fantasy of running away to a desert island with him.

The train slowed for a junction and began the arcing turn toward the ancient city. Medieval Bruges was canals and houses that leaned against each other along narrow, cobbled streets.

"You'll meet him at the Hotel Adornes," Devereaux said. She had not mentioned the hotel until a moment before.

"Yes. Can I trust you? Not to harm him?"

Devereaux said nothing. They think you are involved with Michael, and someone in the bureaucracy in Washington wants you to be sanctioned. But I mean you no harm.

"Can I trust you?"

"There's no choice," he said.

No comfort. Words of comfort were always lies. Why didn't he just lie to her?

He stared at her lovely, pale face. "Michael has to stop running because there is too much danger. You and he. Can go to ground." Devereaux paused. "Why did Michael get the stolen tape?"

She was so startled that she brushed her purse from her lap to the floor. She bent to pick it up. Her cheeks flushed. "What do you mean?"

He noted everything in that moment and did not understand what he saw. "You brought the question to me. Why did this happen to Michael? If this was no accident, why does Michael have the secret and not someone else?"

"I said that because I was afraid for Michael."

"Were you?"

She had to look away. She stared at the comfortless fields bare under the bleak clouds, stripped by the rain.

"I don't want him to be hurt," she said so softly that it was a whisper or a prayer.

"Can you do anything to stop it?" Devereaux said.

"No. Do you think I would hesitate?"

Devereaux merely continued to stare at her.

"Everyone assumes this is an accident. It was not." He waited for another reaction, but she was now as still as silence.

"Perhaps Michael had to be the person to have the tape.

Specifically Michael and no one else. Who does Michael work for?''

She hesitated again. ''I have no idea.''

''Come on, Rena,'' Devereaux said.

Of course she would know. It was stupid to lie. This man had the eyes of a policeman. There was a cold flatness now to replace the bleak look he had shown a moment before.

''You act like a policeman. I am Belgian. You have no right here. I could call the conductor, I . . .''

He said nothing.

''He worked for people in the Middle East.''

''He worked for them in Malmö?''

''Any settlement between the U.S. and the Soviet Union is important to the Middle East.''

''He told you that?''

''He told me that.''

''Is that true?''

''You see, exactly like a policeman.''

Another silence. The car was filled with dozing, late-morning passengers. A businessman folded his *Le Monde* and slipped it into his attaché case and closed the lid with a snap. Two nuns sat aloof from each other, sharing only their old-fashioned manner of dress. The speaker announced in two languages: ''Bruges . . . Brugge.''

''Tell Michael to stay with you,'' Devereaux said. ''I can arrange safety for you. For him.''

''I am in such danger? But I don't have whatever you seek—''

''How do they know that? You were lovers, Rena.'' Gently this time, not like a policeman.

''Who are they?''

Much the same, Devereaux thought. They are the people without faces who make the world.

''People in London said he was in intelligence, in the U.S. Army, that he received a dishonorable discharge,'' Devereaux said.

"He was forced to work for them," she said. "He told me. He hated it, hated the secrets he had to know."

"And now he has another secret," Devereaux said.

"He didn't want it," she said.

The words, Devereaux thought. He tried to memorize the words she used and the tone in her voice. What was it she really said?

She said, "He had a brother he loved, was killed in an accident. It embittered Michael. He said he had heard too much, too many secrets and lies. . . ." She remembered his past clearly now but could not see him as he was, running from assassins. He was her lover, her pet, a gentle man. But didn't she use him for her pleasure because he was beautiful? Of course. It's what lovers do all the time while pretending they are being unselfish.

And the gray man stared at her while she had these thoughts, and it made her want to blush. Still, there was a pleasure to be derived from his gaze as well. She remembered him holding her in the courtyard, pretending they were lovers. Felt the strength of his embrace that insisted on crushing her against his chest, felt the strength of shoulders and arms and hands. She had closed her eyes for a moment, to feel the pleasure of her breasts pressed against him. And then he had fired, killed a man as he embraced her. She shuddered now.

"You and Michael are the only ones who know about Bruges?"

"Yes. We were discreet . . . at the beginning," she said.

"Michael has to hide in a place where they won't find him. Might as well be Bruges. For three days. I can get the tape. Get it back to those who want it, settle this."

"How can you settle this?" she said.

"I'll listen to the tape. As Michael did. As they know he did."

"What if he didn't?"

"Michael took a train to Stockholm. They knew that, the people who put the tape in his bag." He watched her as he spoke and saw her mouth open in astonishment. Perhaps she really was surprised, he thought. "Seven hours on a train in Sweden. He read the paper, he read a book, but he must have been curious about the extra tape. He had to be. He had to listen to it to pass the time."

"He might have flown to Stockholm."

"The train was cheaper. Michael had to take the train," Devereaux said. In that moment, he saw Michael turning on the tape player, listening to the secrets. "He had to listen to the tape."

"But why?"

Devereaux said, "Because the plan was designed that way."

EIGHTEEN

Rome

Cardinal Ludovico was impressive in stature, in attire, in the possessions with which he surrounded himself. He moved with a graceful inevitability through the rooms of his apartment. The rooms were large, and the windows had thick, red drapes so that the summer heat could be shut out during the long Roman days. The drapes were open now for the thin light of Roman autumn. The sun was pale, a dot in the sky, and the sickly yellow light cast a surrealistic wash over the stones of the old buildings. All the city was full of noise, but it was muffled by the gravity of the walls and furnishings of these rooms. Perhaps muffled by the presence and majesty of Cardinal Ludovico.

The journalist was English, which meant there was a certain seediness to his character and credentials. This is what Cardinal Ludovico believed, because he had a firm opinion on the nationalities of others; he was descended from the original Romans, who still lived in the Trastavere section of the ancient, disordered city. He felt the eternity of the old Romans in his bones.

For his part, Evelyn Jaynes thought he was being extremely

clever. Yes, the Sunday London paper was quite interested if there really was something, and yes, they had the money, enough advance to pay off Gustafson and get Jaynes on the first flight south to Rome. Jaynes had been polite but blunt in getting through the bureaucratic layers that protected the center of the Congregation for the Protection of the Faith. The people of the layers admitted nothing, were as truculent as scolded children, but Jaynes was sending a message through them to the intelligent source at the center of the congregation.

"I am grateful, Eminence," the Englishman began. It was best to be humble in the presence of so much obvious power. "The urgency of my—"

Cardinal Ludovico spoke right through Jaynes's words. His English was strained, full of disdain for the barbarisms of the language; his voice commandingly soft: "I believe you mentioned Michael Hampton. I believe you suggested that Mr. Hampton, a translator by trade, is somehow connected with the congregation. I can assure you that is not true. I assure you, not for yourself, but for your newspaper. The world well knows the peculiar institution of the British Sunday newspaper and the inaccuracies which form the core of its mass presentation."

There. There and there. Words like points, lilting in the Roman way, but pointing and slashing nonetheless. Cold leonine eyes behind the words, offering not shelter, sanctuary, or forgiveness.

So it's hardball, Evelyn Jaynes thought. His journalistic adrenaline was rising. He removed the paper from his jacket pocket.

Jaynes flourished the paper with a grand gesture.

The eyes of the lion did not waver but kept staring at the puffed pastry face of the English reporter.

Jaynes continued: "Records of telephone calls between Mr. Hampton and the Congregation for the Protection of the Faith. Actually, in the process of digging, I found other connections."

Cardinal Ludovico remained standing in the center of the room. The soft light replicated the atmosphere of a cathedral during Solemn High Mass—everything was candles and incense and Latin chants, while a heavenly choir in the loft at the back of the church strained to be angels. Ludovico understood the effect, understood all his effects. He had been the eyes and ears and hands of the pope for thirty years— five popes with different agendas and needs, even needs they sometimes did not know they had until Cardinal Ludovico pointed them out.

"Why would the congregation be interested in a conference held in Sweden?" the cardinal said. "Concerning, I believe you said, a discussion of the sea rights of the superpowers in the Baltic?"

The lion made a thin, grotesque smile. "You see, what you suggest is absurd, even by the absurdist standards of the British Sunday press. I cannot explain further—"

Jaynes let the hackles strain against the tweed of his coat. "Eminence," he began again, "I am a simple journalist and must report on what I see and what I hear. I have established the connection between Michael Hampton and the congregation . . . as recently as last week, with telephone calls to Rome from Sweden during the Baltic conference. I have done my homework, Eminence, and even a little detective work. There is a large Catholic population in Lithuania, Latvia, even—"

The cardinal raised his hand gently. The gesture demanded silence. "There are Catholics even in Sweden, but the church has no navies and no need for freedom of the seas, even Baltic seas. There are Catholics in Poland on the Baltic, as well as Germany. You make no connection—"

"Telephone records are not lies. And now a tape is missing," Jaynes hissed, his eyes glittering. "A top-secret tape stolen by a correspondent for the Congregation for the Protection of the Faith, a top-secret Roman Catholic organization directed by the pope's unofficial spy, Alberto Cardinal Ludovico. . . ." He was writing his lead as he spoke it, seeing the headline clearly splashed across the top of the front page, watching the American services picking it up and spinning the ball around the world. All from Evelyn Jaynes, your humble Harris-tweed reporter, who has walked personally into the lion's den on Borgo Santo Spirito, just up from Ponte Vittorio Emanuele—by God! He'd given them Rome on a silver platter with all its priestly corruption and cynicism!

In that moment, Cardinal Ludovico decided something. "Where is Mr. Hampton now?"

"Not in his apartment in Stockholm," Jaynes said.

"Then, where is he?"

"On the run, I suppose."

"He is not here, Mr. Jaynes," Cardinal Ludovico said. He looked about him. The yellow light of the room revealed emptiness.

Jaynes said, "He will be here. If he can get here. There are inquiries made, you know. By intelligence operatives from the United States and the Soviet Union. What is this about? I am only a British journalist who happened upon my little bit of information by dint of effort, by digging for the real story buried beneath the apparent story. What is the involvement of the church? You have no navy, you said it yourself, Eminence. Then why did Michael Hampton call you seven times from Malmö last week during a naval conference? Why did you finance his trip to Malmö?"

The last was sheer guessing.

Ludovico's eyes flickered a moment. Just a moment.

Jaynes saw. He did not move. His rounded shoulders beneath the Harris-tweed padding became very tense, preparing for battle.

Ludovico made a gesture. "Perhaps you will sit down, Mr. Jaynes?"

They settled into velvet and mahogany armchairs more suitable for the posteriors of kings.

"The congregation has, from time to time, employed Mr. Hampton because of his abilities as a translator," Cardinal Ludovico began, the soft voice even softer now. Jaynes did not react to the admission of a lie a moment earlier. "While translators are a large body in Europe, there is a great need both for those able to translate and interpret Middle Eastern dialects and Far Eastern dialects. With European languages, of course. The church has many contacts in the Middle East. This is quite natural, it is the cradle of our faith."

Lull me to sleep, Jaynes said to himself. He was writing it all down, but it was just the commercial message. "Mr. Hampton is skilled in Arabic languages. Did you know that?"

"No," lied Jaynes.

"It is for that speciality that we engage him from time to time," Ludovico said.

Silence.

Is that all? Jaynes put down his pen.

Ludovico waited, hands folded on his lap, eyes serene.

"My dear Cardinal," Jaynes began. He stopped. What does one say to the lion in his den? "My dear Cardinal," he began again. "The documentation is irrefutable. Mr. Hampton was employed by the one unit of the Vatican which has a reputation for conducting . . . affairs of intelligence, should we say? At a conference between the Americans and the Russians? Come now, sir, I really think your explanation is no explanation at all."

"But it is all the explanation that I have, Mr. Jaynes."

"First, you lie to me about the relationship between Hampton and the church, and then you retract that lie and offer another in its place," Jaynes said. He had chosen the naked word "lie" to inject reality into this staged setting. "I am not a fool." I am an Englishman, by God, you papist dago.

"I would hope not. Speculation such as you offered a moment ago would be the work of a fool." No quarter now, no act of accommodation.

Jaynes licked his sandpaper lips. The point was, of course, it was all a bit thin. Not that he couldn't pull it off if he had been one of the overpaid analysts the papers were so fond of who sit in towers and think thoughts and write down their drivel as if it was Revelation. "Afraid, Evelyn, old boy, this is all very well, very well put, but we're dealing in facts here, not idle speculation about an unknown translator who may or may not have stolen a tape recording. I mean, your source is nothing more than a glorified janitor.''

"Eminence." He tried to make his eyes sincere. "I have no quarrel with you or the Roman church. I am not an antireligionist, if that's your concern. I am not interested in sensationalism for its own sake. I am concerned for the safety of Mr. Hampton, if he is in some danger—"

"Are you certain he's in danger?"

There. Just a flicker of the eyelids. What was it betraying?

"I think there is a distinct possibility," Jaynes continued. He watched the eyes. Would this line of speculation reveal that which the previous line had not? "I do not know Mr. Hampton—I met him briefly at the conference—but I do know the danger of knowing secret things."

"Do you, Mr. Jaynes?"

Evelyn Jaynes felt chilled in that moment. Was there irony behind the question?

"What secret things do you know?"

Yes. Irony. And threat. Was this priest threatening him? But the voice was still soft.

"I know Michael Hampton has a secret tape recording from the naval conference and that he has simply disappeared. I know that he works from time to time for a secret organization within the Vatican, you have admitted it."

"Nothing, Mr. Jaynes, is admitted within these walls."

Jaynes blinked.

"You came to me to ask questions on behalf of your newspaper, which serves the British public. I told you that in three weeks time the Holy Father will announce a new era of . . . what word shall we use? . . . rapprochement with the English church."

This was news to Jaynes and the world.

Slowly, the old lion gnawed on, and the journalist in Jaynes did as the lion told. The story was a good one, an interesting one, and one certainly within the purview of Cardinal Ludovico. Oh, favored Evelyn Jaynes! A story that was English to the bone, full of Canterbury and cathedrals and healing of schisms, a story spun as delicately as flying buttresses, as beautiful as stained windows. On and on and on, and Jaynes scribbled his Pitman shorthand notes and then he was outside the rooms that do not admit, he was on the Borgo Santo Spirito, heading to the bridge over the shallow Tiber, beholding the November afternoon of the eternal city on the hills. . . . He found a taverna almost at once and was soon plunged into confused, happy, unsatisfied drunkenness, knowing he had been used as badly as a whore and yet relishing the experience, using the story in his notes as future credit with a future editor and future advance, buying the expensive whiskey on credit against all his future.

Michael Hampton was on hold for the moment. Jaynes had gone to Ludovico for one story and been sidetracked by another one. He couldn't ignore a scoop put in his lap, even when he knew he was being sandbagged.

And the lion stood at the tall window and looked at the street and the bridge and the city.

Dear Michael, he thought. Is it true that I have put you in the way of harm?

But he knew he had.

NINETEEN

Bruges

Rena waited for Michael in her room. She sat at the open window and watched rain fall on the canal and the narrow, cobbled streets. Bicycle traffic was heavy and the riders, covered with slickers and canvas, bent to the rain. Rain polished the cobblestones and streaked the grimy old buildings. Everything was ancient, immovable; she sat at the window like a pale, beautiful statue, as though she had always been there. There was a heartsick feeling to the day, to the rain, to her thoughts of Michael and her loyalties. She wasn't even loyal; she would have yielded for the American agent if he had demanded it. Yielded gratefully, to feel those arms again around her and feel him press her until she opened completely for him. *She would betray Michael like that*.

The window was open. Now and then, in a sudden gust, rain would splatter in and touch her beauty. She scarcely knew what she was thinking about. Michael. Dear Michael, naked in that bed before all this trouble, innocent and beautiful. The man who had held her . . . Suddenly she blinked, because the insistent intrusion of Devereaux colored her daydream of Michael. There was no sun, no innocence in him, in those eyes that had seen everything since the Creation. . . .

She stared at the Devereaux of her imagination and imagined his oak-tree arms around her, pressing her to him for his own need. Dealing death. Unloving, ungentle, raw as spring earth turned in black Belgian fields.

She felt stirred with desire. But for what? Better, for whom? Devereaux was gone. She was to meet Michael alone, when Michael made it to Bruges. Damn. Michael should not be harmed. . . . She thought of Devereaux staring at her, of the soft sound of his hard little questions and the long, arid silences between the questions. Did he trust her? It wasn't a question of that, Devereaux had said. He seemed distracted. He had left her to sit alone by this window and wait for her lover. Perhaps Devereaux was out there in the rain, watching her waiting for Michael. She felt nervous at the thought of being under his gaze. Even now, she plucked at an imaginary bit of lint on her sweater. Was she blushing? Would he think her vain if she brushed her hair? She reached for a brush and began to make long strokes. She brushed and raised her arms over her head and exposed the delicate form of her body. She sometimes stared at her body after the bath, standing in front of the mirror while the soft sheen of her skin glowed from the warm waters. She sometimes was amazed that this was her, amazed at her physical perfection. Here she was, fragmented in thoughts, confused by a thousand memories and emotions. Yet her body was exquisite, so perfect. Men stared at her and she loved them to look at her, to desire her. How perverse of her!

The strokes of the brush pushed her back into childhood. Her deep blue eyes began to fade into dreams.

And at that moment, she saw Michael in the rain.

He was bareheaded and wearing a parka. He walked along the canal coming from the center of the city. He was not looking left or right, but there was a tentative quality to his step. He seemed changed. Only two days since she had last lain in his grasp. Michael. She stopped, put down the brush, almost spoke his name, which would not have been heard above the traffic sounds.

At the bridge he stopped and looked up at the hotel. It was just three stories high, a hotel made by connecting three smaller buildings. He saw her in the open window and his lips said her name. His eyes were haunted. Her heart, in that moment, went out to him. Michael suffered, she saw, and she hated whatever made him suffer.

She watched Michael cross the bridge. Bicycles splashed through puddles, and she felt impervious, for the first time, to cold or rain. She got up then to meet him.

She came down the steps and ran to him and embraced him. Felt his arms around her. He whispered her name in an exhausted voice. He was shaking with fear or cold now, in her embrace. She covered his neck with kisses. She pressed against him and said his name in her deep sensuous voice.

"My God, I didn't think I'd make it. There were men in Berlin. . . ." He stopped, looked at her. What could he say? She was a century ago, and he had lived to be a hundred in the past two days and nights.

"Are you all right, Michael? What about the tape recording?"

"Damn the tape, damn them all." A different voice, frustrated and angry because of the frustration. "I've been on the move all day. We got out through East Berlin, a plane to Geneva, it was horrible, a mess. . . . I finally figured it out. Marie figured it out. She suggested we get out through East Berlin. I wouldn't have made it. The damned credit card, they're tracing me because I'm using the credit card, the tickets at the counters—" He was distracted, his voice broke.

"Who is Marie?" Rena still held him, but in that question there was just the slightest edge of apartness.

He looked at her blankly.

"Marie Dreiser. She saved my life in Berlin. I ran into an alley. Two men were after me. They had guns. They fired. She pulled me down a coal chute." He began to giggle. The woman who ran the hotel stared at him from her little desk. The fire was lit in the dining room. The hotel was warmth and safety, like home.

"Michael," Rena said his name to calm him. "It's all right."

"It's not all right. I have to get away, I have to get to Rome—"

"Rome? You have to get to Rome?"

"It's too complicated, but everything leads to Rome," he said. "I have to call, I have to arrange . . . my reception. Once I give them the tape, they can do what they want. They're powerful enough—"

He was babbling. The woman of the hotel was staring at him. Rena wanted to slap him to bring him back to the present, but she realized he was hysterical. He had held onto himself for two days and nights, but now this temporary relief was too much. She felt him shudder. Oh, Michael, she thought.

"Michael, a man came with me to Bruges. I didn't want you in danger, I never wanted you in danger. . . . An American agent—"

He froze. He held her in his grasp, but he had turned to stone. She stared at his eyes and saw the horror.

"The American agent. I had no choice. There were two men watching me, the American agent killed them. I think he killed both men. He shot them." She saw it all again, felt the pistol, felt the sound of the shot tearing through fabric and then flesh, felt the shudder of the pistol under her coat, her arms wrapped around him in sensuous embrace, his arms so strong, the smell of him, the male thing that roused her as surely as kisses and touches, and in that moment, death dealt out in a single shot.

"This is a trap?" His eyes grew wide. He stared at Rena as if he had never seen her before.

The words didn't register for a moment.

She felt his hands fall away from her. He took a step back.

"This is a trap?"

"No, Michael, no, I brought money, he wants you to hide

while he arranges what to do with the tape. I believe him, Michael, I really do—''

''Why? Because he showed you a badge? One of the good guys?'' Michael's face flushed. ''I asked you to meet me, to bring me money. My God, Rena, what do you think this is about? If you heard that tape, you'd know there was nobody you could trust.''

''Michael, you can't keep running, not if there are men who want to kill you.''

''Marie said to be careful, that they might have set you up. Not Rena, not my Rena, she's no fool, she wouldn't betray me.'' A step back, then another, almost to the door of the hotel. The woman behind the desk rose. Rena stepped forward. Michael was full of hatred, and she saw it. She had never been hated. Michael was her lover. She was love, her heart was his to warm himself with.

''You bitch,'' he said. The voice was full of contempt. ''You stupid silly bitch, you've given me to them. They're going to kill me. Don't you see that?''

''He won't hurt you, Michael, I swear to God—''

''Stupid bitch, you traitor—''

Saw all their love shattered in the eyes, the sound of the voice, the color of the words. She stumbled toward him, and he slapped her.

The blow stunned her. Colors turned red and yellow and then black.

The woman of the hotel said something in Flemish. Sounds on the stairs. She blinked and felt tears and a ringing in her head. Michael hit her again, this time with his fist, wanting to kill her.

Stumbled to her knees.

Michael turned. Flung open the door and hit the cobblestones at a run. Saw the figure across the canal coming toward him. Ran along the narrow street. A shout behind him.

He expected explosions, expected bullets in his back.

Ran to the next street where a warehouse opened on the

canal. Turned toward the wall that encircled part of the old city. Ran slapdash on the street, threading through bicycle traffic, slickered riders, old men walking with umbrellas. . . .

He pushed a fat woman blocking his way, and she went down with a startled, angry shout.

Expected death at any moment. He had turned white with fear.

The man chasing him was threading through the same crowd of traffic, slowed by a bicycle that suddenly turned in front of him. Devereaux slipped, fell on the cobblestones, rose. He saw Michael turn at the corner and disappear. Devereaux felt the breath burning out of him.

His feet slapped at the wet stones, slipped again, recovered. At the corner he stopped and then saw Michael emerging from a courtyard into a side street next to an old church. Devereaux ran at an angle for the church, and the bicyclist smashed into him from a blind alley. The rider was heavy and middle-aged, the black bicycle frame old and bent, and Devereaux went down in a tangle of spokes and slickers. The rider landed on top of him. Devereaux cracked his brow on the stones, felt his hands scrape the earth.

The rider shouted in Flemish.

Devereaux, faintly dazed, pushed him off. Got up. Wiped his head and saw blood on his hand. It didn't matter.

The goddamn fool thinks I want to kill him.

Devereaux started again for the church and reached the corner. He looked down the narrow street that twisted in a slow arc that hid its end. He ran along the street and he shouted Michael's name. He ran to the end of the street. He looked around and there were six streets off this intersection. They were filled with bicycles and riders and walkers and women with string shopping bags. The skies were dark, and for the first time Devereaux felt the chill of the rain on his head. His hair was soaked, the rain mixed with the cut on his forehead, and the blood dripped to his eye. He wiped his forehead carelessly. He stared at the narrow streets. There was nothing he could do.

Devereaux trudged back to the hotel in the rain. Michael had fled with the tape and would not trust Rena again. Rena was watched by the opposition, and Devereaux had rescued her from them. He had killed two men to do it. And he had been instructed by Hanley to get the tape and to eliminate Michael Hampton, who had listened to the secrets. So someone would kill Rena, and someone would kill Michael, and the secrets would be safe, and the faceless people who ran the world would say it was worth this many deaths.

All for the sake of friendship with Moscow. Yesterday, Moscow was the enemy. Now it was the comrade in killing. Would Devereaux get the blame? Of course. Things worked that way.

It was a quarter hour later when he reentered the small hotel where Rena had waited for Michael. His coat shimmered with raindrops. He wiped his feet on the rug provided and started toward the elevator.

His way was blocked by the woman who ran the hotel. She looked stern in the way only the Flemish can.

"I don't understand what you intend to do, but I would appreciate it if you and the lady will leave my hotel," the woman said.

"I don't understand," Devereaux said.

"What are you running? I have friends with the police. I don't want to call them, but I have a respectable establishment."

Devereaux stared at her and waited.

"First you bring her here. Then she waits in the window like . . . like a prostitute, showing herself. And a man comes in and embraces her and then runs away. And then, five minutes later, another man comes in and he takes her away. I do not want prostitution here, I will not have it."

"What are you talking about?"

"You know very well."

"Who was this man? The second man?"

"Just another type. He took her away. Does he have to buy her a meal before they go up to the room?"

Devereaux said nothing. He felt damp in his joints, cold in his bones. He had lost Rena to them. They had come to Bruges after all and found her, and now he had lost Michael as well.

The thoughts made him frown, his eyes went cold, and the woman who ran the hotel took a step back because his look was frightening.

He had lost them both, but Rena was more important because she was innocent of this matter. Michael had put her in the way of harm because they were lovers.

He remembered the smell of her and it obliterated any other thought. He felt her breasts against his chest again.

Rena. He had to save Rena, even at the cost of Michael.

Hanley would say, Not at all.

To hell with Hanley, Devereaux thought.

And patiently he began to ask the woman of the hotel all the necessary questions.

TWENTY

Paris

They sat in the brasserie across the wide street from the Gare du Nord. They sat in the window and could see the crowded, littered street.

Marie Dreiser ate with the eternal hunger of the gamine. She ate greedily and without particularly good manners. The waiter seemed amused by her. Michael Hampton did not touch his steak or fries. When she had finished her portion, she started on his.

"You have to eat," she said once, between bites.

Michael stared at her. He had been in this state since Bruges. Since he had stumbled into the tavern off the square where Marie had waited for him. Marie didn't hesitate. She knew what to do. She pulled him out of the tavern. They rented bicycles and pedaled in the rain along one of the canals until they came to a little town called Damme. They abandoned the bicycles when she found a car, an old Renault Five. She amazed him. He did not protest anything, and she drove in the rain back to Brussels, on the wide four-lane highway full of tandem trailer trucks pushing to and from the North Sea ports. The little car was buffeted in the wind, but she drove with her eyes fixed on the road and with a certain manic glee. It was wonderful, everything he told her. She had expected something like this. "Don't worry, lamb," she had said. "I'll take you wherever it is you are going, wherever this sanctuary is."

She was amazing. She picked the pockets of three men in the space of five minutes in central station in Brussels. There was more than enough for the ride to Paris. And just enough for a meal in this brasserie and a cheap room in one of the hotels that clustered in grimy slums around the station. Paris was sad in November because of the chill that made the brasseries pull in their sidewalk tables. Marie had handled everything, as though Michael was a child.

"It's good steak," she said, finishing his portion. "Ahh." Just as though none of this had happened, as though they were on a vacation together.

Michael said, "Are you going to steal some more money?"

"Of course, my lamb. Without money, we can't go on to your mysterious sanctuary."

"Marie . . ." Words failed. It was so hopeless, all of it.

She put her hand over his on the table and leaned forward. Her eyes were large and playful, and she was smiling up at him. "Little lamb," she said.

"Don't say that."

"Then what do you want me to say?"

"Don't say anything."

"All right, Michael, I won't speak. Not ever. When you want me to do something, just order me like a dog, and I'll do it."

Still smiling.

Michael shook his head slowly. "They got Rena."

"That was easy to see, now that you explained it to me. They knew you were lovers."

"She betrayed me."

"Are you in love with her?"

Michael stared at the childlike face. "Maybe she didn't understand. . . . I hit her, I was so angry—"

The face hardened. "Oh, she understood all right." The Berlin accent was tough, the way it can be. "She sold you out, Michael. Maybe it was for money. But you knew it—"

"I thought he was going to shoot. There were too many people in the street. I looked back once. A gray-haired man, he was running flat out after me."

"You make yourself sick thinking about it, Michael," she said. "I helped you, didn't I? I didn't betray you, did I?"

"Marie," he said. It was all true. He softened. What could he say to her?

"Lamb," she said. Softly. "Come on, you need sleep. They won't find us tonight. We use our brains, we use cash. How far is it that we have to go?"

"Far. It depends. The reception . . . I have to call to-morrow morning, I have to get through to my . . . source," he said.

"I don't ask you, Michael, I don't want your secrets, not if they make you that unhappy."

"It's true, Marie, you helped me."

"Come on," she said.

They left francs on the table. The girl zipped her dark jacket. Her soft brown bangs fell across her forehead. She took his arm. They walked along the broad Boulevard de Magenta and then turned into the side street where they had booked a room. They climbed the steep, uncarpeted stairs to the fourth level and went into the room. It was a sad room with faded wallpaper and a single tall mournful window shut against the cold.

The room depressed him, but she smiled and closed the door. It was her palace for the night.

The bag was on the bed.

"Aren't you curious? I am," she said.

"About what?"

"About what's in the bag."

"I don't understand why you had to steal a bag—"

"Hotels want people with bags and passports and all that, don't you know that?"

''We showed our passports on the train. They'll know we're in France.''

''They'll even guess we're in Paris. But not until morning. They can find us, but they need time,'' she said.

She opened the bag. With luck, it might have belonged to a woman who was her size, but the case was pretty.

She opened it and found the things a woman carries in a small, weekend bag. The clothes had been worn; the woman had returned to Paris from a long weekend in Normandy, perhaps with her lover. Perhaps the clothes still smelled of their lovemaking. . . . Marie took a nightgown and held it to her nose and breathed through the satin. Lovers and the odors of love. She closed her eyes to sense the smells better; pretty smells and soft clothing, and there was lovemaking in her mind. She opened her eyes and saw other treasures. There were silks and satins and pretty underwear. She closed her eyes and let her fingers touch the clothing of another woman.

Michael sat down on the bed while she went through the clothes. Then he lay back and stretched, his hands behind his head. Fully clothed, he lay staring at the cracked ceiling.

''Are you going to sleep like that?'' she said. ''At least take your shoes off.''

He did as he was told. The raincoat was on the single chair in the corner of the room. He wore the same shirt he had worn since Saturday.

He thought about it. He decided to take the shirt off.

''Oh, take your trousers off too,'' she said. **She** was still waiting.

''Marie—''

''You think you'd shock me? I've seen enough men in my life, I thought I told you that.''

Michael looked at her. His eyes were dull. He was tired, worn by shock after shock to his system. He had scarcely said a word to her.

''Come here, lamb,'' she said. She had stopped waiting.

He went to her.

She unbuttoned his trousers. They fell to the floor. He

stood in his shorts. She looked at him and then at his face. She caught his eye. Her eyes were soft with desire. She reached up and kissed him, and he kissed her in return. In a moment, they were embraced.

"I am skinny, I really am," she said.

She slipped off her sweatshirt and jeans. She wore no underwear. She *was* skinny and her ribs showed. Her breasts were small. She put her arms around him again, and he surrounded her with his arms. He bent and kissed her neck, and then she pushed him back on the lumpy bed, was on top of him and taking his desire in kisses. She covered his body with kisses and licked his nipples.

He groaned and wrapped his arms around her small body. His hands rested on the curve of her buttocks and she was over him and they were making love. Thoughts of all love-making past flooded him. He closed his eyes and smelled the peculiar smell that was Marie Dreiser and remembered the smell of Rena and the other women. . . .

They made love for a long time. They made love as never before, because every experience of love is different, with its peculiar odors, noises, touches, even in this different place of a shabby hotel room in the middle of Paris. They made love until exhaustion made them lie still on the bed, touching body to body, breathing together, eyes closed, dreaming of lovemaking.

TWENTY-ONE

The Ardennes

R ena Taurus said, "Where is Devereaux?"
    "Looking for Michael, honey," Henry McGee said.
    They sat in a cabin in the deep black woods of the
Ardennes. The rain had changed here to a tentative snow,
falling with majestic silence in the forests around the cabin.
Rena was terribly afraid, had been terrorized since the mo-
ment they shoved her into the car on the street by the canal.
When she had asked a question, they had told her to shut up.

Rena said, "This was a trap after all. A trap for Michael.
I was part of it." Her voice carried the dull tone of confession.

"That's it, honey. Now where did he tell you he's going?"

"He didn't say."

"I see."

Rena sat in a straight chair at a wooden table. No one else
was in the cabin. The other two men had driven away.

Henry McGee said, "I really enjoy certain things—I want
you to understand that, honey. It's nothing personal, but I
like to get information from people who really think I'm not
going to get it. Some people are into torture and all that, but

that doesn't do much for me. I like to be a little rough some-times, but the rest of it doesn't do anything for me."

He talked like this for a while, letting the words make the matter clear to her.

There was still a ringing in her ear from Michael's slap. She had betrayed him.

She shivered at the things this strange man was saying. He was walking back and forth in front of her. She had no restraints, but her hands were rigid on her lap. She was tired and hurt and confused and she felt very alone.

"So that's the commercial, honey, and this is the meat of the program: where was it that Michael said he was going?"

She shook her head.

He hit her more than once. She fought back, and he hit her until she rolled into a fetal ball on the wooden floor to stop the blows. Then he stopped and asked again.

She said, "Rome."

"Where in Rome?"

"He didn't say."

He hit her some more until she passed out. When she woke up, he asked her again. She pleaded with him, she said she was telling the truth. After he hit her some more, he believed she was telling the truth.

"What are you going to do?"

"Do? Nothing," Henry said. He was smiling at her. "You are a pretty thing. Not delicate, but you got a delicate face. And pretty hair, reminds me of Narvak's hair, she was a native girl up in Alaska, just sixteen and could kill a man just like that." He traced her chin with his fingers. She trem-bled. "You ever kill anyone?" He smiled.

"Why don't you let me go?" she said. She strained to keep her voice under control though it was just on the rational side of hysteria. "Let me go."

The fingers paused. She felt the pressure of his fingers against her flesh. He smiled down at her. "All right," he said. His smile was wonderful.

She blinked. She really had heard that.

"You. All of you were in this. Devereaux—"

"Sure, sure. Working for Uncle Samuel, we're all one happy bunch. Devereaux was supposed to get Michael, and we were supposed to back him up—snatch you in case Michael got away. Well, now we know where Michael is going, so it ought to be a bit easier. The next trap. You've done your part for us and we're grateful, and I hope you won't take offense at my beating on you. It wasn't personal."

He said it flat. She didn't know what to say. She was beginning to think he was crazy because his black eyes held the light in a funny way.

She realized he was staring at the wall and she no longer existed in this room. "You start to smell it when someone is setting you up. Ain't Devereaux this time, no sir. Someone is setting up ol' Henry McGee, and it seems a shame because he's just gonna end up hurting himself because he's so damned clever. Devereaux wants you and Michael and the tape. We want the tape, and you and Michael dead. That's the way I figure it."

She said, "You are not on his side, then?"

He blinked; they were back in the present, and she was in the room again.

"I was in prison nearly two years, had to do hard time," he said.

She stared at him.

"Before you go, I'd like to fuck you, if that would be all right."

Rena stared at him.

"Would that be all right by you? I mean, you aren't a virgin or anything, are you?"

She stared at him.

"Just a straightforward fuck," Henry McGee said. "I can like variations, but I appreciate you might not stand for that, and I just figure we should all be friends from this night on. Especially later, when I got to figure out about Devereaux and what he wants. So how about a straight fuck, for all those lonely prison nights when I was keeping myself heterosexually chaste?''

''Then you'll let me go.'' Voice dull, accepting the nightmare, waiting for morning.

''That's the deal,'' he said. Grinning.

''But what if you don't let me go?'' she said.

''Then you will have fucked in vain,'' he said.

''Should I believe you?''

''Honey, I haven't told you a lie yet.''

And she sat in silence a moment and felt his fingertips on her chin. She stared at him and felt loathing and shame. She had no loyalty; none of this should have happened. . . . She saw Michael so clearly, saw the sudden, confused hatred. This is the price for betraying Michael.

''Take your sweater off,'' he said.

She stood and began to undress.

TWENTY-TWO

London

Devereaux sat in the window of the coffee shop and watched the figures in the fog on The Strand. The fog was illuminated by a liverish sun of green and yellow colors. Passersby moved in and out of the swirls of fog like ships entering uncertain harbors.

Devereaux tasted the coffee again. He felt hungry but resisted the urge to order one of the sandwiches already growing stale beneath the cover of a plastic cake box on the counter. The room was damp and shabby. Old men sat at other tables, solitary lumps of clothes, hoarding brown paper packages at their feet.

Hanley came out of the fog, stared at the door of the place for a moment. It was festooned with decals that said it accepted Luncheon Vouchers and was approved by this or that restaurant ratings guide. He opened the door and a bell sounded.

He took his coffee to the table next to Devereaux and sat down facing him. He had no packages with him or old newspapers; otherwise, Hanley might be one of the solitary old men.

"Damned cold. Every damned day it rains." He blew his well-worn red nose and shoved the handkerchief into his pocket. "Morning fog, afternoon rain. I have listened to the weather on the telly. It's always about 'bright' patches, but it just means it rains and rains and rains."

Morning traffic rattled the windows of the shop. Devereaux sipped at his coffee and noticed a thin, crazed crack that ran from the handle up to the lip.

"Why do we meet here? Where's the woman?"

"Rena Taurus. She's gone. She was taken." Slowly, Devereaux gave his oral report on the failure of the mission. He almost told everything, but there is an instinct in the field agent never to give headquarters or control every advantage; it is like the instinct not to be naked. The woman at the hotel in Bruges had a good eye; she had once been an artist. She described the man with black eyes and darkened skin, and Devereaux knew who it had to be. But Hanley did not need to know.

Hanley said nothing. The coffee gave color back to his cheeks.

Devereaux said, "Who authenticated the message that Viktor Rusinov took off the Russian radio operator on the *Leo Tolstoy*?"

Hanley blinked. There was no context to this question. For a moment, he was silent as the juggernauts of memory lurched into reverse. "Is this a trick? You did. You examined Viktor Rusinov."

Devereaux said, "But who authenticated the message? We authenticated the messenger, but who examined the message?"

"Actually, the Puzzle Factory authenticated some things. The paper used, it was standard—"

"Who said the message had been sent at all? I mean, to the ship?"

Fog pressed against the glass. The world was shadows and vague forms, buses and cabs looming along the wide street.

"Why did we have to meet here?" Hanley said. It was an

annoying habit to push aside questions with irrelevant questions, but it aided his memory.

Devereaux did not answer. He'd spent another sleepless night after deciding to get back to London, to Hanley, to see where the real trail lay and not the damned trail that had led to Bruges and to failure. It should not have been so difficult, but Rena had failed to reassure Michael and enlist his cooperation. What could have been on the tape to make him so full of suspicion? To not trust Section? But then, no one trusted Section at the moment, not in Moscow, not in Washington. He had thought of Rena all night, and it kept him awake with the gnawing edge of worry. He saw her sitting in the window of the Hotel Adornes, brushing her hair. She had brushed her hair and her eyes were wide and full of clouds that turned to blue as the sea shifts its colors during a storm. What was Michael and the memory of him that could make her lose herself in thoughts that changed the color of her eyes? He saw her over and over, brushing her hair, staring at the rain on the canal. . . . He could touch her hair in memory; she was that close.

"We presume it was sent to the ship and not fabricated on board. What reason would they have to make a false message?" Hanley asked. "Or perhaps it was prepared to be sent and had not yet been transmitted. That was never determined. There's so damned much radio traffic, you know we can't possibly monitor it all. It could have been sent days ago, weeks ago, months ago. Checking the paper was not exactly a matter of carbon dating. The point was to check out Viktor Rusinov. To make a human judgment. The judgment you made that he was genuine."

"But the message itself . . ." Devereaux let the sentence fragment hang in the air. "Viktor Rusinov and then Rolf Gustafson, and in both cases the messenger becomes the way to guide us to the message."

Hanley put down his cup.

"Why did Rolf Gustafson make a mistake?" Devereaux

asked. "And why was Michael Hampton chosen to receive the mistake?"

"What's important is the tape," Hanley said.

"Who said that?"

"The Russians. I spent an unpleasant hour with a disagreeable man from Langley named Vaughn Reuben. They have put Langley on our case, Devereaux. It is unthinkable, but there it is. He wants to know why you did not off the woman and why you killed two Soviet agents."

"I told you: I don't kill people," Devereaux said.

"The Russians think this is a trick, that we're doing the old cold-war booga-booga."

"It is difficult to have difficult friends."

"Are you telling me all of the truth? Is there trickery involved?" Hanley asked.

"Whose trick?"

"You're asking questions without answers."

"We just don't know the answers yet," Devereaux said. And then he decided to tell Hanley part of it, part of the larger puzzle that had occupied him since his interview with the woman who ran the Hotel Adornes. "Who resembles a slight man with very black, very mean eyes and dark hair and large hands? And a scarred cheek where some shotgun pellets embedded themselves?"

"Henry McGee," Hanley said in the way of a man acknowledging a death.

"They took Rena. Henry is working."

"He had a witness," Hanley said.

"And didn't seem to care. What do you think Henry is in all of this?"

"Henry was one of the names on the message the sailor stole from the *Leo Tolstoy*. Our genuine sailor," Hanley said. "Linked to something called Skarda."

"And he escapes from a federal corrections center," Devereaux said. "And now he's involved in this tape business. We have to find out what was on the tape."

"That's why we're after—"

"No. It has to go back. To Sweden. We have to go back and find out what was on the tape."

"There's no way. Mrs. Neumann is finding out how little clout she has. National intelligence is getting squashed by the secretary of state. He has become bigger than God, and I think the president sleeps with him. They won't tell us what's so damned important about what we're looking for, but they're going to hold us to blame if we don't find it. I want to save Section, Devereaux—that's the only important thing. And if we can get our tit out of this wringer by murder, we will do it."

Devereaux had decided something. He had decided it on the plane from Brussels to Heathrow. He could not explain it to Hanley, because Hanley was at the other end of things and this was something Hanley could not approve. Covert actions in intelligence are done all the time, but there is an understanding in intelligence that they are not spoken of. Covert operations are performed by intelligence agencies because they are the garbage men of government, the ones left to clean up the messes and take the garbage away and bury it.

"I have to do some things," Devereaux explained.

"You have a trail?"

"Two of them," Devereaux said.

"The girl. And Michael Hampton."

Devereaux shook his head. "I don't have a clue on either of them right now."

"Then what's the trail? I have to tell Mrs. Neumann something."

"Tell her to hang on," Devereaux said.

"I can remove you."

"You can do whatever you like," Devereaux said. "The point is, it won't solve your problem."

"We can involve Eurodesk," Hanley said.

"Eurodesk handled security at the Malmö conference. It was so successful."

"Sarcasm," Hanley said.

"I have to go."

"I'm supposed to tell Vaughn Reuben we met and that you told me nothing?"

"We didn't meet," Devereaux said. "Hold him off, tell Mrs. Neumann to hold them off. There were two or three things, things said and things left unsaid. There was carelessness at Malmö."

"What are you going to do?"

"I can't tell you yet. In a little while."

Hanley watched him get up and go to the door. He wanted to say something. He was control, not Devereaux. This was his mission. The day was past when agents . . .

He said nothing.

The door opened and fog swirled in and swallowed the man he had not come to meet and did not see.

TWENTY-THREE

Malmö

The two men were named McCarthy and Weiss. They were both case officers inside Central Intelligence with a combined total of nine years of experience. McCarthy had been recruited into Langley from the campus of Notre Dame, and Weiss had been persuaded to join the service by his political science professor at Georgetown University. They had never worked together.

McCarthy worked days, Weiss worked nights. Watching Rolf Gustafson was not very difficult. They used an apartment window down the block and two floors up. Vaughn Reuben himself had put them on it. Make sure that no one bothers Rolf Gustafson.

Rolf Gustafson had two jobs and did not work very hard at either one. In the first job, he was "equipment manager" at the Malmö city hall. In the second job, he was a procurer.

He had a list of women who were willing to make money on the side. Three were secretaries in the city hall, one lived in Helsingfor and worked in a small grocery, another was happily married to an engineering consultant with a Saab who was always out of town. In his way, Rolf knew everyone in Malmö and a good number of people in Copenhagen. Of course, it was impossible to compete with the organized prostitution rings that inundated the pleasure-loving Danish city across the Kattegat, but Sweden was a different country. It was true that Swedes had an open attitude about casual sex, but there was just enough tourism in Malmö—lazy tourism, as Rolf put it—to arrange contacts between sensible, quite attractive professional women and men who could afford them. The police knew about it, of course, but like police everywhere, they were not interested how Rolf made money as long as he made it quietly.

McCarthy and Weiss were not at all interested in Rolf's role as pimp. They recorded everything and gave it to Vaughn Reuben through an eyes-only courier.

Rolf's rooms above a bicycle shop were also bugged. They had been bugged since the conference. McCarthy and Weiss had a telescopic camera on a tripod as well as continuous reel-to-reel tape.

Each agent was armed with the standard 9mm Beretta. When they relieved each other—the shifts were six hours long—they ate sandwiches, drank beer, and talked about sports.

It began to snow lightly on the fifth morning of their watch, when they saw the man in the street outside Rolf's apartment. The apartment entrance was to the right of the bicycle shop. It was just after dawn, and Weiss had come into the room with coffee and sandwiches.

"Is that him?"

Weiss clicked off three shots with the telescopic camera while McCarthy stared down at the man through Bushnell binoculars. Their room was dark, and they were certain they could not be seen at the window.

Weiss looked through the lense of his camera and said, "Yeah. That's the asshole." He looked at the sheet of photographs in front of him.

"You call," McCarthy said.

Weiss picked up the telephone. He gave a number to the operator. He waited a long time and hummed to himself while he waited.

"This is Bluebird. Our party arrived at 0809 hours outside the Resident's apartment. It's Designated Hitter. Yeah. We're sure it's him. We're watching. He's not gone up. Yes. Yes. OK."

He replaced the receiver.

"What did Uncle Vaughn say?"

Weiss's eyes glittered. He couldn't help it. It was the moment you knew could come if you were willing to take the chance. When they went into counterintelligence, they knew there would be black jobs like this, and it was the same feeling you got being a paratrooper or a marine hitting the beach. He removed his weapon and clicked the safety. "If he makes contact, we make our determination," Weiss said. "Designated Hitter is going to have friends he didn't know he had."

The man in the street called Designated Hitter on the photo proof sheet had disappeared.

The snow was leaving little traces on the sidewalks. Gray reluctantly moved into black shadows. Malmö was frozen and still.

"You think we're gonna need that?" McCarthy asked. There was the same glitter in his eyes and it showed in his voice. He looked at Weiss's Beretta.

"What do you think this is about? A fucking traitor. A guy with a piece, a hitter . . ." Weiss never swore.

"Yeah."

"He's killed. He took out one of ours ten years ago in London, but he had the clout, he could wipe it out. That's the way it works."

"Fucking dirty son of a bitch," McCarthy said to make himself feel better, to get pumped for the game.

The tapes started up at the sound. A door was opened. Rolf said something they couldn't make out.

"I want to talk to you about the tape," said the other voice.

"That's it," Weiss said.

"That's it," McCarthy said. They looked at each other. They almost quivered with the force of the adrenaline surging in them.

"They knew this was gonna go down."

"This is going down now."

"This is going down," Weiss repeated. They were very excited. Weiss popped up and put the gun in his harness. McCarthy buttoned his coat over his own piece. It was going down now. They were eyeing each other, making sure they measured up, making sure that no fear was showing.

Down the stairs and across the street. Weiss slipped on the snowy street and caught himself.

A car turned into the street, went to the corner, disappeared. The bicycle shop was closed.

Inside the door, they were very quiet. Up the stairs carefully. The walls were painted brown.

They had guns drawn. They stood on each side of the door.

McCarthy kicked it in, gun covering the room, down on one knee, Weiss standing right behind him.

Devereaux turned.

He saw the guns and the faces of young men. He stood very still, his arms apart from his body.

Rolf was white.

"You're under arrest," McCarthy said.

Devereaux stared at him. His face showed curiosity.

After a moment: "Who are you?"

"You know who we are," Weiss said. "Hit the floor, do the spread."

Devereaux knelt on the floor and then spread out his hands. He was very calm and slow in all his moves.

He felt the first cuff and then the second. They removed his piece from the belt holster. Also the knife he always carried in his right pocket.

McCarthy pulled him up by the right shoulder. McCarthy was big, almost linebacker size, though he had never played in college.

"You're coming with us," he said.

"Do I get to call my lawyer?"

For a moment, McCarthy stared. Then he let the dead thing overcome the glitter in his eyes. Devereaux saw the change.

"You think this is funny."

"My identification. You can get it, left-hand pocket. Where's yours? Or doesn't Langley trust you to carry cards yet?"

McCarthy hit him, and it staggered Devereaux. Rolf stood in his undershirt and shorts in the middle of the first of three rooms and didn't say a word.

"Fucking smart guy. You wasted one of ours."

Devereaux said nothing.

"London. Ten years ago."

"So you're Langley."

"So you're shit out of luck," McCarthy said.

"Let me give you a number in London," Devereaux said in the same flat voice.

McCarthy said, "Come on, asshole."

Rolf said, "What is this about?"

"Come on, asshole," Weiss said.

They went down the stairs with Weiss in front and McCarthy in back. McCarthy slapped Devereaux on the head, just because he was so pumped up and he had to make contact and hurt someone.

"Kidnapping is against the law in Sweden," Devereaux said. "You've heard of the law, even at Langley."

"You're a riot, a regular fucking riot," McCarthy said. The vulgarisms were coming on fast now.

"I don't get to call my lawyer?"

McCarthy wanted to hit him, just to shut him up, but they were on the street now. They started toward the corner. They had the rental Saab at the corner, and he would go into the trunk and be taken out to the airport, where he would be turned over to the others. They both guessed he would be shipped back to Washington by extraordinary means. They didn't know about that part of it, but they wouldn't have cared if they did.

"You get in the trunk."

Devereaux decided. "No."

McCarthy took a step, but he didn't have the gun in hand. Devereaux's hands were cuffed behind his back. Devereaux kicked McCarthy in the lower belly. The tip of his shoe caught the soft flesh between the navel and the scrotum. The pain was profound. McCarthy retched onto his black shoes.

Weiss, who was thinner and smaller, moved to one side and grabbed Devereaux's right arm. He was very strong and pulled at Devereaux to knock him off his feet.

To his surprise, Devereaux willingly left his feet. The weight of his body crashed against Weiss, and Weiss was partially impaled on a protruding fin from an ancient Peugeot. The chrome went one inch into the flesh of his lower left back. He cried out. Devereaux fell against him again and shoved his knee into Weiss's groin, compacting his testicles against the fender of the same Peugeot. Weiss felt white pain for about two seconds.

McCarthy staggered into Devereaux, and Devereaux kicked him in the belly again with the toe of his right shoe.

The little spectacle was over in twenty seconds. Weiss was crumpled on the walk, clutching his back and balls, groaning. McCarthy was on his feet now, deathly white, his Beretta held shakily in hand.

That is when they heard applause above the silence of the snow.

One man stood across the street, slapping his palms together. Grinning.

Devereaux stared at him.

But there was no mistaking him.

McCarthy turned the muzzle on the audience of one,

and the applause died until it ended with a final, funereal clap.

"Get in the fucking trunk," McCarthy said to Devereaux. The tough tone wasn't there to carry the words.

"Jesus Christ, son, don't you see he doesn't want to go?" said the man across the street.

McCarthy, frightened and sick, stared at Weiss on the ground and at the witness. Don't worry about witnesses, Uncle Vaughn had said.

"Get out of here," McCarthy said.

"I know guys like him," the witness said. "You just can't convince them all the time to do what they're told. Stubborn streak, son, you gotta back off from it."

This was absurd.

McCarthy grabbed Devereaux's arm and spun him around and slammed him against the car. McCarthy opened the trunk.

The witness crossed the street.

"You back off," McCarthy hissed. He had practiced that for years. He had learned the technique of coldness in Langley, and the cop's technique of showing absolute violent hatred to get all but the craziest or bravest out of the way.

And he saw the eyes of the witness.

Mean little eyes even if the face was smiling.

"Get outta here," McCarthy said. Weiss groaned.

He kept coming.

"You want trouble?"

Henry McGee hit him. McCarthy had a pistol in his hand, but Henry busted him in the mouth and broke four teeth. McCarthy knew he did not have the pistol anymore and was on the sidewalk and the back of his head hurt worse than the front. Jesus, it hurt all over.

And then he was up in the air and down, crashing into the trunk, blood on his nose.

And just as suddenly Weiss was dumped on top of him.

The trunk lid closed with a click, and they were in cold, frightening darkness, tangled with legs and arms and the stench of vomit. A minute before it had been all adrenaline and toughness, and now it was fear in the dark, groaning bodies on top of each other. McCarthy squinted with shame. Locked in his own fucking trunk!

Henry stared at Devereaux.

Devereaux waited. His hands were still cuffed behind his back.

"I got here just in time."

"The Lone Ranger."

"You surprised?"

"No," Devereaux said. "Not from the moment you kidnapped Rena Taurus."

Henry smiled. It was a good smile that made women like him at first. Only later did women understand the irony behind the smile.

"Good witness back in Bruges, huh? The woman at the hotel. Well, I was hoping she'd remember me, but I wasn't gonna count on it. Got your girl friend. You got taste, I can see that. Fine piece of ass, if you ask me."

"She's not involved."

"Bullshit, Devereaux. I'm an old bullshitter and I know it when I step in it. So. We reached the same conclusion, you and me."

"What conclusion is that?"

"Shit," Henry said again, shaking his head. "I guess these keys in the trunk lock . . . yeah, this here looks like the key." He unlocked the cuffs.

Devereaux did not make a move. The snow was harder now. They heard noises from the trunk. Henry smiled at Devereaux and pitched the keys across the street. He banged the palm of his hand on the lid of the trunk, and the noises stopped for a moment.

"CIA? Puppies. Watching Rolf, huh? Whatta you think this is about, then, Devereaux?"

"I don't know."

"I don't know, either. I thought I knew but I don't know. That's the truth for a change. I was going home to Mother Russia, and then I got my chain jerked a couple of times, and now I get deeper into something I don't quite understand. I think I'm getting set up to take a fall, and I'm just not comfortable with that. Then I thought about you in that room in Chicago, asking me about Skarda. Now, what the fuck would you know about something like that, that wasn't even operational? Then I thought, Why the fuck am I Mr. Guy-in-the-Middle?"

Devereaux waited. Henry lied. Henry told the stories that kept changing, and Devereaux never believed a word he said. But what if he wasn't lying now?

"I don't like to be the hare at the dog track, even if it's for the noble causes of revolution and *perestroika*. I been just trying to get a handle on this thing myself. You aced those two assholes in Brussels, and now I returned you the favor with these Langley puppies in the car trunk. Hell, I'll kill them for you if you want to make it really even steven. That was careless of you, letting them get the drop on you. You must be getting old."

"Why was Langley watching Rolf?"

Henry McGee's eyes glittered with a storyteller's enthusiasm. "Yeah, now you're starting to ask the questions in the right way. What were these puppies supposed to do?"

But they both thought they knew the answer to that.

Devereaux said, "Where is Rena Taurus?"

"Bless you, she's safe enough. That girl is really pretty, you know that. Got those big eyes can look so lost and scared my heart just goes out to her. She looked scared at me, and it was a turn on, I can tell you. Like to think of them as the frail sex, you know."

"You're a little sick, Henry," Devereaux said.

"Goddamn. I know that, openly admit it. But that isn't what we're talking about. Not right now. Right now we're talking about you and me and maybe Rena and certainly ol' Rolf Gustafson up the street a ways.''

"What are we talking about exactly?''

And Henry's voice was flat, without corners for a moment. The tone surprised both men.

"About a deal, Devereaux.''

TWENTY-FOUR

Rome

"E minence?"

Softly, with deference.

The voice cut through the dusk of sleep.

The old man opened his eyes in bed and stared at the dark as though he did not comprehend it. He blinked as he sat up.

The young priest, dressed in black cassock, bowed to the prelate and carried the telephone receiver to the plug on the ocher wall.

The cardinal sat in shadows. The red drapes were closed but a slit of light peeked through between them.

"Who is it, Antonio?"

"Signor Michael Hampton," the young priest said.

Alberto Cardinal Ludovico reached for the receiver. The young priest held the rest of the phone as if it represented a chalice.

"Hello?"

"Thank God," said the voice at the other end of the line.

The cardinal glanced at the young priest and made a motion for him to put the telephone on the coverlet. Antonio bowed again and withdrew from the large, dark bedroom.

The cardinal wore an old-fashioned nightshirt with a faintly ruffled collar. He rested a bony hand on the rich fabric of the coverlet and waited.

"I am at Milano, at the train station," Michael Hampton said. "It was the express for Rome. From Paris. But when we got through the mountains, the engine broke down, just my damned luck. . . . I have to get to you."

Cardinal Ludovico closed his eyes to better see the young American translator. So the English journalist had been right in all his parts—Michael was in trouble, and there was the matter of the tape recording. Above all, the matter of the tape recording.

"Michael," Cardinal Ludovico said. "How may I help you in your trouble?"

"At the conference in Malmö . . . I was given a secret tape recording, something they didn't want to let out. I can explain it later, it's so bizarre. . . . Men in Berlin tried to kill me. And running day and night—"

"Michael, Michael." Gently. "When can you be at Rome? Take an airplane."

"No. It's safer. Cheaper, actually, we're running on cash because they've been following me through my credit card —"

"Michael, is there someone with you?"

Pause. The voice was clouded with sudden suspicion. "Why? Why do you think someone is with me?"

"You said 'we.' I thought someone might be with you."

Another pause. He heard the background noise of the train terminus in Milano. Most of the trains that linked the rest of Italy and Yugoslavia and Greece with the countries of northern Europe found their way through Milano, and the terminal never slept.

"A girl with me. She helped me."

"Miss Taurus," the cardinal said.

Another pause, this time lasting more than a few seconds.

"Michael? Are you there?"

"Cardinal?"

"Michael . . ."

"Why did you say that name? You said that name."

Cardinal Ludovico felt the chill of morning in his old bones. He'd been too eager and made a simple mistake, and Michael had caught it. There was no lie at hand to cover it. "Please, Michael, come to Roma and talk to me."

But he heard Michael talk to someone. The background muffled his voice, and then he heard Michael speaking German.

Then he heard another very specific sound. A German voice that was harsh and sudden. He did not speak German well and he could not understand.

"She says I shouldn't trust you."

"Who? Who are you speaking of, Michael? How can I help you if you don't trust me?"

"I'll have to think about it," Michael said. The voice was tinny now. "Maybe there is no sanctuary."

"What have I done to make you mistrust me?" The cardinal gripped the ornate ivory-colored receiver very tightly. "My son, our dealings have always been honest."

Michael said, "You knew I was in trouble. And you mentioned Rena. Rena betrayed me, and for all I know, they've got to you."

"You must trust me, Michael, because I have never lied to you," Cardinal Ludovico said. He waited.

Again, the harsh young German voice could be heard, and then Michael turned to the phone again. "I have to think, Cardinal."

"All right." Gently.

Cardinal Ludovico purged the anxiety from his voice and tried another approach. "As you wish, Michael. I have no intention of ever forcing you. I mention Miss Taurus to you because I know of her. Of your . . . interest in her. I have not been the secretary of our congregation for these years without being careful."

The soft words were like a sponge dropped into the sea. Each sponge soaked a little of the sea and became like it. "I must trust you as you must trust me, but since you are the giver of information, I must know your friends. Miss Taurus is your friend and she is a translator at the European Commission in Brussels. I had to be careful when I . . . hired you, Michael. Miss Taurus interested me to that extent. Only that extent.''

Cardinal Ludovico lied with all the sincerity he mustered when telling the truth.

"Miss Taurus, Michael, is from Lithuanian parents, and the church is concerned by everything that goes on in that most Catholic country. We had to be careful."

"I see," Michael said.

Silence on the line.

"Michael," Cardinal Ludovico began and paused. Michael had been picked precisely because the Central Intelligence Agency had made a liaison with the congregation and because the CIA said he would be a useful "watcher" for the congregation. And ultimately for the CIA, though Michael would never know that. Cardinal Ludovico had long before abandoned candor and truth in the pursuit of what was best for the church on earth.

"Michael, do you suspect me of anything?"

Another silence lay between them.

"I have to go now, Eminence," Michael said in a dull, distracted voice. "I have to think."

"Let me assure you, Michael—"

The connection was broken. For a moment, the Cardinal held the receiver and then pressed the buttons on the old-fashioned cradle.

"Tomaso? I must speak to our agent in Milano. . . . Yes. Quickly, Tomaso."

He put down the receiver and waited. Darkness filled the room with velvet shadows. He felt hunger and thirst but did not stir. It was stupid to have mentioned Rena's name, he thought. If Michael does not trust, then the matter is lost. And his life is lost in the bargain. He grieved at both losses but did not make a sound.

The telephone rang once. He picked up the receiver and heard the sleepy voice of the agent in Milano. He made his instructions simply and then hung up.

There was no misunderstanding the instructions. They were brutally clear.

TWENTY-FIVE

Malmö

Rolf Gustafson sat in his underwear in the middle of the room. His chair was made of unpainted pine. The electrical cord torn from his favorite lamp was wrapped around both wrists and the back of the chair. The man across from him was staring into his eyes without any sense of curiosity. This was a matter of instilling fear. Devereaux did it in a lazy, natural way. He provoked fear by not seeing the object before him but by staring through the object to a point some distance behind, as though already foreseeing the future of the object. His eyes were bleak, as though the thought of Rolf's future made them bleak.

There was no one else in the apartment. Henry McGee was gone. To prove his need to make a deal, McGee had agreed to Devereaux's terms. He was waiting for Devereaux to finish here, and then he would have an errand to run. It was an important errand, and they had both understood it.

The car containing the two CIA agents was still parked on the snowy street. If they figured how to get out of the trunk before they froze to death, they would only be embarrassed.

Devereaux had not spoken to Rolf until he had found the bug and dropped it in a pot of water on the stove. He had torn the cord from the lamp and tied Rolf without a word, though Rolf protested. The cord cut into Rolf's wrists.

Devereaux went through the rooms while Rolf waited. He found the address books and the photographs of his stable of prostitutes. He put these on a table opposite Rolf. He also found the cash sitting in a plastic bag in the back of the refrigerator, behind the milk and cheese.

The snow was very heavy and wet flakes clung to the warmth of the windows until they melted.

"Tell me what you want." Rolf said it over and over. He also said his hands were growing numb because of the binding.

"Listen to me. Tell me what you want. You can't treat me this way."

Devereaux said, "Who are these women?"

"Friends."

"Are they whores?"

"They are respected women."

"This one? In the teddy and garter belt? Is that her wedding picture? Is this her working outfit?"

"Look. It's a sideline with me. The police know about it."

Devereaux stared at Rolf for a long time again. Then he put the photographs back on the table.

"Tell me about the tape," Devereaux said. He was very cold, without hope in his voice.

Rolf had understood from the first moment.

"I made a mistake."

Devereaux said nothing.

Minutes passed. The snow fell. Silence filled the rooms until it was suffocating.

"Tell me about the tape."

"I made a mistake."

Devereaux let it go. He stared out the window and said, "Tell me about Michael Hampton."

"I know nothing. He's a translator . . . an interpreter as well. He lives in Stockholm." The denial was too abrupt, too total. Even Rolf saw that as soon as he said it.

Devereaux said, "Rolf. There are two possibilities. The first is that you will tell me everything and then I'll decide about you. The second is that you will tell me everything, but the decision about you will have been made along the way."

"I don't understand."

"Tell me about the tape."

Rolf started to say he knew nothing. Devereaux grabbed his nose and twisted it until it broke.

Blood streamed down his nostrils and filled his mouth. Rolf screamed and tried to rise, but he was tied to the chair. He kept screaming.

Devereaux said, "No one will hear you. The bicycle shop is closed."

"Blood," he said in a sobbing voice. "My God, you broke my nose."

Devereaux sat still and let the man taste his own blood.

Rolf said, "I was given the tape to give to Michael."

Devereaux got up and went to the kitchen and found a cotton towel. He soaked it with cold water, wrung it, and brought it into the other room. He pressed the towel against Rolf's nose and freed his left hand. Rolf held the towel, still sobbing, his thin shoulders shaking.

Devereaux sat down again and waited.

The tears ebbed at last, and Rolf looked at Devereaux while holding the bloody towel.

"For five hundred kronor. I am to give this tape to Michael, to pack it in his bags."

"What man gave you the tape?"

"I really can't say, sir."

Without a word, Devereaux took Rolf's left hand in his own. He broke the little finger.

Rolf stared at his hand, felt the throb of pain from his finger through his arm to his brain, linked to his broken nose. He thought to scream but only managed a strangled sob.

"You are a madman. They'll kill me or worse."

"No, Rolf. I'm the worse, not them. I'm here and that is real pain, isn't it, Rolf?"

"My God."

"Not God or them is in this room, only me."

"My God."

Devereaux waited. Tears filled Rolf's eyes again. He tried to wrap the wet bloody towel around his hand and hold it to his nose.

"A man I do not know. A man came to me, and I thought he was Russian. Certainly not an American man. Although I cannot be sure of this. A thin man with a limp. An older man, very distinguished, dressed very well. He gave me the tape. It was unusual, but I have done unusual things. It's not easy to make a living in a place like Sweden. They take all your money away. I have to do things to make a living."

"Did you listen to the tape?"

"No, sir."

Devereaux considered this.

"Five hundred kronor is not worth that much curiosity?"

"No, sir. It was done quickly on the last morning of the conference, and I had to pack the bags. I took the tape right away with his bag to the hotel. The Savoy. To her room. The man said he would be there. He was getting it off with her, very pretty woman, I can tell you. They were in bed, I think, when I arrived. I tried to see her." His voice changed. "She was naked, I think."

"That's not important. Why were you supposed to bring the tape to Michael Hampton?"

"I don't know, sir."

"Is that true?"

Silence.

"Don't hurt me, sir."

"I don't want to. But you compel me."

"Please. If I can understand what you want."

"I want everything, Rolf. Didn't I make that clear when I broke your nose and your finger?"

"But how will you know when I have told you everything?"

"Trust me, Rolf."

"Sir, I don't want any more pain, sir."

"I know, Rolf. No one wants pain."

"If I had known, I would not have involved myself. Not for the money."

"No. I'm sure you wouldn't, Rolf. But you are involved now, and that's the problem."

Rolf thought about it while the gray-eyed man watched him. "I will tell you everything. The same man said to me to go to Evelyn Jaynes so that he would go after Mr. Hampton. I didn't understand any of this. The man gave me a thousand kronor this time, and this Evelyn Jaynes was a British journalist."

"What did you tell Evelyn Jaynes?"

"I told him about the telephone record. The record of calls by the journalists. The record of calls by Michael Hampton."

Rolf paused, daubed his nose with the bloody towel. There were tears in his eyes. "Sir. I told him that Michael Hampton was employed at the conference by an agency in Rome. This is the Congregation for the Protection of the Faith. I suppose this is a Catholic group of some sort, but I don't know. He called the number in Rome seven times during the conference. I told Mr. Jaynes this."

"Why?"

"Because I was told to tell Mr. Jaynes that Mr. Hampton had taken this tape recording that everyone attached importance to."

Devereaux stared at him until Rolf dropped his eyes. His undershirt was bloodstained. "I am telling you the truth, all of it, but how will you know when I have told you all I know?"

"Is this all the truth?"

"Yes, sir."

"Who does Mr. Jaynes work for?"

"Several newspapers in Great Britain. I can get their names. He is . . . what do you call it?"

"Free-lance."

"Yes. Free-lance."

"What do you think is the reason they wanted this journalist to go after Mr. Hampton?"

"I have no idea, sir."

Devereaux used the silences to stare out the window at the snow. He might have been passing time. The silences worked on Rolf Gustafson.

"Sir, I am telling you the truth, and I wish I never had seen that damned tape recording."

"What do you think was on the tape?"

"I don't know, sir."

"I believe you, Rolf. What do you think was on the tape?"

"I think it was a secret, sir."

Devereaux stared through him until Gustafson felt shards of ice pierce his heart.

"Please, sir."

"Tell me about the man who gave you the tape."

Rolf tried to describe him. Gently, Devereaux led him back over the ground of his description. He tried to see the eyes, the shape of the face, the color of the hair. But Rolf was a poor witness. He only remembered the limp. The man had limped.

"And no one at the conference seemed to know him."

"No, sir. He contacted me one night in my bar. I was drinking beer, and I was . . . making an arrangement with a visiting German."

"You were pimping."

Rolf stared at the floor.

"He contacted me," Rolf said.

"Rolf. What do you think was on the tape?"

"A secret, sir."

"A secret for whom?"

"I don't know."

Devereaux watched the snow on the rooflines across the street with the same detached, peaceful feeling he had once had as a boy watching the snow cover Chicago and make the city full of magic. The thought of snow comforted him.

"Rolf. You'll have to leave for a little while."

"Leave, sir?"

"You have a passport."

"Of course, sir."

"I think you should catch the next plane to London. Someone will meet you at the airport. Do you think you can do this?"

"But I have work, sir, at the city hall—"

"Make some excuse. You might suggest you had an accident and fell and hurt your hand and face."

"Why must I go, sir?"

"Because I say it. You understand, Rolf? If you go, you'll be met by a man in London, and it'll be all right for you. If you disobey me, then your life is ended."

So flat, so soft, so overwhelming.

Rolf closed his eyes.

Snow covered the city, covered the old Peugeot parked downstairs. The bicycle shop was closed because there were no customers for bicycles on a snowy morning in Malmö.

"I have no money—"

Devereaux opened his wallet. He put the krona notes on the table. "Take the rest from the bank where you keep your legal money. Or from the illegal money you keep in the refrigerator. People always keep their illegal money in the refrigerator. It's a strange thing. Maybe a refrigerator is like a safe in the mind's eye."

Devereaux untied him and stared at him. Rolf looked miserable and battered. His nose and finger were swelling.

"You didn't have to break my nose," Rolf said.

"Yes, I did," Devereaux said.

TWENTY-SIX

Washington, D.C.

Twenty-one hours later, they sat on a bench in Lafayette Park across from the White House. The park also was occupied by two men who said they were homeless and wished to protest their homelessness. They had constructed a crude shelter for themselves using three wire shopping carts stolen from supermarkets and some sheets of plywood. The two men were very drunk on vodka.

The men on the bench stared at the homeless men. They were not interested in the homeless; it was just a place to rest the eyes.

"The next liberal platform will be the right of every person to have his or her own shopping cart," said Vaughn Reuben, who still resembled a professor at an eastern college but whose voice was now full of a deep, utterly black contempt. "Then, for the handicapped homeless, we'll have motor-driven shopping carts."

"You have a lot of sympathy," Douglas Court said. He held up the hickory cane and sighted down its length as though it might be a rifle. The tip of the cane was pointed at the larger of the two homeless men. Douglas Court was assistant secretary of state for intelligence liaison. That title, typical of the overstated titles rife throughout the bureaucracy, was the reason for his curious friendship with Vaughn Reuben.

Vaughn Reuben lightly rubbed his plumpish belly and fiddled with his bow tie. Both gestures, mightily affected, were his ways of dealing with tension, along with sucking at the dry stem of his pipe. He was very nervous and very tired. He wasn't even supposed to be back in Washington, but in London, "riding Hanley's ass," as the National Security director had put it.

The other man was older, more patrician in appearance. Having shot the two homeless men with his cane, he now put it point-down on the sidewalk and leaned on it with the weary security of the longtime lame. He needed his old cane, and it showed in the familiarity of his gesture. As always, the federal city surged with life and Pennsylvania Avenue crawled with traffic. There had been too much traffic for at least thirty years. Across the street from the park, the broad lawns led to the White House. Antiterrorism concrete barricades surrounded the lawns, as well as an elegant black fence, but it was the absurdity of the wide lawns holding back the shabby density of the rest of Washington that made it seem the White House was as isolated as a farmhouse suddenly surrounded by an interstate cloverleaf.

"What's gone wrong now?" Douglas Court said.

"Two case officers in Malmö. They were watchers on our Swedish friend, and they nearly got iced. Rather, they caught pneumonia. Seven hours locked in the trunk of their own car. It was the man from R Section and a passerby, which doesn't make sense at all. He is a murderous son of a bitch. He killed two men in Brussels. They deny it, of course. But the Soviets know. They know it was him. I saw to that."

"That's terrible, Vaughn, simply unacceptable."

"It gets more unacceptable. Rolf has disappeared. The

bug was drowned in his apartment and there was blood, and our two watchers think the man from R Section did that too."

"Brilliant," said Douglas Court. "I must say you've handled this brilliantly so far." His lame leg ached.

The two homeless men sat under the plywood boards and stared at the two officials in long, dark wool coats. The day was washed out like an Impressionist painting done in thin watercolors.

"You spare a dollar for some coffee?" It was the second homeless man, the bigger one, and he was standing about ten feet from Vaughn Reuben. Vaughn stared at him. The homeless man shrugged and turned back to his shelter. A bumper sticker that urged a vote for the last liberal candidate for president was stuck to one of the shopping carts.

"We'll assume that our friend talked to the man from Section. So we'll assume we have to go at this from another end. The point is to get that tape usefulized." The final, bureaucratic word lay between them.

"The secretary doesn't want a fuckup," Douglas Court said.

"The secretary is ready to shove the Firm down the toilet. I give a fuck about the fucking secretary," Vaughn Reuben said. He used the obscenities with elegance, as though reciting a bawdy but ennobling sonnet. "The fucking secretary called this on by himself. The point is to get the fucking secretary to find the right villain when the shit hits the fan. The fucking secretary is supposed to be looking at Section, not across the river at Langley. The fucking secretary is supposed to think this is all an R Section fuckup from beginning to end, but Section sends this son of a bitch in and he's fucking us up."

"You said 'fucking' about sixty times."

"I am so pissed off with that whiny rat Hanley. And that goddamn Devereaux."

"Is that his name? What kind of a name is that?"

"What do you mean what kind of a name is that? How do

I know? I just know that name. That son of a bitch was fucking around back in Viet Nam days when he was there. That son of a bitch is smart, I give him that, and he's tough enough—but he's only one son of a bitch. I got a whole agency, and what do I get out of it? I get two assholes locked asshole to asshole in a trunk in a car in fucking Sweden who got to go on sick leave and maybe even disability because they caught pneumonia.''

"You got problems, Vaughn. I helped you in Malmö and I'm trying to help you now, but you're making your own problems.''

"I know, Doug. I appreciate it. I really do.''

They were silent a moment and became enveloped in the noise of the city. Douglas cleared his throat. "Is Michael Hampton . . . is he going to get to his goal?''

"There's every likelihood. In fact, now that Devereaux has decided to backtrack his trail, he's out of the picture on the Continent. All Hampton has to do is to pull his head out of his ass and fly home.''

"What happened in Berlin?''

"KGB. They almost got him. That was too bad. KGB thinks they're supposed to zap him. On the other hand, why zigzag when it's what? two hours by air to Rome?''

"I don't know. I suppose he's afraid. I suppose he has a right to be afraid. Poor fellow.''

"Yes. Poor fellow. But when he makes it, he'll do all right for himself. And we've got the backup insurance in that drunken sot, Evelyn Jaynes.''

"The inevitable journalist,'' Douglas Court agreed. "That was a good touch.''

"Yes. They're all good touches. Except that Hanley is dragging both feet, and Devereaux is his old murderous self.''

"You've thought of most things, Vaughn. I can't believe you haven't thought of this.''

"I won't let the Soviets shove the Skarda computer system down the Firm's throat,'' Vaughn Reuben said in the quietest of voices. "And if we have to take it, I'm going to have a patsy at least set up. R Section. If Devereaux kills Hampton and recovers the tape, we leak it. If Devereaux kills Hampton and doesn't recover the tape, the KGB and the secretary of state blame R Section. I don't honestly see how we can lose on this."

"Better get back to the Big Fellow." This is what Douglas Court called the secretary of state. He was the assistant-in-charge to the secretary, and he knew and appreciated the position of the secretary and the position of the Central Intelligence Agency. Douglas Court was an old schemer in Washington, and he thought no death could be sweeter than the way old John Mitchell died, just dropped dead on the sidewalk one day doing the things he liked to do. Or even Adlai Stevenson, just dropped over dead in the prime of political life, not that he ever gave a damn for Adlai Stevenson. Douglas Court intended to go the same way.

"He's still putting the heat on Section to get back the tape?" Vaughn said.

"Yes, he is. He's got Mrs. Neumann set up for a nervous breakdown."

"It couldn't happen to a nicer old bitch."

"You know so many sweet words, Vaughn."

"Only one of them matters for now."

"What's that?"

"Devereaux."

The two men got up from the bench and started away from each other, each back to his chauffeured car, each back to the endless traffic that was snarled around the White House grounds.

The two homeless men watched the two government men part.

"Motherfuckers," said one of the homeless men to the other.

"Check the one dude, could hit a dude like that."

"The dude what's limping? I thought about that," said the

first homeless man. ''Got himself a real limp. I'm surprised someone don't knock him up side his head and take off. Just knock the dude down.''

''Yeah,'' said the second homeless man, thinking about it, thinking about the limping man.

TWENTY-SEVEN

Milan

Rain drummed against the roof of the great galleria. They sat at a table and drank cappuccino and watched the gloom and rain rub against the roof and the entrances of the old building. The galleria was a tall, nineteenth-century building lined with shops at two levels. On the ground floor, two broad pedestrian malls intersected at the café where Michael Hampton and Marie Dreiser waited.

They had been lovers in Paris for a night.

Michael felt guilt, of course. He had betrayed Rena with this strange, savage woman. Yet, what he felt had changed him. Rena in lovemaking seemed cool and remote; he could feel it even when he did not look at her, even when he smothered his face into her breasts to inhale the scents of her body. Rena was always a little apart from him. Not this girl. She clung to him, forced him deeper into her, urged him with a savagery that thrilled him.

She had bitten him in lovemaking. When she came, she had cried out. Her cry had been half shout, half sob. The cry was so intense—it radiated from her belly through her lips —that it might have frightened Michael if he was not clinging to her at the moment, if he had not caused this cry of joy and pain.

"This is some sanctuary," Marie said suddenly. She shivered in the cold damp that blew through the galleria from the open ends. "Why would this priest help us? For what's on the tape? I had hopes for you, lamb."

But she really wasn't as angry as her words. She sat across from him, wide-eyed but lacking in innocence from the day she was born. She wanted to provoke him to defense because she still wanted sanctuary. She thought of his arms on her and shivered at the thought, as though no man had ever made her cry like that.

"I—I was confused because he knew about Rena. It's logical. He could have known about her. I could have mentioned her, he would have known. . . . But I was suspicious."

"And Rena betrayed you."

"She was . . . she thought she was doing the best thing. She couldn't understand the importance of what was on the tape."

"Michael, I begin to wonder if you're just crazy or what. Except I know those two men were after you in Berlin and that they shot at you. I know that, lamb, so I know whatever you heard was too much to hear."

He was struck by the words. He looked at her, and she took his hand, like a child who clings to an adult. Except who was the adult? He felt reassured by her touch.

"The train for Rome leaves in thirty minutes. I have to take the chance. The cardinal . . . well, I've worked for him in the past—"

"And what does this cardinal do that has to do with what you heard on this precious tape?"

"The congregation . . . you might say it's the intelligence apparatus of the Vatican, of the Holy See."

She gave a short, Berliner laugh.

He smiled at her.

"I'm sorry, lamb. The thought of religion having any intelligence struck me. So they are spies in cassocks? Cassock and dagger?'' She made the last joke in English, and he smiled again. There was a comforting quality to Marie that was larger than her tawny eyes, larger than her slight frame. Was she the real sanctuary that he had never found?

Suddenly, there were two of them, burly and swarthy, wearing long dark overcoats that glistened with raindrops. They wore black hats and they sat down at the table.

"You weren't at the train station," the first one said to Michael. The second one kept his eyes on the girl.

Michael started and then seemed to slump.

"It's over," he said.

"Yes," said the first one in accented English. He looked at his companion, and they seemed to nod to each other.

The table must have weighed eighty pounds. It was made of iron and had a small amount of marble at the base. They never took the tables inside at night, only threaded a chain and padlock through the legs. It was impossible to believe this thin, little girl with the orphan's face and those large, appealing eyes and those dainty little hands—

The table overturned against the two in overcoats, and she was up, kicking the second one square in the face. There was the sound of teeth cracking. She reached out and grabbed Michael's hand, and they were running away, down the marble corridor of the galleria through the side entrance that led to the square in front of the Duomo cathedral. There were steps behind them, but they didn't look back.

The rain swept the square.

"Do you know where you're going?" Michael shouted above the rain.

"I don't know a damned thing!" she replied, her voice raised in triumph.

Michael saw her face and she was smiling. She was happy to be running in a strange city, running in the rain across an unknown square, chased by unknown men who meant them harm. My God, she was happy!

They rounded a corner and saw a carful of police.

Marie slowed to a walk and entwined her arm in Michael's.

"Lovers in the rain," he said. His heart was in his mouth.

"Of course. That's what we are in fact."

Michael looked behind him but did not see the men. "Maybe I'm getting better at running," he said.

She stopped in a doorway and drew him in. She kissed him. Her lips were wet and hungry.

He kissed her and held her frail form against him.

"You are getting better, Michael," she said. "If we have to run and run and keep running, then we can do it."

"Cardinal Ludovico," he said.

"Why don't you think the priest sent those men—"

"That's absurd. He couldn't have."

"Everything is possible. The priests always say that. Maybe it turns out it's true."

She was grinning again in the darkness of the doorway.

"I have to get to Rome, Marie. But maybe it's better if you waited. You could get a room here—"

Her grip was suddenly fierce. Her face was close. "No. I won't let you go, not for a moment, not to go across the street. You are my lamb, my life. I won't let you be harmed."

He looked at her. There was such passion that he felt melted by her. He kissed her again.

"We will go to Rome," she said. "Together. Now."

"But how? They're at the train station—"

"Michael. How would they know you were at the train station?"

It occurred to him right away. His face twisted. "Damn. Damn him."

"Did you tell the priest?"

"Yes."

"That was foolish."

"Damn him. I trusted him."

He saw the light dying in her eyes at that moment. She was self-sufficient, but she had yearned so for what he promised to give her. To be safe and not to be running. A moment before, he had seen her joy of combat running across the unknown square; now he saw this childlike disappointment.

"So now we just keep running," she said. She clung to him but without passion. In the darkened doorway, they were lovers who had stepped out of the warm Italian rain to kiss and taste the raindrops on each other's flesh.

"No," he said.

She looked up at him.

"The cardinal will hear my confession," Michael said. "Let him bear the same burden if that's what he wants. But he has to do it with me there. I'm going to give him the tape whether or not he wants it. Let them go after the cardinal and the church, not me."

Again, the tight grip against him, her body pressed to him.

"We go," she said. "I know a way. . . ."

TWENTY-EIGHT

London

The first call came at 0713 hours, which meant it was 0113 hours in Washington.

Mrs. Neumann's voice was raspy.

Hanley pressed the receiver tight to his ear. London was still dark beyond his window. The predawn stillness added to his sense of being utterly alone in a hostile world that would eventually find him and kill him. This was absurd, of course. No one would kill him. He was the control, the man who placed pins on the flat map of the world. He was co-cooned behind paper and jargon. But where was he now? He wondered if there was a pin of him on some map in Washington: this is Hanley; this is control; this is the paper shuffler become agent in the field.

"The National Security Council has decided to pull us off the chase," she began.

"I don't believe it."

"The secretary of state convinced the president that Section is purposely botching the case. He thinks we botched security from the beginning of the Malmö conference. They're talking about sabotage and they want an investigation. They . . . say

. . . we haven't cooperated with our Russian friends in hunting Michael Hampton.''

Hanley closed his eyes.

"He wants his own people to go after this Michael Hampton person," Mrs. Neumann added.

"State?"

"Yes."

The silence ran across the ether, touched the satellite, fell back to earth, waited on its human masters.

State. The Department of State had its own intelligence apparatus, of course. There were so many intelligence agencies operating in the country that it was sometimes difficult to remember all their nomenclatures. But State did not have operations as far as anyone knew. State was not prepared to take part in aggressive pursuits. As far as anyone knew. It was much more logical, if R Section were to be replaced at this late date, to put the Central Intelligence Agency on the matter.

Hanley knew all this, and so did the head of R Section, Mrs. Lydia Neumann.

They were silent because it seemed so incredible.

"This smells," Hanley said.

"A week-old fish," she agreed.

"This makes everything look so much different," Hanley said.

"The other oddity is Langley," Mrs. Neumann said. "They threw in their cards early. They don't want to protest this. This whole thing is absurd—and from Langley's point of view, as much an insult to them as it is to us."

"And they didn't protest."

"Vaughn Reuben. Your good friend."

"My good friend," Hanley said.

"He sat there with that little hateful look on his face. He just sat there, and when the secretary was done, he didn't say a word."

"So Langley is silent. This gets more curious."

"Langley has been very active the last few days in putting

the bad-mouth on us," Mrs. Neumann rasped. "Why suddenly give up when the secretary decides on an asinine course like putting State Department intelligence on the trail of Michael Hampton?"

Hanley had been thinking about it. "Because they know State will fail."

Mrs. Neumann did not speak.

"They know State will fail to retrieve the tape. That Michael Hampton is not running aimlessly but has a specific goal and it is not the Soviet Union. He knows where he wants to go. Langley—they know too much, don't they, Mrs. Neumann?"

But she said nothing.

The second call came at 1112 hours London time. The phone rang a long time in the shabby, nearly empty rooms that comprised the "safe house" for R Section on Fleet Street.

Hanley stepped from the bathroom, zipping his trousers on the way. "Yes."

Devereaux began a fill. The fill started from the moment of Rolf's confession. He said that Rolf was on his way to the safe rooms on Fleet Street and that he would probably need some medical attention. He then spoke of Michael Hampton's principal employer at the conference in Malmö.

Hanley repeated the name: "Alberto Cardinal Ludovico. That old schemer. What on earth is the connection with the Malmö conference on naval shipping?"

"There was a secret agenda," Devereaux said. "And it must be recorded on that tape. That's why the Soviets want it back and why the secretary of state wants it back. *Glasnost* has finally happened, and everyone is working on the same side."

"Sarcasm," Hanley said.

Silence. Hanley blew his nose, crumpled the tissue, and threw it into a basket full of dozens of crumpled tissues.

"Who is the limping man? The man who gave Rolf the money to pack the tape into Michael Hampton's luggage?"

"Who indeed?" Devereaux said.

"We'll run it through the 201 computer, but there are probably dozens of limping men on file."

"Probably. Try to narrow it down to someone who might have been in Sweden last week."

"American or Soviet?"

"Or Armenian for all I care. But the logic says he has to be an American."

And then Hanley told him about the telephone call from Mrs. Neumann. He did not have Devereaux's memory for exact things. He did not have the precise words, but he knew the order of thought. He conveyed this and waited.

Devereaux was silent for so long that Hanley thought the connection had been broken.

"I think I begin to understand," Devereaux said.

"Enlighten me," Hanley said.

"You don't want to know. In fact, we've never spoken."

"You have to check in sometime—"

"And sometimes I'm too busy—"

"Don't cross any trails with Langley. Or, now, with State. We don't want to make waves, just uphold the Section."

"Sometimes you can't do both."

Hanley suddenly wondered what the weather was. It was a concrete question in mind, not ephemeral like this conversation with Devereaux. His nose was red; the food was atrocious, even to someone whose lunchtime habit had always been a cheeseburger with raw onion, and a single martini, straight up. He wondered what the weather was and then thought of Devereaux's remark: "Sometimes you can't do both."

Hanley spoke: "What are you going to do?"

"Go to Rome, obviously. Cardinal Ludovico, however crazy it sounds, has to be in this thing. Or Michael Hampton is trying to put him in this thing. The congregation must have financed Michael's trip to Malmö. Or Michael learned something of great interest to the congregation. Ships in the Baltic? Who is the stationmaster in Rome?"

"Mr. Dobetti," Hanley said in clearspeak, not using the code name of the Italian agent. "Number 7, Via Icilio on the Monte Aventino."

"Alert him."

"All right. What do I tell him?"

"Why would the Vatican be interested in a naval conference on security in the Baltic?"

"Because there was something else on the agenda," Hanley said.

"That seems perfectly clear. But what involves the Vatican? Or is a connection to the Vatican?"

Hanley waited.

Devereaux said: "I spoke to Henry McGee. In Malmö. This morning."

Hanley felt curious. "You did?"

"Henry wants to make a deal."

"A deal? A deal? Are you sure you're all right? What does Henry have to do with this?"

"Yes. I'm curious about that too. We're working out an arrangement. It doesn't involve you, Hanley, it doesn't involve Section."

"Stop it. Stop it now. If you were close enough to talk to him, you were close enough to sanction him. Or do you have scruples about that as well?" His voice was rising.

"No scruples. Curiosity. I want to see where he's going to run to next."

"You can't compromise Section—"

"I have to go now. I'm in an airport."

He heard the announcements as background noise to the conversation.

Hanley held his forehead. "Devereaux. You must not compromise Section."

There was silence.

Hanley closed his eyes to hear better. But there were no more sounds.

TWENTY-NINE

Copenhagen

Number 9, Krystal Gade, was near the university. It was a typical Copenhagen apartment building, with a wedding cake facade above the roofline and tall, narrow windows.

Devereaux entered from the rear because he was expected at the front.

The apartment was in darkness, and the man sat at the kitchen table with his back to the back door.

He put the muzzle of the pistol in Henry McGee's right ear. Henry did not even flinch. "I figured you to come in the back. Contrariest man I ever met. Won't believe a thing till he's taken it apart three or four times."

"Where is she?"

"Rena, honey, come here."

Rena Taurus entered the kitchen. She was dressed as she had been in Bruges. Her eyes looked tired.

She stood at the door and stared at them. She saw the gun in Devereaux's hand and Henry McGee's leering grin.

"He said you worked together."

"That's right. That's what I told her, Devereaux. Just being proleptic, I guess. I told you you could trust me."

Devereaux unsnapped the safety on the automatic. He stared at the dead eyes of the girl. He had so long controlled himself that he was always surprised when this gut feeling began to overcome him. He had lived with disappointment and defeat all his life, but they could not suppress him; once he had been in love, and that had nearly destroyed him. What was this other stranger rising in him? It was the uncontrolled emotion of the street kid he had long suppressed. He was angry.

Henry felt it. Felt the cold muzzle of the pistol press his ear, press to enter, press to block out any sound or sensation but the thought of death.

Devereaux stared at Rena as though he wanted her to say it. To say, "Kill him," and it would be done. But she did not speak or move. All his senses bristled to pick up a signal from her. A word, a gesture, the way her eyes would signal him by their mere color. But there was nothing. Nothing at all.

"Rena is all right. I didn't hurt her."

She stared at Henry because the grin was fading.

"She's all right. Tell him, honey."

"Tell him what?" The dead voice almost did it.

"I'll kill you," Devereaux said. What did it matter if he killed Henry McGee? McGee was an escaped prisoner, a former spy against his native country. He had no scruples; he had assured Hanley of that.

And he thought of the two CIA agents in the trunk of the snow-covered Saab on the street in Malmö.

Rena stared. "I told him about you, Devereaux. I told him about Michael. I told him everything I knew. He didn't hurt me very much. I thought it was bad at the time, but he scared me. That's what he did, he scared me. I'm not a child. I don't want to be afraid. I'm not afraid of things, you know." She said this in a monotone.

"Rena, sit down."

She sat at the table. Devereaux still stood with the pistol muzzle in Henry's ear.

She stared right through Henry McGee. The eyes seemed so wet that there would never be fire in them again.

Devereaux said, "How did he hurt you?"

"Why? So you can do the same thing?"

"How did he hurt you?" He had to push the anger down or he was going to blow out Henry's brains. He had to talk to her. Words would numb anger.

"It doesn't matter."

"Tell me."

"He slapped me. He slapped me in the face. He did it until I was crying, and he kept doing it very slow until my head was ringing and my face was hot, and it hurt so much and he kept doing it."

And she started crying, and Devereaux saw the fire burn again in her eyes, saw they were not dead pools. She was alive and there was anger and there would be all other things again.

Eased the trigger.

Pulled the muzzle from Henry's ear.

Henry felt tension drain from his shoulders. He sighed and turned to Devereaux.

"It wasn't that much," he said.

Devereaux brought the pistol muzzle across Henry's face once and then twice and then again. The muzzle made marks, and they all heard a tooth crack and they all saw the blood from Henry's nose.

Henry wiped at his nose but did not speak for a moment.

"Well, I had to take my chance on you," Henry said. He said it wetly through the blood on his lips. He smiled at Devereaux. He had all the balls in the world.

"Just knew you had to go sweet on a sweet girl like Rena, so I had to take my chance that you'd kill me when you heard I beat on her. But that was just professional, Devereaux, same as you'd do. Just beat on people till they tell you what you want to know. It ain't the approved way of interrogation—and God knows the United States of Lovely Fucking America would never sanction such a thing—but it is the most efficient way of finding out what you want to find out, ain't it? You beat on me, Devereaux, that time. You beat on your share of people. What makes it so different if I do it?''

"Because you're on the wrong side." There. The anger was back in its cage, back down in his belly where it belonged and where it could do no harm. If her eyes had stayed dead he would have killed Henry.

"Only side I ever been on is Henry McGee's side," Henry said. He was still bleeding, but it was as though nothing had happened. Rena stared at his face with fascinated horror.

"So what do we do, partner?"

Rena looked at Devereaux. "Is this true? Are you partners after Michael? You let him take me and rape me—''

Devereaux went very cold. Even Henry became still.

"You weren't supposed to tell him that, Rena, honey. It wasn't exactly rape, Rena, honey. I asked you for a straight-forward fuck and you agreed. A bargain, Rena, wasn't it?"

Rena saw it in the gray eyes of the tall, gray man. This time it was not anger. It was as though Devereaux had decided something, and Henry McGee saw it too.

"Who are you men?" she said. She looked at McGee, at Devereaux, angry and confused. "Why must you hurt Michael? Hurt me?"

"Michael was attacked in Berlin," Devereaux said. "That's Soviet. He knows about it. He's a Soviet agent."

Henry smiled. "That's right, Rena. Soviet agents wanted to waste your boy friend. Except I'm in the process of changing sides again because there's more involved here than your toy-boy."

Again Devereaux pressed the muzzle against Henry's right ear. Henry stopped talking and waited.

"You have to have proof, Henry, you know that. No stories this time. Proofs, bona fides.''

"Like that message the sailor on the *Leo Tolstoy* brought?"

"Like that."

"But it could be just a plant, just like that was."

"That's your version of history, Henry."

They spoke as though Rena was not in the room. "I guess I cried wolf once too often," Henry said.

"I guess so. It has to be very good, whatever you bring out. Then we'll talk."

"I told you Rena was safe. I did my bargain. What does it take?"

"Effort," Devereaux said. "You have to keep trying."

Henry said nothing for a moment. He stared at Rena. Then he started to grin again, and she looked away.

"I get up now?"

Devereaux pulled the pistol back.

"Where and when?" Henry asked. "I don't have much time."

"No. You don't. The changing of the guard at Buckingham Palace. Forty-eight hours."

"Damn. That cuts it close," Henry said.

"I don't really give a fuck," Devereaux said.

Henry considered that and decided it was the best he could do. He buttoned his seaman's jacket and smiled again at Rena. "I enjoyed it, I surely did," he said.

"You are a monster."

"That too, honey," he said and threw the grin at Devereaux. "I reckon I can make some money out of this."

Devereaux said nothing.

"Everything has a price."

"Including your life," Devereaux said.

Henry stared at the man and the pistol for a moment and then shrugged. What the hell, it was worth a try. He closed the door and went down the steps. It wasn't much time, but Devereaux had known that, didn't want him to get the time he needed.

Upstairs, Rena stood at the window. The streets were wet. It had rained, it would rain again.

"What are you going to do?" she asked.

"Make you safe. This apartment isn't safe. Their watchers are out looking for you if Henry double-crossed me."

"Why do you trust him?"

"I don't."

"Why do I trust you? Tell me one reason."

Devereaux touched her shoulder. She turned to him. She had never seen his eyes so cold, distant, almost like the eyes of another form of life.

"Tell me one reason," she said again.

He looked at her for a long moment and then turned. "Come on. We'll have to find a safe place for you."

"Tell me one reason to trust you."

He smiled then, but there was no pity in it. And no answer to her question.

THIRTY

Washington, D.C.

The secretary of state was a lean, dark man with a soft Southern accent and the reputation of a man of confidence. He and the president sat in the Oval Office because the president liked to work there and not just use the office for ceremonial occasions. It was turning to dusk, and the sky was brilliant with orange city lights reflected on low clouds.

The president sipped tea laced with honey because he had a bad throat.

"We've notified the Israelis. They aren't that crazy about that many people, but they'll have to go along with it. We'll take our share as well," the secretary said.

"But it will mean something. Getting out that many Jews from Russia. My God, this is something to pull off," the president said. "Every time we meet with Moscow, we get a new surprise."

"See it from their point of view. They get a chance to be the good guys, letting all those Jews out of the country, and they strike a blow against Star Wars at the same time."

"Do we really want this Skarda thing, this security computer thing?"

"We've known about it for two years. We want it, believe me. National Security Agency can't wait to examine it."

"How can Moscow be technologically ahead of us? Especially in computers?"

"Thanks to our Japanese friends, who sold them computers they weren't supposed to have," the secretary said. "And that spy ring in Silicon Valley that sold out. What they never had before was a certified genius to put the things together, make the software work. That's what Skarda is. A program and a man behind the program. Emil Skarda. Born in Prague. A fucking genius. We give up information on Star Wars, they give up information on Skarda, and we program it through the computers to see if it's bona fide."

The president sipped his tea and frowned. "The one thing that bothers me is about this aid thing."

The secretary waited. The president was always talking about "things," and he had to know which thing the president meant now.

"We cut off our funding into Lithuania, what happens?"

"Nothing is forever, but Moscow has a point. Lithuania, Latvia, Estonia—the Baltic states—are never going to leave the Soviet Union, no matter what. Like the vice premier said, 'You wouldn't let your Southern states secede, we will not let our Baltic states secede.' So instead of letting CIA throw money down an aid rathole, we agree to something we might have decided on just for budget reasons. We can't get enough aid to Nicaragua, where we have real interests. What's our aid reason to channel money into the Lithuanian dissidents' movement?"

"It must bother Moscow, though. Throwing that in at the last minute."

The secretary smiled. Sometimes the president didn't understand those people. "Soviets. It's the Soviet mentality, Mr. President. They bargain like Persian rug merchants—

you forgive the slur. They do tit for tat, and just when you figure you got a deal, they throw in one little thing to show that they're really getting the best of you. It's the Russian psyche, it can't be helped. How much aid does CIA channel into Lithuania? Two hundred mil a year. So CIA has its nose out of joint, so who gives a shit? They've got a few measly networks in Lithuania and a couple of smallish independence movements. I mean, if they told us to cut off our channels to Poland, that's a different kettle of fish. But Lithuania?''

''That's what Moscow keeps saying, no matter what they say in Lithuania,'' the president said. The tea felt good, and he wondered if he should ring the kitchen for another cup. ''Well, two hundred million is not that much, I suppose.''

''A drop in the bucket,'' said the secretary of state.

Douglas Court and Vaughn Reuben sat together in the backseat of the limousine in the driveway of the big house in Chevy Chase. The limousines of powerful and rich people lined the curb. The driveway curved across the expansive lawn to the columns of the portico, where the party was in full motion. The *Washington Post* reporter had just arrived in her satin gown. The social season was at its most intense now, and there were parties like this every night.

Douglas Court and Vaughn Reuben wore black tie, though Reuben's tie was a bit careless, rather in the way a professor might wear it. The purposefully rumpled look was a prop too important to Vaughn Reuben not to carry it over into formal settings.

There was no one else in the car. The drivers were all gathered at a side entrance, smoking cigarettes and commenting on their masters.

''State will fumble this, I got a feeling. Our little courier is about to deliver his message,'' Vaughn Reuben said. ''I was amazed that blowhard you work for decided he would finally take over the chase of Michael Hampton.''

Douglas Court smiled in the darkness. He had traded his hickory stick for a more formal cane of polished black wood with a silver-inlaid handle. "I suggested it to the Big Fellow," he said.

"It was smart, very smart."

"Thank you."

"Two days and this thing is a done deal. The tape gets in the right hands and then to the world. The secret agenda is quashed. We save our Lithuania network and keep out that horde of refugees. Christ, can you imagine the security problem in checking through ninety thousand people, looking for a few spies."

"Of course, we don't get Skarda."

"That's all right. I'm not as convinced as everyone else that Skarda is such a neat computer program. Our people are working on it. We'll have our own version of Skarda before long."

"In a way, I feel we've betrayed something," Douglas Court said. "But then I think of the alternatives. We can't have the secretary chop into CIA operations in Eastern Europe. We can't let this *glasnost* wool be pulled over the eyes of the president."

"No, we can't. Someone has to stand at the bridge and deliver for him."

"And get no credit for it."

"None at all," Vaughn Reuben agreed. He felt ennobled to be so anonymous in such an important matter. Perhaps in a few years, the truth would come out. Perhaps he would be honored then.

He felt very warm and very pleased with himself in that moment.

THIRTY-ONE

Rome

Michael and Marie abandoned the stolen Fiat after dusk across the street from the Spanish Steps. There was a McDonald's open, and they grinned at the familiar grease smell. They went inside and ordered a Big Mac, fries, and a shake. Berlin had McDonald's.

The gamine was smiling at him. In the intimacy of the last two days, they had understood each other in ways that years of words could not improve upon.

"Is your name really Marie?"

"Do you like it? Does it matter?"

"No."

"You like it?"

"I like you. I kept thinking of the look on their faces in the galleria—"

They laughed like old lovers whose laughter is triggered by a single word, a glance, a remembrance of shared intimacy. "They never would expect we would make it to Rome. Now what do we do?" Marie said.

"We go to see Cardinal Ludovico, just like before. You

have to trust. There's a bond between us. He's a churchman, for God's sake," Michael said.

"Hopefully 'for God's sake,' " she said.

"You don't trust him."

"I trust no one, lamb. That's why I have survived."

"You trust me."

"I could not help myself. You are too honest not to trust. We reach Rome, and you buy me an American hamburger."

"Not like the ones we had in Wyoming." But he blushed anyway. A babble of Italian surged around him and even the clerks could not control their expansive gestures.

"What is Wyoming?"

"Where I came from. Originally. A state. Cowboys. State symbol is a cowboy on a bronc."

"What is that?"

"A horse. A wild horse."

"A cowboy on a wild horse." She stared at him, saw the gentle eyes and gentle face. Gentleness was not weakness, not at all. It was the edge of civilization. Marie saw this in his eyes, saw the kindness that did not seek any reward at all or any advantage. She had seen it before, in the coal cellar, in the light of a flickering candle. Held the knife to his cheek and saw the eyes. There wasn't fear in them— though he was afraid—but a curiosity that bordered on gentleness. He had made love to her in a shabby room in Paris. He was strong, stronger than he knew, and he gave her his body as a gift. She was a young girl in a pretty dress, sitting in the parlor. He was the young man in bow tie, on one knee, offering her flowers. Offering love. Offering a ring and marriage. Offering faithfulness and a house with pretty wallpaper.

As she thought these things, her eyes glistened.

"I will go with you," she said.

He took her hand. "No. I don't want you in trouble, Marie. I know how to get there, just over the bridge at the Castel Sant'Angelo. . . . There's a code I can use. I make a telephone call, he'll know where to meet me."

"And if he meets you as he tried to do in Milan, what will you do then?"

"I think that was a mistake."

"You trust too much."

"I trust you," he said.

"I trust you," she said. They were exchanging vows. They might have been in church, and there might have been religious music and not the mindless din directed now over the speakers. They sat at a plastic table altar.

"So I give you the tape," he said. And handed it across the table to her.

She took the tape in her small hands and turned it over. It was like a gift, a keepsake, a gift from love. Was she imagining all this? But he had his own woman, didn't he? Didn't he mention her name? But she had betrayed him in Bruges, and where had he to turn? It didn't matter if he had belonged to some other woman. It was good enough that he trusted his girl, his little rat girl found in a cellar in Berlin, his little thin girl with a plain face and plain brown hair. It was good enough if he trusted her.

"Why are you crying?"

"I don't know, Michael. I never cry. I thought I never knew how to cry."

"I trust you," he said again, ritually repeating the vows.

"I will keep it, and I will come when you call me. I will do anything you want me to do."

"We should find a room first. Then I'll call. Then I'll meet with him. I'll make sure he understands about the tape. That I don't have it with me."

"All right, Michael. You must be careful—"

He kissed her. That was so unexpected. She blushed, sitting at the plastic table in the plastic restaurant full of light and smells of grease. It might as well have been a church.

They made love again. The bed creaked beneath their bodies. She was so skilled, he thought. She was satin and silk. She rubbed against him. Her body formed against his body.

He felt her buttocks, her stomach, touched her in the place between her legs. He kissed her there. And there and there.

Sleep.

Darkness.

Thunder rolled across the ancient city. Lightning crazed the sky and the ghosts of the Forum were illuminated among the ruins. The Colosseum was filled again with Romans, and the gladiators fought in the pits. Death and the roar of blood. After two thousand years, the blood remained buried in the pit of the stadium, buried in the Forum, stained on the soul of the city.

Thunder awoke them, and they huddled in the warmth of the bed, beneath covers, naked bodies holding each other.

Lightning made her face soft and small. So young. So without fear. So gentle beneath his own gentleness.

He telephoned from the phone at the side of the bed.

Antonio answered and said the cardinal slept.

Michael waited. She lay in bed and watched his naked body. She traced it with her finger, traced his backbone and the gentle curve of his buttocks.

"Michael." The old voice fighting sleep.

"You sent the men in Milano."

"Only to talk to you. You attacked them."

"Yes."

"Where are you?"

"Do you know the place where you can talk to me?"

"Yes."

"In one hour."

"It is raining, Michael. I can hear the thunder. Come here to the congregation. Come to Santo Spirito."

"Let us say I trust you, Eminence. I always have. I had no reason not to trust you. Then, why would you not trust me? I heard a tape recording, Eminence, and I must tell you. But I won't have the tape with me. Not the first time."

Silence.

Thunder. The sound of thunder is much taller in Rome, much more from God than in any other place in the world.

The thunder is God's voice, and lightning is His fire. It illuminates the past. The light crazed above the sluggish Tiber, and across the river was the Castel Sant'Angelo with its brooding bulwarks and immense indifference to the city it faces. On the parapet of the castle is the great figure of St. Michael the Archangel, his sword raised over the city on the seven hills. St. Michael was seen on this parapet by a pope in the Middle Ages during a devastating plague in the city. When the pope beheld the archangel, the plague came to an end, because God had sent the archangel as a sign that he heard the city's prayers.

Michael had left his lover.

Michael remembered the warmth of her body as he hurried through the rain.

Down the slick streets to the river that flowed like a sewer beneath the great, ornate bridges. Lightning, and he saw St. Michael above him, the patron saint of all named Michael. Would his father or mother have understood this when he was named at birth, would they have thought that on this night would come his salvation as he crossed beneath the statue?

Rain and thunder so that the ruins of antiquity shivered beneath the sternness of God. Pagans in their graves were bones, and so were Christians stacked in catacombs along the Via Appia.

He thought all these things, one thought after another, jumbled like a dream, thought connected to thought by flashes of remembrance.

Remembered the thighs of Rena Taurus that morning in the Savoy Hotel in Malmö. Remembered the child-woman groaning beneath him in Paris. Love and love, smells and smells, each different. . . . Women were all smells and tastes, the touch of silk or satin or skin the same.

He paused at the Ponte Sant'Angelo and then ran across.

St. Michael, pray for us.

A black Fiat on the Lungo Vaticano turned at the gate of

Hadrian's great castle and started across the bridge for the city.

Michael thought of Cardinal Ludovico waiting for him beneath the colonnades of the square of St. Peter's. The cardinal preferred to speak of intimate things in the fresh air, away from rooms that listened. They would stroll the square together, the priest and the translator, the priest with his hands locked behind his back, his eyes seeing the vision of his words and instructions and not the man strolling next to him.

Lightning froze the action of the world for a moment.

Michael saw the car and three men inside.

Two pistols.

Windows.

Shots.

Automatic fire.

He was in Viet Nam.

He thought of Will being hit by a truck in Bangkok.

THIRTY-TWO

Brussels

Rena slept a long time, through the night of rain and lightning.

Devereaux sat with her.

She slept in a room at the Amigo Hotel behind the city hall. The lightning illuminated the beautiful Grand Place in front of the hall and all the spires of the medieval buildings around it.

Devereaux waited. He waited for her to awake and for a telephone call. There was nothing to do. Rome was completely socked in and so was Milan.

A night of stupid waiting. He wouldn't let Rena go home, because it wasn't safe. He asked her again and again to see if she could remember a limping man hanging around the conference in Malmö.

The call came in a buzzing ring.

He listened for a long time as the international operator chatted to Rome, and then he heard Mr. Gobetti.

"Mr. Devereaux. It is quite sunny in Rome."

"But there's rain predicted, Mr. Gobetti."

"I'll return in a moment."

The Rome stationmaster broke the connection. The greeting and response were satisfactory. He wanted to make no mistake, because he had never met Devereaux.

In fact, it was still raining very hard in Rome and in Brussels and across the face of Europe. The Rhine was surging along its banks, and Cologne was facing the threat of flood. The Seine was also surging, and there was talk about the worst autumn rainstorms in Europe in fifty years.

The telephone rang again. This time, Devereaux had pressed a key on the phone and attached a small electronic device that cost $3.59 to manufacture and which was purchased in wholesale lots by agencies of the United States government for $690 each. The scrambler beeped once to show it was activated.

"Mr. Devereaux."

"Mr. Gobetti."

"There is terrible news. This Michael Hampton is dead. He was shot to death about midnight on the Ponte Sant'Angelo. He was going to the west side, presumably to the Vatican."

Devereaux let the words sink in him.

"The tape."

"There was nothing on the body. Cardinal Ludovico was awaiting Michael Hampton in the Piazza Santo Pietro."

"Are you certain?"

Gobetti snorted. "How long have you been in this business, *signor*? I am as eternal as Roma."

"So they have the tape—"

"No, I do not think so, *signor*. There was a woman with this man. We're quite certain of that. There was a tap placed of course on the house on Borgo Santo Spirito."

"A woman? Are you certain?"

He saw Rena stir in the bed. She wore a satin gown she had purchased in Copenhagen while they waited at Kastrup for a flight out. Everything was late. Planes were forbidden to take off and to land. The world was reduced in the storm to crawling on its stomach across the earth.

"Nothing is certain, but this was surely a woman with him. There is an ambiguity to the last conversation Michael Hampton had with His Holy Eminence, the great spy." Gobetti stopped to let his prejudices air. "Michael indicates the tape but indicates he will not have it at the meeting. So there is a possibility he entrusted the tape to his confederate."

"Are you sure there was a woman?"

"Unmistakably. I had three dozen men waiting for him. Naturally, I put such a man in the one place where most Americans go when they first come to Rome. To see the Spanish Steps and look at the bad paintings of the bad artists. We have, if you can imagine this sacrilege, a McDonald's across from the Spanish Steps. The great gift of American culture."

Devereaux waited out the irrelevant indignation.

"Nevertheless, my agent saw the couple. He even took their photograph. And there was something exchanged, but it is not clear from the photograph. It could be a tape recording. It is difficult at the moment to do a proper examination of the photograph, if you understand me."

"You did fine," Devereaux said. He had no time for praise, for himself or others, but he sensed that this was a good thing to say to Signor Gobetti.

"Unfortunately he lost them, and we presume they went to a hotel. There are so many hotels, but we are going through them, one by one, with patience. If she stays in the rooms until dawn, it will be all right."

"Is there a way to run down their passports and get identification?"

"Of course." Gobetti sounded insulted. "We have her name, which may or may not be true. Marie Dreiser of Berlin."

He was coming from Berlin. He was coming to Bruges to see Rena. He was coming for help.

Lightning.

Rena stirred again, rose to a sitting position. Her skin was ivory in the lightning bursts against the window. She seemed serene, aware. She looked at him with those eyes.

"I remember the limping man," she said in English. "It was in my dream."

Devereaux stared at her and listened to Gobetti. The scrambler made his voice very thin, very high.

"They entered on the Rome Express at the Swiss-Italian border at six-thirty in the morning. The train, unfortunately, suffered a breakdown in Milano. They apparently made a contact to Cardinal Ludovico's residence from Milano. That is when he mentioned the girl, on the telephone, but it was not this name but another, Rena Taurus."

Michael was dead.

"When will you be in Roma?"

"I don't know. I have calls in to the airport. Both airports."

"The weather will break here in the morning."

"Then in the morning."

"Do you need directions?"

"No. I'll trust the cabdriver."

"Tell them on the Monte Aventino. The idiots can at least find mountains. Then ask at the local trattoria for Via Icilio. Don't think they're cheating you. There's too many streets in Rome, and most of these people are illiterate."

Devereaux saw her get up from the bed. He could see her and then be unable to remember the curves of her body except as smells and remembered touches.

"I'll be there. If you can, get the girl."

"By any means?"

"In any way."

"And the tape."

"Of course. Keep the watch on the prelate."

They broke the connection. Devereaux removed the scrambler and put it in his pocket.

He stared at her for a moment. She didn't speak at all, but she sensed the thing he had to tell her. He stood up, and she ran to him and held him and began to cry.

"Michael," she said. "Michael."

"He was killed. I was too late. If it hadn't been for the storm . . ."

He felt her sobs.

When she was finished with tears, he led her to the chair at the window. She sat down and stared up at him with her extraordinary eyes. They were shining in the lightning, wet and sad.

"You know the limping man now. You know what he looks like," he said.

She shook her head. "What does it matter? Michael is dead. It doesn't matter now—they have the tape."

He stared at her.

They have the tape.

He stared at her for a long time.

"Why did you do it, Rena?"

She trembled.

She did not speak.

"You set him up. You could have stopped this. Even in Bruges. You wanted him to run."

"No, I never wanted him to die. I never wished him harm. They said there would be no danger at all."

"Who told you? The limping man?"

"I didn't tell you. Yes. He is an American, but it wasn't him. He was part of it. Two weeks ago in Brussels. . . . Michael is dead, and I killed him."

"You were one of them who killed him," Devereaux said.

"Don't you have pity for me?"

"No. Not now."

Thunder clapped and lightning danced. The city was under siege.

"The damned rain. You would have stopped him. But the tape . . ."

"What was on the tape?"

"I don't know."

He slapped her as hard as Michael had slapped her that

afternoon in the lobby of the hotel in Bruges. She felt the sting of it for lingering seconds, and there were tears again in her eyes.

"Go ahead and hit me again," she said.

"What was on the tape?"

"I don't know. They said there would be an agreement in Malmö, that my Michael was there at the behest of a secret society. They said it was very important that Michael carry the true agreement to that secret society. They told me this."

"Who told you?"

"I won't betray them."

He saw her eyes in the light of the sky. "You killed him, you know."

"You want to hurt me. I know I killed him. And the tape . . . I hurt them as well."

"Who?"

"It doesn't matter to you. You're an American. You love Moscow now, it is the fashion. Americans are so fickle. They forget Estonia and Latvia. They forget Lithuania. I am Lithuanian, not Russian. I am Catholic, not like the Russians. I am not a barbarian like the Cossacks. You let them take my country and then you turn the other cheek when Moscow demands that you sell us out. Do you know how many lives are at risk in Vilnius alone? Do you know how people live while they work for our freedom?"

"Are you a patriot, then?"

She let the question answer itself.

"Was it worth Michael?"

"You think nothing is worth a life?"

"You betrayed your lover."

"I betrayed him the moment you put your arms around me. Yes. I betrayed him to carry the message, but I didn't want him in danger, I did not want him to die. I'll punish myself for his death all my life. But I betrayed Michael, not in Malmö but here in Brussels when you put your arms around me and held me and I could feel your body and I wanted you. I wanted you to hold me and make love to me. I betrayed him then and kept on betraying him. We all betray each other, isn't that true?''

Yes. It was true. It was perfectly true.

She touched him and clung to him.

It was perfectly true. She had smiled in pleasure in the window of the Hotel Adornes that day, and it was not Michael that gave her pleasure in that moment but the thought of Devereaux. He could feel her desire rise just as she could feel his. God stopped the world with rain and storms, and a boy died in Rome who was completely innocent, the only innocent in the world. Innocence had to be punished in some way, and it was carried out on a night of storms.

He looked at Rena. There was no innocence at all. He was too late, and she had delayed him for the sake of some cause she did not even understand.

''Not innocent,'' she said, reading his thoughts.

He took her for a long time, and she took him. There were kisses, and the passion was horrible because it satisfied them, both of them, to sin against God and Michael and their own innocence and to smear their passion over each other's body until they were both drenched with lovemaking. When he broke into her body, he was a barbarian without any thought but cruelty and the taking of pleasure. Michael was dead, and she didn't care. She had to have Devereaux now and had to have him completely possess her. She smelled him like an animal and saw forests, silences, snows, great mountains, the panorama of existence frozen in his touch. She didn't care, she didn't care. . . . She bit him on the shoulder, and he bit her neck, and she didn't care. . . .

And when it was over, when it was finally over, and the storm was still raging, they lay in exhaustion like battle casualties.

Guilt?

Yes, it burned her, she was tied to the stake and the flames licked at her. Was it the same for him? But then, innocence was long gone for both of them.

When it was finally over, she began to tell him things. She began to describe the limping man. She relived the last days of Michael Hampton, and she told him many things.

THIRTY-THREE

Rome

Marie knew he would not come back.

She put the tape in her pocket.

She took his passport and her own passport and put them in her purse.

He wasn't coming back. She didn't know how she knew this. It was sullen morning and the rain clouds were gone, but it was not very bright or clear, as though the sky had left traces of tears in its eyes.

She had waited all night for him. He did not call her. He wasn't coming back.

He was dead, she thought.

She turned the thought over. It was well examined by the time she accepted it.

She had to kill the priest at least.

Get a good knife and go to him.

Maybe he would listen to her confession. She would kneel and bless herself. When he leaned forward, she would put the knife in his eyes. That was for pain. That was to make the blindness real to him.

And cut off his ears and puncture his ear drums.

And then, finally, cut out his lying mouth and fill his nose with blood.

She was grinning like a demon as she rode the elevator down to the lobby. She saw the mutilated priest in her mind, begging silently for mercy with his bloody tongue on the carpet beside him.

Kill the priest. And then kill the man who had given Michael the tape. And then the agent in Bruges, the gray-haired man. . . .

Should she kill Rena Taurus as well?

Her grin became a frown. This was a puzzle.

The elevator opened, and the operator slid back the gates. She walked across the dusty, reddish lobby with its overstuffed chairs and little tables. The night clerk was still on duty. The rain was gone, dawn crept across the Forum of Rome.

First of all, she had to get a knife.

There must be knives in Rome, she thought.

She did not know her direction, but she was heading for the Tiber River without any reason or thought. She crossed the bridge, and then she saw the mark on the sidewalk in chalk. The chalk had run a little, but the mark was of a man in death. She knew these things; the pigs used the same method in Berlin.

A man in death.

Knelt. Saw the little brown stains that must have been blood.

Saw marks in the stone. These had been bullets and that was blood.

The area was sealed by plastic tape looped around temporary barricades. A policeman watched her from the other side of the little monument to sudden death.

Michael.

Her eyes filled with tears.

The policeman saw this and was puzzled and came around

to her and spoke to her in a language she didn't understand. When she looked at him, her eyes were glistening again, as they had been for Michael the night before.

The policeman spoke more loudly this time in Italian.

She shook her head. "*Ich bin ein Berliner*," she said.

"I do not speak German," the policeman said in Italian. "Do you speak English?" he continued in English.

But there was nothing to say to him. He was a pig, and pigs were all the same race of fascists. She jammed her hands into the pockets of her coat and gave him a sullen look. He had seen that look a thousand times.

He turned away.

"*Ich bin ein Berliner*," she said to herself. And walked away, reluctantly, from the place on the ancient bridge where Michael had been killed.

THIRTY-FOUR

Stockholm

Viktor Rusinov was quite angry with this United States
government and the fools who ran the embassy at 101
Strandvägen and with a number of other people who
now populated his pantheon of hated objects. The gods in
the pantheon had shifted since his days as a Soviet sailor on
the freighter ship *Leo Tolstoy*.

The anger showed in many ways. He was silent at his
meals, and he did not eat his mashed potatoes.

They rarely talked to him anymore. He asked them over
and over when he would be allowed to go to the United States
and, in particular, New York City. They smiled at him, mut-
tered vaguely about complications, and each day was like
another.

For example, during the period of his exercises—he wished
to keep his body whole and healthy—a marine accompanied
him to the yard behind the embassy and watched him as he
did situps and pushups and jogged around the little walkway.
He was not a prisoner, of course, and was free to leave the
embassy if he wished. But the problem was with the Soviet
government.

The Soviet government alleged he had struck a Soviet merchant marine officer and had severely injured him. It was one thing to defect; it was another thing to hurt someone in the act of defection. This greatly worried everyone, including the fool who was ambassador from the United States.

Viktor knew that God sent him these troubles because his escape from Soviet life had been too easy. Viktor was certain God would reward his suffering by avenging his enemies, starting with the fool of an ambassador and perhaps extending to the smug young American marine who accompanied him on his exercises.

And the vodka. When he could get it, it was American vodka, quite watery and without any taste at all, not unlike the exported Soviet vodka. They called that vodka.

The women were pretty, and many of them were Swedish. He knew Swedish women. They liked to do it almost as much as they liked to breathe. But these were women who must have been told to avoid him. Once, in a corridor in the residence wing of the embassy, he talked to this black-haired Swedish woman who resembled an ikon of the Virgin, and she had blushed at his suggestion rendered in passable Swedish and had reported him to the ambassador. So the fool of an ambassador had a talk with him. God, these Americans liked to talk. He had talked to all the intelligence agents, and they had been so kind and persistent and so stupid that he had almost lied to them to make it more interesting.

On this afternoon, after a night of violent storms with thunder and lightning dancing above the sacred spires of the Gamla Stan, Viktor Rusinov took his stroll along the waterfront. The great night of storms had inspired him to prayers, and he had earnestly suggested that God, in His wisdom, burn down the American embassy. But morning had come and the embassy stood, and Viktor, though disappointed, accepted God's judgment as a sign that Viktor's time of suffering must continue a while longer.

He had a particular route which took him along the waterfront Strandvägen to the Djurgards Bridge, which led to the island called Djurgarden. On this pleasant island in the Stockholm harbor was the battered remains of the *Wasa*, a Swedish ship that had unceremoniously sunk on launching three centuries earlier. For some reason, the Swedes had raised the ship from the harbor floor and housed it in a museum, where it was kept constantly wet so that the planks would not crack and wither. The ship had rolled over and sunk because it was top-heavy, and this was hardly a tribute to Swedish engineering. It amused Viktor Rusinov to go through the museum and to look at the hulk of the ship and study all the ancient naval artifacts recovered with the ship. He was in touch with those sailors who had drowned because of the stupidity of the people who had designed and launched the *Wasa*. Wasn't life endlessly repeating itself? Wasn't stupidity always the ruler of humankind?

The day was clear after the rain. The cold sun was bright. People walked about in heavy clothes, their breath preceding them in puffs. Men in fur hats with briefcases and girls in bright parkas and jeans. God, he would love to have a woman right now.

He walked down the Djurgardsvägen, past the Nordic Museum (which did not interest him at all), to Alkarret. The Wasa Museum was just ahead.

He did not recognize the man who stopped him.

The man stopped him with a hand on the shoulder. He glared at the man. Viktor Rusinov was a big man, and he had big sailor's hands.

The man spoke Russian to him: "Do you speak English?"

Viktor nodded. His English had been pretty damned good to start with, and now with the endless days in the embassy, it had gotten better. What was it to this guy anyway? The big sailor's hands were bunched in his jacket in fists.

"Then that makes it easier for me," the man said. He had small, mean eyes and dark hair and dark skin. He was a lot smaller than Viktor. Viktor thought he could take him easily.

"I want to know how you got that message and how you got my name on it," said the stranger.

"I don't know what you're talking about."

Henry McGee hit him so hard and so fast that Viktor was on the frozen earth, staring up at the cold bright sun and the bright, mean eyes at the same time. He didn't even hurt. He had no idea why he was on his back on the ground, but he figured that this man had something to do with it. There wasn't anger on the other's face, just a sort of lopsided smile.

"What did you do?"

"Hit you, Viktor. Which is what I am going to keep doing until you tell me the things I want to know. This ain't the embassy, Viktor, and I'm no Boy Scout from Central Intelligence."

"Who are you?"

"The man whose name was on that message you took off the ship. The thing is, how did you get it and who did you get it from?"

"I told them I stole it from the radio room."

"Damn, Viktor." And the little man kicked him so hard in the belly that Viktor retched his American breakfast of Wheaties, fried eggs in margarine, and link sausage.

When he was done with that, Viktor scrambled away to regain his footing.

They were in a park with bare trees and browned grass. The ground was frozen and crispy to the touch. Viktor got to his feet and swung and missed. No one was around, and that began to bother Viktor. In case anything serious developed.

The little man stepped inside and dropped him with another sledgehammer, this one to the chest. Viktor thought his heart stopped. He shuddered at the blow and fell again to one knee. This time the little man followed up and kicked him hard, again in the chest, again to stop his heart.

Viktor turned blue and coughed and coughed. When he was done with that, he thought about dying.

"You wanna tell me now or you wanna dance again?"

"Tell you what?"

"Who you got that piece of paper from and how you got it."

"I told them over and over. I stole it from the radio room."

"If that's all you really got to tell me, you're gonna be dead."

Viktor saw it was true. Not only had the man brought him to the point of death, but now the man had a pistol. The mean eyes were glowing as if the pistol and the thought of what it could do gave him pleasure.

There was no one else in the world. In the summer, the park is full of children. This was in the middle of the week, in the throes of November, after a night of rain and thunder. The ground had refrozen at morning, sealing the earth from the cold, moaning wind across Stockholm's harbors.

Viktor was cold and alone in the world. He said a name. "Arkady Yazimoff."

"That a brand of vodka or someone's name?"

"The radio officer on the *Leo Tolstoy*. He sold me the message for money. I had money. I had a lot of it."

"Is that right?"

"If I tell them, they will suspicious the letter."

"Get suspicious of."

"Yes. That. I cannot say this. I do not want to go back to Soviet Union."

"I appreciate that sentiment, Viktor, I really do."

"Can I get up?"

"Not at the moment. Tell me about the message, Viktor."

"What can I say? I do not know this message. It is code."

"Tell me about Arkady. You and him shipmates and buddies?"

"Not buddies, like you say."

"Come on. Did he cop your joint for you? Or you for him?"

"What?"

Henry said it in Russian.

Viktor looked tough for a man lying on the ground. "I do not do this, this fairy-boy thing you say. I am man. I fuck girls all the time and fuck them good."

"Good for you, Viktor."

"I talk to Arkady to buy this."

"How did this come up? I mean, you were at the same dance together and you dropped a hint you wanted to buy a message?"

"No."

"Then how did it come up?"

"I do not understand."

Henry spoke in Russian. It wasn't perfect Russian and the accent was strange, coming by way of Siberia, but it was good enough to puzzle Viktor for a moment. He had forgotten that. He had thought so long about getting off the *Leo Tolstoy* and defecting to America that he had forgotten the origins of the thought.

"I do not remember."

Henry McGee kicked him in the groin. The act was so quick and natural that Viktor did not react until a moment after the white pain hit his brain and the yawning sickness in his belly told him it was time to vomit again. He did, this time on himself. He couldn't help it, he really couldn't.

"My God, never do that to a man."

"I'm not even sure of that—you might be a pussy sailor. Tell me about you and Arkady Yazimoff."

"I try to remember. . . . Arkady is drunk. I make the vodka, good strong vodka, not this weak American vodka. Arkady is drunk and we are aboard. It is when we are in harbor at Göteborg. . . . I remember that Arkady is drunk in the radio room, and the ship is almost deserted, only a few of us left because it is the day of the Revolution and the sailors are in Göteborg to march in the parade. . . . I can't remember, but Arkady says to me that if someone could steal some traffic sheets, some second sheets where the traffic is written down—he means the radio traffic—that someone would have a good passport to the West because the West is always about stealing secrets. Yes. Arkady is drunk and he tells me this. All the political officers on the ship are making me nervous just then, always watching me."

Henry McGee stared at him.

"Yes," Viktor says, his face as pale as snow. "It is this that he says, to bring a secret message."

"And you told no one this thing."

"If I tell them that I pay Arkady Yazimoff for papers, they suspicious the papers and they suspicious me."

"They surely would suspicious you, Viktor, they surely would. So you kept your big dumb mouth shut."

"I only tell you. Now."

"Now I want you to tell me all this again, just go over it nice and slow and talk into the tape recorder."

"Will you use this against me?"

"Hell, no, Viktor. We can get along now that you're telling me things I want to know."

So Viktor did it again, for the tape recorder. When it was finished, Henry put the tape into the pocket of his jacket. He stared at Viktor. "Everybody's got a secret, you know that, Viktor. Ain't one creature alive in the world ain't leading a secret life. If we get enough tape recorders going, we'd find out everybody is a liar."

"I do not understand you," Viktor said.

"And that creates a problem too."

"Why?"

Viktor stared at him hard to understand what it was this man was thinking.

"Why, Viktor. I'm sort of caught in the middle of things. I don't mind telling you, because it puzzles me. I might just want to go back to Mother Russia, and I might just want not to do that if the Big Mother is setting me up, which I think she is. So, either way, I got what I came for, and that means it's too bad about you, Viktor."

Henry shot him then in the head at very close range. The

first bullet shattered his left eye, and the second bullet shattered his skull. Viktor Rusinov stretched out on the frozen earth, arms thrown out in a quiet plea. The pistol cracks reverberated above the frozen earth, but Henry McGee was already walking away.

THIRTY-FIVE

Rome

Alberto Cardinal Ludovico stood before the side altar and finished the words of the Mass. He spoke Latin because it was the tongue of the church and because it was now permitted again and because it most moved his heart. His heart had been lost with the death of Michael.

"*Agnus Dei, Qui tollis peccata mundi, donna eis requiem.*"

Again and again, striking his heart with his hand. *Lamb of God, who takes away the sins of the world . . .*

But what sins could be forgiven?

Michael Hampton was dead, shot to death on a Tiber bridge at midnight, all because of Cardinal Ludovico.

His hands trembled as he picked up the wafer.

The immensity of St. Peter's Cathedral was all around him, the immensity of the statuary and the high altar by Bellini and the immensity of pillars reaching hundreds of feet to support the dome of the roof. On the prow of St. Peter's stood the stone Christ and the stone Apostles, and they gazed with somber eyes across the piazza and its columns, where

Cardinal Ludovico had waited for Michael Hampton beneath the storm.

Ite, missa est.

But there were only three standing at this side altar, early tourists or worshipers who wished to hear the Latin words again. Go, the mass is ended. *Ite, missa est.*

Only two left.

Cardinal Ludovico bowed to the altar and genuflected before the sanctuary on arthritic knees.

He started for a side door.

The pilgrim waited.

He opened the door that led to the changing rooms where he would shed the chasuble and alb of worship for the ruby gown of office.

He turned into the corridor and the pilgrim was behind him.

"Cardinal Ludovico."

He turned.

The face of a child, not a man at all but a girl, perhaps a woman, thin and haggard. He began to smile, and then he saw the knife.

"I come to kill you," she said. "The way you had Michael killed."

Cardinal Ludovico understood. This was the woman with Michael, the one who had overturned a table in the galleria in Milan. He had not intended to frighten anyone, least of all Michael. He had loved Michael. Didn't she understand that?

But he said nothing to her.

He waited for her and the knife and his death. He tried to think of God.

And he knelt on the stone floor to receive his death.

The knife glittered in the dim electric light of the hallway between the church walls.

"Why did you kill him? I loved him," Marie Dreiser said. Her eyes glistened with all the tears she had been saving for this moment. The tears dug little paths on her cheeks.

"I did not kill him."

"This. You killed him for this."

She held the tape in her hand.

The cardinal blessed himself. And then he raised his hand and began to bless her. "I forgive you," he said. "You do not know what you do."

"Do not forgive me. Forgive yourself forever for this murder on your hands."

And he looked at the pale, elegant fingers of his hands, and he thought he saw the blood, saw the same thing this girl saw.

She did not move.

Cardinal Ludovico closed his eyes to better feel the blow, to feel the blade sink beneath flesh, between bone and sinew, to find his heart. All his life as a priest he had waited for this moment, for the first of the final four things. To die in this church, after that act of worship, comforted him. He did not intend his death, but it pleased him to die because he had felt so badly about Michael Hampton and felt the guilt of Michael's death as surely as if he had ordered it.

He opened his eyes, and still she had not moved. She stared at him but could not see him because her eyes were so blinded now by tears.

"I want Michael!" she screamed and threw the knife down on the stones. The knife clattered and skidded across the stones and stopped at the kneeling figure of the cardinal.

Then she threw down the tape.

The cassette clattered loosely on the stones and skidded as well. It was almost within reach of the ancient, bony hands.

"Take it. Michael died to give it to you. He only wanted to give it to you, he didn't want anything, he wanted to be free of it. He said I could have sanctuary with him, he said I would be free, and I loved him for that, for the kindness he gave me. Take it! You evil man, you utterly evil man. I hope to God, if there is God, that He will come down and smite you and you will roast in hell for eternity for what you did to Michael."

"I did not kill him. I swear to you, child, I did not kill him and I did not want his death."

"Go ahead, you've got the knife. I don't care, I won't kill you, you hideous frog. I hate you. I thought about you, about tearing your eyes out with my hands. I could do that, I could do that. *Mein Gott in Himmel!*" And she leaped at him and knocked him to the ground.

The cardinal struck his head on the stones.

Her hands were on his throat.

"Sanctuary! You would not give him sanctuary!" she screamed in German, but he did not understand a word. He felt the vise of her small hands choking down life, holding him under. There was blood on his forehead.

Was this from God?

But the blade was beneath his hand.

Was this a sign?

He struck her, and the knife slipped into her back as easily as if she had intended it this way.

The hands slackened.

Her eyes grew wide. Her eyes were large enough to see everything in the world.

"Michael," she said. Her voice was soft. She saw him rise from the chalk outline on the bridge and smile at her gently. He was the kindness of the world, reaching out his hand to her.

"Michael." She said it with love and tenderness. "Lamb."

And her back arched, and then she had to fall—she knew it—and she would have to fall on this man who was lying on the stones beneath her. She would have to strike her head upon the ground, but there was no pain to any of it.

"I did not kill him."

He said this over the crumpled body of the German girl. "I did not kill him." He reached down to touch her neck, to feel for any pulse. The knife protruded from her back. And then he saw the cassette. He reached for it first. He held the cassette.

The cassette transformed him back to cardinal from priest.

Michael was gone, the moment with the mad girl was gone. He held the tape recording. The secret deal a man had given his life for. To know it was to have the power to use it, and Michael, poor Michael, could not understand the uses of power.

Almost against his will, he was suddenly filled with soft contempt in that moment for his son in the church, Michael Hampton. He had not harmed Michael, did not wish him harm, had said a Mass of the dead for him this morning in the holiest church in Christendom. But Michael did not understand power and was afraid of it, from the moment he had run from the army and then from the CIA. Michael did not want to know, he did not want to hear. What a pity. God gave him his talent, and he did not want to use it. Except for the church. Michael was naive enough to believe the Congregation for the Protection of the Faith was merely an agency of innocent intelligence, bent to give the pope and the hierarchy the best possible information about the welfare of the church in the various countries of the world.

Poor Michael.

The leonine eyes of the cardinal glittered now.

Pulse fluttered like a dying bird beneath his fingers. She was alive, but what was the point of it? We all end in eternity.

He raised his fingers and blessed her. The Latin ritual for absolution came next: *"Ego te absolvo, in nomine Patri, et Filii, et Spiritu Sancti. . . ."*

What was he absolving her for?

She was a child, and she might have sinned with Michael. Sinned before he was killed on the bridge.

Did he believe in such things after thirty years of deception and treachery in the name of the protection of the church?

Yes, he must believe.

He pulled out the knife and raised it above the child as he had done a moment before, raising his hand in blessing and absolution.

Forgive me.

The side door opened and threw bright light into the narrow

hall. He looked up at the tall man. Did he know his eyes glittered in that moment or that the tall man saw every intention in his eyes?

"Will you murder again?" the tall man said.

"I did not . . ."

But he looked at the knife, and it accused him. He saw now there was blood on his hand, not the imagined blood of Michael that the girl saw, but the real blood, this of the girl he had not intended to hurt.

"Put the knife down," said the tall man, and Cardinal Ludovico thought he must obey.

The knife clattered on the stones again.

"Get away from her."

He staggered to his feet on creaky legs. He felt age and weight and the weariness of many burdens. He held the tape in his hand.

"How many would have to die for the tape before it's been paid for?" the tall man said.

"Who are you?"

"The man who wants the tape."

And the side door closed, and they were alone in the semidarkness of this hall between the walls of the church, standing over the prone, bleeding body, staring at each other and considering the worth of lives.

THIRTY-SIX

Helsinki

A scum of ice floated on the blue, still waters in Helsinki harbor. The *Leo Tolstoy* groaned at the ropes that restrained her, rubbed against the dock, struggled to be free in the waves at sea. She was here too long, and she felt it in her hull, in the quiet of her engines, in the agony of her empty gangways. The ship yearned for all the ports of the world, and this could be seen in the undulation of steel and wire pulling at the immense ropes that held her.

Arkady Yazimoff dozed at the radio table. There were no messages; there had been no traffic for hours. He was the prime radio officer and had to take his turns, but he had really wanted to spend this afternoon getting drunk in Helsinki.

He had missed Viktor Rusinov's vodka. That was the only thing everyone agreed on: Viktor was a pain in the ass—and good riddance to rubbish when he had slipped over the side that day in Stockholm—but he knew how to brew the very best homemade stuff. God, it could put you out.

Arkady wanted to be put out. Oblivion was almost complete pleasure to him. He liked to drink, liked the raw taste on his tongue and throat, but most of all he liked the dreaminess that came just before oblivion. In those moments—it might be minutes, it might be hours—a warmth like sex overcame him and caressed him.

"Officer Yazimoff."

He started in his chair, turned to the open hatch. A civilian in raincoat and hat.

He thought of KGB immediately and snapped to as much attention as you can manage in a chair.

The hatch closed.

"I am Garishenko, KGB."

"Yes, Comrade."

"Comrade. Be at ease, please."

"Yes, Comrade." Yazimoff strained for a little more attention. He thought his shirt buttons would pop or his neck would explode from the pressure.

"Comrade, this is in regard to the matter of Viktor Rusinov." The KGB man sat down in the second chair of the cabin. He did not remove his hat.

"Yes, Comrade."

"I have reviewed the whole matter, and I want to go over it again with you, at least your part of it, so that I can understand perfectly."

"I don't understand, Comrade Garishenko."

The freighter was so silent. There were only groans, sounds of metal against sea, sounds of ropes squealing and the hull scraping like a lover against the wharf. Not a sound in the world because every sound was familiar and was in their souls already.

"Tell me how you approached Viktor Rusinov."

"This is all in the report—"

"Tell me again."

The voice chilled him. The voice was of the state and the cells of Lubyanka and the cold depth of Siberia or the bauxite mines deep in Kurdistan. Yazimoff had heard all the stories, because sailors get around and sailors live on their stories.

"As I was instructed, I became an associate of Comrade Rusinov. I was told to tell him certain things, that certain messages could be carried away if he wanted to defect to the Americans, and that the messages would give him a gift to give them that would ensure his acceptance into their confidence.''

''As who instructed?''

''But surely, you know that.''

''I want to know it as you know it.''

''Well, I know, but I don't understand—''

''Who gave you this instruction?''

''One of yours. His name is Skarda, that is the name he has given me.''

''Of course,'' Henry McGee said in Russian with a Siberian accent.

Yazimoff looked at him. He had a dark complexion—he might be an oriental Russian in part. It was hard to tell anymore. The damned foreigners were everywhere; they had jobs in Moscow and ate their filthy Eastern food with their fingers, like peasants. His eyes were black and small and mean. Mean. The mean look put fear into Yazimoff more than anything else.

''When Viktor decided to defect, he paid me, and I gave him the arranged message. The message is in my mind.''

''Is it?''

''Yes, Comrade: 'Skarda. The time of Henry McGee is not past. Eagle will be penetrated. The operation . . .' ''

''That was the whole message?''

''Well, it was a broken message. It was intended that way, as though he had stolen one of the pads.''

''I see,'' said the agent.

Yazimoff tried a smile. ''But you know all this. Does my memory recollect with your report?''

''In every way,'' said Henry McGee.

THIRTY-SEVEN

London

The reports came in all morning. Every listener and watcher and chaser made his or her report. They came in cipher or by digital code or by sound blip, with the message squeezed into a fraction of a second of radio transmission and then "ironed out" later in the receiver to its normal length. The reports were noted on flimsy paper and put on Vaughn Reuben's desk. He looked at every report before he consigned it to the paper shredder at the side of his desk.

Vaughn Reuben was back in London, in the corner office of the subdirector of the CIA station at the United States embassy on Grosvenor Square. The fog was gone, and the sun was crackling bright above city and river. The streets looked fresh with new people on them and newly painted cars and buses. As usual, every inch of road was taken and no one was going anywhere very quickly. London was full, but it had been full for years, and the British philosophy was that to build more roads would only encourage more traffic.

Reuben picked up a sheaf of flimsies, weighed them, put

them down. He looked at his visitor and said, "You don't listen to your marching orders so good."

Hanley said, "This doesn't concern you."

"By God it does. It does if the director says it does. You're not running with some goddamn renegade agency that can set policy and do as it damned well pleases. You got an order, didn't you?"

"Internal affairs of Section are not the business of anyone in Central Intelligence."

"You pompous asshole, what do you think this is about?"

"I came here out of courtesy."

"You came here because Mrs. Neumann ordered your ass to liaise with me, so you better start doing some liaising." Vaughn Reuben was just letting the words steamroller out of his mouth. "Goddamn agent Devereaux— Don't protest to me about your fucking security. I know goddamn well who you got running right now. Goddamn agent Devereaux shot and killed Michael Hampton at midnight. In Rome. Your Rome station was involved as well. You were supposed to pull Devereaux off of this, and you didn't do it. You think we don't have a station chief in Rome? You think we're the three blind mice?"

"Hum me some of it," Hanley said.

"I really don't like you, Hanley," Vaughn Reuben said.

"Really?"

"I am going to tell you once. Get your goddamn man on the first plane back to London, and then we'll talk to him about things like murdering people in foreign lands. And I want that tape delivered personally to me, you got that?"

"I thought this was a matter for State. For State Department's intelligence," Hanley said. "I don't understand this intense interest by Langley in matters that don't concern Langley. Why don't you start by explaining that to me?"

"Hanley." Vaughn Reuben was definitely doing his John Houseman imitation. "None of this would have happened if Devereaux hadn't been on the loose, and that's your responsibility. Two dead Soviet agents in Brussels, and he kidnaps this . . . this Rena Taurus, and no one knows where she is, and there's a report he was supposed to ice Michael in Bruges but he let him go—"

"So now you are convinced he killed him in Rome. That doesn't make sense, Vaughn."

"Hanley, where is the tape?"

"I don't know."

"Where is Devereaux?"

"I don't know. I haven't made contact."

"Hanley, are you fucking with me?"

"Yes," Hanley said. Very cold, very distant. Vaughn Reuben was sweating it. He really wanted that tape. But why? Why did any of this involve CIA?

And why had Devereaux suddenly made contact with Henry McGee? What did any of this mean except danger to Section?

Section was getting all the heat in the world because it had not called off one of its agents and because the orders for Section seemed to be coming from a dozen sources and a dozen points of view.

To hell with it, Hanley thought at last.

He stood up and buttoned his coat and pulled a wool scarf around his neck. He had a cap too, with a little brim, all made of wool. British November weather had made him a believer in wool products.

Vaughn Reuben gaped at him for a moment. "Where are you going, Hanley?"

Hanley blinked. To hell with it. "Out."

"What are you going to do about this?"

"Nothing," Hanley said.

THIRTY-EIGHT

Rome

The surgeon was gifted. His fingers were strong and sure. The surgeon was young, and his scowl of concentration was enhanced by the darkness of his beard. He moved very quickly because the life of the girl on the naked operating table demanded it.

The problem was in the bleeding.

The single knife thrust had cut through muscle and intestines and touched the liver, and there was great damage. The girl had strength—they could see her strength on the heart monitor, on the screens that showed her blood pressure—but she was weakened by the loss both of blood and of that other, unmeasurable thing that doctors sometimes called the will to live. A curious lack of it in one so young.

All of the skill of this peasant child who had gone to university and medical school through the gift of his intellect was now bent to the task of healing this bleeding body. The girl's face was soft and waxy, as though composed for death. She lay naked on her stomach and was draped with sheets, and only the wound of her back—enlarged by surgical incisions—was exposed. The operating room, like the hos-

pital, was old and high ceilinged and not the most efficien
place of its kind. But there was a spirit within the heart o
the surgeon and in the attending nurses and nuns that coul
not be replicated or purchased. Others had seen it in thes
grim dungeons called hospitals in Italy, which seemed con
structed as monuments to mortality; this human spirit wa
still alive amidst the ruins, and it would not accept men
death. It did not matter, none of it, except that this chil
should not die.

When it was over, the surgeon walked from the room wit
a drained look in his eyes. His thin body drooped as he walke
down the lime green corridor to the room where they waitec

There were two men—one was a priest, the other was a
American.

The priest in his plain black cassock might have been fro
some slum church in the ancient city. His face was ravage
by age and his hair was dull. He stared at the surgeon an
did not speak, but his look asked a question anyway.

The surgeon shrugged. "It's up to her. The bleeding i
stopped. She can heal herself or not. She seems . . . s
composed. As if for passing on."

"Did she speak?"

"Not at all. She was nearly dead when she got here. D
they know who did this to her?"

"It is a complete mystery," said the priest.

"Are you a friend?"

"Yes," Cardinal Ludovico said. "A close friend."

"Well, this will certainly be a scandal," the surgeon saic
He was very tired from the act of healing. He looked a
Devereaux. "And what is your interest, *signor*?"

"I have no interest. I found her body in St. Peter's. I calle
the guard."

"Muggers and murderers working even in San Pietro
There is no safe place anymore," the surgeon said.

"No," Devereaux agreed.

"I have done my best. It's up to God," the surgeon saic
He meant only civil piety and intended the words for th

priest, because he had long concluded that if God existed, He was a Being the surgeon did not wish to know.

The priest nodded as though he understood, and made the sign of the cross to continue the fiction of piety.

The surgeon walked away from them. There were others in the waiting room, others full of jokes, whispers, sobs, all waiting for life or death to be announced. The hospital was full, the corridors were crowded with litters and wheelchairs, as though some great disaster had just been visited upon the city.

"I will pray for her," Cardinal Ludovico said.

"How decent of you."

"I did not intend—"

"I know. I was mistaken in what I saw."

The old man turned to the American, and there was a cold thing in the leonine eyes that was meant to be disdain. It was a look that had terrified servants and staff, but it withered in the face of this American.

"I do not know the tape or what Michael intended," Cardinal Ludovico said at last in precise English.

"He intended to give it to you. He intended to be safe after he gave it to you."

"I did not kill him."

"No. It would have been foolish to kill him when he would have given you the thing. Whoever killed him did not want you to have the tape. Or Michael's memory of what was on the tape."

"Then who did kill him?"

"We must listen to the tape."

The cardinal stared at Devereaux for a silent moment. He said, "Will you know the secret then? Adam will have knowledge and will know the difference between what is good and what is not good. Will you eat the same fruit?"

Devereaux almost smiled.

"A madness seized me," the cardinal said. "I will pray for her the rest of my days. I will commend my soul to God for her sake. It is madness, whatever is on that tape is madness and evil for its own sake. I think we should destroy the tape—''

''No. I don't think that at all,'' Devereaux said.

Devereaux held the tape cassette in his left hand for a moment and then slipped it into the Sony recorder on the large, walnut table.

Devereaux pressed Rewind. The key clicked immediately.

They sat in the most secret room of the Congregation for the Protection of the Faith on the Borgo Santo Spirito. Bright morning had faded to the gloom of afternoon, and there were more clouds scudding in from the Alps. Along the western coast of Italy, the waves swelled and there was a smell of the coming rain in the brittle air.

They had no amenities between them. The cardinal finally remembered Devereaux from the matter of Father Tunney in Florida years ago, when R Section and the congregation had first found themselves at odds. The man had not seemed so cold then, only hostile. The man had not seemed so detached then, as though the events of the world did not touch him. He had been touched since then; that was certain.

Cardinal Ludovico had no illusions about Devereaux or what Devereaux might do to achieve his ends. He studied the other man as he thought of the possibilities that might exist for the congregation—for the church—depending on what was on the tape.

But Devereaux sat there without playing the tape.

Cardinal Ludovico said, ''Are you afraid, then?''

''Tell me about Michael Hampton.''

''He was a free-lance. He was employed by us from time to time.''

''This tape was intended for you. For your use. Someone intended it. If Michael Hampton was the innocent courier, then who gave him the tape? Who knew he worked for you at the conference in Malmö?''

Silence. Thunder suddenly rumbled across the hills of the city, and the cardinal seemed startled. He rose and went to the window and closed the glass and locked the frame. The room was still for a moment, and then thunder insisted again. Cardinal Ludovico looked down at the Borgo, at the traffic, at the people hurrying along the walk to get to their destination before the rain.

"Michael was recommended to us by Central Intelligence a long time ago."

The words were quiet. The cardinal did not turn to look at the American agent.

"Do not believe that Michael was our agent. He was a translator and interpreter. He knew the congregation was an intelligence apparatus in the church, but he was not our agent. He was our eyes and ears."

"Until he heard too much."

The cardinal stared at his fingers. His hands trembled on his lap.

Devereaux said, "What is the relationship of the congregation to the CIA?"

Ludovico finally looked at him. "We have no . . . relationship. The Central Intelligence Agency is aware of our existence only, as we are aware of theirs."

"That isn't true, priest," Devereaux said. He said it as though he was not guessing this time. "You sent Michael Hampton to a naval conference in Malmö with expectations. The church has no navy. What did you expect?"

The cardinal opened his hands to show his honesty. "Intelligence is to be gotten in unlikely places at unlikely times."

"You commissioned him. He called you seven times in five days. Someone at the conference gave him the tape, even if he might have been reluctant to have it. Someone knew he would take the train home to Stockholm. It's a long trip across Sweden. He would listen to the tape at some point, and as soon as he knew the contents, he would know he had to get the tape to you . . . for his own safety. It was a very cynical plan and you were part of it." Devereaux paused. "And it cost Michael's life."

The old man pressed thumb and forefinger against the

bridge of his nose. He squeezed his eyes shut so that he would not cry for Michael. When he opened his eyes, the American was sitting still, staring at him.

"I did not wish the death of Michael."

"It doesn't matter what you wished. You were part of the maneuvering. But what had to come to you, what information could you use that would benefit the CIA?"

Thunder rattled the windows. It startled both men.

"I cannot remember so much rain in November," Cardinal Ludovico said.

"Perhaps it's the deluge," Devereaux said.

"God promised never to flood the world again."

"Perhaps God was joking."

The two men stared at each other. Then Devereaux shifted in his chair and sighed. He pressed the play button, and the silence of the room was filled with the clear, concise voice of the American secretary of state, reading from a memorandum. The secret agenda of Malmö was laid before both men.

There were four points, all interconnected.

First, the Soviet Union agreed to lend to the United States the antiterror computer program called Skarda, which would insure that records kept by secret agencies would be "immune" from outside viruses, that "hackers" would not be able to imperil the ability of the United States to keep its programs and memories secret. This was in the interest of the Soviet Union because a blinded American government, stripped of memory in records, would become a dangerous American government, suspicious and impotent against world order at the same time. The Soviets wanted to deal with a strong United States.

The second part of the agreement said the United States, in return for the gift of the program called Skarda, would back down on its research into the Strategic Defense Initiative. Specifically, $200 million already targeted for missile testing research would be rescinded.

Third, the Soviet Union, in the spirit of *glasnost*, would enable ninety thousand Soviet Jews and other dissidents to have visas issued them in the coming calendar year.

Finally, in the same spirit of openness between the great powers, the United States agreed that continued funding of the Lithuanian dissident movement through the CIA would be halted.

Devereaux listened to the secretary's words and watched Ludovico through it all. Only at the last point did he see the cardinal make a movement. It was involuntary. The cardinal's right hand started to tremble. And Devereaux thought he began to understand.

He switched off the tape at the sound of the Russian voice. The Soviet foreign secretary was repeating the memorandum of agreement just read by the American secretary of state.

Silence for a long moment and then thunder again. The rumble filled the room for a moment, and then there was another dead silence.

"Hardly enough to kill a man," Devereaux said.

Ludovico looked at Devereaux. "You do not understand, Mr. Devereaux. Lithuania is important. To the West and to the church."

"So that's the CIA connection," Devereaux said.

"I don't understand."

"You understand everything, priest. The church was the connection to Lithuania. The conduit for the CIA funds. The funds are drying up, and in exchange, the Russians will let some of its dissidents go."

"Networks. Agents. Dozens of networks in Vilnius, throughout Lithuania. Set up by patriots willing to risk their lives, and all of it washed away in a stroke by a secret agreement. Last year, forty-nine thousand Soviet Jews were let free. This year, ninety thousand. I am glad they will be free. . . . But at the cost of Lithuania's freedom?"

"The church was funding the movement in Lithuania. With CIA monies. Is that it? Is that why CIA arranged to get the tape to you, so that you could make it public? And making it public, kill the deal. And Michael was the innocent in all this," Devereaux said. He stood up and put the tape in his pocket.

"What are you going to do?"

"Not pray," Devereaux said.

Ludovico shook his head. "I grieve for Michael."

"Tears are easy at the end. You grieve for the loss of this tape. You were going to make it public, Ludovico, sabotage the agreement."

"They have no right . . . to agree to disarm Lithuania, to destroy the movement for freedom. . . ."

Devereaux stared at him another moment. "It's their money, Cardinal. Not yours. Not the CIA's."

"It is more than ending something that exists. There are lives involved, more lives than Michael's or that girl's. Is all this to be done for . . . for a computer system?"

"You were the man removed," Devereaux said. "You could reveal the secret tape as long as the Soviets and the Americans were convinced that Michael stole it for you. Michael was set up from the first moment in Malmö. Even before Malmö, when you agreed to send him there. Who told you to send him to Malmö?"

"I sent him . . . for intelligence—"

"Both sides would officially believe that this was the act of a third party, the Congregation for the Protection of the Faith. But it was directed by you, Cardinal, and you got your marching orders from someone. Who was it?"

"I cannot say—"

"Someone in Central Intelligence."

"I cannot say."

"Who do I blame this on, Cardinal Ludovico?"

"Please." He held up his hand. "Before you turn this tape over to the Soviets, at least you must contact your superiors. At least you must contact the CIA—"

Devereaux said, "Who do I ask for?"

"You must . . . contact . . ." The old man wiped his forehead and was surprised he was sweating. Rain drummed at the windowpanes. So much rain, it was unbelievable. The days were all full of gloom now.

"You must contact Mr. Vaughn Reuben," the old man said.

Devereaux stood still for a moment. He absorbed the name, saw the connection, saw how everything connected in that moment. Reuben did not want the memory program called Skarda; he didn't give a damn about the Soviet Jews or the Lithuanian network. The important thing was to queer the deal on Skarda in exchange for Star Wars. Let the old priest steal the tape through his agent in Malmö and let the bricks fall down on the congregation. Not on CIA. It was at least two steps removed from Langley, and no one could blame Langley for interfering with American negotiations. So Vaughn Reuben kept shifting blame to R Section for not protecting the conference in the first place and for not getting Michael in the second place. The administration would blame Section, would blame the church, would blame Michael . . . in fact, would find blame everyplace but at the building in Virginia that housed Central Intelligence.

Devereaux turned from the priest without a word.

"You must not betray Lithuania."

"I owe nothing to you. Or Lithuania." And in that moment, he saw Rena in his mind, saw the flawless cold beauty of her perfect face, saw her small act of betrayal against Michael. No one wished Michael dead. Not the cardinal, not the woman he loved. But they had betrayed him to the death dealers.

Devereaux took a step toward the tall doors at the far end of the room.

The doors opened, and two large men stood shoulder to shoulder and stared at the American.

"You must not," the cardinal said.

Devereaux took out the Beretta and snapped the safety.

"Tomaso. Guglielmo." The cardinal stood and waved his hand. "Do not put yourselves in the way of harm. He has a gun. It's not worth a life."

And Devereaux turned at that, pistol in hand, and stared at the priest.

"Not even Michael's," he said.

THIRTY-NINE

Copenhagen

Skarda himself sat at the thin-legged rickety table on the second floor of the house in Copenhagen. It was the same house Henry McGee had been brought to before by the blond girl named Christina.

This time, he was brought by the fat leather spy. The fat leather spy had picked him up as he left the terminal building at Kastrup, and there had been a driver and another man who was strictly for muscle. Henry let himself be muscled. He tried to talk to the fat leather spy, but there was nothing but silence from the other end.

Up the old-fashioned staircase. Grandmother was still downstairs, still carrying her Uzi.

They searched him at the door and took away his pistol and the knife. He went into the room and sat down in a straight chair opposite Skarda. Skarda motioned with his hand, and the fat leather spy closed the door on the two men.

Skarda stared at Henry McGee for a moment, and they both understood the silence, understood there was some finality hidden in this moment.

"The tape recording was retrieved two hours ago," Skarda

said. "We have an assurance from the Americans in London that it will be returned, that no damage has been done. Can I inquire what you were doing the past twenty-four hours?"

"Inquire away. I was in Stockholm, Malmö, trying to go back over the trail."

"You did not make contact."

"Happens."

"We had men in Rome, they contacted Mr. Michael Hampton. But he did not have the tape recording on his person."

"So he was going to Rome with it," Henry said. He was staying one step behind because Skarda was one of those arrogant kind of explainers: you asked him what time it was, and he explained how a watch works. Besides, Henry was just now measuring the cell of the room, trying to see where the walls were and how much time he was going to have.

"He was in Rome. He had a confederate, a girl named Marie Dreiser. She is the one who saved him in Berlin. We investigated her thoroughly, and she is in a Roman hospital. It isn't clear, but she did not have the tape. The Americans recovered the tape—I cannot say how. They have contacted us through the embassy in London. Soon it will be delivered to us."

"What was on the tape exactly?"

"You have no need to know," Skarda said.

"No. I suppose not." He waited.

"You murdered Viktor Rusinov. For what purpose?"

Henry just felt the chill in the walls, felt the words shut like a prison door. "I don't know who you're talking about."

"What is on the tape? Do you have so much curiosity? Then I'll satisfy it."

Henry went cold. The door was locked and they were throwing away the key.

Skarda tented his fingertips and smiled. It took him less than a minute to tell him the contents of the tape.

"And so when you get the Americans to start programming Skarda, they'll screw up their communications system."

"Is that what you believe?" Skarda said.

"That's what Skarda was supposed to be, wasn't it? Something or other to put a virus in American communications with the Europeans?"

"The Americans will examine Skarda as a primitive culture might examine . . . what should I say? Exactly as the Trojans examined the wooden horse. Carefully. Unbelieving at first. And then accepting it. They will program Skarda in bits, slowly, turning each bit over to see if it fits and is genuine. It will be very genuine, Henry McGee, that is the genius of it. Skarda is exactly what it seems to be."

"Then I don't get it. Sounds like a good deal for the Americans."

"No. You don't get it."

"Whatever this Lithuanian thing is, can't amount to very much," Henry said.

"But it is important to the CIA. We suspected them immediately. CIA sabotaged the conference in Malmö. CIA stole the tape. CIA set up this courier run to Rome."

"Why Rome?"

"The Catholic church is the financial mule for the CIA money into Lithuania. They take their . . . what is the Americanism, the slang word?"

"They take their skim," Henry McGee said. He was grinning to show how relaxed he was with all this knowledge. He was studying the window right behind Skarda.

"So," Skarda said. "Why did you kill Viktor Rusinov?"

"Who is he?"

"Are you working for the Americans?"

"He someone the Americans want to kill?"

"You were seen."

Henry said, "Why set me up? Why put me in charge of hustling after Michael Hampton when it was all just a day late and a dollar short. Hell, you knew he was going to Rome in the first place."

"We knew."

"And you had your hitters set in Rome from day one. What was all this garbage about hitters in Brussels, putting them on that girl Rena, setting up in Berlin."

"Berlin was an honest effort meant to retrieve the tape," Skarda said. "Our target disappeared, only to resurface in twenty-four hours in East Berlin with a girl. A West German girl with a passport. Marie Dreiser. She was not expected; everything else was expected."

"Including me fumbling along, chasing after someone I was not going to be allowed to catch."

"We did not trust you, Henry. Your trail was dirty. We had reports from Washington from the time of your trial, about how you betrayed our secrets to R Section, how you betrayed Skarda, or what you believed Skarda was."

"Devereaux. R Section. They dirtied the trail. You people should have been smart enough to see that I never betrayed you, and you let me rot in prison."

"The dirty trail was genuine."

"Genuine horseshit," Henry said.

Skarda shrugged. "It doesn't matter, Henry. Whatever you said then or say now. You were seen in Stockholm, and you killed Viktor Rusinov. Believe me, we know this. We had observed Viktor from the first day. He was useful to us. And you will be useful to us as well, when we return you to Moscow and when you explain to us in painful, even excruciating detail, how much you betrayed during your American captivity and how they managed to drag it out of you. It is always useful to examine a traitor, however odious the task, rather as a doctor examines stools."

Henry McGee smiled.

Skarda frowned. "There is no joke here. Everything has been cleaned and examined. This Marie Dreiser is in a Roman hospital. She is of no importance to us. The last important thing is the American agent, this Devereaux, who has the tape. He is in Brussels and he will be dealt with, and the tape will be retrieved before the Americans can have one of their famous, unpredictable debates about returning it and change their minds.''

''And I'll be tagged as the hit man,'' Henry McGee said.

''Of course. Everything legal and logical. We and the Americans must not engage in mistrust. Let them look for you, not for us.''

''*Glasnost*,'' Henry McGee said.

''It is quite genuine, I assure you.''

''Sure.''

''Lithuania. It is a concession to us. It shows how genuine we are in the bargain—we cannot give them too much, or they will be overly suspicious.''

''You gave away the program called Skarda.''

''And Skarda is genuine, believe me. I devised it.''

''So why give them secrets?''

''When you have a healthy man, a man with a strong heart and lungs, and you see his perfect health in every way, in his confidence and his smile, you cannot believe for a moment that he is dying from a cancer.''

''Skarda is a healthy man.''

The wizened man nodded. ''And Skarda is a cancer.''

''What is the cancer?''

Skarda couldn't help himself. He was so clever.

''Skarda works at one level in programming, but the program itself is encoded to work at the level of the American programs to rewrite a program. Do you understand that?''

''Vaguely. Sounds like a lot of shit, but if you believe it, fine.''

Skarda glared. ''A lot of shit. Let me tell you about a lot of shit. *Glasnost* and *perestroika* are genuine. We must reduce our arms, our mutual wariness. But the Americans are so unpredictable and so suspicious. They still push too hard. They put too much money into research, into their ridiculous concepts like the Strategic Defense Initiative. What can we do when we have so many problems? The Americans must convince themselves of their dangerousness.''

"And you're going to convince them?"

"They must convince themselves."

"How do they do that?"

"What if a missile, an ordinary nuclear missile with a nonnuclear warhead, were being tested next month in Utah?"

"Utah?"

"Next month," Skarda said. "On December twentieth. Five days before Christmas."

"Sentimental time," Henry said.

Skarda grinned now, and it was as ghastly as his frown. "What if this missile changed course at the command of its own computer network and landed on a place like Quebec City?"

Henry thought about it. "An American missile."

"That lands on a Canadian city."

"That cannot be explained except for a system malfunction. Some malfunction in computer command. But steps and steps away from Skarda and your simple little computer defense shield. My, my. You are a genius, no doubt about it."

The compliment pleased the old man. He nodded at the bright pupil and did not see the gleam in the small, black eyes. The gleam had not been there a moment before, but it was heating up now.

Henry said, "The Americans suddenly get into one of their numbing debates about weapons systems and who pulls the trigger and all that other horseshit. And the Canadians are mad and probably even the Frenchies, because there's so many Frenchies in Quebec. Well, it sure sounds wonderful to me, Skarda, really wonderful."

Skarda reached for the button under his desk. The interview was over.

Henry saw it was over. No trade, no getting out of it, no yin-and-yanging anymore.

He leaped across the fragile desk, breaking it, and put his hands around Skarda's neck and broke it as if Skarda were a bird.

Skarda's eyes bulged as he felt the hands, heard for one moment the snap of bones, heard nothing after that.

The crash brought clatter on the stairs. Henry ran to the door just as the fat spy opened it, and kicked him in the groin. The fat leather spy went down with a strangled moan, and the pistol fell on the bare wooden floor. Henry picked it up as the next one came into the room. He fired point-blank, and the second man's nose widened into a bloody clot before it disappeared. He fell back against a third man coming up the stairs.\

Grandmother had her Uzi at the bottom of the stairs, and the bullets sprayed the neatly patterned walls.

Henry ran to the window he had measured a moment before, and broke the glass and jumped. He cushioned his fall on the snow-covered lawn by bending both knees and rolling with the fall.

Grandmother poked the Uzi out the broken window and fired. Her rounds made the snow dance.

Henry kept rolling and then was on his feet, crashing through a wooden gate that led into a connected garden. The machine gun chattered behind him, but he didn't think about it, thought about running and making his feet fall smoothly on the snow and not slipping and not making a mistake like running into a dead end.

The *dit-dit-dit* of the machine gun was lost in the heaviness of snow on the quiet neighborhood.

Henry leaped to catch the top of a nine-foot brick wall. He pulled himself up against the bricks and reached the top of the wall. He looked down into yet another snowy garden and saw the face of a growling German shepherd. He stared at the dog. The dog took a step back and then forward again.

Henry leaped down into the garden.

He bared his teeth and raised his hand. "Get the fuck outta my way," Henry said to the dog as though it might be a reasoning animal. The dog unexpectedly wagged its tail and took two steps back, growling all the way.

Henry opened a wooden gate in the wall opposite and then the dog charged, but it was too late. It slammed into the gate as it closed.

He ran from yard to yard. The chatter of the machine gun had ceased, and they were probably running around, trying to find their cars, organize a search. . . . Henry smiled at the thought.

When he reached Norrebrogade with its wide road and pedestrian crowds, he slowed down.

He had left the tape at the airport, the tape with the last words of Viktor Rusinov and the recorded voice of the radio man aboard the *Leo Tolstoy*.

Too bad he couldn't tape Skarda, but that was unexpected. He had in mind all along just to buy himself insurance with the tape, maybe make a trade, maybe not, see what way the wind was blowing. It had smelled bad to Henry from the first, from the moment they had set him up with the fat leather spy and the booga-booga stuff on the *Leo Tolstoy*. They had wanted him to dangle out there for some reason and now he knew what it was. They believed all along that Henry had betrayed them, and they wanted to use Henry to make the chase after Michael seem genuine. But they *had known* Michael would go to Rome with the tape, and they had expected him.

Smart Skarda.

Henry grinned so hard that a passing girl stared at him, but he didn't see her.

He was inside himself. Trying to see what kind of a deal he could finally make with Devereaux. Thinking about the girl, the German girl, down in Rome, thinking about how he could maybe use her in this.

FORTY

Rome

Evelyn Jaynes was uncomfortably sober—no more than three or four tots of Famous Grouse whiskey had crossed his lips since breakfast—but the story was enough to keep him that way.

Cardinal Ludovico led him through the intricacies of it.

The journalist took Pitman notes, and his hand danced across the pages of his notebook. Usually, his hands would be shaking by now, but there was the reserve strength in him that all the old pro newspapermen share, to get on with the story with the reckless abandon of football linemen.

On and on, unfolding the intimate agreement between the Americans and the Soviets, presenting the unique moral dilemma—he loved it!—of trading the future of a lot of Soviet Jews for the future of the whole liberal movement in Lithuania. And some other stuff about a computer defense system. It was tedious, and he wrote it down as well, but it was clear to him that was not at the heart of the deal. The deal was to sell out Lithuania for a cheap political triumph by the corrupt American administration. That's the way Ev-

elyn Jaynes saw it, strictly another cynical American man-
uever. . . . And what sort of debate would this story inspire?
Ah, Evelyn Jaynes, journalist of the year, perhaps now it was
time to seek regular employment. But why think small? Britain was a little country, and there was America just over there
and the great British press lords who were now recolonizing
the land with their splashy newspapers and magazines and
publishing empires. . . . Of course there would be a place
for Evelyn Jaynes in such a world. He cut too great a figure
to stay on the provincial stage. Evelyn saw the headlines,
saw the bylines, saw the photographs of famous people called
upon to decorate his revelations.

He licked his lips as he wrote, and felt the dryness of his
tongue. Perhaps just a celebratory glass or two after he left
the dear old Cardinal of the Secrets?

"You understand, my son, the implications of all that I
have told you?"

"I understand perfectly, Eminence. You should have told
me at the beginning, perhaps it would have—"

"I knew nothing at the beginning." He held up his hands.
"My dear Michael Hampton was our agent of intelligence to
see if the church would be harmed by whatever agreement
came from the Malmö conference—"

"Then you suspected the conference was about other
things."

"We had our suspicions." He put on the guise of wisdom.
He nodded his head. "The church has eyes and ears in many
places. Alas, it is the price we must pay for our survival."

"I understand perfectly, Eminence." Evelyn Jaynes had
taken the first flight from London after receiving the aston-
ishing phone call from Cardinal Ludovico. The previous
story—the story about the pope reaching out to the Anglican
communion—had gone over well, and they joshed him in
the Pig and Whistle about turning religious in his declining
years. But what the hell, it was a good enough story to earn
a Sunday banner.

"You must keep this matter in secret until you are safely back in London."

"I'll go to the airport directly."

"This is very, very grave material, Mr. Jaynes. I shall not rest easy until the truth is published. For a long time, we have observed the American operations in Lithuania. It is a disgrace that the Lithuanian movement would be traded in such a callous way." He said this to see how the Englishman would take it, to see if the Englishman would put the correct spin on it. But it was going over very well, the cardinal saw.

"I will—"

"Do not seek out the Americans, they will deny everything. I stand behind you—"

"Eminence, I am humbly grateful for all you have done for me." It was true. Evelyn was grateful in that moment, so grateful for this second chance at a new career that he might have kissed the cardinal's ring or done whatever bit of papishness the old man would have demanded. But the old man, the dear old man, demanded nothing but the truth, and Evelyn Jaynes would let the truth make him free.

The gratitude poured out of him as he shook the hand of the cardinal at the portico of the great house on Borgo Santo Spirito. The gratitude continued as he waved down a taxi to take him to the airport. But it was the time of day when taxis were occupied and the whole world needed to go to Michelangelo Airport, and there was nothing to do about it. He stood on the avenue with the best of intentions for ten minutes, but every bloody dago in Rome was queueing for cabs at this time of day—not queueing, mind you, but bloody running into the street and flinging down old ladies to get a cab—and what the hell was he doing but standing here like a bloody fool? There was nothing to be done. . . .

Except have a drink.

He popped into the bar near the bridge and had a whiskey down before the bottle was put away. He had another with a glass of Peroni beer. Better, much better.

Evening. Lights along the Tiber.

Not far from the place of Michael Hampton's murder, Evelyn Jaynes walked out into the night air to find a taxi. The lights along the river were festive, because the time of Christmas was coming. The wind was cold but not demanding, and Evelyn felt very warm with a belly full of whiskey. He was sated with the story, puffed up with an expansiveness he had not felt for some time.

Across the river, in a little black Fiat, two men sat. The third man came down the embankment and got into the car.

"Well, there's some kind of a mess in Copenhagen," said the first man. "Skarda has been replaced as number one on this. They said to go ahead and make sure we clean the body in case he has the tape or notes. They said to wait on the old priest—that would have to be cleared. Probably back to Moscow."

"What about the American agent?"

"They said he went back to Brussels. They said they'd watch him in Brussels to see if he jumps one way or the other. Someone's got to have the goddamn tape."

"Yes," said the driver. "That girl—she just disappeared. You notice that? Both of the women disappeared. The girl disappeared in Rome. The gray man—he iced our men in Brussels. He killed Mikhail. I knew Mikhail, we were in Kabul together."

"I didn't know that."

"It's true. Mikhail was all right. He would have liked to get that girl in Brussels. You should have seen him."

"Well, all the girls are disappeared."

"Well, you know how it is." And the third man related a bawdy story that was very popular in Moscow those days. The other two men had heard it before, but they laughed in any case. It eased the tension of their job.

"He's on the street, looking for a cab." The laughter of a moment before was gone. They were all steel again, flat and dulled by use, waiting on the time of the dead.

"Yes," said the driver. "Well, we might as well do it here instead of at the airport."

They thought about that.

"Yes. We might as well," said the third man. And the car began across the bridge.

FORTY-ONE

Brussels

"Who is it?"

"Me."

She opened the door on the chain. She saw him and closed the door and reopened it. They stood apart for a moment. It was done, she thought, whatever it was. She saw the coldness, saw it in eyes and the pale color of his face, saw it in the slump of his shoulders. What would warm him?

She embraced him. Was there anything else she could do? There was no power in her to resist him, not for a moment, not from the moment he had come to her rooms in the rue du Lavois, when he opened her case, not from the moment he had ordered her to embrace him in the courtyard at the moment of dawn. *I love you*. But did she love him, or was it that he was only life? She could not obliterate dead Michael from her mind. Not Michael. She had betrayed Michael from the beginning; she had helped kill him as surely as if she had been the one shooting at him on the bridge in Rome. . . . All for a cause.

She stood apart from him when his arms no longer pressed against her back and when she felt the coldness of him.

She looked at him in the half darkness.

He said, "I got the tape."

She understood then. The tape cassette was between them; it would always be between them. Because she had made a small betrayal of Michael's trust in her, and it had cost him his life. She took a step back and folded her arms across her chest. Her beautiful face was now cold and stoic. She would not be hurt by him; he could not do it.

"What will you do now?"

"What do you want me to do?"

"Give me the tape."

"What would you do for me then?"

She did not waver. "I will do anything you want. For as long as you want."

"Is that true, Rena? Is it that important?"

"It is a cause—"

"Cut the crap, Rena. Your only cause is yourself."

"I hate you."

"But you gave yourself to Henry McGee to get free. Did you resist long? Did he have to rape you? And you gave yourself to Michael that morning in the Savoy Hotel because it was important that he not go back to pack his own bags, it was important that he get the tape in his bag and not be able to give it back. Did you think of him listening to the tape on the train to Stockholm, listening to it out of boredom? How many times did you have to make love to him to betray him for your cause?"

She hit him then in the face, and he smiled at her because he had hurt her so much. There. She could feel pain and it pleased him.

"I loved Michael."

"I'm sure you loved him. Right up to the moment he started running to Rome. Maybe he might have made it, and you wouldn't feel so guilty, and you could thank him with a courtesy fuck."

"And you, from the moment you forced your way into my rooms," she said, "you wanted me. You didn't give a damn if I loved someone else—you just wanted me. You have no worth, Devereaux, remember that.''

"I never said I did," he said. The words were soft and curiously introspective.

She saw a sense of loss in his eyes and was touched by it because it was exactly her loss.

"What will you do with the tape?"

He stared at her for a long moment. "The right thing. If I can."

"What is the right thing?"

Devereaux said, "Yes, that's the question, isn't it?"

"Oh, damn the tape and damn me for killing Michael. Damn me for needing you. Will you forgive me?"

"I have nothing to forgive anyone." His words were at the edge of the universe, and she understood that.

And understood why she embraced him then in the mutual suffering of a kindred lost soul. Clung to him but did not expect comfort from the feeling of his body.

She had known all her life this moment would come, without expecting it. She wanted him to possess her in a way that she had never been possessed before, to fill her while only taking his pleasure.

Yes, he held her. He wanted the satin of her belly beneath his hand. He felt the silk between her legs then, felt her velvet in the darkness, felt her yielding, felt her draw him into her. He could feel and hear her breath on his neck, against his ear. He could touch and not see her, the fingers of the blind man reading her need for him. She said his name and he said hers. They made love to each other. She was the smell of flowers and the darker smell of loam turned in spring after the rain.

The two KGB men wore black coats and berets.

"Do we take them in the hotel or out of the hotel?"

"Well, we take them and it's up to us. I'd just as soon wait until they came out, because that way, we got a better exit."

"That's true, but if we take them inside, use the silencers, it might be hours before anyone finds the bodies. And looks for the damned tape."

"That's true," said the second one. They were standing at the corner of the city hall, watching the entry of the Amigo Hotel. "Well, we ought to make up our minds, because I don't want to stand around all night in the rain."

"Well, I say we take them inside. Like you say, we don't want to stand around all night in the rain. I hate this fucking rain. Let's do it now."

"He probably is screwing her anyway. That's a good time. When they get to screwing, nothing else matters."

"Remember, this is the guy who took out those two guys in Brussels. Just remember it."

"This is Brussels, stupid."

"I mean before. Christ, I lose track of the cities. It seems we've been on the road for weeks."

"It hasn't been that long, but I know what you mean. You get tired of being on the road. A lot has happened."

"I'll say. Well, here. I put in the special charge. Two good shots and they'll look like steak *hachette*."

"Oh, don't get carried away."

They went into the quiet lobby. There was a Mexican or Spanish influence to the decor of the hotel, which they thought was very odd. They went to the elevator and rode to the third level.

They knew exactly what they were doing. They knew everything down to the room number. They had picked up the room number that morning, and they had made a key to fit it. Every little trick in the trade is special and has its own expertise, but they were good at what they did.

The first one opened the door with the special key. Not a sound. Just like clockwork.

Into the bedroom.

They were on the mattress, the covers over them. The hitters pulled out their pistols and fired through the silencers.

Thump.

Thump. Thump.

Thump.

They walked into the room to find the tape. They pulled back the covers.

Blood over everything.

The first one stared.

"Christ," he said.

"Christ," said the second one.

"It isn't him."

"It's some other guy."

"It's two other guys. Two fairies. This one is bald even. What the hell are they doing in this room?"

"How could we get fucked up like this?"

"Let's get the hell out of here."

To the door, down the corridor, taking the stairs this time. Into the lobby and past the concierge, and they were both running now.

"What do you want from me?" she said.

"Describe the limping man to someone in London."

"Why? Who is the man in London?"

"The limping man at the Malmö conference must be working for the CIA. It's the connection."

"What about this other man, Henry McGee?"

"Henry McGee may deal, he may not deal, I can't depend on him. Henry puts out a convincing case that he's being set up. I don't understand it. I don't understand the secrets on the tape. This all seems trivial, but perhaps that's all it is. Trivial. A lot of stuff gets set in motion for trivial reasons. I don't understand politics, but I understand there could be some political advantage to having the Russians free a lot of people. Advantages. Little edges in the game. That's all it is maybe."

"And you will let Lithuania die."

She was naked against him, lying in bed, speaking in whispers. Their sheets lay tangled around their bodies.

"It isn't a matter of that. I have to return the tape to my masters, and they determine the political morality."

"Are you so unable to have a conviction?"

He looked at her. She was beautiful, she made love with power and passion, she filled him and drove away apparitions. She wanted to have him possess her; even now while they spoke, their bodies were poised.

"The spies don't set policy," Devereaux said.

"Is Lithuania such a little thing?"

He did not speak to her.

For a long time they lay against each other and searched through all the words in their memories to find the words that would make it clear to them. What were they supposed to think?

"I am not a member of the movement. I was asked this through my father," she said. "My father is not a member of the movement. But it is no small thing, to be from a homeland that you cannot be part of again, that does not even exist in the eyes of the world. Russia. It is a terrible thing to be in the embrace of a bear, to feel its paws on you all the time, to feel its teeth marking your flesh."

"Come here," he said.

She put her hand on his sex and felt it and said, "I want only that. The other thing—those are words and we will not understand each other, not ever. You make me act like a spy, change hotel rooms, want me to make a call to that man in London. . . . I am not a spy, I am a woman only. I know languages as easily as I know that I want you, I have always wanted you, I have waited for you to come and possess me all my life. Do you understand me?"

He didn't, but he was beyond caring.

FORTY-TWO

London

There were the sounds of bagpipes, beautiful and clear in the still November air. The sun stood straight up in the sky and flooded the ancient city with unexpected light. Every brick and stone was polished by the sun. The day was as fresh as a child beginning his life.

Devereaux stood among the tourists, not looking for anyone, not expecting anything until the moment he saw Henry McGee. Henry grinned at him.

Henry followed him into the park, and they found a bench and sat on it. The day was cold enough to make their words form puffs of breath.

"I need a deal."

"What kind of a deal?"

"I need money."

"Everyone needs money. It's the one thing capitalists and communists agree on."

"I saw Viktor Rusinov. I iced him, but I got it on tape. It was a setup, like you thought. I got the same from the radio man on the *Leo Tolstoy*. On tape. The only thing I ain't got on tape is the main thing. What this whole thing was really about—even I didn't know.''

''Is that right?''

''That's right.''

Devereaux stared at him. ''You're a congenital liar, Henry. Why should I believe anything you say?''

''I thought about that all the way here. Then it seems obvious to me. I iced Skarda. They're all going to come after me like a wolf pack. That won't be a setup. They want to ice me, and that ought to prove myself to you. Except if I wait until then without taking precautions, I get iced and you stand there at the grave and say, 'Well, I shoulda listened to ol' Henry this time, because this time he was goin' to tell the truth.' That doesn't do either of us any good.''

Devereaux thought about it. Hanley had already learned of Skarda's death in Copenhagen. The shit was hitting the fan.

''All right. What would be worth it to me?'' Devereaux said.

''Skarda is a software program designed to prevent viral attacks on computer systems. Years ahead of what the Americans have. Except it is also a viral attack by its very nature, and when your people program it, it is going to direct a missile, a fucking missile, to land in the middle of Quebec City. Kill SDI. This is going to fuck up the American military program for months, for years—I can see that. But it will never trace back to Skarda. Skarda will just be there, in place, working fine, and it will never trace back to the Russians. The Russians want their *glasnost* and friendship and all that, and they want it bad enough to use Skarda to get it. The man is dead but not the program.''

''When is this going to happen?''

''December twentieth. A missile-launching test in Utah.''

''Is that right?''

''I gave you the day and time and target. What else do you want?''

"The only thing that makes it sound genuine is that you didn't produce a tape of it."

"It is genuine."

"And what do you want?"

"I got maybe ten thousand left after all my expenses. I got to have some money to run on."

"You're a convicted felon. You escaped from prison. You should turn yourself in."

Henry grinned. "I used to think about killing you. Inside. Cutting your nuts off or something. I see why you had to get me, but I didn't see why you had to dirty my trail so that they believed it, believed I betrayed them."

"Just a personal touch, Henry. I don't like you."

"I also don't like you," Henry agreed. He slipped his hand out of his pocket just enough to show Devereaux the grip of the revolver.

"What are you going to do?"

"I coulda come to shoot you, but I need money."

"How much money do you need?"

"Twenty-five thousand."

"Ten thousand," Devereaux said.

"Jesus. You're talking the bottom of the basement."

"Government austerity," Devereaux said.

"I really hate you, you know that. I could just kill you now and walk away. I don't owe you anything."

Devereaux waited.

"Fifteen," Henry said.

"And both tapes," Devereaux said.

FORTY-THREE

Washington, D.C.

The problem at first was with the tape recording itself. R Section managed to override the no-copy signals imbedded in the tape, but it took nearly thirty-six hours of work and the Soviets were howling for the tape. When the tape was finally copied, the original was turned over to the Soviet Union.

Within three days, the first part of Skarda was transmitted to the United States Central Intelligence Agency. Also, the president of the Soviet Union, in a stunning gesture of goodwill, announced that the first of thousands of Soviet Jews who had applied for permission to leave the Soviet Union would be allowed to do so and that the number of departures would reach ninety thousand by the end of the following year. The Soviet Union said it had made this decision after intensive negotiations with the United States as part of the Malmö meeting of the superpowers.

The newspapers were filled with stories of the emigration of Soviet Jewry. The refugees were being processed through in Vienna as well as in Stockholm. Everyone had praise for the negotiating skills of the U.S. administration and, particularly, the secretary of state.

The president announced a new Soviet-American summit would be held in New Jersey in early spring.

The world reveled in the spirit of the Christmas season, in the apparent friendship of the two great powers, in the good feeling it felt toward the Soviet Union for living up to the spirit of reason and *glasnost*.

Among the 90,000 exit visas would be 1,298 visas for members of the Committee for State Security, the KGB.

Douglas Court sat dining alone in the great restaurant in the Willard Hotel. He ate with delicate enjoyment of the small portions of very rich food. He ate in the European manner, fork in one hand and knife in the other, because he had spent so many years abroad.

He was only slightly annoyed when the two men came up to him and stood before his table. He looked up at them. One he had never seen before, the other was only vaguely familiar. He hated to remember a face, but he tried. Who were they?

"Yes?"

"Yes, that's him, all right."

Douglas Court remembered the face then. He even connected it with a name. Rolf Gustafson. He remembered the name and face and time and place, and he understood then that the second man, the one with gray eyes, would not be a friend.

"We have a car outside waiting for you," the second man said.

Douglas Court, with the good manners born of a lifetime of civility, dabbed at his lips with his napkin and put it down. He saw the way it was.

"Which agency?" is all he said.

"R Section."

"Yes. It would have to be, wouldn't it?"

* * *

In the second week, a GS14 in Computer Analysis in R Section showed, through charts, how Skarda was designed to work. Everyone agreed it was very clever, including Mrs. Neumann, who understood computers, and Hanley, who was completely baffled by the demonstration but did not acknowledge it. The only way they had discovered the secret of Skarda was that they knew what they were looking for; otherwise, the computer program would have passed any minute inspection.

On the same day, a secret grand jury in Washington, D.C., filed a true bill naming Vaughn Arthur Reuben on fourteen counts of conspiracy to commit espionage against the United States by misdirecting CIA personnel in Europe and conspiring to steal a government tape recording. The true bill was signed into an indictment at 1:45 P.M., and two hours later, when officers arrived at Reuben's house, off DuPont Circle, they were not especially surprised to find him dead, a large pistol in his right hand and a large hole in his forehead. There was a note, a long one of explanation and regret, and it was turned over to the U.S. marshal's office, which, in turn, sent it to the CIA. It was destroyed at Langley, after a suitable number of conferences.

On December 20, during a routine field exercise in Utah, a Strategic Defensive Initiative test missile veered suddenly off course. All this was monitored at Moscow Center communications. The missile appeared to cross the border into Canada before it was destroyed. No one was injured in the incident, and the administration denied that any such test had occurred or that a missile had been destroyed. The consensus in Moscow Center was that Plan Skarda—to send a U.S. missile off course and into a Canadian city—had not worked, despite all of the late Skarda's brilliant posturing. Gorki of the Committee for External Observation and Resolution concluded that Skarda had oversold his masters inside KGB on his software expertise and suggested that, in the future, KGB stick to more fundamental methods of infiltration and sabotage.

In the funding of covert counterintelligence activity, it is not uncommon to bury authorizations inside more routine budget allocations.

This is done less to fool the intelligence enemy, who might stumble upon such material, than to obfuscate facts in the face of scrutiny by Congress and the more professional interest of the General Accounting Office.

Thus it was noted that $200 million in funds to the CIA that were used for "research and liaison with religious bodies in foreign countries" were stripped from its budget. The CIA so informed Cardinal Ludovico within two weeks.

The following day, an agent from R Section called at the house on the Borgo Santo Spirito and explained the new facts of life to the cardinal. He reluctantly agreed, and the secret lists of Lithuanian networks was turned over to Section, which had, surprisingly, come up with a $200 million surplus in its fiscal budget to enable it "to expand crop reporting techniques to Scandinavia and nearby regions."

Thus Devereaux had convinced Hanley, who had convinced Mrs. Neumann and the power structure of the American intelligence community, to "do the right thing."

FORTY-FOUR

New York and Brussels

S he loved him like a schoolgirl; she followed after him; she took his arm with the eagerness of a child. Why did she fear once that he would not come back to her? He had come back to her, back to her rooms on the rue du Lavois, come back to sleep with her and share her life, to put his strong arms on her and feel satin and silk and lace and velvet, to reach and reach until he had all her secrets. She had feared he would never come back to her.

But he needed her, because New York was too full of ghosts and this was the gloomy time of year when ghosts revealed themselves throughout the world.

There had been a message on the answering machine in the safe house in Manhattan.

"Call me."

The voice was the same, the voice was exactly as he had always heard it in his dreams, as he always saw Rita Macklin. Rita's voice was an angel's, clear as a bell at midnight on the coldest night of winter.

"Call me."

When he heard it, he rewound the tape and played it again

and again. "Call me." A simple request, a command—he felt all the love welling in him again. She could not live without him. "Call me." She needed him despite everything, despite her decision to walk away from him.

New York was full of ghosts, and they were all the same, all red-haired women with melting green eyes, all full of sweet flowers and milky breath, all full of desire that was wet before they touched each other. What would he do now but run to her, hold her as he had held her that afternoon in the hotel?

Instead, he took the Sabena flight to Brussels. It raced across the ocean toward the coming light. When he went to Rena Taurus's apartment, it was only an act of strength that others might see as an act of weakness. Cold Rena and cold Devereaux seeking to warm themselves in aimless passion, they deserved no better than they got. Got no better than they deserved.

Rena was the schoolgirl of a romance that had always eluded her. Devereaux was life, strength, a story she told herself that was almost true. They ate at a little café on the Grand Place and watched the snow fall, and when they walked up the hill to her rooms, they were in love with each other. Perhaps it was not love as defined by some, but it was what they had and they both needed it to stave off the cold. They rarely spoke to each other, as though they had both heard too much for too long.

Would it last?

Even the world would not last, but they did not speak of the end of things, did not speak at all as they urged each other on with touches and kisses and every familiarity. It got to be that just to see him coming to meet her after work would fill her with such desire that she wanted him, insisted, right then and there, demanded that he fill her.

Oh, she loved him and she knew what love was. She had always known, though it had been a secret until she met him

FORTY-FIVE

Berlin

O h, yes, there was no question about it: he was a good-
looking man, and he treated her in a way that pleased
her. He was plenty rough all right, but she was used
to that. He was really able to take his pleasure with her, and
sometimes it hurt, sometimes she had to hold him off for a
day or two, but he understood about things. He needed her
—she knew that. He really needed her. She was in love with
him because he needed her.

The other thing that made her love him was thinking about
that dirty old priest, the one who had tried to kill her.

Henry said he would kill the priest for her. That it wasn't
a problem at all. Henry meant it too, you could see it in his
eyes. She wasn't afraid of mean eyes, not at all. The pigs
had mean eyes. Some of the men who had abused her had
mean eyes.

Henry looked nice, it was nice to be out with a man who
presented himself well.

Not that they went out very often. Henry said he had to
stay in the shadows. Well, Marie was just the girl to show
him how to do it. How you could hide yourself away for

years in her old city, her mother, Berlin. It was the perfect match they had, and she would almost forget about her lamb on some days.

She would never call Henry a lamb.

She had known a lamb once, a little lamb, innocent as the first day of the world.

She could cry sometimes.

When Henry was sleeping, she might sit in the second room and stare out the window at the old, sleeping city, and her eyes would make soft tears as she thought of Michael.

And then she would think of Cardinal Ludovico, and she would think of Henry, and she would think of so many things, and it would dull the edge of pain that Michael, the sheer thought of dead Michael, tore out of her.

Who said she could not love or feel?

She could feel. She knew pain because she had known love.

Only once, but she had known it.